Julian C…

…and Kent.

Praise for *Briefs Encountered*:

'*Briefs Encountered* is quite as hilarious, clever, stylish, charming and wickedly witty as Noël Coward . . . It would easier to stab a puppy or slap a baby than to dislike such an utterly lovable book' Stephen Fry

'Julian Clary is a smart and as funny as ever . . . a delicious airy treat' *Sunday Times*

'So clever, so funny, so romantic, and scary too. I don't know how he does it!' Fay Weldon

'So funny...Clary switches effortlessly between eras and demonstrates an inspired eye for comic detail'
Daily Mail

'Clary has produced a surprisingly complex, artfully constructed and mostly very convincing novel, which isn't bogged down by its intelligence or his obvious research. Indeed, it's all dressed up in delightfully accessible, sharp prose that's full of gags'
Daily Mirror

Also by Julian Clary:

Non-fiction
A Young Man's Passage

Fiction:
Murder Most Fab
Devil in Disguise

Briefs Encountered

Julian Clary

EBURY
PRESS

3 5 7 9 10 8 6 4 2

Published in the UK in 2012 by Ebury Press, an imprint of Ebury Publishing
A Random House Group Company
This edition published in the UK in 2013 by Ebury Press,
an imprint of Ebury Publishing
A Random House Group Company

The Random House Group Limited Reg. No. 954009

Addresses for companies within the Random House Group can be found at:
www.randomhouse.co.uk

A CIP catalogue record for this book is available from the British Library

The Random House Group Limited supports The Forest Stewardship Council (FSC®), the leading international forest certification organisation. Our books carrying the FSC label are printed on FSC® certified paper. FSC is the only forest certification scheme endorsed by the leading environmental organisations, including Greenpeace. Our paper procurement policy can be found at:
www.randomhouse.co.uk/environment

Printed and bound by CPI Group (UK) Ltd, Croydon, CR0 4YY

ISBN 9780091938857

To my nephew, Christian

'I believe, the more you love a man,
The more you give your trust,
The more you're bound to lose.
Hey-Ho. If love were all . . .'
Noël Coward

DRAMATIS PERSONAE

Present

Richard Stent	a famous actor, handsome but slightly past his prime
Fran Chilman	Richard's long-term partner. Clever, independent and considerably younger
Jess Campbell	Richard's efficient and loyal personal assistant
Albie Campbell	Jess's son
Marcia Brown	Richard's eccentric, blousy agent
Gary Lucas	Richard's best friend, an out-of-work and out-of-shape actor
Julian Clary	annoying camp comic and renowned homosexual
Paul O'Grady	TV personality from Birkenhead
Cheryl Dawkins	a beautiful model-turned-actress. No stranger to the party scene

Past

Noël Coward	actor, playwright, composer
Jack Wilson	his American lover, a chisel-jawed jock
Violet Coward	Noël's adoring mother
Aunt Vida	Violet's troublesome sister
Arthur Coward	Noël's moody, neglected father
Lorn Loraine	Noël's loyal and long-suffering secretary
Mrs Ashton	the housekeeper, big boned and all knowing
Alice Creyse	the maid, timid and rather clumsy
Stanley Lewis	the gardener, a man of few words, if any
Jude Perkins	the young, good-looking under-gardener
DI Cecil Keaton	a middle-aged, balding, tenacious policeman. Might as well be northern
Natasha Paley	a Russian princess and Hollywood starlet
Graham Payn	Noël's partner in later years

And sundry spirits

PROLOGUE

Scene: a beautiful, idyllic manor house in Kent. Present day.

Richard

I've been lying here under the mulberry tree, spread-eagled on a sunbed for hours. But if anything I'm paler now than I was a few hours ago. I can't move. I feel as if I'm in a painting, positioned just so, the dappled evening light catching my cheekbones and giving my blond-and-grey-speckled hair an ethereal glow. The house lies a hundred yards or so to my right: a serene, knowing presence. It looks smart and well kept now but this wasn't always the case.

Fran is inside, reading the *Guardian*. He says there are too many flies about in the garden today. Occasionally he looks out of the window to check on me. We both need some quiet time after all the awful events that we've been through lately. He is probably savouring the calm of the two of us, alone at last, in the house's restful embrace. We deserve some peace.

It was such a different house when I first saw it on a summer's afternoon two years ago: crumbling walls, sagging ceilings and knackered guttering. It whimpered at me like a whipped puppy, pleading for help. This house knew I had cash to spare and a rebellious personality that would ignore the surveyor's doom-laden report. Indeed, while I paid for the report, received the thick package that contained it, I never read its many gloomy pages. I knew what I had to do: like a wealthy businessman under the spell of a beautiful Jezebel, I signed the papers and prepared myself, willingly, to be fleeced. I accepted my fate: that I would be the one to bring the house back to life, to restore her to her former glamour and magnificence.

The house is very old. In fact, during their exertions, the builders uncovered a hitherto boarded-up fireplace, which has the initials PB and the date 1742 carved into the wooden beam above it. Sometimes, when I can't sleep (and as you shall learn there has been a lot on my mind lately), I lie awake listening to the creaks and groans the house makes. If the mice are being frisky in the rafters, instead of counting sheep I attempt to calculate how many generations of mice have lived and died here since 1742. If mice have six babies every few months then it's somewhere in the region of billions. Equivalent to the population of China, probably. It is admittedly a rather highbrow way of getting to sleep but each to their own.

People have lived here for centuries. It is mentioned in the *Domesday Book*: Falconhurst – residence of the King's falcon keeper. Then it became Goldenhurst Old Manor, and it stands to reason that the lord of the manor lived here, bossing around the lowly serfs and drinking brandy for breakfast. This is smugglers' country, part of Romney Marsh, so no doubt masked men on horseback roamed everywhere; gold, silver, copper, lace and brandy were brought in by boat under cover of darkness and hidden in houses such as this one. There were all manner of dodgy types and I'm just the latest.

I bought the house from Julian Clary (of whom more shortly.

I'll try to keep his appearances in this book to a minimum, but we must bite the bullet and give him the odd name check at least. Let's just say that, when it came to the house, I think the poor old queen rather overstretched himself). He changed the name to Priest's Hole House – no doubt something he and his louche friends considered humorous. I restored its dignity by giving it back its name, or at least part of it. I settled on the Old Manor and so it has remained. It was my duty of care to bring the old place back to life, and, at a price, I think I have succeeded.

First I had a new roof (original Kent peg tiles, a pound each) and lived for months under steel scaffolding. The ancient oil-fired boiler dwelt in the basement like a mad old dragon, flames licking dangerously out from under its rump. That had to go. The electrics sparked and fizzed whenever I turned on a light switch, so re-wiring was essential.

The window frames were so rotten you could push your fingers through them like putty. A clever, old-school craftsman came, nodded sagely and in his own, Kentish time, replaced them with new sturdy oak, blond and brash when first fitted, but within a year aged and organic, melting into the original brickwork like butter into a wholemeal crumpet.

Meanwhile I employed a visionary gardener who set about thinning out the endless Michaelmas daisies that had taken over every flowerbed. Delphiniums, lupins, hollyhocks, iceberg roses and rambling rectors were cultivated.

After a merciful break that allowed me to refill the coffers by means of any acting roles that came my way, the interior was tackled, ceilings rebuilt, walls re-plastered and bathrooms modernised and created where once evil asbestos tanks lurked.

Now, at last, it is all rather perfect. Inside and out. I've got antique napkins and everything. But please believe that the house rules my life like a domineering lover. My friends tut and raise their eyebrows, smile benignly and frown when I look away but what can I say? What can I do? I am under its spell and at least I'm not spending my money on cocaine or heroin. Not that I'm telling you, anyway. Anything is possible and we all have our secrets.

But enough. Tired as I am, I quiver with anticipation as I take a deep breath and begin to tell you the story sired by this extraordinary dwelling. It's not a house, bear in mind, but a monument, host to all who have dwelled within its walls, a saturated rag of damp, breathing spirits. And my tale is one of ghosts . . .

ACT I

Scene One

Richard

In buying this house I set off a chain of events that otherwise would never have happened. I have found myself at the epicentre of strange, sordid, violent, dangerous happenings. But finally, after everything, I am enlightened. That's a relief.

Why this house? Why move to Kent at all, you might well ask? Well, a famous actor in his mid-forties whose career is fading as quickly as his looks is often inclined to get out of town. I'm not the first. There were, after all, certain facts to be faced. Although I had more than a few quid in the bank from my golden years on the big screen, the parts were drying up. The last call from my agent, the formerly respected Marcia Brown, was a tentative offer of a walk-on part in a TV drama about sex rituals on the Isle of Wight called *The Silence of the Limbs.* I, who was once cast as a young Michael Hutchence in the multi-award-winning Disney spectacular *Dead Man Wanking*, had lost my sex appeal along with my trim waistline. Goodbye, rock-star parts. (Unless, of course, the Duran Duran bio-pic idea takes off. Which seems unlikely.) Moving to the country was already an idea floating around my mind when a number of things happened in quick succession that led me to this particular house at this particular time in my life.

I had always felt a connection with Noël Coward. By pure coincidence, I was born in Waldegrave Road, Teddington, Middlesex, in a flat right opposite the very house in which Noël was born, one of those square-fronted, red-brick Victorian villas with a pointed gable roof and white trimmings everywhere. Years later, after I'd long moved on, they put up a circular blue English heritage plaque in his honour that read:

NOËL COWARD
1899 – 1973
ACTOR, PLAYWRIGHT AND SONGWRITER
BORN HERE

As a boy, though, I heard of our famous former neighbour from my mother. She played me his songs and we watched his films. Noël took hold of my imagination. As I skipped down the garden path at seven years old, I would picture a seven-year-old Noël skipping towards me, on his way to his destiny as a famous actor and writer. I wasn't sure what an actor was, but it sounded impressive and clearly made one loved and revered. No doubt my own desire to become an actor stemmed from those childish daydreams about Noël.

In my final showcase performance at RADA at the age of twenty-one, I was cast as Elyot in *Private Lives* and I was a smash – a he's-the-best-thing-since-Michael-Crawford genuine hit. Marcia Brown, the most impressive agent in London at that time, signed me and the rest is history. It was perhaps a rather romantic notion, but I began to feel as if Noël was watching over me. I just felt blessed.

Blessed by Noël or not, ever since I'd left RADA, equipped with my piercing blue eyes, cheekbones to die for and a rather shining talent, I'd never stopped working. I started out in the theatre, then starred in art-house films that got me critical respect, did a season at the RSC, and a few, well-received cameo parts in more mainstream flicks, usually playing the British baddie. I'd arrived. Then, when I was established, well-reviewed and thirty, Marcia advised me to shock everyone and take a role in the Hollywood blockbuster, *Wolfman*. We knew it was rubbish but said yes. It turned out to be the kind of unpredictable world-wide phenomenon that no one can explain, and I was screamed at everywhere from Tokyo to Taunton. It was exhausting. Fame was something I'd craved but this was a little too full on, even for me.

'Go with the flow,' Marcia advised. 'It will only last a couple of years and then you'll be lucky to get a guest role in *Midsomer Murders*.'

And so I persuaded myself to reprise my role in *Wolfman 2*, *3* and *4*. I made unspeakable amounts of money and was what you call 'global'. After that, much to Marcia's horror, I had another complete career change and returned to serious theatre.

Obviously, some in the profession were aghast at the way I had sold out and then tried to return to the fold, theatre's very own prodigal son, but they had to admit when I toured Chekhov's *The Seagull* to packed houses all over Britain, that I had brought art to those whose real interest was in seeing Flay Claw, the Wolfman's deadly foe, in the flesh and who would not have otherwise have considered watching nineteenth-century Russian drama.

For my part, I loved my taste of Hollywood stardom and the mighty pay cheque it brought with it. Freedom from financial worries meant I could take my pick of roles, not minding if it was a minimum-wage gig or even a labour of love. Theatre was where I belonged and I knew that.

Then, just five years ago, my agent told me that Channel 4 were making a big-budget three-part series about Noël Coward called *Noël, The Vegas Years* dramatising the Master's remarkable comeback in the 1950s, and that the starring role was up for grabs. My heart beat faster. I was prepared to do anything for this part and made Marcia signal my interest to the producers. They were far from sure about casting me as Coward: I was younger and better preserved than Noël at the age I was required to portray him, and, some would say, considerably more handsome. But they agreed to a meeting and I went along, determined to show them that I was born to play this part. My passion must have impressed them – the role was soon mine, and with some clever prosthetics, vocal coaching and the adoption of a slight stoop, I managed to be almost eerily convincing. I would stare at myself in the mirror before I went on set and I swear I could feel Noël fluttering inside me.

I prepared for the role with great fervour. I read Noël's published diaries and letters, immersed myself in his plays, songs and films and felt, during the six weeks of filming, that I was channelling him, night and day. Fran sighed with exasperation during our nightly chats when I spoke in witty epigrams, called him 'my dear boy' and took to carrying an ivory cigarette holder. He cautioned me that my stoop would become a permanent feature if I wasn't careful.

During my research, my personal assistant Jess had made a few discreet phone calls on my behalf and I had been permitted access to the Waldegrave Road house in Teddington where Coward was born, and also to 17 Gerald Road, Belgravia, where he would preside over exclusive soirées. I was allowed to prowl both premises, inhaling his ghostly presence. Yet phone messages and letters to his country refuge in Kent, now called Priest's Hole House, had produced no response. One morning, just before filming was due to start, Jess handed me a torn-out page from *Woman's Own* magazine. Grimacing slightly, she said, 'This might explain a thing or two.'

There was a full colour picture of Julian Clary, the camp comic and renowned homosexual (as he liked to call himself), standing in front of a beautiful Elizabethan-ish farmhouse, arms wide open as if to say 'all this is mine'. The place was none other than Noël's old residence. To add salt to the wound, the headline was 'Homo of the Manor'.

Noël would be turning in his grave, I thought. My professional path had never crossed with Clary's, which was hardly surprising. But back in the early nineties, I had once visited a gay club called the Phoenix in Cavendish Square. I was standing innocently at the urinal when several bouncers burst in and banged furiously on a cubicle door. Aghast, I just managed to zip myself up as a red-faced, white-nosed Clary was escorted off the premises with not one but two wild-eyed youths whose appearances might best be described as dishevelled.

After that, I was not all that keen to be introduced, and once I discovered that this was the very man who was now in possession of Goldenhurst Old Manor (I couldn't quite bring myself to call it by its new name), I didn't pursue a visit there any longer.

That year, to my great delight, my performance as Noël was nominated for the Best Actor award at the BAFTAs. It was a typically stellar evening, with the brightest lights of film and television gathered in their finest gowns and dinner suits, and I was feeling excited and confident. The only downside was that, to my dismay (and I wasn't alone), the presenter of the award was none other than Mr Clary himself. (One can only imagine he was standing in for someone at short notice.)

'I'm thrilled to the marrow to be here this evening,' he began. 'How lovely to be amongst so much talent. But enough about the security guards.'

When he opened the gold envelope, he raised one eyebrow, simpered and said, 'Oh, *bona*! It's the divine Richard Stent.'

I was delighted to win and with the cameras on me, I made sure that I received the award with a smile and accepted the kiss he dropped on my cheek with good grace, but inside I couldn't help feeling a tiny sense of resentment that I hadn't been allowed to visit the Old Manor as I'd desired. Later, at the post-ceremony party, Julian pranced up to me and apologised for ignoring Jess's letters.

Jess, who was my escort for the evening, stiffened beside me and butted in before I had the chance to reply. 'I expect you were busy rehearsing for panto in Crawley,' she said haughtily. 'Now if you'll excuse us, Dame Judi Dench is taking Richard to supper.'

She pulled me away by the arm, leaving Julian staring after us. Jess had a tendency to be overprotective on my behalf, especially if she felt someone had slighted me. Soon, I was surrounded by people offering their congratulations and in the excitement, Julian slipped from my mind.

The next morning, however, as we placed my award in the glass cabinet with the others, Jess told me she'd had a private chat with him before she left.

'He's selling that house,' she said casually. 'He now has the nerve to wonder if you'd be interested.'

'Selling? Really?' I replied, immediately roused by the idea. The pictures I'd seen of the house had made the place look delightful: a romantic country idyll of weathered brickwork, old timbers and a lush green garden. But more than that, I felt the familiar flutter within – maybe Coward wanted me to rescue his home from Clary's unsuitable clutches. Perhaps the ghostly seven-year-old Noël who had waved at me across the road had been preparing me for this opportunity. Knowing how cynical Jess was about fate and suchlike, I did my best to keep my tone calm.

'What did he say?' I enquired casually.

Jess raised her eyebrows. 'He's barely been in it for five minutes. Reading between the lines I think he's broke. Says it's too big for him.'

'Not something Miss Clary often complains about,' I said.

A few days later, without even telling Fran of my plans, I drove down the M20. I don't know why I didn't want to tell him – after all, by this time we'd been together for six years and he knew everything about me – but I felt that this would be my secret, just for a while. He was away on business anyway, as he so often was. I enjoyed the thrill of something almost forbidden as I drove into Kent, a part of the world I knew hardly at all, and through the village of Aldringham. I was already half in love with the soft green countryside and the mellow brick houses before I arrived at the Old Manor, and I suppose I was ready to be entirely seduced as I pulled my Jaguar up to the white five-barred gate.

There it was – an old country farmhouse, kooky and rambling, with three upstairs dormer windows jutting out of the sagging brown-and-terracotta roof like a sleepy serpent's eyes. Below that the walls were faded vanilla-cream plaster, frequently crossed with ancient, uneven timbers, all bearing the scars of summer sun and winter rain endured over hundreds of years. And everything was speckled with living lesions of pale yellow moss, like the bristly warts on an old crone's chin.

I got quietly out of the car, as if frightened of waking the old girl, but a couple of the small latticed windows glinted in the sunlight and I guessed she was awake and contemplating me.

I imagined I heard a quiet, high-pitched sigh, but it was only the side gate opening. Two excited, rather unfortunate-looking mongrels came dancing towards me, followed by the familiar features of Julian Clary as he swanned over the gravel to open the gate.

'Park over there on the lawn!' he commanded, gesturing towards a spot, and I obeyed. When I climbed out of the car again, he greeted me with a kiss to each cheek and the words, 'You're the most interesting guest I've had since Denise van Outen, and she had a hangover!' and led the way back into the house. 'Mind the fig tree,' he said, as we brushed past some exotic foliage that seemed to be growing out of the side of the house. 'It's a magnet for wasps.'

The first room I saw was a kitchen, very dated and with more Cath Kidston polka-dot curtains than strictly necessary but notable for the original flagstones and a 1920s Rayburn range.

'A present from Paul O'Grady,' Julian said, following my gaze to the Rayburn. 'Bit of a gas-guzzler, but a comfort on a winter's evening. Now . . . some Lady Grey tea after your journey? And can I interest you in a chocolate finger?'

I managed a weak smile and nodded.

'I'm so glad you've come to see the house, I'm sure you'll love it. And it's a very friendly village,' he continued. 'They'll all make a fuss of you but they won't intrude. That's what we celebs want, isn't it, at the end of the day . . . ?'

I winced at the way he managed to place himself in the same category as me – had *he* ever starred in four blockbuster Hollywood movies and been photographed on the Kodak Theatre red carpet between Catherine Zeta-Jones and Jennifer Aniston? I very much doubted it. I zoned out his witterings and instead tried to imagine Noël pottering about here in days gone by, while Julian boiled the kettle and filled a green-spotted teapot then loaded a tray with cups. When all was ready, he led me through to the reception room, but walked swiftly through the low door via the lounge towards a study at the back of the house, where the sun was streaming through the open French windows. I caught glimpses of low ceilings dissected by beams and huge soot-stained fireplaces.

'Mind your head,' he said. 'Come through to the garden and we'll sit down.' When we were settled at the table on the paved terrace that overlooked a long stretch of green lawn, he said, 'I suppose you'd like to know a little about the house. Um . . . it's very old. Fifteenth century. But it's thought there has been a dwelling of some description here since Roman times. Just think, all those leather skirts!' He giggled suggestively, before assuming a more reverential tone. 'And then, as you know, Noël Coward lived here for thirty years from 1927.' He gave me a meaningful look. 'Imagine the goings-on. If walls could talk! Parties with Gertrude Lawrence and Joan Crawford, though I think I read somewhere that she didn't care for country life and left early. I expect it was raining. I won't lie to you, it can be terribly miserable here when it rains. The lawn turns to mud and the skies bulge with grey, tangible misery.' His face took on a poetical look. 'I rather like such moodiness,' he said dreamily. 'I embrace it, inhale it.' He paused for a moment and then snapped back into life. 'But the spring! Oh, it's just glorious. First the snowdrops, then primroses, daffodils, bluebells, and narcissi. They were planted by Noël himself, as was the fig tree.'

I interrupted him before he could get too lyrical. 'That's Coward's Jaguar on the drive.' It was true. I'd bought it in auction only the month before. I'm not sure why I felt the need to share this information with Julian – one-upmanship perhaps – but it did the trick.

'No!' he exclaimed, his eyes widening. 'That's really strange and weird! I expect the car knew the way here, didn't it? Home at last after all these years. I didn't have the chance to tell you the other night at the awards – your escort seemed rather keen to spirit you away from my presence – but your performance as Noël was quite remarkable.'

'Thank you.' I nodded, accepting his compliment.

'You looked and sounded just like him. Uncanny. You wouldn't do a little bit now, would you?'

'Oh, I don't think—' I protested, but Julian was insistent.

'You doing your Noël turn here in Noël's house would be too much. Stephen Fry came to tea last year and launched into "Mad Dogs and Englishmen" but between you and me, it was a little bit *Stars in Their Eyes*. You're much classier. Go on. Say something. Anything.'

'Very well,' I sighed, then adopted my best Coward voice. '*You're looking very lovely in this damn moonlight, Amanda.*' I added in my normal voice, 'That's all I can manage without costume and make-up, I'm afraid.'

'Brilliant!' said Julian, apparently satisfied. 'Do you do anyone else?'

'I'm afraid not,' I said firmly, finishing my tea. 'Would you mind if I had a little wander around? Alone.'

'Of course,' said Julian. 'You need to soak it all up without me chipping in. I'll stay here and you go inside. Take as much time as you like. The dogs might follow you but they'll be fine. If Albert rolls on his back it means he wants his scrotum tickled. Don't we all!'

By the time he'd finished laughing at his own joke, I was through the French windows and almost out of earshot. There was a stillness inside. I could almost feel the house pressing me to its heart, urging me to come to its rescue. Big, rectangular rooms led one from the other, sometimes with a step up or down between them. The light was different in each but the atmosphere the same: peaceful, almost holy. I went upstairs and stood at a window, looking out towards the front lawn and the gate with paint peeling off it like a snake shedding its skin. I looked at the vintage Jaguar sitting happily there, like a big hippo resting in the sun. Of course I could see that the windowsills were rotten and the ceilings were holding themselves up with great effort, like a duchess about to burst out of her corset. But everything seemed to whisper to me, thanking me for coming, tearfully hoping I would stay.

By the time I returned to Julian in the garden – who was picking at a bit of skin on his knee and muttering 'Folkestone gay fun night. Never again' – my mind was made up. As a matter of urgency, I had to get him out and myself in. I couldn't be bothered to play the games you are supposed to play in such situations. I wanted it and that was that.

'It is a very beautiful house,' I began in my most business-like voice. 'And I think I would like to buy it from you.'

'Oh. Good,' said Julian, looking somewhat stunned. 'But . . .' He seemed to be struggling to find the words.

'But what?' I asked impatiently.

'Well, it isn't all Douglas Fairbanks Junior and Mrs Worthington's Daughter, that's all,' he said in a strange voice.

'What do you mean?'

'You'll see,' he said. 'And I ought to warn you, it needs a lot of work. I'm afraid I've quailed before it, but no doubt your surveyor will tell you everything so there's no point in hiding it. You'll need a new roof, and—'

'Yes, yes,' I said. 'That's all perfectly obvious.' I stood up. 'Now—'

'You slipped into Noël then!' exclaimed Julian happily. 'You didn't even realise it!'

'My PA Jess will call you first thing in the morning, if that's convenient? And I suppose my solicitors will need to speak to your solicitors and so on.'

'Yes, of course,' he said, clearly delighted to have made such an easy sale. He dictated his number and I typed it into my mobile phone.

'I just love it when things happen as if pre-ordained,' he said, as I slipped my phone back into my jeans pocket. 'By the way, I ought to let you know that I'm buying a bungalow just by the village green. So I won't be far away.'

That should be worth another ten grand off the asking price, I thought to myself.

Scene Two

The summer of 1926

Noël

'Let me know if I'm talking too much,' said Noël, driving with careless speed through narrow country lanes, leaving hedges trembling in his wake. The little black motor roared as he made it fly around corners and swoop up hills, and he had to raise his voice to be heard over the engine. 'Although it's only fair to point out that what I say is quality and quantity combined. A rare thing, I think you'll find.'

'You go ahead,' replied Jack, smiling. 'I'm not glazing over.'

'Well, we're about to enter Kent. I can feel the sap rising in me like mercury up a thermometer. Take a deep breath. That is England's garden. That's hawthorn blossom,' Noël said, heedless of the road while he was pointing out the flora. 'Isn't it too lovely?'

The pair of them were motoring from London to Kent in a convertible Crossley with the roof down, Noël at the wheel, Jack in his shirtsleeves sitting beside him.

'Are you going to tell me where we're going?' asked Jack in his easy New York drawl, which somehow managed to squeeze an 'r' sound into every word.

'Certainly not. But I can tell you that our destination is also our destiny. Which rules out Chatham.'

'What's Chatham?'

'Do be quiet. If you're going to interrupt me constantly it will be a very dreary journey. I need to be left to chatter away like a parakeet if we're to have a memorable drive. A deaf mute would be my perfect travelling companion. If I could trouble you to smile and nod occasionally, like royalty, we'll get on terribly well. Otherwise I shall leave you at the roadside like a squashed hedgehog.'

Jack held one finger to his lips to indicate that he would not say another word. Noël moved his hand from the gear stick to his friend's knee and gave it a squeeze.

'This is all so thrilling, dear Jack. That is the long and the short of it. I'm taking you somewhere special. Our very own Utopia where we can have fun and then fun, followed by more fun. What do you say to that?' Noël's fingers made a little tinkling run up Jack's thigh, as if it were a keyboard.

'I've been told to shut up, haven't I? But it sounds like . . . fun,' said Jack, giving his lover a wry, sexy smile and flexing his leg muscles as an indication of his willingness to provide as much fun as Noël could take.

Noël inhaled and was uncharacteristically silent for a moment, staring ahead, before he said dreamily, 'I haven't been this excited since I attended the opening night of Ivor Novello's Fifty-Fifty club in Wardour Street. Light me a cigarette, would you, darling?'

His eyes flickered from the road ahead to Jack as the American turned to reach into his pocket to find his cigarette case. Jack looked back at Noël as he lit the cigarette, and the two of them shared a moment as he took it between his thumb and finger to

Noël's mouth, his finger brushing Noël's lower lip as it completed the transfer. A shiver ran through them both simultaneously.

'How about we pull off the road for a bit?' said Jack huskily, as quietly as an American can.

They had met for the very first time in London, where Noël had been starring in his own play, *The Vortex*, a scandalous portrayal of drug addiction and an uncomfortably intense mother/son relationship, and naturally a huge hit. Jack Wilson, an American stockbroker, had been brought back to his dressing room to meet the toast of theatreland. Young Noël Coward, only twenty-six, was being hailed as a bright new genius of the stage, and the good and the great flocked to see not only the witty, amusing play, but the man himself; after every performance, there was a queue of celebrities, film stars and lords and ladies outside Noël's dressing room.

It had been a brief meeting but Jack had made an impression. He was just Noël's type: handsome and masculine, with a hint of a cruel streak about his mouth. Jack, well connected and a theatre enthusiast, was visibly nervous to meet the great man but managed to suggest lunch if Coward should ever find himself in New York. Noël was very taken with the elegant, athletic American with shiny black hair and deliciously dark eyes, and when he did arrive in New York that autumn to open *The Vortex* on Broadway, he was secretly thrilled to receive an invitation to lunch, though he said carelessly, 'Jack who? Oh yes, that rather uppish American who wore his evening shirt with the collars turned down. But I think I may be free . . .'

Noël had scribbled a reply, and then on the day waited in vain for Jack to appear. He was enraged at being treated in such a manner until he discovered his reply had never been posted.

A contrite note was sent, and then Jack came to the first New York matinée of *The Vortex* and was invited back to dinner. Jack's first love was theatre and he only practised finance because his acting had come to nothing – he was witty and clever and well read. Rather pleasing in every way, Noël thought. They were both instantly smitten, the false start to their relationship only serving to heighten the thrill when they did eventually meet alone. Soon they were living it up in New York, drinking in clubs and bars, every door open to Noël's celebrity, both enjoying the hedonism and the liberalism of the cosy world of art, fame and money.

When the run in New York and then a tour had come to an end and it was time for Noël to return home to England, love and lust had him in a headlock and the idea of being separated from Jack was torture. He suggested his lover come back with him and it hadn't taken much for Jack to be persuaded. He, too, was in love, and besides, he had no ties to keep him in the States. His work as a stockbroker only occupied him when he chose that it should.

'Will I get to see Buckingham Palace?' he asked.

'See it?' said Noël. 'I shall buy you a Buckingham Palace paperweight and a tea towel. Does that settle it?'

'I guess so.' Jack put his hands in his pockets and smiled. 'England, here I come.'

They had travelled back together in adjoining first-class cabins on board the SS *Olympic* and the three-week crossing had cemented their relationship, for they could spend almost every hour together. Noël loved to stroll along the decks with his handsome companion, receiving admiring glances from the ladies sitting under their sun hats. They took lunch privately in their cabin, served by a knowing waiter who refilled their glasses and retreated discreetly after laying out the cheese board. The afternoons they would spend in bed, doors locked in case of interruption. Afterwards they dressed for dinner and appeared in the champagne lounge for cocktails at eight. Here, with a secret look of longing, they would part, Jack to flirt with the ladies and Noël to work the room, flitting from one titled couple to the next. At dinner, though, he made sure he and Jack sat with their own little set: Lady Diana Cooper, Syrie Maugham and Rebecca West. They were apart from the rest, their little group marked out by talent, high birth or exceedingly good looks.

Noël and Jack might exchange a few words after dinner in the smoking lounge, possibly, but they wisely kept their distance during the dancing or a concert in the ballroom and more cocktails. Occasionally Noël would take command of the piano and sing three or four of his popular ditties to an enthralled audience, all knowing how lucky they were to enjoy the company of the terribly famous Noël Coward, whose plays dominated the West End, whose songs were on gramophones in every parlour. Noël, ever the showman, would always judge his departure perfectly, leaving them wanting more. He would make a point of saying goodbye to everyone in the room, and then, pausing by the door, he would give a wave, deliver one final *bon mot*, smile affectionately and bow, trilling, 'Goodnight, my darlings!'

If he had one complaint about Jack, it was that he didn't follow him soon enough to the privacy of their adjoining cabins. Noël would return to his room, enter the day's events in his diary, pour himself a brandy and wait. One hour, two hours. He would pace up and down. Here he was, the darling of society, being kept waiting by his American stockbroker! What could Jack be doing? No doubt that strumpet Lady Whatever-her-name-was was making cow's eyes at him again. It was positively vulgar. Once he summoned the bellboy and had him deliver a terse note to Jack.

Ten minutes later Jack flew through the door. Noël had arranged himself seductively on the bed in his dressing gown but Jack was having none of it.

'You little shit!' he said, scowling, his eyes glittering dangerously with a mixture of anger and Scotch. 'Who the fuck do you think you're sending notes to? I'm not some absent schoolboy and you're not my master!'

Noël sat up, clutching his chest. 'There's no need to overreact. I thought you may have needed rescuing.'

'I can rescue myself, thank you, Florence Nightingale.' Jack was slurring his words. He ripped off his jacket and bow tie and poured himself another drink from the decanter.

'Haven't you had enough to drink, darling?'

'Maybe I have. Maybe I've had enough of you, too.' Jack downed his whisky in one gulp and poured himself another.

Noël was instantly penitent. 'I'm sorry. I didn't mean to be petulant. I was missing you, that's all.'

Jack's shoulders relaxed and his expression softened. 'That Amelia Field is a fucking leech. She kept standing so close to me I could see all the hairs up her nose. She wants a man so badly Cecil Beaton would do.'

Noël laughed. 'Poor, dear Cecil. I doubt he could rise to the occasion. Sit down and I'll rub your shoulders for you.'

The row had passed. Peace was restored. But Jack had made sure that Noël knew he wasn't to be treated like a plaything. No matter how famous and influential Noël was, if there was a master in their relationship it was to be Jack.

*

In London, Jack had set about meeting – and charming – Noël's family and friends with his easy style and his obvious good looks.

'Jack is the real thing. That's all I can say. He fulfils all of my requirements,' Noël told his devoted secretary Lorn Loraine one morning. They were in his sitting room, Lorn at the ready with his diary of engagements.

'How nice for you to be fulfilled,' replied Lorn, staring at him through the glasses perched on her nose as she sat at the table by the French windows. She was a solid, dependable woman with sharp intelligence and a honed wit, and she doted on Noël. 'And I'm so glad to hear he's real, and not some apparition.'

'You're making fun of me, Lorn, which is wicked of you.' Noël pouted.

'Please accept my humble apologies and strike my last remark from the record book,' said Lorn, bowing her head in supplication. 'If you're happy, I'm happy.'

'I am happy,' replied Noël, with a sparkle in his eye. 'So happy that I shall very probably write an elegant new three-act play before elevenses.'

'I'll inform the Lord Chamberlain and have him clear his afternoon appointments,' returned Lorn.

'My only desire is to make enough money to pay your extortionate wages,' Noël retorted, reaching for his cigarette case. 'A constant worry, I'll have you know.'

'And my only desire is to receive them,' said Lorn, raising an eyebrow.

Noël lit his cigarette and exhaled a long stream of smoke. 'By the way, you shall have to do some organising for me. Basil Dean is bringing *Easy Virtue* over from New York to open at the Duke of York's, cast and all. There's nothing for me to do. As my coffers are full to bursting . . .' He smiled at Lorn, who gave him a warning look . . . 'I think that Jack and I will do a little travelling in the next few months. Paris, Palermo, Venice – and some gorgeous hot places where we can feel the sun on our skin and turn dark mahogany.'

'Sounds dreamy,' Lorn said, smiling. 'You deserve some time off. You've been working frightfully hard. I worry about your health sometimes. You're looking all thin and pale.'

'I may well break in two like a cheese biscuit,' said Noël, sighing.

'If you don't rest, you'll never be able to write.'

Noël leaned forward. 'That's why Jack is so good, darling! He looks after me.'

'Yes, dear, he's a saint and we must erect a statue of him in St James's Park without further ado,' his secretary said, making a note of it.

Noël and Jack embarked on a wonderful, languid holiday, playing with high society when they weren't alone together in Sicily and Tunis, admiring the bronzed bodies of the local youths. In Venice, they partied with Cole Porter, the three of them sunbathing in their belted trunks while Porter thought up clever rhymes and Noël began conceiving his new play, *This Was a Man*. It had been depressing to return to London, so sunless and joyless compared to the sparkling Mediterranean and without the delightfully relaxed attitudes to two men enjoying each other's company. They had been forced to remember to man up, drop hands, refrain from kissing one another's cheek, to pretend they weren't in love.

It was then that the idea of the house had come to Noël: a secret retreat for just himself and Jack, where they could simply be themselves without worrying about anyone watching. Before long, he had found the perfect place and had signed an open lease so that they could go there whenever they liked.

'So where are you taking me?' asked Jack as the roads got narrower and the trees either side grew older and wilder, meeting above their heads so it seemed they were driving through a sumptuous green tunnel.

'I have rented a cottage in the country. Somewhere we can be alone.'

'How come you know where the fuck we're going?'

'This is a part of Kent I am familiar with. Full of childhood memories for me. It's a magical place I'd like to share with you. The Romney Marsh.'

'A marsh? Jesus!' Jack looked worried, as though he half expected the car to sink immediately into the bog and for them both to be lost forever.

Noël nodded, and narrowed his eyes. 'Witches live on the marsh, so they say. And ghosts on horseback. I have found the most divine house. Darling little latticed windows, low wooden beams, a cat-slide roof.'

'A what?'

'A roof that doesn't stop until it reaches the ground. You'll see. It's rustic heaven, trust me. I've taken it with an open lease. We can make it ours for as long as we want.'

'Can we get gin there?'

'I have a boot full, silly. Is that all you're concerned about?'

'We'll be alone?'

'Completely.'

'No socialising? No parties and cocktails? No at homes and dinners? No rehearsals, no first nights, no theatricals? No dressing up in bow ties?' Jack said suspiciously. Their time in London had been marked by the same frantic pace and social obligations that they had known in New York and then on board ship. Noël never seemed to stop. Jack loved parties and could drink with the best of them, but even he found that unceasing socialising took its toll.

'Nothing more troublesome than a stag beetle to disturb us for two weeks,' Noël replied with satisfaction. 'Darling Lorn has arranged it all. My diary is completely clear. Only your name is in it, in thick black ink. This is Jack and Noël time.'

'Who's gonna cook and do the dishes?'

'Well, I have provisions for a few days, but we can hire a cook and a maid from the village once we're settled. Won't it be blissful? Just think – no pretending.'

They were driving slowly now, along a bumpy track through woodland. Suddenly the track left the woods and sunny fields spread on either side of them. Involuntarily they both tipped their heads up towards the sun and smiled contentedly. Noël let the car roll to a stop.

'There it is,' he breathed, and they both gazed at the house, looking comfortable and mellow under its speckled slate tiles. It seemed to gaze right back at them, just as a beautiful, tempestuous stallion might contemplate its new jockey.

'Well, just look at that,' said Jack approvingly. 'As pretty as a kitten up a Christmas tree.'

'A snowy *white* kitten wearing an emerald collar,' corrected Noël. 'Now, go and open that gate, there's a dear.'

Jack leapt out to obey and Noël watched admiringly as his lover wrestled the gate open, letting it swing back so that the way was clear for them to enter. He sighed with pleasure, got out of the car and headed for the dear little door that led, he felt sure, to a new, happy chapter in his life.

Scene Three

Richard

When I told Fran about my impulsive decision to buy the house, he was in favour of the whole thing. I'd feared he might think I'd been hasty and rash, but it seemed to appeal to him.

'Maybe it's time we had a country pad. Tweed jackets, Wellington boots,' he said down the phone from Cologne, where he was away on business. 'I'm rather taken with the idea.'

'And, of course,' I enthused, 'we wouldn't have to wash or shave. Country folk don't bother with personal freshness.'

'Of course they don't,' agreed Fran. 'They even drink tap water. Imagine!'

I was glad that Fran was behind my plan, but Jess had to be on my side if the project was going to meet with any success at all. And at first, she had been firmly against my move to the country. She liked London and the order and convenience of my Chiswick house, where everything was at her fingertips. Although I hadn't been bothered with the surveyor's report, Jess had read it and been aghast.

'You can't buy it. It's going to cost you thousands. Hundreds of thousands!' She looked truly appalled. 'And think of the time it will take! And I'm not prepared to commute down there every day, I'll tell you that now.'

'You don't have to,' I said. I'd already put a plan in place to deal with her resistance. 'The house comes with a little cottage – the old chauffeur's place. I'd like you to have it. You can live there in the week and go back to town at weekends if you like. Or stay there the whole time. There's room for you and Albie. Just think, won't it be lovely? All of us in the country? Don't you feel ready for a change, Jess?'

I watched her face carefully, knowing that the next few seconds were decisive. Once Jess made up her mind, it was hard to change it. But the mention of the little cottage had given her pause for thought, and my invocation of Albie's name had been a masterstroke. I was certain that Jess was picturing herself and her son together in rural bliss; perhaps she was in a gingham apron pulling a tray of freshly baked scones from the oven while outside young Albie chopped logs for the fire. I leapt in to push home my advantage.

'I'll get the cottage done first,' I coaxed. 'You can choose everything and have it done just as you like. Wouldn't that be nice? Roses round the door, a fire blazing in the hearth, a budgie snoozing on its perch.'

'If there's any snoozing to be done, I expect it will be Albie lazing in bed,' Jess said, but her face had softened. 'Maybe it wouldn't be so bad. Perhaps Albie can grow some vegetables. My own choice of everything?'

'Down to the last tap!' I declared. 'Just think, a wonderful new stage in our long and happy relationship.'

Jess was convinced, despite her misgivings. She made short shrift of Mr Clary and the deal was signed and sealed in record time. Priest's Hole House was mine.

*

My relationship with Jess had indeed been long and happy. She had been a constant in my life, my loyal personal assistant, since I first sniffed real success at the age of twenty-three. We had met when I was performing two shows a day in a rather crumby theatre in North London, and she was in charge of the front of house. Even then she was the same: highly organised and efficient, always neatly turned out, and very keen to help me. At the end of every show, Jess would come backstage to the dressing rooms for a long natter over glasses of warm white wine and the occasional spliff. Even though others often couldn't see it, she had a certain sweetness that appealed to me: under the cool-looking exterior of pale-blue eyes and soft shoulder-length fair hair, there lurked a sharp mind too, and she was always an appreciative audience. She soon became a devoted friend and, when success beckoned, it had seemed a natural step for her to take on the role of my personal assistant. She was brilliant at it, of course, with her organised nature, and she was utterly loyal, my protective gatekeeper.

I came to depend on her more and more over the years and by the time I was installed in my Chiswick home, the basement had become Jess's domain, converted to a large, open-plan office from where, each weekday morning, she organised my diary, accounts, pensions, finances and future commitments. I couldn't imagine my life without her. I truly knew nothing about what I called the 'dreary' aspects of my fabulous life – meaning bank accounts, tax demands or anything whatsoever delivered in a manila envelope. Jess kept it all going without my having to worry at all. She made sure she had tabs on everyone and everything. There was a hint of dominatrix about the black, high-heeled boots she favoured and her preference for leather skirts, and it seemed to keep everyone in line nicely. She would peer coldly over her sparkling, gold-rimmed glasses as she tasted the chef's soup and declare it too salty or not seasoned sufficiently. She would inspect bedrooms after they'd been done and if they weren't up to scratch she would fire the cleaner on the spot. The staff in the house would quake when they heard Jess's footsteps approaching, tip-tapping briskly along the corridor. Consequently, on the whole, everything ran smoothly.

Even if a cook or cleaner or dog walker was everything one could hope for, Jess had a rule that they couldn't stay for more than two years. After that, she told me, complacency and over-familiarity would creep in.

'And what about you, then?' I once asked, after one of my favourite cooks had said her tearful goodbyes simply because Jess had found a fork in the spoon drawer. 'You've never considered replacing yourself for the same reasons you dismiss others? You're over-familiar, aren't you?'

'I am your personal assistant, silly!' laughed Jess. 'It's my job to be familiar in every way. I have to be an extension of you. I do all the things you don't have time or inclination to do. I'm here so you don't have to worry. This is completely different from cooking your lunch, frankly. No one else could cope with my job. So let's not have any more silly talk from you or I'll be off and then you'll be sorry. I don't just post your letters and file your fan mail, you know. I run your life. I enable you to be Richard Stent.' Jess waved her arm towards the shelf full of film and theatre awards. 'You wouldn't have collected half of those if I hadn't been around, and don't you forget it. I never will.'

She was right. I liked a strong, no-nonsense woman, and Jess was certainly that. I sometimes wondered if we weren't a little too close but it was a bit late for that. The line between personal and professional had been blurred long ago, after all. When I'd hit the big time, I'd discovered that along with the fame and money came the sex. I went through a wildly promiscuous phase – inevitable, I suppose. But if I was like a kid in a candy store, then I was more Pick 'n' Mix than Ferrero Rocher, it has to be said. I wasn't looking for love and love wasn't looking for me. My star was rising and I was enjoying the ascent. If anyone attempted to get too close I would simply give them a cheery wave and tip them over the side, back to oblivion.

Jess knew about all of this, just as she knew about everything. One memorable morning she arrived and dutifully picked up a used condom from the living-room mantelpiece and a bottle of amyl nitrate from the table. Then she came into the bedroom to check on me. While I, mortified, pretended to sleep, Jess hauled a hung-over Moroccan out of the bedroom by the scruff of his hairy neck and ejected him from the building without so much as a mint tea.

'He's gone home. It was for the best,' she said briskly, smiling a tight smile when I appeared a little later, asking where Abdul was. 'I have to worry about your Rolex, you know, even if you don't.'

Which I thought bordered just a little on the racist, though I didn't say anything.

While Jess knew almost every aspect of my personal life, she gave very little away about her own. In fact, she hardly ever spoke about herself. I knew she was three years older than me and that she lived alone in a flat in Earls Court she'd inherited from her father, but she didn't talk about her home life or her social circle and I sensed her discomfort if ever I tried to find out anything, which wasn't often, to be honest. Like most actors I wasn't terribly interested in anyone but myself. Jess didn't seem to mind and was happy to chatter about me and my affairs for as long as I liked.

Jess was seven and a half months pregnant before I even noticed. I was thirty, with my career nearing its peak, and I was so completely taken up with my latest role as Stanley Kowalski in the National Theatre production of *A Streetcar Named Desire* that I'd barely thought about anything else for months. It was only when I saw Jess's swollen belly entering the room a good ten seconds before she did that it occurred to me she might be expecting a baby. I gathered up my courage and asked her if it was the case.

'It's not a problem, is it?' she said, as if she'd passed wind.

'Er . . . no . . . of course it's not a problem,' I said uncertainly, immediately thinking only of myself.

Jess knew me too well. She didn't bother mentioning varicose veins or morning sickness or trepidation at giving birth. She cut to the chase. 'I'm due in six weeks and I've worked out that I'll need a couple of weeks off to begin with, but I've already arranged a full-time nanny and I should be back at work in no time at all.'

'Please don't worry about it,' I said, embarrassed that I'd been so self-absorbed. 'I'm a bit surprised, that's all, but I'm very happy for you. I just wonder why you didn't tell me before.'

'I was worried,' said Jess, biting her lip. 'I didn't want you to think it means I'm leaving you. I thought you might start looking for my replacement.'

I put my hand out to her, horrified she might think I would treat her that way. 'No, I wouldn't, of course not! And you must take as much leave as you need. God. I'm just so shocked. I didn't even know you had a boyfriend.'

'I don't.'

'Oh.'

'One-night stands are not exclusive to famous gay actors, you know.'

'Good for you, girlfriend!' I replied, thrilled at the thought of Jess having just the sort of rough and tumble she seemed to disapprove of whenever I indulged myself. I tried to imagine her having a personal life beyond work, but it was difficult. Picturing Jess romping in bed with some random man was impossible. I shook my head to clear the picture. 'This is so exciting! I couldn't be more thrilled.'

Jess smiled, looking relieved, and I felt guiltier than ever.

I was determined to make up for my laggardly behaviour. For the remainder of her pregnancy, I think I was more excited about the forthcoming arrival than Jess herself. I bought baby clothes and a crib from Harrods and an impossibly soft little toy llama from an exclusive shop in Chiswick High Street. Jess was delighted, evidently thrilled that I was taking such an interest. I suppose it was a novel feeling for her.

Then one day, she left a message saying she was working from home. I called her mobile later, assuming she must be feeling tired now that she was in the very late stages of her pregnancy. Jess started telling me about changes to my diary and some meetings I had scheduled, when she broke off to grunt rather uncharacteristically.

'Are you all right?' I asked.

'Oh, yes. I am . . . but . . . my waters broke half an hour ago. I'm now at the hospital. You'll have to excuse me if I have to ring off suddenly.'

'How fantastic!' I said, secretly hoping she'd made it to the bathroom or at least managed to put some newspaper down. 'You'll be wonderful! Break a leg.'

'Listen, Richard, I must go. The midwife says I'm nine centimetres dilated.'

'Right. I'm off. Thinking of you. But tell me quickly, did you reserve my table at Sheekey's for tonight?'

'I . . . er . . . oooowwww,' was Jess's decidedly unclear response.

'Was that a yes, darling? Only I've got Joan Collins in the diary and we wouldn't want to abort the evening.'

'Yes, done,' managed Jess breathlessly.

'Thank you,' I said, relieved. 'I'll go now. I'll be in to see you tomorrow. Hope it's not all too mucky. Bye!'

Two weeks after giving birth to her son Albie, Jess was back at her desk, the baby asleep in a Moses basket on top of the filing cabinet, the nanny waiting in the hallway, filing her nails in case she was needed. As soon as he stirred, the nanny whisked him off with a bottle and fed him, or tucked him into a pram and took him for a stroll around the park. I loved having him about, and rocked him in my arms and cooed over him almost more than his mother did. He really was the most gorgeous little thing, with navy-blue eyes, a fuzzy down of soft blond hair and that baby-button nose and rosebud mouth all infants seem to have. I'd never had the slightest desire to be a father myself, but now I realised I could have all the fun of being paternal with none of the burden of responsibility. And as there was no word of who Albie's father really was, I didn't have to worry about making someone else resentful. When Jess asked me to be Albie's godfather (an honorary role – she wasn't the churchy type), I accepted very happily.

When he was a toddler, Albie and I would spend hours playing hide and seek. As soon as he and Jess arrived, I would pluck the boy from his pushchair and swing him around, making him giggle and gurgle with delight. While Jess opened the mail and made important phone calls, we would chase each other around the garden. I bought a swing and a climbing frame. When I was filming abroad, I flew them out too. Jess knew it wasn't so much that I needed a PA but I wanted to see young Albie. The pair of us were best buddies.

As Albie grew older and I became more successful, I asked Jess if she'd let me pay for his schooling.

'He's special to me,' I said honestly. 'I don't have any family of my own. I have plenty of money. I'd like it very much if you agreed.'

'That's so sweet of you, Richard. I accept. Thank you,' she said, smiling happily. She chose a boarding school in Norfolk.

'But I'll never see him!' I cried in dismay.

'I knew you'd say that, but it's the school where my father went. If you want to withdraw the offer, then . . .'

Of course I didn't. I only saw Albie in the school holidays after that, and sometimes not even then. Jess would whisk him away on some trip, or send him to his grandparents, or arrange for him to visit school friends. I once wondered if she was actually trying to keep me apart from the boy, and even if the bond that had been developing between us had made her jealous. Perhaps she didn't want Albie loving me like a father, or me playing the role of the fairy godfather in his life. It was true that Jess seemed to treasure the special relationship the two of us enjoyed. Boyfriends had come and gone for both of us, but no one had disrupted the smooth passage of our professional and personal relationship. We were firm friends, after all, and although Jess was always assiduous about doing her work, we spent hours gossiping and chatting.

Albie's arrival in particular, and my involvement in his life, meant that we became even closer. It was Jess I turned to when my father died, and on my shoulder Jess cried her tears when six-year-old Albie was in hospital with pneumonia.

Sometimes I sensed a hidden side to Jess's personality. Darker moods could settle on her occasionally and for weeks at a time she would be quiet and curt, not her usual self. I would be fearful that I was in some way the cause of these upsets, and would buy her flowers, ask if she needed some time off or, if all else failed, simply keep my distance and leave her to get on with it. The black clouds would pass eventually, and harmony restored. I could see no rhyme or reason to the black moods; the only thing I wondered was whether Jess – so organised and in control – found it difficult when things became unpredictable and stressful. And, of course, she was bringing up Albie alone – how could I possibly understand the pressures of being a single mother? But Jess always got back to her old self in the end.

As far as I was concerned, she ran my life excellently and I was very fond of her. I had no complaints.

'You're the wife I never had!' I would say often, and Jess would glow with pleasure.

Then I met Fran on a yacht in Ibiza. It was a set-up arranged by a well-meaning friend from the world of fashion, though I didn't know it at the time. He probably intended us to have a holiday romance or twenty lust-filled minutes in the broom cupboard, not move in together and become life partners.

It was Fran's cool, intelligent eyes with a hint of neediness that attracted me over the canapés. He was very tall and slim, dressed with stylish restraint: nautical pale blue-and-white striped T-shirt and faded, expensive jeans. His hair was artfully cut: very short mostly, but with a longer fringe, gelled and teased up and out to draw attention from his generous nose. When we went for a stroll on deck later we kissed but when I tried to lure him into my cabin, he shook his head.

'I like to take things slowly,' he said, gazing down into the water. This was a novel change from most of my conquests and sharpened my interest. And slowly is just how we progressed through life together: no dramas or fights, just steady and reliable. Some sort of instinct kicked in when I met Fran, informing me that happiness and contentment this way lay. I'd had relationships in the past where the moment things became remotely serious, they also became costly and stifling; suspicion and jealousy reared their ugly heads. But Fran put up with my touring or filming schedule and I had to accept that Fran's work teaching high-flying corporate types how to fly even higher also kept him away from home for weeks at a time. We spoke every night on the phone and saved up amusing stories of the day's events to tell each other. We laughed a lot.

When it became clear that Fran was going to be an important part of my life, I was worried about how Jess would take it.

'She's a bit . . . possessive, I suppose,' I said to Fran, as we lay in bed together one day. 'It's always been just the two of us. None of my boyfriends has lasted that long and none of them were like you. She's going to know you're a different proposition from the off.'

Fran smiled a knowing smile. He understood perfectly. It was why I loved him, I suppose. 'Don't worry, we'll make sure Jess is happy.'

Winning over Jess wasn't easy, but Fran was clever about it –

he was restrained but friendly with her, and slowly he established himself in my world, taking care not to step on her toes. Jess thawed gradually as she realised that, despite his permanent place in my life, Fran was not going to oust her. In fact, because he was so busy and frequently away – not to mention openly uninterested in any kind of celebrity or show business – I still needed Jess to accompany me to opening nights or award ceremonies, which was something she'd always enjoyed.

Jess's curiosity about our unconventional relationship surfaced on my birthday after Fran and I had been together for over two years. Fran was away in Geneva, so Jess had taken me to the Ivy for dinner.

'It's such a shame Fran couldn't be here,' she commented as we waited for the oysters to arrive. 'I feel like a very poor substitute.'

'Oh, you're not at all,' I replied at once. 'I shall see him next week and I'm not fussed about birthdays.'

'You must miss him though.'

I sensed Jess was digging in an area that clearly concerned her.

'The odd stab, yes,' I answered. 'But I think missing someone is rather enjoyable. It puts your emotions in order. If you're with someone you love all the time, and you felt boredom rising up inside you like damp up a wall . . . well, I can't think of anything more heartbreaking. If we were joined at the hip we wouldn't have lasted all these years.'

'Do you trust Fran?'

'Completely. That's the whole point of our relationship. We have trust and love. But you know, there is the rest of life, too.'

'Work?'

'Seems an inadequate word for the rest of life, but yes.'

'I think the romantic side of my brain was underdeveloped somewhere along the line,' said Jess, fiddling with her napkin. She was looking typically restrained in a plain black dress, her fair hair pulled back into a tight ponytail.

'Have you ever been in love, Jess?' I asked. In all the years I'd never asked her this question and, even now, it was bold of me, but she had started the conversation and besides, I wanted to know. I sensed at once I had gone too far. Jess clutched her neck as if trying to stop the hot rush of blood from colouring her cheeks. Just then the waiter arrived to top up our champagne and she didn't need to answer. Seeing her discomfort, I didn't push the point. I still wondered about Albie's father. He was such a good-looking boy; why couldn't she tell me about him?

'How is Albie?' I asked, thinking that it was a while since I'd seen him. He was growing up fast, already a teenager with gangly limbs and unfortunate hair. I was delighted that he had seemed to flourish at school, developing into a fine lad with an appropriately plummy accent to go with his boarding-school education and rich friends, but I had seen so little of him lately. Although I still spoilt the boy with expensive presents for Christmas and his birthday, I regretted that the early connection between us had faded.

'He's fine,' Jess said with a smile. 'Getting on well at school. Though I do worry what he's going to do with his life. He seems somewhat unfocused. Still, there's plenty of time yet.'

'I really must catch up with him one of these days. It's been ages. Far too long.'

'Mmm. Yes. One day soon.' Jess looked at me steadily for a moment, and picked up her glass of champagne. 'Here's to you!' she said brightly. 'Happy birthday, Richard.'

We each took a sip.

'And here's to you,' I said, smiling. 'The wind beneath my wings.'

Jess grimaced at my crass line. 'The beard beneath your flings, more like,' she muttered, and looked decidedly pleased with her humorous riposte.

Scene Four

Summer 1926

Noël

Goldenhurst Old Manor was everything Noël had hoped it would be. Here, he had Jack to himself completely and those first two stolen weeks were bliss. There were no debs or duchesses batting their eyelids at him for one thing, and Jack seemed able to relax and be himself. Of course they'd had to return to the bustle and whirl of London life, but they escaped to their retreat as often as they dared.

Noël's heart leapt each time he drove slowly along the lane towards the house. Indeed he felt a twitch of sexual anticipation, an involuntary tightening of his buttocks: under that darling, bowed roof he and Jack would romp to their hearts' content, with no need to stifle their whelps of pleasure or whisper their declarations of love.

It was no easy task conducting a passionate affair in London, and Noël was so tired of being furtive and secretive about it. Of course he was known to be 'that way' and it was hardly unusual in theatrical circles. No one ever asked why he wasn't married. Even the public, by and large, accepted that he wasn't the marrying kind, and Noël had studiously ignored the rare insult muttered within earshot as he left the stage door. The law declared his physical love of another man to be illegal and that was that. In his plays and his presentation of himself, Noël went as far as he dared. He wrote 'I'll follow my secret love my whole life through' – as clear a statement as he could make without getting arrested. Of course he didn't hang around parks or public conveniences looking for sordid encounters – that was hardly his style and he disapproved of such carryings on. He'd had fun with a number of men, enjoyed late-night visitors to his rooms and had a thoroughly pleasurable time. But things were different with Jack. This was a meeting of minds, hearts and souls. Noël felt almost overwhelmed with love for him, wanted to be with him for ever, to spend his life with him.

'I expect there is a place somewhere,' he'd said to Jack in New York soon after they met, 'some little island just off the coast near Papua New Guinea where you and I could live together quite openly and lovingly. Wouldn't that be divine?'

'And they wouldn't set fire to our grass skirts and skin us alive?'

'Only on Sundays.'

The renting of this house was really part of that dream. They were able to show their affection for each other without glancing about first and checking that no one was observing them. They sat around until lunchtime in their dressing gowns if they felt like it, kissing and canoodling. They wandered through the woodland holding hands, stopping to hug each other or sit, holding hands on a fallen tree. Together they watched a young owl testing its wings high up in a sturdy oak tree, hopping precariously from branch to branch.

'I keep hearing myself sigh,' Noël told Jack. 'Just with the sheer pleasure of being alive and here with you. This is the England I wanted you to experience. Away from London and the theatre and all the fuss and nonsense that goes with it. You feel it too, don't you? Don't you?'

'I feel it,' said Jack, looking deeply into Noël's eyes. 'This is magic.'

Real life could only be kept at a distance for so long, even at the Old Manor. Noël had a telephone installed and no sooner was it connected than it never stopped ringing, or so it seemed to Jack. *Easy Virtue*'s London run was a hit and the next of Noël's plays opened, a gossamer-light Ruritanian romance called *The Queen Was in the Parlour* and audiences seemed to like it too, so that, for a brief golden moment, there were two Coward plays running in the West End. Noël's producer Basil Dean hadn't wanted to produce *This Was a Man,* despite the fact that Noël was proud of it, but opening the play proved impossible in any case. To Noël's great annoyance, the Lord Chamberlain had refused to licence *This Was a Man,* declaring its depictions of adultery lacking in morality.

'What a thoroughly unpleasant, small-minded man he must be,' a furious Noël had declared when he'd learned the news. 'I expect he eats fried food and is married to a woman who wears her hair in a bun.' After pacing up and down for a few moments, his mood lightened. 'Well then, shunned by the mother country, we shall simply open on Broadway,' he declared carelessly. 'God bless America, with its enlightened stage censorship. Now that really is the land of the free!'

Jack had liked that idea of returning to New York where he was more at home and where they could resume their life of theatre by day and glamorous clubs by night. But now Dean had suggested that Coward take the lead role in *The Constant Nymph*, which would mean delaying a return to New York, and yet more frantic preparation and work. It made Jack want to growl with frustration.

And, he thought jealously, if it weren't producers and agents on the line to Noël every day, badgering the star for his next play, then Noël himself was on the telephone, absorbed in his nightly hour-long billing-and-cooing calls to his mother. The post brought letter after fat letter from Violet, wondering if she was ever going to see her darling boy again.

'Not another one,' Jack said, frowning as over the breakfast table he watched Noël slit open an envelope addressed in his mother's sloping hand. He leaned back in his chair and took a gulp of strong black coffee. 'What can there be left to write about?'

'Plenty,' Noël said, pulling out a wodge of writing paper covered in dense handwriting. He scanned it, his high forehead furrowing with concern as he did so. He looked older than his age, Jack thought, as though he'd already lived through more than most. But then, he'd been acting on the stage before he was twelve. Noël looked up at him, his expression half apologetic and half haughty. 'You know how she cannot live without me. Nor I without her. Love needs to express itself, we find. Take note.'

'Yeah, I'm taking notes. Twenty-pound notes,' muttered Jack. He had met Violet in London and found the mutual adoration she and Noël had for each other decidedly disconcerting. Noël addressed his mother as 'Darlingest' for starters, which seemed to place her above any other mere mortal in his affections, and signed his letters to her 'Snoopie'. He had a penchant for nicknames and had christened Jack himself 'Bay-bay' or 'Dab'.

Violet had been polite enough with Jack when they met but her face had said more than her lips. Violet's appearance was as strong as her personality: with dark eyebrows heavy beneath a fluff of grey curls, and the same nose as her son over a wide thin mouth, she was an intense small package of a woman. She seemed to Jack a sort of miniature version of Noël, with a bird-like face and piercing eyes that seemed to laugh inwardly, unless she was looking at her beloved son, when they glistened and glimmered with passion and pride. But there was suppressed rage there, Jack could see. It was quite obvious, too, that she knew the exact nature of their relationship and she didn't seem to mind this at all – not the physical aspect, at least. Jack felt she was suspicious of his motives and concerned about how embroiled in her son's affairs he was becoming. Jack felt himself watched, assessed and found wanting. But as time went on and Violet began to accept his presence at Noël's side, what hurt Jack most was that he was considered unimportant. Violet was careless of him, not bothering to ask after him or include him, radiating the inescapable sense that he would be gone soon enough.

That was another reason he loved being at Goldenhurst: the proper order of things seemed established here. He was Noël's partner and here Noël's mother was kept at a distance, only able to reach out to her son via those endless letters and nightly phone calls.

Jack watched Noël reading, his eyes flicking quickly across the page as he ate his toast and marmalade.

'She loves the fact that you're queer,' he said. 'It means she doesn't have to face any competition. Imagine if you fell in love with a woman. Darlingest would poison her tea and bury the bitch in the garden.'

'Mmm,' Noël replied, not listening.

'If only she had a cock,' Jack said, emphasising the last word, 'she'd be the perfect woman for you.'

Noël glanced at him. 'You are being deliberately nauseating. Please stop. Toast is difficult enough to swallow as it is.'

The other woman in Noël's life watching and waiting for a false move from Jack was Lornie, Noël's secretary and bookkeeper. But when he met her in Noël's London office, Jack could see that she was more than this: lavished with affection by Noël, she was the key to his support network and he was terribly fond of her. Their relationship was so idiosyncratic – all pet names, coded words and mock insults – Jack declared it beyond his understanding.

'Must be an English thing,' he said. 'It's like you're a schoolboy and she's the matron. I don't get it. Can't she just do her job and go home? Do you have to have silly names for the filing cabinets and leave each other rhyming ditties all over the place? It's all so bloody arch.' Jack shook his head in confusion.

'Are you feeling shut out, dear Jack?' asked Noël. 'It's hardly Lorn's fault that you're American. Please be quiet and think about baseball or something you understand.'

'I don't understand this, for example,' said Jack, producing a note written in Noël's hand. He read it aloud:

> *'I couldn't cope without her –*
> *Though I'm not one to fawn,*
> *I simply can't imagine*
> *My life* sans *graceful Lorn.'*

Jack laughed. 'I mean, if that broad is graceful then I'm Nijinsky's understudy.'

Noël snatched the note away from him. 'You are rather missing the point, but never mind,' he said wearily. 'Lorn is a woman without vanity, who has accepted the plain face and large nose nature has given her, much as she accepts the weather. I refer to her grace because only I can see it. This must be difficult for a man as blessed as you to understand.'

Jack sensed that Lornie felt insecure when he appeared on the scene, and feared for her position in the hierarchy. He was sure that there was also a snobbish, almost racist dismissal of his status, simply because he was American. This was confirmed when he read one of her four line poems to Noël:

Just because he's charming,
And takes you up the knoll,
Don't forget this debutante
Still enjoys a stroll.

She was doubtless referring to his sexual prowess, Jack concluded, feeling a touch of smugness. Noël must have alluded to it somehow. Nevertheless, the secretary's reference to her social superiority infuriated him: she was obviously reminding her employer that she'd been received at court by Queen Mary and belonged to the world Noël wished to inhabit. He immediately felt the desire to shut her out and keep her away from his lover as much as possible.

More than once, he had lifted the ringing telephone and replaced it gently in its cradle, feeling a sense of satisfaction at silencing the voices that were clamouring to get into Goldenhurst.

As summer grew to a close and the evenings cooled and shortened, Jack could sense the vultures circling. Violet, Lornie, the producers, the press, the hangers-on and the admirers were all crowding in, demanding their share of Noël and he feared there may not be enough to go around. It seemed that they were all waiting in the wings for Noël to forget his dalliance with Jack and consign him to the rubbish heap of past loves where he belonged, the forgotten American, while Noël returned to his creative, money-making life in London. He loved Noël, was enchanted by him and adored him with all his heart, even when he sometimes tired of the tantrums and tears that seemed to come along with genius. Surely beyond the bubble of the Kentish cottage, away from the fields and the birds and the rustic bliss they had immersed themselves in, real life would spoil everything.

They were spending one of the last warm afternoons of summer in the garden, soaking up the sunshine. They lay on an old wool rug, both wearing linen trousers and white shirts with the sleeves rolled up, lazing in companionable silence as they read. Jack stopped reading and closed his eyes, relishing the feel of the warm breeze across his bare feet, and listened for a while to the rustling leaves in the trees and the constant, gentle hum of a thousand insects so busy with the adventure of their short lives. Jack realised that Noël was studying him, his eyes watery with emotion.

'What are you thinking about?' Jack asked, smiling.

'You. About how much I love you. Promise me you'll never go away? I don't think I could bear it.' He put one hand out towards Jack as though wanting to clasp him tight.

Jack rolled to face him, discarding his book. 'I'll never go. Unless you chuck me out.'

'That I'll never do.'

'And what if—'

'Don't let's talk about "what ifs". Let's just sit here in this garden and try not to think about the future or the past. I love you and that is all that matters.'

'I love you.'

'No one can spoil this.'

'I can think of several who might give it a damn good try.'

'Hush now. Quiet. Hold my hand.'

The two men sat together, fingers entwined, shoulders touching. After a few moments they embraced and kissed, then simultaneously, as if flattened by the euphoria of love's finest moment, reclined, lay back on the grass to study the blue sky and squint at the sun. Without meaning to, they synchronised their breathing. The dry earth beneath them shifted to caress their shoulders and the grass parted, then moved imperceptibly to fondle their toes. The sun shone through the green leaves and offered a cool, dappled warmth and soul-feeding energy. It was a moment that would bind them together.

A few days later Noël and Jack were having a lunch of boiled eggs, anchovies and lettuce on the front lawn by the kitchen.

'Darling, I've got something to tell you,' began Noël, dabbing the corners of his mouth with a napkin.

'Are you pregnant with twins?' asked Jack.

'No.'

'Oh, what a disappointment.'

'This is important. Be quiet and listen, would you?'

Jack laid down his fork and put on his serious face.

Noël frowned thoughtfully, then looked up at Jack, his eyes earnest. 'You mean the world to me, and I don't want this party to end. But we both know we cannot stay here for ever.'

Jack felt a nasty poke of apprehension in his stomach. Was this the moment he had been dreading? 'Actually we could,' he said quickly. 'You could write plays in the back bedroom, send them off to London and Broadway and wait for the cheques to come tumbling through the letter box.'

Noël waved aside his suggestion. 'No, no, I've got a better idea. Why don't you become my manager? I don't have one, and you'd be brilliant at it – you understand me completely, better than anyone else, and you have your stockbroking background so you know how business works. Don't you see? We'd have a legitimate reason to be together, without any frightful busybodies asking unwanted questions.'

Jack stared back at him, amazed and moved. 'You trust me?'

'That is what I'm trying to prove to you, darling. I will give you complete control. It's rather erotic, don't you think?' Noël smiled, his thin upper lip curling up in amusement. 'When *The Constant Nymph* is finished, we'll go to New York together and open *This Was a Man* there. After all, I dedicated it to you. What could be more perfect? Well, what do you say?'

Jack smiled and waved his empty teacup at Noël. 'I've always said you're a genius. Shall we drink to it?'

Scene Five

Richard

I was so excited the night before I took possession of Priest's Hole House, I didn't sleep a wink. This was the start of a new chapter in my life, something private that neither Fran nor Jess really understood. I knew that deep down both, in their own ways, thought it was just a folly of mine, the latest distraction for someone rich and famous enough to indulge his fancies and probably something that would soon pass. Fran, to be fair, wasn't as cynical as Jess, but then he also wasn't going to be around very much.

Not long before the purchase was complete, he broke the news that he was off to Los Angeles for an extended period as part of his job.

'You mean, longer than a week?' I asked, frowning. He'd cooked me a delicious supper that we were enjoying in the kitchen of the Chiswick house.

'I mean longer than a month,' replied Fran. He looked a tiny bit guilty, which was unusual for him. 'Probably as long as six months. I've been offered a long assignment and it's a fabulous opportunity. I'm going to take it.'

'Oh,' I said, feeling flat. I pushed away the remnants of my osso buco, suddenly realising why he had taken so much care. It was an apology on a plate. 'We won't trouble ourselves with a conversation followed by a mutually agreeable compromise then.' I sighed, feeling crosser. 'You'll miss all the fun of moving into the new house, helping me do it up, all the things I was looking forward to us doing together.'

'You can send me pictures.' Fran gazed down at his own food and put down his fork. 'And I'll be back on visits.'

Visits? Was this what our relationship was reduced to? 'But you'll miss all the exciting things,' I said sadly, realising that the freedom and independence we prized in our relationship meant I was facing a prolonged period of time alone – and alone in a new and rather isolated place.

'We've had this talk before,' Fran said, his hazel eyes almost reproving. 'It's work, remember? These years are important for me.'

I said nothing more. We had talked about this many times, and I knew that the one thing in the world Fran would resist was the idea that I and my career might, by virtue of my fame and success, be the more important. He would stubbornly resist being at my beck and call, I knew that. Equality was everything. And I was acutely aware that while I might be at a place in my life when settling in the country seemed appealing, Fran's relative youth meant that he was still in the whirl of work where the professional took precedence over the personal. I didn't want to dwell on that, or remind him of the fact. So I bit my tongue and accepted that he would be going, though I knew I would miss him horribly.

'Be good, won't you?' Fran said as he pulled his suitcase along the hallway the morning of his departure.

'I'll try,' I said wistfully, 'but some of the sheep in Kent are damned attractive.'

He left me a pair of green wellies as a house-warming gift before he flew off.

On the big day itself Jess said she needed to be in London to deal with money transfers, so I was very much alone as I drove down the M20 that freezing January morning to meet Julian Clary at midday and be handed the keys to my future. Just as I entered the village of Aldringham Jess phoned me to say she'd had the nod from the solicitors.

'It's yours. Enjoy!' she said, as if she were a waitress delivering me a sandwich, and then hung up.

As I drove around the corner, the house came into view looking somehow emaciated and in a trance, like an elderly horse appearing out of the mist on the moors with frost on its back and just a sliver of white condensed air escaping from its nostrils. I couldn't help gasping at the sight as I parked on the gravel drive.

Julian was in his car with the window wound down, waiting. I pulled to a stop, got out and went over. He reached out and tossed me a heavy bundle of keys. 'They're all labelled. Be careful of the steps down to the cellar, they're slippery,' he said hurriedly, revving his engine. 'I've got to dash. Having lunch in Chatham with Brian Dowling. Look after the old place! See you on the green!' And with that he sped off.

The removal van had already arrived and, as I got out, the men jumped out, ready to start work, while I unlocked the door and entered my new home. It was chill and empty but I knew unpacking would sort that out. I felt a thrill of potential: what would I make of this new home of mine?

The movers were swift workers, well practised at manoeuvring furniture around tight corners and hauling heavy boxes, but things did not run as smoothly as I would have liked: one of the removal men, carrying in a sofa, banged his head so badly on the low beam across the front door that he had to be taken to casualty with concussion. A box of glassware was dropped, smashing every blessed thing inside. A tap was turned on and left running with the plug in the sink, though no one could remember using it, and I was soon mopping the kitchen floor with tissues and newspaper, as the mop itself was nowhere to be found. A curious old lady wearing dark glasses and a headscarf and riding a mobility scooter passed the drive at least six times in each direction. On her last 'drive-by' I strolled towards her to introduce myself, assuming she was a neighbour or possibly a fan, but she sped off down the hill and did not return.

The removal men unloaded all the furniture and piled unsteady pillars of cardboard boxes in the kitchen for me to empty. Then they left and I was alone in the place for the first time. I stood in the middle of the lounge and tried to imagine it furnished and ordered and lovely. A low, ominous creaking sound came and went, like the branch of a weary old tree bending in the wind. I pulled my coat around me. The house was freezing and I turned the central heating on, but the thoughtful Mr Clary had left only a thimbleful of oil in the tank. I rang Jess to order a new supply urgently but she said it would take several days to arrive, so I lit a fire in the huge hooded inglenook fireplace and huddled by it. A curious feeling crept over me, as if I were standing before an ancient oak door that was about to open, not knowing what was on the other side. I shuddered and decided I had better set to work. Jess had wanted to get a team of cleaners in before I even set foot in the place but, to her surprise and almost to mine, I had insisted on handling it all myself: I wanted to get to know every nook and cranny of the place personally and what better way than to go over every inch? It was already late in the afternoon and the winter light was fading. I chose the large ground-floor bedroom with the brown striped wallpaper for myself and made up the bed with lots of extra blankets. There was a tiny bathroom next door with a stained toilet and an old-fashioned bath. I put my toothbrush and some soap by the sink. To cheer the place up, I got a hammer and some nails and hung three large portraits of Japanese Buddhist monks on the walls – paintings by an artist called Bombolo that I'd had for years and was rather fond of.

I lay on the bed to admire my handiwork and test the ambience of the room. Again I had the curious feeling of apprehension, as if I had taken an irrevocable step into a new but not entirely happy world. Tired and a bit confused, I closed my eyes and must have fallen asleep. The next thing I knew, I was frightened out of my skin by several loud crashes and the sound of glass shattering. I sat up, catching my breath, and turned on the light. It was three o'clock in the morning. The three large pictures I'd hung had all plummeted to the ground simultaneously.

'Stay calm,' I said to myself as I got up and examined the fist-sized holes in the ancient plaster. 'It's just that they were too heavy. You mustn't let yourself be scared. There is a rational explanation for everything, even a monk face down on your bedroom floor in the middle of the night.'

I went to the bathroom and brushed my teeth, but I was soon shivering with the cold so I climbed back under the duvet and endeavoured to go back to sleep. I'd feel better about everything in the morning.

In the silence of the night I heard the sound of what I assumed were mice, although as I listened I realised I couldn't hear any scuttling or squeaking, but rather a sound above the ceiling: something moving, propelled, like a cotton reel being rolled playfully across wooden floorboards. From the room next door I could hear the dying embers of the log fire spitting and sighing like an elderly cat having a bad dream.

Where was Fran when I needed him? He had no business swanning around LA talking incomprehensible nonsense about 'client deliverables and ideation workshops'. I wanted him here. Fran was always very still when he slept, and I had to listen very intently to hear him breathing. He never wriggled or turned over. It's like sleeping with a corpse, I used to tell him. It suddenly occurred to me that perhaps our relationship might truly be dead, or at least dying, since he'd gone off to America for an unspecified period, work permit in hand. What would become of him, living in that strange, unnatural place? It did weird things to people. I'd refused to let Hollywood change me but Fran? He'd probably develop an awful accent and start every sentence with 'You know what?' as if the listener were psychic. He'd get strange ideas about fashion, too, I wagered. Lose touch with reality. Become the sort of person I despise. Forget the meaning of sarcasm and irony. Have plastic surgery. Date someone rich who worked for Disney and buy a silly little pedigree dog.

Of course, we hadn't actually broken up but things always seem worse in the dead of night. As I lay there I became quite tearful, convinced our relationship was doomed. I should never have let him go, I thought. Or I should have got Marcia to get me a job in LA so that we could be together. But I couldn't take myself away from this old house now and besides, if Fran had wanted to be with me, he would have stayed.

The noises in my roof appeared to have stopped. The mice, or whatever they were, had gone back to sleep. Outside a dull, icy grey dawn was beginning to break. My first night in the Old Manor was almost over.

It took me almost a week to get the house in some kind of order. Jess was busy in London, organising my life as usual and preparing builders for the updating of the chauffeur's cottage that she would eventually move into, so I tackled the house alone. It was a much bigger job than I'd expected, especially as I hadn't so much as washed up my own cups for years. I was aghast at what I'd taken on, and almost considered ringing Jess and begging her to send in the professionals, but I was too proud to admit I couldn't manage, so I ploughed on. Every cupboard I opened was filthy and swathed in cobwebs, so simply finding a home for crockery, glasses, pots and pans involved dusting and scrubbing and bleaching. I made many trips to the supermarket to buy mops and cleaning products. I worked so hard I barely noticed the cold, and I wore frightful baggy, sweaty leisurewear. Unshaven and unwashed, I went unrecognised except once when the girl at the checkout reddened as she saw the name on my card. I looked pleadingly at her and raised a hand to silence her exclamations of surprise and she pressed her lips together and nodded, obviously enjoying our complicity. I knew that news of my arrival would soon spread, however. Every village between here and Maidstone would soon be writing to me, inviting me to open their fêtes and loiter for a mix and mingle.

But for now I was left alone, absorbing the personality of my new home. I began to become accustomed to the strange noises that muttered and murmured through the house at all times of the day and night. Timbers stretching and contracting in the changing temperatures of the day, I told myself. The old girl heaving her muscles about and exercising her limbs a little. Nevertheless, sometimes I had the distinct impression that sounds were coming from a nearby room or floating down the stairs, as though there was a little gathering somewhere in the house from which I was excluded. My vivid imagination, I told myself. I might have felt blessed by Noël in the past, and had a vague notion of fate and destiny, but I wasn't sure I really believed in the spirit world – to my mind, there was always an explanation firmly rooted in this one. I tolerated the strange noises easily enough once I was familiar with them, but there was an occasional faint coughing sound, like a newborn puppy struggling to breathe, that always stopped me in my tracks. Mercifully it never lasted long and I put it down to the old plumbing.

At last, with all the necessary rooms cleaned and made as comfortable as possible, and with logs and oil duly delivered so that the ancient central heating spluttered into life, I felt able to receive my first visitor. Marcia Brown, my agent, came to lunch, on the strict understanding that Jess would not be there. The pair of them had both been vital parts of my life for several decades and had loathed each other since day one. It was the most spectacular of personality clashes. Marcia was ten years older than Jess and drank like a fish. While Jess was efficient and formidable, Marcia was scatty and cuddly. She was a big-boned woman who wore stylish kaftans (or tents, as Jess called them) with brightly patterned scarves and pashminas slung theatrically about her shoulders. Jess was all neat and trim and reined in, while Marcia's big hips and billowing sleeves were a hazard to small children and fine china alike.

Marcia was married to a wealthy eccentric socialist called Lord Ballard, who had given (most of) his inherited millions to charity. Blissfully childless, she and Percy lived in a rambling mansion flat in Primrose Hill full of cats, empty bottles and mismatched furniture. She was a gifted but unusual agent: she only had three clients, all of whom were household names and consistently successful, like myself. Marcia's 'office', which she had occupied for the last thirty years, was a virtual broom cupboard above a notorious drinking club in Fitzrovia called Feeney's.

'I shall come down on the train tomorrow,' she announced to me. 'But I'm only coming if the Fag Hag isn't there.'

'Jess is in London,' I said. 'She's not moving into the cottage until it's all decorated.'

'Will her witch's cauldron be gas or electric?' Marcia enquired.

'Get a taxi from Ashford,' I advised, ignoring her barbed remark.

I couldn't help but be excited. Despite Marcia's avowed preference for London, I knew she was curious and concerned, in her maternal way, and I was glad she was to be first over my threshold. Her warmth and humour were just what I needed. I hoped Marcia would appreciate the feral beauty of the Old Manor, as I had now dubbed it, unable to bear the silly Priest's Hole connotations any longer, along with its history and magical qualities.

The following day I heard the taxi pull up, crunching over the gravel, and went out to greet Marcia just in time to see her emerge from the passenger door, as heavy and regal as a whale rising up out of the sea.

'Thank you, dear,' she said to the taxi driver. 'And I recommend some steroid cream for your personal itching issue. And maybe pop your fleece-effect seat covers on a warm cycle? Goodbye!' She tossed him a twenty-pound note and looked up at the house before she even said hello to me, and her jaw dropped. 'Oh. Oh my,' she said. 'What have you done?'

'Don't you like it?' I said, crestfallen.

'It's not that,' she said, a long strand of silver-white hair escaping from her bulbous velvet hat. 'I just didn't expect it to be quite so *Wind in the Willows.*' As the taxi drove off, she enveloped me in a big, jasmine-scented bear hug. 'Let's go inside. I've brought Laurent-Perrier Rosé!' she said, releasing me and holding up an off-licence carrier bag. 'It's icy cold too, all ready to christen the house.'

I led her into the kitchen where Marcia sat at the ring-stained pine table I'd acquired at a local antique shop for a small fortune (only to see an exact copy in the window of the Dymchurch Hospice shop for £12) and, breathing heavily, waited patiently for me to open the champagne and pour it for her. I handed her a glass.

'Congratulations!' she said, lifting her glass to me and looking about. 'May you be as happy here as a pig in excrement.' She took a long slurp, then stood up and slipped her black-and-red tartan cape off her shoulders. 'Now show me the house, darling, before I become incontinent with excitement. Lead the way, or did you want to sing something rousing by the Wurzels first?'

'I don't think that will be necessary,' I said, preparing to give her the proper guided tour. 'Well, this is the kitchen as you can see—'

'Indeed,' said Marcia. 'And is this the very sink where Julian Clary washed the grass stains from his knees after a trip to the local lorry park?'

'Very probably. Now come on.'

I led her through the low doorway but as we went into the next room, Marcia stopped, raised her hands and sniffed the air. 'Oh my goodness. This house is haunted!' she announced, astonished but with absolute certainty.

'Oh, I expect so,' I said airily, though I was a little taken aback at the Marcia's fervency. 'There've been quite a few bangings and crashings. But you know what I think about these things – stuff and nonsense.'

'Ah,' said Marcia, ignoring my scepticism and nodding. 'Bangings and crashings? I should say.' She pressed her hand to her forehead and staggered slightly. 'This house has stories to tell and residents to tell them.' She shook her head and flapped her hands before her, as if hushing a class of noisy children. 'One at a time or not at all!' she snapped.

I watched in astonishment. 'What is it?'

'I'll be able to tell you in a minute,' said Marcia. 'Did I mention I recently discovered I'm a little bit psychic? Percy and I have been researching our family trees and I have a touch of Romany in me on my mother's side. That's probably where my second sight comes from. Mind you, my great-aunt Sybil was a medium, and quite successful too. Always thought it was a parlour trick but recently something seems to have kicked in. And as it happens, I never leave home these days without these.' She passed me her champagne glass and then dived into her shoulder bag and whipped out a red satin purse. She opened it to reveal some elderly looking brass-coloured divining sticks, each about six inches long.

She held them in front of her and half closed her eyes with concentration.

'I didn't know you could do this,' I said, surprised but intrigued.

'It's a curse, really.' She sighed. 'If I take them out on the Underground I just jerk all over the shop like Gloria Hunniford connected to the National Grid: Roman spirits, ghouls from the Black Death, the ghost of Darius's career, they're all swanning around down there like it's first day of the sales at Primark. Awful. But this place isn't much better.'

I followed her around the kitchen as she moved slowly, arms outstretched, sticks twitching. Her first discovery was just a few steps from the kitchen to the reception room.

'All right, dear, I'm listening to you . . . How awful for you!' she said brightly, and then she murmured to me from the corner of her mouth as though protecting the spirit's feelings. 'A rough old girl. She's telling me she was the cook. Complaining about the hours she had to work. Sixteenth century, I'd say, from the way she's speaking. Hands all chapped and sore. Poor old thing. Quite feisty.' Marcia cocked her ear again. 'Made a lovely steak-and-kidney pie, she wants it known. Let's move on, there are more here, I can tell.'

Fascinated, I kept quiet, not wanting to disturb Marcia's stream of consciousness, but followed her as she progressed through the house, her sticks held out in front of her. In the lounge, she suddenly leant against the wall and lowered her voice. 'There's a girl here, but she won't speak. She's staring at me. Rather alarming. Now she's pointing to the fireplace. I think. What is it?' Marcia glided across the room, led by her divining sticks and stood staring at the wall just to the side of the large open fireplace.

'Has she spoken yet?' I asked, a little worried by Marcia's expression. Her face had fallen and she looked as if she might cry.

'No, she won't say anything. But she's terribly cut up about something.' After a few moments of contemplative silence, Marcia shook her head. 'She's gone. Just as well. Something was troubling her.' She stroked the hood of the fireplace tenderly and bowed her head. 'Oh dear, so very sad,' she whispered. She stood very still suddenly, like a cat hearing something inaudible to humans, then began to move. 'Now there is something through here . . .' She set off quickly, leading me through the house towards my bedroom. Just outside the door, she began panting like a dog in a hot car.

'I've found it! This is the vortex!' she announced, clearly rather thrilled. 'The place where the spirits enter and exit the house!' She paled. 'There is a man here. Sits on your side of the church. John? Jeffrey? Is it Jack? He's dressed up as the Laughing Cavalier . . . looks like a rather bad fancy dress outfit. I can't really make out what he's saying, to be honest. He's very interested in the champagne you're carrying around. Says he's gasping.'

'Should I offer him some?' I said, feeling a little helpless and waving the glass around in mid-air.

'Don't be silly,' replied Marcia scornfully. 'It doesn't work like that. Anyway, he has a sickly yellow aura. Liver problems, I'll be bound. Now let's move on. He's getting on my tits.'

We proceeded on through several rooms where nothing happened, but upstairs in the middle bedroom there was 'a confused youth'. Marcia backed out almost immediately, declaring she didn't want to get involved with him. Then finally, in the front bedroom to the right of the stairs, there was someone else. Her sticks quivered so much I thought she was going to drop them.

'Yes. Yes, dear,' she said, nodding furiously. 'I'll tell him.' She turned to me, her eyes shining with excitement. 'Noël Coward is here,' Marcia breathed reverently, sitting down on the side of the unmade bed as if in shock. 'How extraordinary! You'd think he'd prefer Jamaica or New York. He's trying to shake your hand. Thrilled you're here . . . Worried about the . . . what . . .? What's that?' She cocked her head on one side as if unable to hear him properly. 'Downstairs, he keeps saying. *Down* the stairs.'

I stared at Marcia, amazed, waiting for more but her shoulders slumped suddenly, and she shook her head. 'No. He's gone,' she said matter-of-factly, popping the divining sticks back into their pouch and standing up. 'Any bubbles left? Let's go downstairs and replenish our glasses. I'm going to need a cigarette.'

Back in the kitchen Marcia gulped down several refreshing glasses of champagne in quick succession and smoked a rejuvenating Benson and Hedges, sucking on it as if it were connected to an oxygen tank.

I was twitching with curiosity. Had Marcia really just been in direct conversation with Noël himself? Did the spirit of the man I admired so much, had recently portrayed on screen, still reside in this old house? How amazing! I was quite prepared to be fully converted to the spiritual side if it meant I'd get to cosy up with my idol.

'What did Noël look like?' I wanted to know. 'Did you see his whole body or was it just his face bobbing in front of you like a toffee apple? Was he wearing a smoking jacket or what?'

'Very hard to describe, darling,' said Marcia dismissively. 'He was all soft around the edges. Like a duvet. It's all very tiring for me, you must understand. I need to clear my chakras. Let's get out of here. I saw a lovely little pub in the village as we drove in. Let's go there for lunch. I can feel the need for a rack of lamb coming on.'

Over lunch, I tried to probe Marcia more about the spirits in my house, the cook, the girl who wouldn't speak, the drunk party man and Noël in particular, but she became irritatingly vague, brushed off my enquiries and changed the subject.

'And what was it you found by the fireplace?' I wanted to know.

'I've no idea. The girl didn't seem able to tell me. All very odd, but they often are, these spirit types. They lead you a merry dance and then they slip through the wall, like bit-part players in a David Bowie video, and leave you wondering. I'd put some fresh mint in that room if I were you. That'll see them off.'

'But—'

'Now listen. We need a change of subject matter. I have a new project I want to talk to you about.' Marcia's eyes twinkled with mischief.

'Oh, yes,' I said warily. 'What is it?'

'Darling, now you've moved to the country, why not sit at a big oak desk and spill the beans about Richard Stent and his fabulous career?'

'What do you mean?'

'Write your autobiography. We'll call it *Heaven Stent* or something like that.' She clinked the ice around in her gin and tonic. 'I know some lovely people at Ebury who will print any old nonsense and give you a whacking great advance. They've got more money than they know what to do with, believe me. They've hit on the formula of asking fat people to write recipe books. As long as there is "essence of anchovy" on every other page the chattering classes will snap them up.'

'I don't know,' I said doubtfully. 'I don't think I could write a book.'

'Darling, it's a doddle: sensitive child, artistic inclinations, losing your virginity to Robson Green or someone fabulous like that, drama school, your three-day crystal-meth bender with one of those slappers from *Loose Women*. That sort of thing. It'll fly off the shelves, trust me.'

I was rather indignant. 'That was a long time ago and besides, I was so out of it I can't really remember. Which one is it that looks like Francis Bacon towards the end?'

Marcia waved away my comment. 'We can get you a ghost-writer if you can't be arsed. Forest Hill is chock-a-block with them. Penniless Oxbridge types who think they're the next Muriel Spark. They'll do all the graft and slog for the price of a new stair carpet. Give me the word and if there's phone reception here, I can arrange your book deal before the crème brûlée arrives.'

'I'll think about it,' I promised, but more to keep her happy than with any resolve to do what she wanted.

Later, after Marcia had been dispatched back to London and I was alone back at the Old Manor (and a little the worse for wear), I couldn't resist going upstairs to the bedroom supposedly haunted by Noël. I lit some incense and several candles, lay on the bed, arms folded across my chest, and listened.

Now would be a good moment for Noël to give me a sign, I thought. Here I was, all alone, concentrating as hard as I could. I hoped he might utter a few ghostly words of encouragement for my endeavours to restore his home, inspire me to become the writer Marcia imagined I might be or perhaps appear briefly as an apparition. I would have even settled for a cold breeze or a book falling off the shelf, but there was not a sausage.

When I told Jess about it all the next morning, she sniffed scornfully.

'Marcia can see ghosts then, can she?' she scoffed. 'And did she slip fifteen per cent of their ectoplasm into her handbag before she left?'

Scene Six

Spring 1927

Noël

Late one afternoon the telephone rang persistently, just as the lovers were nodding off to sleep entwined on the sofa in the drawing room at Goldenhurst. Noël sighed and got up to answer, pushing Jack's weight off him.

'Yes?'

'I have a trunk call for you from America,' said the operator.

'Who is it?' asked Noël, irritated that life outside Kent was interrupting him.

'It's Miss Tallulah Bankhead.'

'How delightful, please put her through.'

It turned out his old friend was calling to congratulate him on the Broadway production of *This Was a Man*.

'I was bowled over, baby,' she declared in that unmistakable deep voice. 'You are a geeee-nius. I always said, even when you were traipsing round New York, trying to sell your work without two dimes to rub together.'

'How perceptive you are, darling,' said Noël happily, the receiver held jauntily to his ear. 'Unfortunately it has been the biggest flop since Lillian Gish dived into the Serpentine. Thirty-one measly performances. And no wonder – they played it so slowly there was time to go around the corner and have an ice cream soda between every line.'

'You're going to go on to bigger and better things!' declared Tallulah stridently. 'You haven't even started, honey! Don't you worry, I can scent big success coming your way.'

'You're quite right, Tallulah.' Noël played with the telephone cord, wrapping it around his finger. 'Perspicacious as ever.'

'And maybe one day you'll create something for us to do together, huh?'

'I couldn't wish for anything more splendid. And how marvellous of you to track me down to a little cottage in Kent. I've always sensed you were a bold woman.'

'You better believe it,' Tallulah said with a throaty laugh. 'Remember what they said to me when I stayed in that little village near Eton College and entertained some of the more delicious boys in my house? "We don't mind you smoking and drinking with boys and perhaps a little sex on Sunday afternoons. But we do wish you wouldn't give them cocaine before chapel."' She laughed again. 'I never listened to them, of course.'

Jack had got up from the sofa and was loitering by the French windows, fixing himself a gin and tonic. He turned and gave a sour look.

'You take your role as an educator very seriously, I can see that,' Noël said. He turned away from Jack. 'Now, my next play is on its way and I absolutely insist that you accompany me to the first night. We shall drink a bathful of Martini beforehand and it will be a stupendous success.'

Jack cleared his throat noisily and stomped into the garden.

Ten minutes later, Noël found him sitting in the shelter of a mulberry tree, his jacket pulled tight around him against the blasts of chilly spring wind.

'I've brought you a fresh drink,' Noël said lightly, handing him the glass. 'I assume you have finished the last one?'

'Thanks,' muttered Jack, taking it and staring into the clear liquid. His black eyes looked darker than ever.

'Well. It seems there is no end to my circle of admirers,' said Noël happily. 'Dear Tallulah. So glamorous and such fun.'

'You don't say,' said Jack, glowering.

'Don't be like that. Aren't you pleased for me?'

'Sure. Everyone loves you. That's just great.'

'Are you jealous?'

'Did she ask after me?'

'Now you're being silly.'

'You're the genius and I'm the silly one.'

'It was only a phone call. It would be rather pleasant if you could share these moments with me,' said Noël with a hint of petulance.

'They're your moments. Not mine. Do you know what? I can feel show business creeping into our life here. Spoiling everything. Like water into the *Titanic*.'

'Don't say that. It makes me terribly sad.'

'But I heard you. The next play. London. Broadway. Rehearsals. When does it ever stop? You'll make yourself ill again.' Jack had witnessed Noël collapse in his dressing room after a performance of *The Constant Nymph*. It had been a terrifying moment but, fortunately, not too serious. A doctor had revived him with a strychnine injection and ordered him to bed. Ignoring the orders of complete rest, Noël and Jack had escaped to New

York where they had enjoyed themselves producing *This Was a Man*, but its comparative failure had brought Noël low again, with all the symptoms of nervous depression. Travel had helped a little – but being back together at Goldenhurst had helped more, healing Noël and restoring his spirits like nowhere else. Was Noël really going to threaten his fragile recovery all over again, send them both back to the dark days of the winter?

Noël looked wistful. 'Darling, I have to work. Someone has to pay for the gin. But that doesn't mean the end of everything. You must know that. We can come back here whenever we need to.'

'I see, all right,' said Jack quietly. 'But as your manager, I cannot sit back and watch you make yourself sick.'

'I can assure you nothing will be better for me than a big, fat hit.'

'I'd better let you get on with it, then.'

'You are too kind,' said Noël, patting Jack's knee.

'But I will wrap you in a blanket, bundle you into the back of the car and bring you back here the moment I see the blood drain from your cheeks.' He pushed away his dark mood and smiled up at Noël. 'God bless Goldenhurst.'

'And all who sail in her,' Noël returned, happy to see Jack's good humour restored.

Jack gazed at the house and felt a wave of love for it. It seemed to grow out of the ground like a tree, breathing and still. The upstairs windows were all open, and, his head swimming a little with the gin, he imagined he was flying upwards, across the raggedy lawn and into their bedroom, dominated as it was by a rather grand mahogany bed Noël had bought at an auction and which they had taken great delight in christening Benjamin Bed. That was where Jack truly felt in charge, on the new mattress that

Noël had sent to London for. There it was that Noël surrendered to him every night and most mornings and afternoons, too. No witty ditties, no talk of any kind, just love and lust and the joy of being alone together, unafraid and uninterrupted.

'This is our place, you know that,' said Noël seriously. 'Now and for ever.' In a sudden swift move, he sat down next to Jack on the bench and took his hand. 'Listen, I have a plan. I intend to buy this place and make it our own – *really* our own. We could cope with life in London or New York and wherever else we found ourselves if we knew we had this place to escape to. Don't you see? This is that funny little island I imagined a while ago. Do you remember?'

'I thought it was in Papua New Guinea.'

'So did I. But it was much closer to home the whole time. How perfectly extraordinary. What do you think? Is it a good plan?'

Jack smiled. 'Another of your masterstrokes, my dear. I think this place should be ours entirely.'

Noël had Lorn make the enquiries at once. As it happened, the house and farmland was only being rented because it had failed to sell at a recent auction. Noël was able to negotiate its purchase easily and swiftly, and excitedly the pair set about planning renovations and more decorative gardens. One of Noël's gifts was that he had an instant vision of the completed thing, be it a house or a play. Three acts of a smash-hit comedy would come to him in a dream sometimes, and he simply had to scribble it down. And so it was that he saw, in his mind, fabulous house parties with the good and the great, the cream of show business lounging about his lawns, dressed for dinner and entertaining each other late into the night. Most of all he saw long summer evenings in the Kent sunshine with champagne and gin flowing, cascading laughter, tinkling piano and beautiful people wearing linen clothes and expensive jewellery. Kent was to be the Hamptons of England, envied, admired and gossiped about. A weekend invitation to Goldenhurst was to be a gateway to the most elite social circles. And gradually the dream of a private retreat for himself and Jack was forgotten.

Noël called in his friend, the chic decorator Syrie Maugham, to overhaul the house, and she created a fashionable white interior with pale green and beige coverings and curtains. One hallway was papered entirely in his song sheets and one room, white with a large open fireplace, contained two grand pianos back to back, where Noël could hold impromptu performances for his guests. Jack, Noël and Syrie drove through the lanes, across Romney Marsh, visited auctions, markets and shops, and even went over to France, buying furniture and things for the house: a Grinling Gibbons carving; paintings; an allegory of 'Winged Time' made from Cornish tin.

There was a full-time housekeeper now, the mature and portly Mrs Ashton, who told Noël meaningfully during her interview that she 'knew about the house'.

'Oh. Have you worked here before?' asked Noël, curious.

'Oh no, sir. But my grandma was born here many years ago, before it changed hands, when it was still owned by a farming family and . . . well . . .' Mrs Ashton went quiet, as if she had spoken out of turn.

'How interesting,' said Noël. 'Did she ever tell you about the place and what it was like back then?'

'Oh, yes, sir.'

'Well? What did she say?'

A dark shadow passed over Mrs Ashton's plump face. 'She used to cry about it. Could never bring herself to tell the whole story but there was a terrible fuss in the family. A baby born out of wedlock, I believe, sir. The eldest daughter of the house. There was a scandal and it had an unhappy end, though I'm not one for gossip.' She folded her hands in her lap. 'And it was many years ago. There's no place for it now, and those who still go on about it should let bygones be bygones.'

'Oh. Yes, absolutely,' said Noël, intrigued and disappointed by the woman's resolve not to enlighten him any further. 'These things happen. Even in Aldringham.'

'Yes, sir, they do,' she said.

'I've always sensed some odd little things about the house,' Noël went on. 'And Jack's noticed strange noises and what have you. He's sworn blind he heard someone crying one night when there was no one here but us. Do you think it's connected?'

Mrs Ashton looked a little worried and glanced around the room. 'I couldn't say, I really couldn't. Perhaps I've said too much. You mustn't believe idle chat and I shouldn't have mentioned it. It would be a great honour to serve you, sir, here in this house. Whatever happened in the past is long forgotten.'

'Quite so,' Noël agreed, not wanting to offend her. Some folk could be very touchy at the mention of ghosts, especially if they were churchgoers. 'We shan't mention it again, Mrs Ashton, if you'd rather not. But if you'd like the position, you can start immediately.'

Besides the new housekeeper, there was also a cook and a gardener, but yet more staff was needed if all ten bedrooms were to be occupied by Noël's dazzling guests. Mrs Ashton suggested her niece, Alice, to Noël as a possible general maid. 'She may not be clever but she's clean,' was her memorable recommendation.

Alice was a thin, nervous girl with stooped shoulders and full red lips that she bit constantly.

'Have you done this sort of thing before?' asked Noël, when Alice stood before him, trembling. Jack watched from his armchair, peering over the top of his paper.

'No, sir,' she managed to say, keeping her eyes on the floor and wringing her hands.

'But I'm sure you can carry a tray and peel a potato? You look to me like an able sort of girl,' he said kindly.

'Yes, sir,' answered Alice, her huge blue eyes not quite able to meet his gaze.

'Very well,' said Noël. 'Mrs Ashton will arrange your hours.'

Alice became a source of great amusement to Noël and Jack after that. They could hear the tea tray rattling in her shaky grasp long before the sitting-room door opened and she made her mortified entrance. She would hover in the doorway unsure where to deposit it, swaying from left to right, her mouth opening and closing like a fish out of water, until Noël said, 'On the table please, Alice.' Then Alice would cautiously advance, as if she carried the crown jewels, raise the tray several feet above the table and lower it with an air of studied concentration. But she would always misjudge the last few inches and there would be a clatter of crockery and a splashing of tea and milk and poor Alice would make a high-pitched, apologetic whinny before scurrying out of the room.

Jack and Noël would cover their mouths with their hands to muffle their giggles, for they couldn't bear to hurt her feelings.

'She never fails to amuse,' said Noël. 'A glorious girl. I shall have a nervous maid in one of my plays and immortalise Alice for ever.'

'Shall we call her back and order some cakes, just so we can get an encore?' suggested Jack.

'Wicked of you!' said Noël, reaching for the brass bell.

They were so amused by Alice that they increased her hours of employment so she could serve them breakfast, lunch and dinner. Guests were forewarned about the silent comedy of the maid's every move and the room would fall silent with anticipation whenever poor Alice entered.

'Simply stupendous!' they would declare once she was out of earshot and sometimes a slight spattering of applause would spontaneously break out.

'She's a find,' Noël would declare, 'but you must all be sweet to her, it's part of the conditions of her employment. And one of these days she'd going to conquer her nerves and then that adorable innocence and gaucherie will be lost, so let's make the most of it while we can. The other condition is you must tip her enormously when you leave.'

And they all did, to Alice's astonished delight. Prince George left her a five-pound note, and the little maid nearly exploded.

'I'll never spend it, sir,' she spluttered, holding the note as though it were precious parchment, while Noël smiled with amusement. 'It's from royalty!'

'Don't be silly, of course you must spend it. Put it in your bottom drawer, at least, and wait till you're married and need it. Now hurry off, there's a dear, and try to calm yourself down.'

The parties went on till midsummer: an endless procession of friends, and stars from the world of film and theatre. The village shop soon ordered in extra gin to keep up with the demand.

*

Jack opened the window of his bedroom. Even here, for propriety's sake, he had his own room, though it was next door to Noël's. The garden was in the delightful bloom of early summer. There were six acres and Noël had decreed white, pink and red roses, and meandering paths where his guests might wander and get up to no good, ponds, fruit trees, a country cottage garden with rustic furniture, a herb garden, a vegetable garden and English flowers enough to fill every one of the bedrooms his famous friends occupied when they came to stay.

Jack laughed ironically to himself. The promise Noël had made him that this would be their place alone had come to nothing. The parties went on every weekend, and they saw the same faces there they did in London. The minute Goldenhurst had become Noël's project, it had ceased being their remote island and become as frantic as Fifth Avenue.

Only last weekend, Katharine Hepburn had come to stay.

'Do you like my little slice of the country, Kate, dear?' Noël had asked as they lounged outside, Noël very casual in linen shorts and espadrilles.

Hepburn had shot him a look from under the wide-brimmed hat she wore to protect her fair freckled skin. 'This isn't the country, Noël,' she said witheringly. 'It's nice and all – but you've brought London with you. This is the city, only the temperature is different.'

Noël laughed, but protested she was quite wrong.

Jack had agreed with Kate but he kept that to himself.

He stuck his head out of the small leaded window and inhaled the scent of a fresh summer morning: grass; fragrant blooms; damp earth. Stanley the gardener had done a wonderful job, though he'd had to employ a lad to help realise all of Noël's grandiose plans.

There he is now, Jack thought, catching a glimpse of the boy through the shrubbery. Unaware that he was being observed, the wiry, good-looking youth whistled happily to himself as he pushed a wheelbarrow full of earth along the path towards the house, occasionally flicking his head to one side to toss his overgrown fringe out of his eyes. His face and neck were bronzed from the hours he spent outside and his flexed muscles showed through the thin rumpled shirt.

'So that's Jude,' Jack said to himself, his eyes glistening. He dressed quickly and went downstairs to offer the men some refreshment.

ACT II

Scene One

Richard

As a matter of urgency, I employed some builders. After several tenders, all of which were much the same, I went for the crew with the best tattoos. If I was going to see these men out of my bedroom every morning for the next few months, aesthetics such a bone structure, muscle tone and body decoration were as important as their given skills, it seemed to me. Besides, the company was called BJ's, which was a cheap thrill that Mr Clary would have appreciated, no doubt.

The cottage where Jess was to live needed much less work than the main house, and, as I'd promised Jess, I asked them to tackle that first. It was painted to Jess's specifications (all white) and a no-nonsense kitchen and bathroom were installed. Jess came down to bark at them once a week and point like a schoolmistress at various areas she considered unsatisfactory, but it was finished in good time. To me it looked a bit like a dentist's surgery, but Jess pronounced herself delighted and that was all that mattered.

'Albie's going to love it!' she declared. 'But I've told him he's not allowed to visit until after he's passed his A-levels. It will be a reward for getting his exams.'

I was faintly astonished that Albie was already finishing his school career. But I had to stop thinking of him as a little boy. He was almost grown up.

'If you're happy, so am I,' I said.

Jess was as good as her word: she went to spend Christmas with her parents and Albie joined her there. I spent the day at Marcia's, which was a tradition of ours, and tried not to think about how much I was missing Fran. When Jess returned in January, we were both established in our new homes, and closer than ever.

The builders began work in earnest on the house, and weeks passed in a blur of workmen, plaster dust, delivery vans and all the mess, confusion and problems of renovation. For a while, I even moved into the chauffeur's cottage with Jess just to get away from the chaos. With Jess cracking the whip, the worst of it was over in twelve weeks and I was able to move back in to the refreshed interior, complete with sparkling new bathrooms, new electrics and chic rush matting throughout. Now I could occupy myself with the pleasanter aspects of refurbishment: soft furnishing, fabrics and the tricky business of padded headboards.

Fran's extended stay in America meant he managed to miss all the drama of both my move and Jess's eventual relocation. Try as he might, he couldn't even manage a visit at Christmas, but I emailed him all the plans and the before-and-after photographs and he sent suitably enthusiastic responses via email. Bricks and mortar were a good, solid investment, after all, and the Coward connection added glamour. That, of course, appealed to Fran's business sense.

'I was afraid your mid-life crisis might result in adopting a baby from Malawi,' he said to me one night on Skype. 'This is a lesser evil.'

'This house is for us,' I said. 'Although you've never actually seen it. A place where we can be together. When you're ready.'

Fran looked a little shifty, but it could have been the poor connection; my Wi-Fi in the old house was not as reliable as it had been in London. 'One day, I hope. You know how things are . . . I'm going to be over here a lot.'

I thought I detected a slight American accent. 'Lot' sounded like 'Lat'. It made me feel slightly sick. We stared at each other over cyber space. Different countries, different times of the day and different moods.

'I'm feeling a little put out,' I said, choosing my words carefully. 'I know work is important to you, but it seems to be taking over. It's a question of priorities.'

'Yes, it is,' answered Fran briskly. 'And if you'd been offered a big TV role that meant you moving to America for a year or more, would you have turned it down? Is it somehow different for me just because I'm not the famous one?' His face changed suddenly and I could tell he was furious. The very implication that I might consider myself the biggest thing in his life always set him off. 'I think you should shut the fuck up,' he snapped.

'No – *you* shut the fuck up!' I shot back, suddenly incensed, and clicked off the connection. The modern version of hanging up. I felt shaky and furious as I continued to stare indignantly at the blank screen, a little shocked by the sudden flare of ill temper we'd both just shared. Being independent and mature was one thing, but there is a fine line between that and just being lonely. Fran might not care about my fame and status in the world, but he still had to care about me, didn't he? Otherwise what was the point of anything? Here I was, in a new house, my whole life transformed and yet my so-called partner couldn't be bothered even to come and see me. I was growing sick of gazing at his familiar face on my computer, complaining about the heat. Sometimes he took his laptop out on to his balcony and sat before me wearing his Chanel sunglasses while I huddled here in a polo neck jumper, my nose blue with cold. There was very little common ground for us to chat about some days: he was usually stressing about some work deadline and I was worried about a late frost getting to my new bedding plants.

The whole situation was becoming more and more depressing.

'Well, yes,' Gary said, lounging walrus-like on my sofa, a beer clutched in one hand. 'Bound to piss you off. But it will all be fine in the end. You'll see.'

Gary was one of my oldest friends. We had our first job together in a Jean Genet play, premiered to bewildered critics at the Lyric Theatre, Hammersmith. We were briefly rather passionate lovers, way back when. As my star rose, so Gary's dimmed, or rather was obscured, behind the fickle clouds of mischance and bad luck. He had the occasional one-liner in a TV drama – usually as a lawyer, which suited his looks and posh voice – but nothing that he could get his teeth into. The last five or six years had been particularly grim, professionally, and Gary had drifted into a job, firstly as a waiter, now as a restaurant manager, which could be why he'd piled on the weight in recent months. And yet he stayed remarkably optimistic. 'Liz Smith didn't even decide to be an actress till she was in her forties! You just never know what's around the corner in this business,' he would declare.

Despite our different destinies we had remained good friends, probably as a result of us having met when we were so young and frisky, and we always talked frankly about our sexual triumphs and disappointments. Now, with the passing of the years (and still no sign of even the most mediocre rep job for Gary), we both considered our friendship as important as ever. Gary was a naughty, sexually voracious and, more often than not, triumphant predator. It was a running joke that anyone he bedded seemed to be 'huge, mate! A monster dick – I almost fainted!' It seemed that lack of professional success was no barrier to his conquering lust, whereas I'd stifled such instincts long ago, even before Fran. The drawback of success was that I had to curb my earlier promiscuity. Such carry on was unseemly – I valued my professional standing too much to risk being caught with my trousers down in some sordid club or notorious cruising spot. I couldn't help envying Gary's sexual freedom, listening with avid attention to his graphic accounts.

One of his current squeezes was known as Doorbell. Gary didn't know his name – the man had followed him home from the Co-op, shopping in hand, one afternoon. Since then he would simply turn up unexpectedly at any time of the day or night and simply ring the doorbell. There were no preparatory arrangements, not so much as a text. They barely even spoke. Doorbell would simply arrive and if Gary was available and frisky, he would invite him in. Once inside the flat there was no preamble, no cup of tea. He would simply be led into the bedroom for sexual congress. Bish, bash, bosh, as they say in Sarf London.

There were occasions when Doorbell had to be turned away. 'Always with a heavy heart, mind,' said Gary. 'He's such an award-winning shag, it seems a shame.' There was one memorable occasion when Gary was in the middle of hosting a dinner party and the bell went just as the potatoes were beginning to boil. Unable to turn down the opportunity, he led Doorbell silently into his bedroom, and while the guests chatted and the spuds simmered, he and Doorbell had one of their silent, fifteen-minute encounters and no one was any the wiser.

Gary had come down for the weekend to admire the paint shades and curtains I'd chosen, and on Saturday afternoon he entertained me with his latest adventures while we drank: beer for Gary and wine for me. He'd signed up to a website called TV Chix where he proclaimed himself to be a 'total dom' and had just hitchhiked all the way to Cardiff to meet Adwena, a seventy-year-old tranny who'd opened her front door wearing a rainbow afro wig and a baby-doll nightie.

'Didn't you run a mile?' I asked.

'Oh no,' said Gary, opening another bottle of beer. 'We had a lovely time. And after I'd rogered her senseless, she revived me with a chicken, leek, prune and Caerphilly cheese pie. Delicious! I'm going back next week.'

I was drinking red wine, which always made me maudlin.

'What's the matter?' Gary asked. 'Out with it.'

I confided my worries about Fran and the creeping sense I had that things were slowly heading for the rocks.

'Hmm,' said Gary. 'Maybe a bit of a sandbank somewhere in the distance. Dangerous waters, certainly. But I don't think you need to abandon ship just yet.'

'Should I send out a distress flare at least?' I asked, endeavouring to see how long we could keep the nautical metaphor running for, and a little put out that Gary wasn't allowing me to wallow in the full shipwreck scenario.

'You two are great together. Everyone knows that. You can

survive a bit of a separation. No one is saying it's easy. But the whole point of love, as far as I understand it, is that it survives. For fuck's sake, some people have their husbands kidnapped or imprisoned or sent away to war. Yours is just swanning around La La Land in a pair of pastel slacks with the crease down the front. Get a grip.'

'Yes, but that is half the problem,' I interrupted. 'He *chooses* to be there, he *chooses* to be away from me!'

'Well, if you can't be doing with it, if it's all too much and your abandonment issues are getting the better of you, tell him to fuck off. You're in charge of your own life, after all.'

'Thanks for your words of wisdom,' I said witheringly.

'You're welcome,' replied Gary, flicking his ash towards the fire and missing. 'You're not a teenager. There's no need to have a nose bleed just because you haven't had your joint prodded for a few weeks.'

I opened my mouth with horror but a sudden wave of laughter erupted and I spluttered with amused indignation.

'Now I'm going for a piss,' Gary announced unceremoniously, staggering towards the stairs.

I liked his brutal honesty. As the 'great Richard Stent' and national treasure, nobody talked to me that way any more. It was one of the many reasons I relished Gary's friendship – he'd never changed the way he behaved towards me despite our differing fortunes. I had been pondering this fact for a few moments when I became aware of a persistent banging from above, interspersed with muffled calls for help.

'Gary?' I called. 'Is that you?' I climbed the stairs to the tiny bathroom at the end of the corridor and stood outside the door. 'What is it?'

'I'm bloody locked in!' came the distressed voice of my dear friend.

I turned the door handle but it didn't open. 'Have you unlocked it on your side?'

'Of course I fucking have! Didn't bother with the lock in the first place, so I don't know how it's got itself stuck. For God's sake, get me out, will you?'

I could tell Gary was feeling claustrophobic in the small, enclosed space. I tugged and pulled at the door but it didn't budge. It was stuck so hard it might have been sealed in place.

'Don't panic,' I called through the door. 'I'll be right back. I might have some WD40 under the sink.'

'Hurry up, please,' said Gary, sounding suddenly childlike. 'I am not enjoying this experience in the slightest.'

'Hold on!' I ran down to the kitchen. There was no WD40. Would Mr Sheen be any help? No, as it turned out.

'Should I call the fire brigade?' I asked Gary, after we'd exhausted ourselves pulling and pushing at the shut door.

'How about an axe? Just break the fucker down?'

Then I had a brain wave. I reached into my pocket for my wallet. 'Here. I'm slipping a credit card under the door. Slide it over the lock. I've seen that done on detective programmes.'

'Okay, worth a try. Yes, I've got it,' said a tense Gary as my card disappeared.

A moment later, with just the gentlest click, the door swung open and we stood in front of each other, shocked at how suddenly the drama had ended.

'Bloody hell,' said Gary, panting with relief and jumping over the threshold as if the door might close again.

We both inspected the troublesome lock and now it behaved

perfectly, turning smoothly with the key, closing and opening like nothing had ever happened.

'Oh well,' said Gary, frowning. 'Perhaps it was just having a funny turn.'

We returned to our drinks in the sitting room to recover ourselves.

I found it hard to get to sleep that night. The stuck door played on my mind. I simply couldn't work out how it would have got jammed like that. Gary had clearly regained his equilibrium if the massive snores echoing through the floorboards were anything to go by, but I couldn't shift a feeling of uneasiness. I lay in bed, listening for the familiar stretches and wheezes of the house but there was nothing. In fact, there was dead, empty silence that was almost more unsettling. I'd become accustomed to the sighings, the rolling noises, and the chilling little cries in the night that I was sure must be foxes; the sound of nothing at all made me shiver.

I got out of bed and went to the window, pulling back the curtains that I'd ordered in a fetching green-and-vanilla toile de Jouy print from Colefax and Fowler. The lawn was dark, the shrubs and trees turned to vague, black massy shapes that loomed from the edges. My eye was drawn to a square of gold: it was a lighted window in the chauffeur's cottage. Jess was still up. I was surprised. She usually headed off to her flat in Earls Court at weekends, taking a break from the house for a while.

I consulted the luminous hands of my watch. It was after three. Jess was much more of a lark than an owl. How odd that she was still awake. Then I saw her, walking back and forwards past the lit window, her shoulders hunched, her arms wrapped tightly around herself, a fist breaking free every now and then to punch her own chest. Her mouth was moving soundlessly.

She's on the phone, I thought with relief. Then I realised that she wasn't holding a phone. Back and forth she went, her lips moving rapidly as though she was declaiming some long monologue to herself. I watched her for what seemed like ages before I gave up and went back to bed.

Huddling down in the blankets, I thought it over. Jess had seemed less ebullient lately and perhaps she was sinking into one of her dark moods. I'd given her masses of work to do – she'd had all the stress of managing the builders as well as her usual workload, and they'd not stinted in coming to her with every kind of hitch and problem. She'd project-managed the whole house, spending hours here overseeing the progress. In fact, now I thought about it, the longer she'd spent here, the lower her spirits had become. I'd found her one chilly afternoon loitering by the fireplace in the lounge, a miserable expression on her face.

'Cheer up, Jess,' I'd teased her. 'You look as blue as that poor ghost Marcia talked to.'

Jess had gone quite white, mumbled something about checking if the insulation had been delivered, and hurried off. Since then, I realised, I had hardly seen her smile at all.

Once Gary's gone, I'll make it up to her, I decided. I'll get her a nice present, tell her to take some time off. Perhaps we both need a bit of sun. We could pop over to Marrakesh for a bit, maybe . . .

With that thought, I slipped into sleep.

The next day Gary and I rose late and lazed about before I cooked him a roast dinner. I've always found homosexuals eating together depressing – we pile too much on our plates and grunt at each other like cavemen as we eat – but I'd also found Sunday lunch depressing since Fran had left. That had always been his territory and he would shoo me into the garden with a gin and tonic while he peeled and basted and prodded the joint.

We had finished and were sitting down inside with our glasses of wine, as it was too breezy for being outside, when we heard the slam of the back door.

'That'll be Jess,' I said, and a moment later, she came wandering through from the kitchen. Her office was at the back of the ground floor and she usually came and went much as she pleased. I always left the back door unlocked during the day so she could let herself in whenever she wanted.

'Hello, Jess,' I said, cheerily. 'I'm glad you're here. I must tell you about the close encounter Gary had with the bathroom door. It's the most bizarre thing.'

Gary lifted his wine and waved it in her direction. 'Wassup, Jess. How's country life treating you?'

She stood in the doorway, staring at us both and saying nothing, her expression simultaneously dour and rather blank. There was a long, uncomfortable pause, broken only by the hissing and spitting from the logs rearranging themselves as they slowly collapsed into ashes on the burning hearth.

'Jess?' I said.

'Bathroom door?' she said in a strange, distant voice.

'Yes, I got stuck there, for no obvious reason,' Gary put in. 'It was as though someone had superglued the door shut. Very odd. Have you noticed anything strange about the door?'

I noticed that she looked dishevelled, her fair hair pulled back into a loose ponytail and her clothes rumpled. 'Are you okay? You don't look quite right.'

'I'm fine,' she said, her voice full of the same distant grandeur. Then her expression changed and she looked both angry and fearful at the same time. 'I've come to tell you I've been up all night worrying about the ivy.'

'What ivy? Jess, what is the matter?' I asked, nonplussed.

'The ivy is *everywhere*,' she said, as if I were an idiot not to understand her already. 'Green, dark, creeping ivy. Ivy that never goes away, that strangles trees, cracks walls, pulls and smothers.' She lowered her voice to a whisper. 'She says we have to get rid of it. It's a menace, don't you understand?'

Gary looked at me, raised his eyebrows and made a silly face.

I ignored him. 'What are you talking about? Who is "she"?'

Jess strode past us and stood directly in front of the fireplace, so close she must have felt the heat from the logs on her shins. She stared at the hood above the fireplace and murmured to herself, 'I don't know . . . I don't know where it's gone! How on earth am I supposed to know that?'

'Jess,' I said again in a tentative voice. She was giving me the creeps; if felt as though Jess herself wasn't actually there, but some odd automaton impersonating her.

She stopped talking and turned suddenly, her eyes fixing on the jumper I was wearing. Her jaw dropped and her complexion turned grey with horror. 'Take that off!' she shouted urgently.

I glanced down at the object of her horror. It was new, a dark avocado cotton-and-linen V-neck I'd bought in Marylebone High Street last December but never worn. I'd found it and ripped off its wrapping just that morning. 'What's wrong with it?' I asked, thinking maybe it was a bit snug.

'It's green. Green! Green is evil. She says that green is not allowed! Ivy . . .'

'Doesn't it suit me?' I asked, noticing that her eyes were red with dark rings underneath.

'I know it means bad things. Trust me. Just take it off. Quickly!' She moved towards me, clearly intent on taking the jumper off me by force if necessary.

'All right. I will. I'm doing it now.' I was unnerved enough to do her bidding, pulling the jumper roughly over my head. 'You can calm down, now. I've taken it off.'

Reassured, Jess stopped her advance. She stared at me for a long moment, then said, 'There's no need to snap at me,' grabbed the jumper from my hands and left. An instant later, the back door slammed again.

I turned to look at Gary, whose expression was both horrified and amused.

'Oops,' he said, wide-eyed. 'Has Jess lost the plot? She looked raving mad. Thank goodness we'd eaten all the green beans. I thought they looked like the devil's work as I ate my seconds.'

'I don't think it's funny, Gary. I've seen her moody – but never so irrational and intense,' I replied, worried. 'It's like she was possessed or something. Do you think I should call someone? A doctor perhaps?' Though I had no idea of where the local surgery was – I usually made appointments for myself with my doctor in Harley Street if I needed any medical advice, but that was hardly appropriate in this case. Besides, as it was Sunday afternoon, he was probably on the golf course.

Gary shrugged. 'Don't know, mate, maybe it was just a fit or something and she'll snap out of it. But maybe you'd better send her back to London to be on the safe side. Supposing she opens a letter with a green card inside? She might attack you with the letter opener. Cut your throat or something.' Gary took another, generous and clearly much-needed gulp of his wine. 'I thought you were retreating to the country to get away from all the strains and stresses of life. But what with Fran and now Jess . . . well, it looks like you've simply taken them all with you. If you can't cry, you might as well laugh.'

Later that night, after Gary had been poured into a taxi to Ashford station, and I had finished off the bottle of Chateau Something-French, Fran called me on Skype. We both chose not to mention our last abrupt phone call. Besides, I was in too much of a hurry to discuss Jess's strange behaviour. I hadn't seen her for the rest of the day, and I hoped she'd gone to lie down and catch up on her sleep. Her cottage had been dark when I'd come out to say goodbye to Gary.

'What on earth shall I do? I'm really worried about her. I've never seen her like this before,' I said, once I had described what had happened.

'Oh, I dunno,' said Fran, yawning. It was first thing in the morning there and he was barely awake. 'She was probably hallucinating from sleep deprivation. She'll be fine tomorrow. I've always thought she was a witch anyway,' he said unsympathetically. 'Can't you just sack her?'

It was true; Fran had always thought my relationship with Jess was unsavoury because of her deep involvement with me. He had never warmed to her and considered our relationship past its sell-by date. I'd always assumed it was because they were both a little jealous of the other's intimacy with me.

'I've told you before,' he said now, 'she should either be your friend or your PA. Not both. It will end in tears. She's too full on. I don't care if she likes me or not, although the answer is clearly not. She sees me as some kind of threat, just as she sees anyone close to you as some kind of threat. It isn't a part of her job to sniff around your personal life like a fox around a chicken house. She gives me the creeps.'

'Now I think of it, she's been a bit strange ever since we moved in here. The atmosphere of the place seems to affect her somehow.' I sighed. 'I wish you were here.'

There was a pause.

'You've obviously been drinking,' said Fran, as though this explained everything. 'Cheer up. I'll be back soon. Another month or two, then I should have some time off.'

'You're not here in my hour of need,' I said petulantly.

'I had no idea your hour of need was approaching when I left, did I?' replied Fran with impeccable logic. 'And I wouldn't be so smug to point out that I foresaw trouble with Jess some time ago. Told ya.'

'I don't remember you mentioning a curious obsession with ivy but there we are. Not particularly helpful to point out now that you've always suspected she might go all botanical, but thank you for taking the trouble,' I said, becoming terribly English in response to his increasingly American turns of phrase. I felt that I couldn't convey the strangeness of the episode to him over the great distance between us. He obviously didn't understand, and could only focus on his usual beef with Jess and her closeness to me. 'We can't all separate our lives into neat compartments.'

'Hey, listen,' said Fran, wide awake now and ignoring the dig. 'On second thoughts, there may be something else going on here. I think you should go to the cottage and see how things are. She may be all right now, or she might need you to get her some help. And . . . I don't want to worry you, but perhaps make sure the doors are locked before you go to sleep? Just in case.' He sounded deadly serious.

'Oh, no,' I said unhappily. 'You don't think it's that bad, do you?'

'It's probably nothing – but no harm in taking precautions. Promise?'

'I promise,' I said, my heart a little warmed by the fact that Fran seemed to care. There was a concern and perhaps even longing in his eyes, I thought to myself as I gazed at him for those last few seconds via my computer.

Maybe as a consequence I found it hard to sleep that night. I thought I heard something moving about outside in the garden, breathing heavily.

Perhaps it's a badger with respiratory trouble, I thought to myself. I expect badgers get hay fever like everyone else.

Scene Two

Spring 1928

Noël

Jack slugged back a gin, trying to control his temper but it was difficult.

Noël watched him, languidly puffing on a cigarette that he'd put into a short ivory holder. They were sitting in the garden at Goldenhurst, the sound of spiky feminine chatter floating across the lawn towards them from the house.

'You said that Goldenhurst was for you and me – suddenly there's five of us,' Jack complained but in a low voice, glancing over his shoulder towards the house. 'Not just weekend parties, either – all the goddamned time!'

'Well, quite a few things are not as they were,' Noël replied, raising his eyebrows.

'And what's that supposed to mean?' Jack shot back.

'Nothing, my dear, nothing at all. Except that I'm not used to what some might call a *cool* reception.' Noël tapped his cigarette on a china ashtray and exhaled a stream of smoke. '*Sirocco* has shaken me up rather. I feel the need of my family around me.'

Jack said nothing for a moment. He was not to blame, of

course, but he couldn't help feeling guilty that Noël's last play had met with a less than warm reception. In fact, it was hard to believe how violently the audience had hated the play with its depiction of free love. Even Ivor Novello as the handsome lead hadn't been able to stop the deafening boos that had filled the theatre as the curtain had descended. Out in the street, Noël had been spat at and cursed. He had pretended not to mind but, in truth, he was deeply upset and had even considered leaving Britain, where once he had been the nation's darling. In the event, he and Jack had escaped to Europe, spending Christmas at St Moritz where they had skated and sledged their troubles away. Returning to star in a hit play, not one of his own this time, had helped salve Noël's ego, but he still felt the need to retreat to Goldenhurst where he could recover himself and work on his new revue.

Recent and unaccustomed failure had not proved a happy opening to the new arrangement of Jack being his lover's manager. He had been delighted with his new role: now he would not only be included in Noël's artistic life, but reap some of the benefits too. He'd said he needed power of attorney over Noël's money, and in London he'd requested to see the accounts, even though Noël protested that Lornie took care of all of that and wouldn't like Jack interfering.

'Sure, no one's stepping on Lornie's toes. But she needs to know I'm sticking around. I'm not here to make the coffee. I need to know how it all shapes up. Get an overall view of things. We'll go for a couple of days and you can introduce me to the money guys. Oh, and I'll need some business cards printed.'

'Things are moving quickly,' observed Noël, smiling at Jack's enthusiasm.

'And your next play needs to be different. Show you're not a one-trick pony.'

Noël had bristled slightly at this. 'Yes, darling. I shall set it in a coal mine in Lancashire.'

In London, Jack had a desk installed in Lornie's office and took to hiring cars and charging dinners and tailor's bills to Noël's 'office'. He failed to see the humour in Lornie's filing system – two cabinets named Poppy and Queen Anne. Lornie had borne it all without complaint but Jack knew she wasn't happy. But it was what Noël wanted, Jack made sure she knew that, and then, she had to play ball with him.

'Are you having fun?' Noël would ask, stroking Jack's head, having just admired his newest suit.

'Lots of fun,' Jack would reply. 'One of these days we'll start our own production company. Really be in business together. Imagine – Wilson and Coward!'

'Yes, darling,' Noël would say soothingly, 'but I think Coward and Wilson has a better ring to it – don't you?'

Now Noël gazed out across the well-kept garden. 'I can't be away from Darlingest for long, you know that,' he said quietly and sincerely. 'That's a fact. As you may have noticed, my father is about as interesting to talk to as an under-ripe plum, so Aunt Vida is here for my mother's sanity. It's all perfectly simple.'

'And what about *my* sanity?' asked Jack, tapping his fingers on the table, though he knew that it didn't matter compared to Noël's need for Violet. He'd spent enough time comforting Noël as he wept with longing for his mother whenever they left her for trips abroad.

'Perhaps if you didn't drink so much you may not have mislaid it in the first place,' responded Noël tartly.

'I gave it to you to look after.'

'Fiddlesticks! I've never seen a hint of your sanity since I met you.'

Jack stared at him, thinking that it seemed a long time since that idyllic summer when they'd had this place to themselves, when they'd wandered hand in hand through the woods and kissed and canoodled in the haystack. It hadn't been long before Violet had visited, accompanied by the obedient Arthur, Noël's father, and Jack could see from the light in her eyes that she rather fancied the place for herself. While he and Noël were away in America, Violet had taken up residence and made herself utterly at home. By the time they had returned from their trip, his Aunt Vida had also moved in to keep her sister company, even though the pair seemed to do nothing but bicker with each other.

Violet's quite a number, thought Jack to himself, watching as she clutched her pearls, patted her hair and looked lovingly at her son whenever they were in the same room together, much as a goose who had laid a golden egg might regard its unusual lay. Jack was no fool. He knew that he had to get along with Violet. If she didn't like him, or Noël thought he didn't like his mother, then their relationship had scant chance of survival. Noël and Violet were completely enthralled with each other, as anyone could see. For all his talent as an actor, playwright and songwriter, Noël never seemed to have grown out of her over-powering ambition for him.

Which had come first? Jack wondered. Could she see in her son when he was just a small boy that he was destined for an extraordinary theatrical future, or did she somehow infuse him with it? Noël had embarked on a career in the theatre at an age when most boys have little idea of what they want from life, and it was indeed fortunate that mother and son's plans and ambitions married together so beautifully.

Now the five of them resided together, a strange little menagerie of creatures. Jack felt himself apart from the others, and observed the Coward family with a kind of detached interest. The heart of it was Noël, who was their sun and moon, who was flattered and cosseted and petted. He and Violet shared an intensity of devotion to each other that no one else could match or even come near. Then there was the relationship between Violet and her sister Vida, a shrewish, somewhat Victorian spinster. There seemed little sisterly love between them; they squabbled ceaselessly, the muffled spats coming through the ancient floorboards. At mealtimes they would be civil, but always with an undercurrent of unpleasantness: passing the salt could almost be akin to a kick in the shins under the table where these two were concerned. And it was always Noël they complained to, Noël who was called upon to arbitrate in their childish quarrels. Noël, as ever, was the trump card – as his mother, the bearer of this rich fruit, never let Vida forget. She would threaten Vida with telling Noël what she had done or said, and the two of them would flutter around him, like two fretful chickens hopping and squawking around the tall, unconcerned rooster. Spiteful, catty exchanges infested the house. The unpleasantness was forever simmering under the surface, neither sister ever forgetting, each keeping the score, filling their days and nights with bitter resentments and plans for revenge.

The least important person in the whole set up seemed to be Noël's father. Arthur was much less of a bother. He said very little, appearing to be permanently locked in his own world, but the veins on his forehead throbbed with irritation each time Violet made one of her superior remarks. He acquired a bicycle and would go off on it each morning after breakfast, returning for dinner, and it was obvious to Jack that he left the house to get away from his wife and Vida, the constant disapproval they exuded for him, and the tense atmosphere they revelled in creating, either between themselves or towards Arthur. He felt sorry for the guy.

'How is your husband?' Jack boldly asked Violet one afternoon when the two of them were sitting in front of the fire, drinking tea. He always made sure to spend a little time every day in a fruitless attempt at charming her, usually when Noël had retired to his room to write or take his afternoon nap. 'I feel kinda sorry for Arthur. He seems lost down here in Kent.'

Violet raised her thin eyebrows. 'That's very sweet of you, I'm sure, but you needn't trouble yourself. He was much the same living in London. He's not a gregarious man. I'm sure the air is more agreeable for him here.' She sipped her tea and then said conclusively, 'Arthur has never amounted to much, either as a husband or a father, unfortunately.'

Jack stifled a gasp at the casual cruelty of her words.

'My husband is like a tomcat,' Violet continued. 'Happy as long as he's fed, but who knows what he gets up to all day? Noël thinks he sleeps in the hedgerows.' She gave a short, derisive laugh at the image. 'It wouldn't surprise me – him lying there like a dead badger.'

'What does he make of his famous son?' Jack asked.

'I hardly know,' Violet answered tartly. 'He doesn't understand that world. He never has. Only I have ever understood. Right from the start I saw that Noël was gifted, special. As soon as he could walk and talk, I knew. The theatre was never going to be passing phase for my son. That was apparent as soon as he went on the stage as a boy – no one could deny his talent, his genius. He lives and breathes it. For Noël, it comes from his heart and soul.'

'What does?'

'His need to entertain. He simply loves to make people laugh.'

'I've noticed that.'

'I dare say you have. You are his . . . er . . . manager, after all.' Violet looked at Jack gravely. 'You must ensure that he eats and sleeps properly, you know. He has a tendency to get overexcited, to exhaust himself. You must guard against that.'

Jack smiled to himself. It was Noël's sexual appetite, not his singing and dancing that was tiring him out. 'Oh yes, quite,' he said politely. In fact sex had become inhibited now they were all living under the same roof. Jack liked to make some noise when they were making love. He enjoyed making Noël squeal and scream too. He hated having to creep along corridors in the dead of night. Where once sex had been loud and prolonged, it had become furtive and urgent. There had been none of this 'Mother might hear!' fearfulness from Noël before.

It was becoming intolerable as far as Jack was concerned. It was no wonder he was finding himself drawn more and more to watching that handsome young gardener as he weeded beds and wheeled the barrow along the paths.

'We gotta sort out these arrangements and quickly,' he told Noël firmly. 'Either they live here or we do. Not both. Got it?'

Later that evening, when Jack came in to say goodnight, he found Noël gazing out of the bedroom window, his eyes resting on the old granary that stood close by the house, only a few yards away, its elderly thatched roof bowed and covered in moss.

'Ah!' he said lightly. 'I think I have a solution. Look.'

Jack came to the window where Noël was sitting on the padded seat.

'What?' he said.

Noël sighed. 'It must be a terrible thing to have no imagination.'

'What am I supposed to be imagining? Versailles?'

'That charming granary. We'll turn it into the perfect residence for the parents. Lovely views across the Romney Marsh, close and yet far enough away to allow us all some privacy. We'll call the builders tomorrow. I can see a little pass door I can scurry through to say goodnight to Mother or borrow a lemon. Don't you see it too?' He turned to Jack, his eyes alight with enthusiasm.

Jack bent down so that he was looking at the same view as Noël. He frowned. Perhaps Noël was right. That old building could be spruced up and turned into something. It might even be possible to connect it to the house . . . but it would be a big job. 'I'm beginning to get your drift. Do you really think they would go for it? Promise we won't hear the cat fights?'

Noël's lips tightened just a little, though that could have been with amusement. 'I'm sure I don't know what you mean.'

'Won't be big enough, will it?'

'Oh, we'll add to it, in charming rustic style of course. It will be as pretty as a delphinium, believe me.'

With that Noël began drawing in his notebook. After a few sweeps with his pencil, he closed the book. 'So, problem solved. Is there any other business?'

'What are you going to do about this?' asked Jack, untying his pyjama cord and standing with his legs apart, hands on hips.

'Heavens,' declared Noël. 'We may have to send for the fire brigade.'

Scene Three

Richard

After a restless night I got up early and went outside to peer at Jess's cottage through the trees but the curtains were all drawn and there was nothing to see. I went to the front door and knocked. When there was no answer, I let myself in and found all the lights on and Jess curled up on the sofa, face to the wall, unable, or unwilling, to speak to or look at me.

'Jess, can you hear me? Are you all right?' I asked, but there was no response at all, just a twitch of her jaw muscle. I felt terribly anxious. It was obvious she wasn't at all well but I had no idea what to do or who to call for help. Jess was usually the one taking charge of me, not the other way around. I made my way outside, taking my mobile from my pocket. I had to call someone and get some advice – but Fran was fast asleep and thousands of miles away; Gary was only any good in a situation where there was a big, fat cock involved. The only person I knew who could blossom in a crisis was Marcia.

'Yes, darling? Have you finished chapter one?' she enquired, answering her telephone on the first ring, as she always did.

'Marcia, I'm in trouble. It's Jess.'

'Trouble as in "hubble, bubble, toil and trouble", you mean?'

'I think she's having some kind of episode.' I explained her recent behaviour and all the things she'd said. 'Can you come down?' I asked, my voice trembling with panic. There was a pause while Marcia re-assessed the urgency in my voice.

'It sounds like a breakdown to me. I think you need to get her some professional help. Don't worry, I'm on my way. Maybe you should go back to yours and wait for me. And maybe lock the doors. I'll be there as soon as I can – I'll call you from the train.'

I wondered why all my friends were warning me of Jess turning violent – had they always seen something in Jess that I never had? It didn't seem possible that the person I'd always regarded as my right hand would wish me harm. Even so, I found myself locking the doors to the house behind me as instructed.

In fact, Marcia raced out of her flat and hailed a black cab, persuaded him to drive to Kent at breakneck speed and was giving me a comforting hug within two hours. There was still no sign of life from the cottage.

As I made some strong tea, Marcia explained that she had been busy on her journey.

'I've found a place called the Monastery, not far from here.' She peered at the screen of her BlackBerry. 'It's a private, high-walled establishment, where, for a price, your problems can be sorted out in luxurious surroundings, away from the prying eyes of the general unwashed.' She looked up at me. 'Well, that's the gist of it. And they've got a space for Jess if we want it.'

'I've heard of it,' I said, relieved to hear that Jess would get some help and, more selfishly, that she would soon become someone else's concern. This sort of thing was completely outside my experience. 'Is it mostly a rehab clinic?'

'No,' said Marcia, carefully wrapping a wasp in a tea towel before carrying it over to the window and releasing it. 'Drugs. Alcohol. Food. Exhaustion. Phobias. Mental health issues. They cover everything and they're very discreet. No doubt Jess will be mortified by all this, so I've found a place where discretion and privacy are all part of the deal. They'll sort her out, I'm sure. But before we make a decision, perhaps I should go and see Jess for myself.'

Several minutes later, having glanced at Jess's huddled non-responsive frame on the sofa, Marcia shook her head, told me she thought it was serious, and phoned for the Monastery to send a blacked-out Mercedes to take Jess into their care. We packed her a bag and I sat down with the Monastery representative to go through all of Jess's personal details. It was somewhat embarrassing how little I knew about her, considering how close we had been for so long, but I did what I could and offered to accompany her to the Monastery. I was told that personal visits were discouraged while assessment was being carried out. They would let me know in due course, and meanwhile, could they please have my credit card details? I handed them over without a qualm. I didn't care how much it cost as long as they could help Jess.

The car pulled off with a mute and blank-eyed Jess inside, and twenty minutes later we were in the Walnut Tree choosing from their '100 Ways to Devour a Saveloy' menu. Marcia had kept the taxi with its meter running throughout the proceedings. Tom, the driver, was understandably all smiles.

'Enjoy your lunch,' he said, smiling so widely his eyes all but disappeared.

'I think it's money well spent,' Marcia said as we tucked into our 'Saveloy *à la* Keith Harris'. 'It assuages my left-wing guilt over the money you'll be forking out for Jess's private health care.'

'Are you going to have him drive you home now?' I asked, incredulous. 'Very extravagant of you.'

'Yes. I need to get back to the office. Will you be all right?'

'I shall be fine,' I said. 'I'm just relieved Jess seems to be in good hands.'

'Perhaps Tom is hungry?' Marcia interrupted. 'I'd better treat him kindly. He may be related to Catherine Middleton. Isn't everyone these days?'

Just as we left the pub Marcia rooted in her shoulder bag and retrieved a large brown envelope. 'I almost forgot. Have a look at this script, darling.'

'What is it?' I asked, suspicious. Marcia had a habit of springing things on me when I least expected them.

'Just a little part in a film. I've marked it for you. Three scenes. Ten days' filming. Start next week. I'm not sure why they're bothering, but it pays well. It's in France, though, so dust off your passport.'

'Next week?' I asked, incredulous. 'Bit short notice, isn't it?'

'Mmm,' said Marcia casually, leaning against the taxi now and lighting a cigarette while Tom went round to get it started. 'Apparently Nigel Havers has pulled out.'

'Why?'

'He's been offered the part of the father in *Billy Elliot* and fancies being stretched.'

I felt slightly crestfallen that I was now being offered Nigel's leftovers. Had it come to that? Marcia must have noticed, because she went on:

'I've managed to triple the original offer for you. It will pay for

Jess's renovations, her hospital care and – if I have anything to do with it – her indefinite incarceration,' she added with a malevolent smile. Not for the first time I was glad that Marcia was on my side.

'Well, I'll have a read this afternoon and call you,' I said, a little sniffily.

'There's no need,' said Marcia, tossing her half-smoked cigarette down on the ground. 'I've already accepted the part for you.'

'But—' I began.

'Quick, get in the car,' interrupted Marcia suddenly. 'Julian Clary is mincing towards us, and I'm pretty sure he's wearing Tesco jeans.'

But it was too late – we had been spotted.

'Coo-eee!' Julian called, breaking into a languid trot. He looked remarkably fresh-faced and bright-eyed. 'Sorry I haven't popped in to see how you're settling in. *So* busy.'

I didn't believe that, but I reluctantly shook his hand and introduced Marcia.

'Lovely to meet you,' said Julian, clocking her Rolex watch. 'And are you impressed by my lovely old house? I see Richard's changed the name,' he said with a sniff. 'Each to their own.'

'It's charming, my lovely,' Marcia purred, all twinkles and smiles.

'Marcia has been talking to the ghosts,' I said, interested to see how he would react. I was beginning to wonder if the strange noises and spirit occupants had anything to do with Mr Clary selling the house just a year after he purchased it. Julian's expression changed and he took a step backwards. He glared at Marcia.

'Oh. Have you? How nice,' he said, as though it was anything but.

'Quite a collection of them, I must say,' said Marcia, her eyes fixed on his trousers and the supermarket logo on the cheap canvas belt that strained to hold them up.

'I didn't say anything before,' Julian began uncertainly. 'Well, some people don't believe in it, do they? Think it's all nonsense.'

'It's certainly quite a noisy house,' I said, trying my best to encourage him. I sensed Julian knew something about these matters but was reluctant to say. 'Did you have any . . . experiences while you lived there?'

Julian bit his lip and said nothing for a moment. When he did speak he looked away from us, across to the distant fields.

'A seance. I had a seance once with some friends.'

'And?' asked Marcia impatiently.

'It probably wasn't a good idea. Not on Halloween, after a lot of drink.'

'Did anyone come through?' I asked.

'Er, yes.'

'Who was it? Noël? The cook?'

'I can't remember. Drunk as a skunk, I'm afraid. Listen, I have to go,' said Julian, looking flustered, a bead of sweat running down the side of his face. 'Doctor's appointment. Bloody candida.' He stroked his throat. 'I'll pop by soon. I've got a diamanté horseshoe for you as a house-warming present.'

'Oh. Can't you remember anything?' I asked, a little cross at his shifty behaviour.

'Afraid not,' he said unconvincingly. 'Laters!' And off he scuttled, at a decidedly hurried pace.

'He'll remember it when I shove that horseshoe up his arse,' said Marcia crossly.

*

With Jess away, I was really and truly alone for the first time I could remember. Even when she was in London, I'd always known she was only a phone call away, with my life at her fingertips, always there to sort out any problems I was having. Now, there was not only the running of things – bills, banks, fan mail and all the rest – but also something else I had to think about. Or rather, someone else. Jess's son, Albie. I had to let him know what had happened to his mother but had no idea how to set about finding him. I knew he was at a new school, having spectacularly failed his A-levels, according to Jess. She'd wasted no time enrolling him at a new institution with instructions not to come home until he'd passed his exams. I knew that I was paying for it, just as I had for all of Albie's education, but Jess was such a model of ruthless efficiency that I never saw the bill or had to write a cheque myself. As a consequence, I had no idea where the school was.

The next morning, with the inexplicable synchronicity only really apparent in retrospect, I received a phone call from a Mr Innes, the very well-spoken headmaster of Stoke Ferry Private School for Boys in Norfolk. Albie had now completed his re-sits and was ready to come home, explained Mr Innes. 'But we've been unable to contact his mother to confirm Albie's return. We have you on the records as an alternative next of kin.'

'Ah, yes, well—'

'Can't keep the boy here, twiddling his thumbs,' explained Mr Innes. 'Amongst other things. His education here is *complete*,' he said firmly. 'We can now release him into the wild, as it were. I believe the family home is now in Kent?'

'Yes, it is,' I said. 'But his mother has been taken poorly. Can't he stay at school for a couple more days until we know how long she's going to be in hospital?'

'Unfortunately Master Albie is a little restless. His, er, *maturity*, makes it essential that he be given access to, shall we call it . . . the wider world?' The headmaster sounded rather strained.

'Oh,' I said. 'I quite understand' – although I didn't.

'In fact, we believe he may have already left the school.'

'What do you mean?' I asked, concerned.

'The truth is we cannot locate him. He didn't turn up for Morning Register. My guess is he went over the wall after Benediction yesterday afternoon. His bed hasn't been slept in, which is more unusual than you might think in an all-boys Catholic boarding school.'

'But I suppose that means he could turn up here . . . at any time?' Just as I spoke those words, there was the sound of footsteps on the gravel and then a confident knock at the door. 'Do excuse me, Mr Innes, I must go. I'll let you know of any further developments.' I put the phone down and went to the front door. I opened it and there on the front step stood a tall young man, his tousled dark-blond hair barely contained by a grey beanie hat, a rucksack slung over one shoulder. He was wearing baggy jeans, a pale-blue shirt and his boots were unlaced. He had intense navy-blue eyes that were staring straight at me.

'Hi, Richard,' he said with a smile that chased away the surly curl around his lips. 'Any idea where my mother is? No one's answering the door at the cottage.'

'Albie!' I gasped. 'I've just been trying to find you!'

He shrugged. He looked like an All Saints retail assistant. 'Well. Here I am.'

We stood staring at each other for a moment. I could hardly believe that this tall, self-possessed young buck was the little boy I had played hide and seek with. It seemed an age since

I'd seen him and he'd changed beyond all recognition.

'You'd better come in,' I said, remembering my manners. 'I'll tell you everything.'

Once Albie was settled on the sofa, drinking a cup of coffee and smoking a cigarette that he'd rolled deftly with one hand from a tin he kept in his pocket, I told him as gently as possible what had happened. I didn't want to frighten the poor boy.

'So let me get this straight,' he said, picking a stray strand of tobacco from the tip of his tongue. 'Mum's in the funny farm at last?'

'Well . . . I don't know if I'd put it like that,' I said, taken aback by his lack of concern. 'They think she's had some kind of breakdown. The Monastery is a well-known, not to say expensive, rehabilitation centre with an excellent reputation in diagnosing and treating psychological disorders.' I had absorbed some of the spiel in the brochure they'd given me as a matter of habit. 'Your mother needed help,' I added more kindly.

'You don't need to tell me that. She's as crazy as a box of frogs.'

Obviously the poor boy must be aware of his mother's strange behaviour, I thought, chiding myself. Goodness knows what he had endured in the past. I had only seen Jess's dark moods on occasion but this was the first time I'd realised that Albie must have seen much more growing up. Was that the reason that Jess had been so keen to send him away to school at an early age? At the time I'd thought it was because her maternal genes were somewhat lacking but maybe she'd actually been looking to save Albie the trauma of witnessing something he shouldn't. 'Albie, are you okay?'

He looked thoughtful. 'She's always been strange. Under the surface, anyway. And above it, sometimes. It comes and goes.'

'I've seen some of her moods . . .' I trailed off, wondering if I could ask him for more details but not sure if it was wise to probe in such a sensitive area. 'It can't have been easy for you,' I said, in what I hoped was a reassuring tone.

'I've never known any different,' he said rather sharply, and then smoked quietly for a while. After a pause he said, 'Well, I guess you know what's best for her.' He stubbed his cigarette out on the hearth.

'They will take good care of her, I assure you,' I said sincerely. 'And let's hope it's not too long before she's back with us, all better.'

'And what about me?' He sounded vulnerable. 'I was going to stay with Mum for a bit while I made plans for the summer.'

'The cottage is at your disposal. I'm sure you can stay there. It's your home after all.'

Albie shook his head. 'Mum wouldn't like me living by myself. Even though I'm nineteen, she doesn't think I can cope. She'd go mental . . . I mean, she'd do her nut . . . I mean . . . oh dear.'

We both caught each other's eye, and then started to laugh.

'You know what I mean,' he said eventually, his head bowed so far forward with laughter that his fringe gave my knees a butterfly kiss. 'She wouldn't like it.'

'In that case, you must stay here, in the Old Manor,' I said firmly. It was obviously my duty to make sure that he was taken care of. 'I've got a very nice guest suite and it would be lovely to have you here. We can potter about the garden together. Would you like that?'

Albie stared at me, his dark-blue eyes glittering slightly in the morning sunlight. 'Very much,' he said.

'Good. Then that's settled.' We sat quietly for a moment, but then the silence was interrupted by a faint high-pitched wail. We both turned to look at the fireplace, which seemed to be where it was coming from.

'Is that an owl or something?' asked Albie.

'I don't know,' I replied. By then the noise had stopped. 'I expect so.' I stood up. 'Now, I'll show you to your room and you can settle in.'

It was rather pleasant having Albie in the house with me. He was immediately at his ease and seemed to enjoy looking about the place, inspecting the garden with me and just lounging about, feet up in front of the telly. I made him a simple lunch of sandwiches and salad, and that afternoon, after I'd rung Mr Innes back to let him know Albie was safely with me, we called the Monastery for an update on Jess's condition. Jess was comfortable, the doctor told me, and quite calm. She was displaying symptoms of a nervous breakdown of some sort and tomorrow they would begin to assess her condition and decide on a course of treatment. She did not advise any visitors for at least a few days but would keep us informed of all developments. The doctor then spoke at length to Albie about his mother's recent behaviour. And that was that. Jess was in good hands, and there was nothing more we could do for the moment.

I took Albie for supper at a local Italian restaurant and we managed two bottles of house red between us – he'd made it clear he was a regular imbiber and certainly old enough to drink. He proved to be a surprisingly entertaining companion, amusing me with stories of his life at school and various high jinks he and his mates indulged in. For my part I shared a few choice showbiz anecdotes and found him a receptive audience. We had a good evening, quite forgetting the shadow of Jess's illness that hung over us. After leaving the car and taking a taxi back, I showed Albie to his room and left him to it while I made my usual late-night phone call to Fran.

'Blimey,' said Fran down the line from LA. 'What a bloody drama. You theatricals.'

That night I slept deeply, numbed by all the red wine. I woke inside a deep and sensuous dream, deliciously erotic and leading me to a delightful conclusion.

By the time I came fully to consciousness, it was too late. I was past the point of no return. It was only when the dark shape popped up beside me from under the duvet that I had any real idea of what had happened – and with whom.

I gasped and reached across to turn on the bedside light, just in time to see Albie wriggling out from under the duvet squinting in the sudden light, his cheeks bulging as if he had just hurriedly eaten a Big Mac.

I recoiled away from him and clutched the duvet to my chest, horrified. 'God! Oh my God. What are you doing?'

Albie swallowed noisily. 'Oh, where am I?' he asked.

Horrified as I was, I still knew bad acting when I saw it. I'd sat through Keanu Reeves movies just like everyone else. 'Albie! Whatever are you thinking?'

'That I could do with a glass of water,' he replied, smiling insolently.

His naked body rose from the bed and went to the bathroom.

I lay there, still struck dumb with horror and astonishment until the lithe limbs and hairless torso loped back into the room, glass in hand.

'Don't let the age difference bother you,' he said lightly, sitting down on the side of the bed. 'I've always liked older men. Between you and me, it's about the same as Madonna and her latest boyfriend.'

'Albie . . .' I hardly knew where to begin. 'You can't just do that to someone . . . I thought I was dreaming! I would never— I have a partner, thank you,' I said haltingly, blinking at him.

'Oh, I know you have a boyfriend. I don't want to usurp him. Not yet, anyway.'

I began to come to my senses. 'Get out, Albie!'

'How rude!' was his reply. He gazed at his own reflection in the dressing-table mirror. 'I'm pretty fit, you must admit. It's not like you've just woken up in bed with Christopher Biggins.'

'OK. Get out. Now.' I used a low but determined voice. 'Do I make myself clear?'

'Would you like me to tell you the truth about my mother before I go?' he asked casually. 'It might interest you more than I obviously do.'

'Go! Your mother would be horrified by what you've just done.' My mind was reeling and I was overcome by panic and anger, shame and self-loathing. To make matters worse, it seemed the boy was revelling in his accomplishment. I didn't want to think about my own – albeit semi-conscious – response to his actions.

He lit a cigarette and sat back down on the bed, leaning back against the pillows, allowing his legs to fall open. I picked up his dressing gown and threw it at him.

'Cover yourself up, for God's sake.' I was about to order him to leave again but hesitated. 'If you have anything to tell me about your mother that will help her to get better, you'd better spit it out. And then go.'

'Ashtray?' said Albie, waving his cigarette around.

'Fran doesn't allow smoking in the bedroom.' I got up, grabbing a blanket to cover my modesty, and opened the window before going to the bathroom and returning with a soap dish. 'Use this.'

'I don't suppose Fran allows anything very pleasurable to take place in this room,' said Albie, tossing the dressing gown on the floor and examining the soap dish. 'Philippe Starck. Very nice.'

'I'm waiting,' I said tersely, ignoring his barb about Fran. I sat back down on my side of the bed.

Albie drew on his cigarette, enjoying his moment of power.

'Gosh. I'm centre stage now. Your ears are burning. Well, so they should be. You may need a visit to the Monastery yourself once I've told all.' He looked me straight in the eye. 'My mother is secretly in love with you. Worse than that – she's obsessed.'

'Don't be ridiculous,' I said, outraged. 'Jess is my friend – my best friend.'

'If she wasn't your PA, she'd be your stalker.'

'I think you're making this up.'

He looked suddenly serious. 'I'm not, Richard. I mean it. You occupy my mother's every waking thought. You always have. It hasn't been much fun for me, growing up in your shadow, I can tell you. I've always felt that I was little more than an annoyance to my mother while you were her main focus. Her whole reason for living, in fact.'

I gaped at him. 'Jess is dedicated and intensely loyal, yes . . . and I love her for it . . . but I can't believe what you're saying. You must be mistaken.' A thought occurred to me. 'Perhaps Jess hasn't been the perfect mother and I'm sorry if you felt ignored. Is this a way for you to punish her? Is that why you crept in here in the middle of the night and—' I couldn't say the words.

'Oh no. I'm not that complex.'

'Then why?'

'Lust, plain and simple. I'm a slave to it,' he said, giving me a sly smile, his blue eyes sparkling. 'It's been a fantasy of mine for years. I couldn't help myself. With my mother locked away and us here together, the temptation was too much. I lay in bed thinking about you and then realised there was nothing to stop me having my way.'

I stared at him, speechless, unable to prevent a tingle of arousal and hating myself for it. Then in a flash he was across the bed and I felt his arms around me, enclosing me, and his chest pressed against my back.

'I'm sorry to tell you, Mr Stent, that I haven't finished with you yet,' he murmured in my ear.

I tried to break free but the younger man's bear hug held me fast. He clasped his hands together across my ribs and for a moment I couldn't breathe, then he loosened his grip a little and I managed to suck in some air.

'Get off me, will you?' I demanded.

'Just relax,' he cooed in my ear. 'This won't hurt at all. In fact you might even enjoy it.'

As Albie rocked backwards and forwards on top of me, slowly, imperceptibly our patterns of breathing gathered pace and became synchronised. I was unable to resist the rhythm, the power of the repetition. My body responded, my imagination skipped beyond the bounds of propriety and decency and soared away into fevered, darkly exciting places. I panted and moaned, and the weight of Albie's body and the harshness of his rapid exhalations in my ear urged me on. I was powerless to resist. I didn't want to resist. I had to embrace it.

Then Albie threw his head back and crowed like a cockerel on top of a feisty hen.

ACT III
Scene One
1928
Noël

Violet and Vita were horrified at the new building plans, when Noël and Jack told them over lunch. Arthur listened without expression, his face still except for the grinding of his jaws as he slowly chewed his veal.

'Am I to be relegated to an outside barn like a donkey?' asked Violet, with a quiver in her voice, clutching a handkerchief to her bosom.

'No, Darlingest,' soothed Noël. 'It's the granary for one thing, and it won't be anything like a barn once we've finished with it. It will be a terribly modern, roomy abode with hot and cold running water, stunning views across the marsh and a servants' hall so close they will simply have to reach in and scratch your nose should you get a tiresome itch.'

'Barns aren't so bad. Christ was born in a manger,' said Jack helpfully.

'And we all know what happened to *him*,' put in Aunt Vida. She puffed out her ample chest and her weak chin wrinkled as she tightened her lips.

'Oh, for goodness' sake!' said Jack impatiently.

'Very well,' said Noël, aware that he wasn't going to win this argument. 'I had hoped you would be pleased at the thought of such an extensive building inspired and designed for your well-being, but clearly I was mistaken. Mother, Father and Aunt Vida shall stay here in the main house, with creaking floorboards, low ceilings and more mice than Gertrude Lawrence has teeth. Jack and I will slum it in the new wing. That is an end of the matter. Now if no one has any objections, I shall retire to my room for the afternoon. I have a new West End triumph to start writing, if you don't mind. At this rate I am unlikely to finish it until Thursday.' He tossed his napkin onto his plate and left the room.

Jack smiled his wicked smile at the two ladies, who were now looking worried. 'Happy now, girls? Got what you wanted?'

'I can't cope with draughts,' said Aunt Vida weakly.

Arthur spoke unexpectedly. 'I think we should live in the new bit,' he said in his gruff voice. 'There's some oddness in this old place that I wouldn't be sorry to say goodbye to.'

Jack looked over at the old man, interested. He was a distinguished-looking old gent in his way, thought Jack. Noël's long face and determined chin had come from Arthur, there was no mistake, as had his expressive mouth, with its ever-present twist towards a smile – unlike Violet's thin-lipped downward curve. 'Oddness?' he asked.

Arthur looked around at them all. 'You've all heard it; don't pretend you haven't. There're noises in this place. Who hasn't heard those cries in the night, eh? Babies howling in the dark . . .'

'Owls!' cried Aunt Vida helpfully. 'Foxes?' She sounded less sure. 'Foolishness . . .' But Jack thought he saw a spark of recognition in the old lady's eyes.

'You think the place is haunted?' he asked, amused.

'I'm sure you Americans don't believe in such things,' sniffed Violet. 'You're far too busy dashing about the place and shouting to each other about how you want your eggs done. Well, we've got a bit of history over here, thank you very much. We live with a resonance from the past that I doubt you would comprehend.'

'Then I'm surprised you're not keen to move out of here and into the new place which, I assume, is free of strange noises and ghostly crying,' Jack returned, wondering if there was anything that would ever dent that English sense of superiority.

Arthur said nothing but carefully cut another piece of meat and set about eating it slowly. Vida muttered under her breath something about being quite comfortable where she was.

'Don't mention infant ghosts to Noël, will you,' Jack said, torn between wanting to laugh and feeling exasperated. 'You know how sensitive he is. We don't want to upset him.'

'He always writes better when he's a little agitated,' said Violet, ringing the small brass bell to summon Alice. 'Anyone for coffee?'

The building plans got underway, with Noël's principal concern being that the new wing should be skilfully blended in with the old. Half-timbered frames and reclaimed bricks were to be sourced, and the roof had to be the same height with matching chimneys and inglenook fireplaces. Kentish builders being what they were, there was a lot of talk and rubbing of chins long before anything got done. Noël planned the build rather like he would one of his plays; it was to be eloquent, seamless and chic, but also daring.

Goldenhurst Old Manor, built all those centuries ago, had been cunningly placed so that the rising sun streamed into the rear of the house, no doubt waking the inhabitants to begin their rural duties at first light. During the day the sun was overhead, so that in the summer, with windows open, the house remained cool and dim, then towards the afternoon it slid over the front and the long rays of evening warmed the west side, bathing the garden in soft balmy light.

To the side of the Old Manor, across to the south, was the Romney Marsh, gently sloping towards the sea, bleak and beautiful and mysterious. So the new part of the house was designed by Noël to make the most of this aspect (at least that's what he told Violet). But it had the added attraction of giving maximum privacy to the new residents, positioned as it was at just the angle to prevent any peering in through windows. And for sound insulation, Noël had the brainwave of building a 'studio' between the old and the new, still allowing for the rabbit warren of interconnecting doors but extending, by several dozen metres, the distance from his new bedroom to the old house. Jack saw the drawings and declared them genius.

'A rehearsal space, an art room, a *border*!' he declared.

Noël looked satisfied. 'Where there's a will, there's a way. Darling parents and Aunt Vida will be close – but not too close. We shall have our privacy and they shall have theirs.'

'You mean we might have a bit of our secret island back to ourselves . . .'

'Precisely.'

'As long as you promise me we won't hear the eternal bickering?' pleaded Jack.

'And they won't hear our eternal anything else,' said Noël wickedly. 'And there will be plenty of that.'

*

As the granary neared completion, there were long periods when Noël and Jack were away, either rehearsing or presenting a new play in London or New York or on one of their spectacular extended trips to exotic faraway lands.

Upon their return from one sojourn, when the house was blissfully quiet owing to the Cowards and Aunt Vida being at the seaside, they noted with regret that their maid Alice was changing.

'I do declare,' said Noël after a prettier, more upright Alice served them their drinks on the terrace without spilling a drop, 'The dear girl is not as gauche as she was. How tiresome of her.'

'A tragic loss,' agreed Jack. 'No stoop, head upright and barely a quiver as she put down the tray!'

'I am positively dismayed by such a sad development. Maybe if I bark at her later the old Alice will come back?'

But it wasn't to be. Alice had grown up, developed a cleavage and a sway to her walk. She even smiled confidently as she entered a room.

'Our guests are going to be terribly disappointed,' sighed Noël after a few days at home. 'I doubt anyone shall visit us ever again. It's like going to Tangiers and finding they have discovered lavatory paper.'

The new Alice had also found her voice, trilling 'Good morning, Mr Coward' or 'Will there be anything else, sir?' in a pleasant Kentish burr.

Jack was passing the kitchen one morning in search of that day's newspaper when he heard Mrs Ashton's voice floating out, echoing off the stone flags. Curious, he stopped to listen and realised that the housekeeper was berating Alice in shrill, scolding tones:

'It's no good coming back from your lunch hour with bits of grass and heads of wheat all threaded through your jumper. People will wonder what you've been up to. I know what you're doing and it's not decent. It's got to stop until you're respectable. Do I make myself clear?' she was saying sternly.

And that afternoon, when he idly watched Alice picking damsons from the tree on the back lawn and witnessed Jude, the gardener's assistant, dart across the lawn and squeeze her in a tight, unexpected embrace, Jack realised the new, confident Alice was a result of her sexual awakening, no less. He smiled to himself. Although he and Noël had lost that first precious, joyful isolation, the many residents of the Old Manor (both principal and supportive) provided – should one care to embroil oneself in the ebb and flow of their relationships – a live soap opera of exquisite twists and turns.

'I think Alice and Jude are being feral,' he announced to Noël in bed that night.

'I beg your pardon?'

'They're fucking. Is that plain enough for you? I saw them together in the orchard, and I'm sure of it.'

'Oh,' responded Noël. 'I do hope it doesn't affect the strength of the tea.'

The next day Jack wandered into the garden and saw what he had been hoping to see: the young under-gardener. Jude was hard at work digging the heavy clay soil and glowing from his exertions. His sweat-stained singlet clung to his broad back and his shoulder muscles jumped and bulged like snakes under his skin with each thrust of the spade. Jack couldn't resist stopping to engage Jude in conversation.

'Good morning,' he said, smiling appreciatively. 'You are obviously working very hard.'

'Yes, sir,' said Jude, bowing his head. 'It's all comin' along.'

'You obviously have the right touch . . .' Jack let his gaze rest on the boy's chest. Jude didn't reply, but carried on hoeing the flowerbed, then reached down to pull out a large dandelion. Jack looked hungrily at his rump.

'Everything is looking lovely. I must say. Very lush.'

'Is it, sir?' said Jude, standing up again and turning to look at Jack, as if he knew very well what he was referring to.

'Call me Jack.'

Jude wiped his forehead with the back of his hand and pushed his hair out of his eyes. He looked uncertain.

'You're happy working here, are you?' Jack asked.

'Yes, si— Jack. I'm very happy,' Jude replied quietly.

'Good. I'm glad to hear it. And do you have a young lady?'

'Alice and I,' Jude said awkwardly. 'Er . . . we're stepping out together.'

'How nice. And where do you go?'

Jude shrugged. 'For walks.'

'Yes.' Jack nodded, still smiling. 'Alice is a charming girl. And you enjoy your walks?'

Jude shrugged again and scratched his head.

'Careful!' Jack said. 'Don't want to get dirt in your hair. Here. Let me get it out for you.' He stepped close to the boy and spent several seconds removing a small lump of earth from the crown of the gardener's head. 'There.' He held out the grain of dried mud between his thumb and forefinger so Jude could see it. 'Now give your head a shake.'

Jude laughed nervously and did as requested.

'Occupational hazard for you, I suppose?'

'Well, yes,' mumbled Jude, colouring slightly. 'Thank you. I'd better be getting along.'

'Yes, I mustn't keep you. Enjoy your day. And your walks with Alice. I go for walks too sometimes. With Mr Coward. But sometimes he's too busy. Maybe I could go for a walk with you instead?' Jack spoke quietly and meaningfully.

Jude seemed lost for words and picked up his hoe and weed basket as if desperate to get away.

'What do you say?' demanded Jack, smiling and taking a step to block Jude's way.

'If you'd like, sir.'

'Jack.'

There was a pause, then Jude said, 'If you'd like, Jack.'

'Yes, I'd like it very much,' said Jack and turned to walk back to the house. Maybe there's more fun to be had down here than I guessed, he thought to himself. One only has to look for it.

Scene Two

Richard

The next morning, I woke to discover that there was no electricity. Well, there were lights, which I didn't need, it being daylight, but no power to any of the sockets. Hairdryers, televisions, kettles: none were working. I discovered this inconvenience when, stumbling in to the kitchen, my mind reeling with the events of the night before, I was unable to make the cup of tea I was so desperate for.

There was no Albie in the bed when I woke, and I was grateful for that, at least. Perhaps I could now pretend that the things that he'd done were just a dream, one that might pinken my cheeks with the embarrassing recollection but that I need not worry too much about. But try as I might to conceal the truth from myself, I knew that the whole ghastly thing had been real. Amongst the sheets, I found the leather wristband that Albie had been wearing. Plus I could *feel* that sexual activity had taken place. (Let's just say that had there been any hot water, I would have been planning a salt-water bath.)

The problem with the electricity was almost a relief – I had something to swear about, something to occupy my mind. I called

John, the builder who had worked on the house, and explained the problem. He said he could get me an electrician round by 2 pm.

'Do you mean to tell me,' I said earnestly, 'that I'm to miss all two and a half hours of my Phillip Schofield fix?'

'Try not to break out in hives,' said John dryly.

The sockets remained stubbornly dead all day while I waited for the electrician. As I wandered about from room to room with no television, radio or music, it felt, through the silence, as though the house were asserting itself, telling me roughly that there was no need for electricity in its day. Electricity was for nancy boys. I paced about anxiously, trying not to think about the fact that Albie was probably only a few metres away in the cottage, and to stop myself wondering what he was doing and what he thought about what had happened. Eventually, unable to bear it for a second longer, I called Gary and told him everything. A problem shared is a problem halved, as Fran always said. I suppose I should have predicted Gary's reaction.

'You can stop pretending it was all against your will, mate,' Gary said, sounding almost gleeful. 'You can turn off your anguish tap. You're not traumatised. Rough trade, girl, that's what it's called.'

'Well, I . . . I . . . I didn't exactly give my consent,' I protested. 'In fact, I've been feeling used and violated.'

'Oh, come off it. You're an openly gay, world-famous actor and you got fucked up the arse by a nineteen-year-old rugby-playing public schoolboy. I hardly think your shrinking violet act is going to go down very well in court. It's like the plot of a smutty novel. And you are not cast as Prince Charming.'

'No, obviously it isn't going to come to court, but—'

'I'm not being judgmental – I'd never do that. But really, Richard—' he chortled '—you've surprised even me this time. Top marks.'

'I know I can rely on you to keep a secret. I just had to tell someone. I've had some weird experiences in my life, but this was something else.'

'It certainly was. The little minx. Very empowering for a teenager, I dare say. And what happens now?'

'God alone knows. He was gone when I woke up this morning.'

'I bet he was. He'd hardly be up and making you bacon and eggs, giving the kitchen the once-over with a damp Spontex. I predict this relationship will be all about sex. No conversation, no breakfast, no dinner, no text messages, just raw, outrageous sex. Then it will all end in tears one day. Quite soon.'

I was horrified. 'Relationship? What are you talking about? No, this can never happen again. Never!'

Gary's voice came mercilessly down the line. 'I'm nothing if I'm not a gay man too, remember. Experienced, some would say. And I know an erotic fantasy come to life when I hear about it. I'm not buying any of this "Alas, poor Richard, he can hardly walk" stuff. You loved it. Let's be real here. You ain't no victim.'

I was stunned into silence.

Gary went on, 'Just go with it. It'll be exciting, make you feel alive. I love the fact that human beings, for all their sophistication, become slaves the moment there is a sniff of carnal activity in the air. If I was being boring I'd tell you that intellectually, socially, morally there are problems with what has occurred but fuck all that. Sometimes the brain wins the argument, sometimes it doesn't. Last night your brain cut out. You felt the tsunami of desire and you were engulfed by it. Nobody died. Stop trying to justify what was at the very least an unusual, very probably regrettable, encounter. Take *responsibility*, Richard. You allowed that to happen. You got off on it. It made you feel young again. I don't know. Maybe you've been lusting after this kid since he was—'

'Stop right there!' I barked, appalled. 'You're so, so wrong. I have never, ever thought of Albie in that way. That is the God's honest truth. I swear on my life.'

'Didn't I see a Justin Bieber CD in your car the other day?' teased Gary.

'No, you did not!' I shouted. 'I won't have this. I *am* the victim. Believe me!'

I could almost hear Gary's smirk across the telephone line. Then he said slowly, 'So why do I have the feeling that tonight, in approximately ten hours from now, you and Albie will be rutting like pigs in shit again?'

I said nothing. I didn't know how to reply to such a vulgar remark.

Carl the electrician (all industrial romper suit and neck tattoos) arrived at 3.30 and managed to get the power working again, though he was puzzled as to why it had cut out in the first place.

'There's no real explanation for it,' he said, munching on a custard cream.

'This house tries it on,' I explained. 'Never satisfied. Like David Gest's plastic surgeon – nothing is ever good enough. She doesn't seem to like my modernising ways, but I have to let her know who is boss. She's an old girl and forgets. I have to keep explaining, very gently, that I'm here to help. The Sky box I had fitted last week seemed to be the last straw.'

Carl finished his biscuit quickly and picked up his tool bag. 'All working again now, anyway,' he said, looking slightly bemused. 'Maybe you should get your pipework looked at, though.'

Psychic or what? I thought, as I sat down gingerly on a kitchen stool.

'That old copper one above the fuse box. Probably not a good idea.'

'I'll tell John,' I said, and thanked him for his advice.

Then he left me to the silent house and my fevered brain.

As evening came, I could think of nothing more appropriate to do than open a bottle of vodka. I had a shower, put on my Alexander McQueen cowl-neck top and sat in the sitting room, self-medicating with the vodka to calm my nerves. The anger and shock at the previous night's events had subsided and, as the Grey Goose flooded my veins and alcoholic euphoria made its brief appearance, I found my feelings for Albie undergoing a number of transformations. Despite my best efforts, an erotic thrill, a kind of electric vibration, buzzed through my body. I couldn't help replaying the encounter and what had seemed at the time to be a sexual assault very much against my will now became exciting, illicit and transporting.

As I became accustomed to those feelings, mulling them over and justifying them, my attitude to Albie began to change too. How was the boy feeling? Suppose he was full of regret and horror at what he had done? His mother was in hospital, after all, and his emotions must be all over the shop. Why hadn't he come over during the day? Perhaps he had run away. Maybe he had done something silly. Another thought struck me. What if Albie had told someone about what had occurred? A journalist even. Panic rose in my chest at the very thought. It could ruin my career if he did a kiss-and-tell on me. I'd been around long enough to know how it worked: being a gay national treasure was possible if I was safely with my long-term partner; buggering about with my teenage almost-godson was not something the great unwashed would stomach so easily! It would be trial by tabloid.

I shuddered and got to my feet with the force of the thought. Should I call round to see him? Should I phone? But what tone should I take? Or should I phone a lawyer? I wondered darkly. Perhaps I should have some sort of super-injunction ready just in case. It was all so complicated. I had another drink and began to pace, or, if the truth were known, stagger, up and down.

At nine o'clock Fran called from LA. 'Hi,' he said, as always. 'It's me.'

'Hello,' I replied, glad that we were not on Skype in case he could see something different about me, or spot the air of panic I was sure surrounded me.

'Have you been drinking?'

'I've only said one word!'

'Yes, but I can tell.'

'Oh, well. Just a glass of vodka. It felt like a good idea. I miss you.'

'I bet you don't.'

'Why do you say that?'

'I don't know. Very suspicious.'

'Yes, you are. Always suspecting the worst of me.'

'Hmmm. What have you been doing? Apart from drinking?'

'Well, we can't all be the Virgin Mary. Just unwinding.'

'Any word from Jess?'

'No. Doctors say she's fine and she's being assessed, whatever that means. I feel much better knowing she's being taken care of.'

'And what about Albie?'

'He's all right. I've hardly seen him, to be honest.' I hoped that I was sounding completely normal. I thought I did, I was an actor after all, but I was never any match for Fran's sharp ears. I concentrated on sounding relaxed, hoping that if I didn't, he'd put it down to the vodka. 'He doesn't seem that bothered, strangely. I suppose he's been living with her madness for some time, unknown to anyone. I feel a bit guilty about that . . .' I trailed off, trying not to think of the other things I had more reason to feel guilty over. 'How arc things there?'

'Oh, the same old, same old. I saw Stephen Dorff walking down the street today. Gorgeous, but so small I wanted to pick him up and put him in my pocket.'

'I bet you did.'

'He's been spending some serious time in the gym.'

'It's easy for these short, wiry types. A couple of weeks working out and they're bulging all over.'

'Well, I'm telling you he was ripped.'

'That's an American expression. I think you've been away too long.'

'You're telling me.'

There was a long pause and then Fran said, 'Apart from that there's really nothing much to report.'

'Here neither,' I said. 'I've got less than a week before I start shooting a film in France.'

'Who's it with?'

'Some model-turned-actress. I forget her name. She weighs

about five stone. I'm going to look like Eamonn Holmes next to her.'

'Don't flatter yourself,' said Fran. He never feigned an interest in my work. He never commented or expressed any opinion. Then he added, 'Well, it's bad luck in a way. I've just been told I can take some time off next week. I've booked a ticket and I'm home in four days so I'll see you for all of forty-eight hours.'

'Four days?' Fresh guilt exploded in my stomach. I wanted to see Fran, of course. I'd missed him. The dark and disturbing events of the last twenty-four hours would not have occurred if he had been present. And yet I was immediately terrified that he'd guess what I'd been up to. A kind of countdown began ticking in my brain. 'That's great. I can't wait,' I said.

We said a hurried goodbye a moment later. Fran had a 'work' call on his other mobile phone and hung up abruptly. It was usually the way our conversations ended.

I poured myself another drink and tried to think about something or someone other than Albie, pretending to myself that I wasn't waiting for him but in my heart, I knew otherwise.

At ten-thirty, the back door opened. I'd left it unlocked half on purpose, I realised now.

Nothing will happen, I told myself, putting my drink down and running my fingers through my hair. We'll just talk. Maybe there will be a few tears of regret, then secret, eternal vows to never let it happen again.

Albie appeared, rucksack over one shoulder, as arrogant and beautiful as ever. I couldn't help but look as he stood silhouetted in the doorway. He unhooked his bag from his shoulder and let it fall to the ground beside him. I watched, unable to stop my mind assessing his body, the slim hips, the jeans with their cat's whisker creases, drawing the eye to the groin and the top fly button casually undone. Then he walked towards me, bandy with machismo, slow and confident. I had to force myself to breathe.

'Vodka,' he said, noticing the half-empty bottle on the table. 'Do you mind if I join you?'

Still I didn't speak. Albie poured himself a drink in the empty glass and sat down on the sofa next to me. He put the glass to his lips and flung his head back, downing it in one.

'Ah, that's better,' he said, smiling a crooked smile and looking sideways at me. He flung his arms over the back of the sofa, casually brushing my shoulder as he did so. 'I've been a bit fucked up all day, to be honest,' he said brightly.

I turned to look at him. Our eyes met, and with a sudden, ghostly movement, his mouth was pressed against mine, his arms sweeping forward, tightly crushing my shoulders once again, and we were back where it all should not have started. As I opened my willing lips to receive Albie's tobacco-tinged tongue, I thought fleetingly of Gary's prediction and of Fran.

This is all wrong, I thought, and then I stopped thinking altogether.

Scene Three

May 1930

Noël

Despite the fact that it was gone midnight, Violet and Vida were both standing on the doorstep of Goldenhurst as the Jaguar drew up, illuminated by the light from within the house: two small women in sensible skirts, jumpers and sturdy shoes. Noël and Jack sat together in the back, the chauffeur at the wheel, and as they approached the house along the driveway between the newly planted (as yet rather small) poplar trees, Jack leaned out of the car window.

'From the way those two are bobbing up and down like a couple of Indian runner ducks, there is some drama afoot,' he said.

'Oh, Lord, no,' said Noël wearily. 'There's always something. Last week Alice served tea with grass stains on the back of her uniform. Mother drew her own conclusions and the entire moral well-being of Kent seemed to be at stake.'

'This looks worse,' said Jack grimly. 'Brace yourself.'

The car pulled to a stop in front of the house and before the chauffeur could open the door for Noël, Violet darted forward.

'Thank goodness you're here!' she cried, wringing her hands.

Aunt Vida came up from behind, peering over Violet's shoulder, eyes wide and staring like a mad owl.

'Goodness, ladies. Calm yourselves, please,' said Noël, climbing out of the car and putting his hat on for the five steps to the front door.

'Your father! Carrying on with Mrs Cheeseman!' said Aunt Vida in a rush, unable to keep it in a moment longer.

'It's the talk of the village,' added Violet, clasping her hands in mortification. 'I can never be seen in public again!'

'Good evening, Mother,' said Noël calmly, kissing her twitching cheek firmly and then bending even lower to reach Vida's. 'Jack and I shall need a plate of cheese and a bottle of Beaujolais before we hear another word. Inside. Shoo! Both of you.' He waved them on, as if they were troublesome geese.

Aunt Vida gave one of her high-pitched squeaks and skipped up in the air as if smacked on the back of the legs. Violet's mouth tightened and she turned regally towards the house.

'Very well,' she said.

'How nice to see you all. Good to be home. Yes, I'm very well, thank you for asking. Isn't the weather clement for this time of year?' muttered Jack as he followed behind, ignored.

There was no sign of Arthur in the house. The two women sat silently as Noël and Jack ate their supper and sipped their wine. Once or twice their need to spill the terrible beans got the better of them and they attempted to speak, but Noël raised a finger and said, 'Not yet, please.' Finally he wiped his mouth with the napkin, re-filled his glass and sighed. 'So,' he said. 'What seems to be the trouble?'

'Mrs Cheeseman,' said Aunt Vida, almost erupting. Her habit of editing her sentences down to just a handful of principal words was trying at the best of times. 'Arthur. Bicycle. Shirtless at the window. Post office. Everyone. Too terrible!'

'Has my father been cycling shirtless to the post office with Mrs Cheeseman on the cross bar?' asked Noël.

Jack stifled a laugh.

'No,' said Violet coldly. 'And it isn't a laughing matter. I am hurt that you first dismiss and then trivialise your father's blatant infidelity. His betrayal of me, of our sacred vows . . .' Violet could not go on. Her head flopped into her hand and she wept bitterly.

Noël immediately jumped up to comfort her. 'Oh, darling, I am so very sorry. Tell me, what has he done to hurt you? That beastly swine of a man.'

'Broad daylight!' wailed Violet. 'Without even drawing the curtains! I cannot live in this place any longer. The shame and humiliation are too much. Mrs Cheeseman can hardly even read and write.'

'Well, I don't suppose that matters, frankly,' said Noël honestly. 'It seems unlikely that they were doing *The Times* crossword.'

Jack felt it permissible to let out a proper laugh this time. 'Ha! The sly old devil.'

Violet jerked her head up. 'Please. There is nothing amusing about this situation. If you knew what I've had to suffer! The postmistress herself told me, she loved rubbing my nose in it, cutting me down to size! "Mrs Coward," she said, "I do hope your husband's bicycle has been mended. It must have a puncture, because it's been propped against Mrs Cheeseman's hedge every afternoon this week. So nice for her to have a bit of company, though. He must be feeling well, for Mrs Carson saw him in the upstairs window without even his shirt on."' Colour rose to

Violet's cheek at the very thought of it. 'The disgrace!' she choked out.

'I'm sorry,' said Jack, finishing his glass of wine. 'But let's look at this realistically. It's hardly the Pope and Fay Wray, is it? I mean, the world may continue revolving.'

'Hush, Jack,' Noël said sternly.

'Your mother. Terribly, terribly upset,' jumped in Aunt Vida. 'Tears. Divorce! He doesn't care.'

'Where is Father?' asked Noël in the tone of a high court judge asking for the black cap.

'Bed. Smoking,' Vida informed him.

'I shall speak to him in the morning,' Noël announced. 'First we must all get some rest.'

'Our marriage is over,' said Violet determinedly.

'Now then,' said Noël. 'Everyone to bed. I shall sort out this sordid affair and Father will have a very severe telling off. Then everything will carry on as normal. As if I didn't have enough to do. Goodnight, Mother darlingest. Don't cry any more. It upsets me terribly. Goodnight, Jack. Sleep tight, Aunt Vida.' Noël stood up and left them all at the dining-room table, bowing his head as he went through the doorway that led into the corridor connecting the now-finished granary to the house. Quietly, he made his way to his bedroom and shut the door.

It was midday before Noël emerged the next day, wearing a rather startlingly bright-blue suit he had purchased in Paris and a pink bow tie. Alice had delivered his breakfast to him in his room on a tray, and he was feeling particularly chirpy as he had just finished the last rewrites on *Private Lives* and something told him this play would be a hit. He and Gertie Lawrence would take the lead roles of Elyot and Amanda, with young Laurence Olivier and Adrianne Allen supporting them as Victor and Sibyl.

The irony of his play being about the power of love over social conventions, and the task in hand – to chastise his father for doing just that – was not lost on him. But, as always, he reminded himself, his chief concern was his mother's happiness, and if Arthur was the cause of Violet's upset, then he must be held to account. It was not a confrontation he was looking forward to. The two men had avoided being alone together all of Noël's adult life, their worlds too different to be ever harmoniously conjoined. Arthur had never laughed and applauded Noël's wit and brilliance, as Violet had. He had remained silent and inscrutable and, people imagined, uncomprehending. Secretly, Noël feared there was more to his father's silence than stupidity – hence the natty dressing and the extra dab of Brylcreem on his hair.

Arthur had evidently guessed or been warned by either Violet or Vida that he was to be up before the beak, as it were, and Noël found his father in the garden sitting on the bench facing the house, a little lost in his dark overcoat, a hat covering his baldness. Noël felt Arthur's eyes upon him as he walked down the path, and found himself checking his stride, placing his feet slightly wider apart with each step. Perhaps the pink bow tie was too much, he reflected, but it was too late now.

'Good morning, Father,' he said, when he was within earshot.

Arthur didn't reply, but looked at his watch as if surprised. Noël widened his lips, not smiling exactly, but using his lips to express a martyred irritation, a characteristic – one of many – he had picked up from Violet. Arthur stroked his chin and looked past his son. Noël hesitated. Should he stand before his father in a dominant stance or sit beside him? The director in him contemplated his options. Why not do a bit of both, he thought. He put his hands in his pockets and struck a pose. 'Right,' he said resolutely. 'This is what I've come to say. Mother is terribly upset and I'm sure you know why. You must stop seeing this Mrs Cheeseman at once. It really won't do.'

'I see,' said Arthur quietly.

'I hope you do,' said Noël. 'You are a married man and should behave like one.'

'I see,' repeated Arthur. His slightly hooded eyes seemed to glimmer in the shadow that his hat brim cast over his face. 'We're all going to behave like we should, are we?'

'Correct, yes,' said Noël, somewhat unnerved by his father's words. 'We neither of us want Mother to be anything but blissfully happy.'

Arthur said nothing.

'I'm sure you agree?'

'Oh, I know *you're* sure,' said Arthur.

'Please don't be obtuse,' sighed Noël, deciding it was time to sit on the bench beside his father. He sank down gracefully. After a moment's consideration, he crossed his legs and lit a cigarette. 'We're all going to live here very happily and that's that,' he continued. 'Now that the granary is finished there is plenty of room for all of us. But if we're going to be harmonious here, you cannot go gallivanting around the village like a randy stallion, unfortunately.'

'Can I not?' said Arthur, sounding surprised. 'Well, if you say I can't then I can't. It's your house after all. You may well own the entire village too, I don't know.'

'Don't be tiresome, please,' said Noël, adjusting his tone to be less emphatic. 'You must know it won't do. Mrs Cheeseman, honestly.' He tutted and rolled his eyes. 'I hear she's only been widowed for a month and drinks cider for breakfast.' He was trying to diffuse the tension with some camp, but it was lost on Arthur, who stiffened noticeably beside him.

'She's got a bed and she welcomes me into it,' the old man said bluntly. He stood up, standing over his son, their positions now reversed. 'Which is more than your mother has done for many a long year. In London, where I belong, she never noticed or cared where I was or what I was doing. All she cared about was you. Do you know what it feels like to not get so much as a smile from your wife for nearly thirty years?'

Noël held up his hands, grimacing, the small plume of smoke from his cigarette floating upwards. 'I don't want to hear this. Please don't say any more.'

'I've not got much more to say,' said Arthur. 'I'll go inside shortly and sit in my armchair, silent and quiet like you want me to be. Like an old dog waiting to die – and you lot *are* waiting for me to die, too. You won't have to so much as throw me a stick. I've got fleas and my breath stinks and I'm no use any more. I won't get over the fence, I won't chase sheep no more or bother any bitches down the lane. Shoot me if you want. It would be a kindness.'

'Stop it, Father,' said Noël, a dark, guilty sensation spreading over him like ink on the carpet.

Arthur turned towards the house and took two steps away from his son. Then he stopped and half turned back, but not enough to look Noël in the eyes.

'I am not the idiot you take me for,' he said, spitting out the words like sawdust from his mouth. 'You and Jack. I've heard you two. At it. And your Yankie friend is not all you think, either

– he's good at pleasing himself. And now you're judging me? Telling me what I can and can't do? May God forgive you. Because I never will.' His last few words dissolved into a shuddering whisper, and Arthur shuffled towards the side of the house, shoulders slumped and head bowed. Noël heard the main gate open and the quiet, fading clunking of Arthur's bicycle as he pedalled up the hill.

He found Jack reading a newspaper in the drawing room. Jack took one look at Noël's ashen face and said 'I take it you've had words with Arthur?'

'It was ghastly,' said Noël, throwing himself into a chair, his fists clenched. 'Probably the longest conversation we've had for years and easily the most excruciating.'

'What did you say?'

'That his dalliance with Mrs Cheeseman was devastating Darlingest and it had to stop.'

'And he said?'

'Oh, that he's an old dog waiting to die and that Mother ignores him.'

'Poor man,' said Jack with sympathy.

'He's not a poor man. He's stubborn and surly. Is it too early for a drink? My heart is going like a woodpecker.'

'I'll fix you one,' said Jack, getting up and going to the drinks table. 'I don't want to take sides, but couldn't you just let the poor guy get on with it?' He put some ice from the bucket into a crystal glass and opened a green bottle.

'Not when Mother is upset, no.'

'Buy her a new mink or something. She's not upset on a real level. Only cos some bitch in the post office was making arch comments.' Jack handed his lover a tumbler full of gin.

'I am simply trying to keep the peace here,' said Noël, before taking a sip.

'A son telling his father how to live his life?'

'That is what it has come to.'

'No wonder it was so awful.'

'I wonder if Mother and Father were once like Alice and Jude?' asked Noël as he felt the gentle sedation of the gin taking effect and melting away his anxiety. 'Young and in love, gazing into each other's eyes.'

Jack whistled lightly. 'Jesus, what a horrible thought.'

Noël cast a look at him. 'He knows about us, of course, and it disgusts him. He said you were very good at pleasing yourself. What does he mean by that, do you think?'

Jack shook his head. 'I haven't got a clue.' He sipped his gin and seemed lost in his own, dark thoughts.

Scene Four

Richard

That second morning when I woke up, Albie was there in bed beside me. Strangely, there was no horror this time, no sense of shame, just warmth and joy. I lay there, still half asleep, watching and marvelling at my secret lover's perfect nose, watching the nostrils dilate slowly as he breathed. The light caught his long eyelashes and his hair seemed artfully tousled, even after sleep, and I thought he looked like a still from a foreign film, one about lust, love and anguish, with, no doubt, an unhappy ending.

I was almost fifty. My thoughts kept returning to this stark fact. Soon I would need Viagra just to listen to Radio 1. There would not be many more occasions like this in my life. Beautiful, poignant scenes in the bedroom at daybreak would no doubt all be memories in the not-too-distant future. It was all the more important to hang on to this moment, to enjoy it for its beauty and unexpectedness. A part of me, a reckless carefree part, urged me on to touch the boy and bring him to life, make love to him, and lose myself in desire and lustful abandon.

My own youth flashed through my mind as I lay there,

considering Albie's profile: my first lover, the school friend who seduced me after a drunken party at the youth club when we were seventeen; then my first 'proper' affair with Gary, while we were both at RADA. We had shared a flat together for a year and, after the early passionate months, had learned to enjoy the art of conversation too, to read books together, to go to the theatre, cook elaborate recipes from the Saturday *Guardian* magazine, and enhance and expand love in every direction so it wasn't just centred on the reassurance and comfort of sex. Then, single again, I made dangerous but erotic forays into the world of casual sex: nightclub pickups, encounters in derelict buildings, on Hampstead Heath, in sand dunes in Greece, saunas in Barcelona. There were cocaine-fuelled orgies in New York, model rent boys in Los Angeles, off-duty soldiers in Tel Aviv, and all the rest. Then, slowly but surely, fame and age had closed the doors of opportunity and the more sensory experiences that are a significant aspect of gay life faded from my recent experience.

Yet now, stirring before me, his eyes slowly opening and his lips rising into a sensual smile, was Albie, the most beautiful of them all. I knew I couldn't deny myself this one last fling. It was mad, scandalous and sure to end badly. I knew all this, but, I told myself, even so it would be worth it, in a tragic 'at least I have my memories' kind of way. Although this was clearly not a memory that would make it into print should I ever finish my autobiography. Marcia might want a bit of scandal to spice the pages but this was too salacious a secret to ever be revealed.

And what about Fran? whispered a little voice in my mind. Fran, my sensible, stylish, funny partner, my gift from God. He had appeared in my life, bringing love and peaceful calm, making all my friends sigh with relief now that I'd found someone to settle down with. Was I really going to risk it all? Guilt nibbled uncomfortably at me, like mice at the mattress.

Yet that morning, after our second night together, Albie and I inevitably started the day with sex, without so much as brushing our teeth first. Afterwards, all pheromones wafting in the air and head rolling on the pillow, Albie suggested breakfast in bed, and so I trotted obligingly to the kitchen and returned with boiled eggs, toast and tea on a tray and even a saucer full of decanted marmalade. We stopped short of feeding each other bits of buttered crust, but only just.

'What are you doing today?' I asked.

'Spending time with you, if that's okay.' His face lit up. 'Let's go for a drive in the country!'

'Excellent idea,' I agreed, and we snuggled together under the duvet, as the breeze wafted over us from the open window. I was almost dozing off again when I heard a clicking noise. I opened my eyes. My head was cradled in Albie's arm, our faces touching cheek to cheek. Albie's other arm was stretched above us and in his hand was his iPhone. There was another click.

'There!' said Albie, bending his elbow to show me the photo of the two of us, naked chests rising from the duvet. I felt a sudden burst of panic.

'Oh no, sweetheart,' I said. 'That's not a good idea.'

'How blissed out do we look?' said Albie, smiling at the picture.

'You'll need to delete that, seriously,' I said urgently. 'Suppose it falls into the wrong hands?'

'All right,' Albie snapped irritably. 'I will if you want. It's not child porn or anything.'

'I know – but it's *dangerous.*'

Albie sat up in bed, roughly pulling his arm out from under me. He tapped a couple of keys on the phone. 'Gone,' he said. 'All evidence of our disgraceful liaison has been deleted.'

'Albie,' I began, but he jumped angrily out of bed.

'I'm going to wash away any forensic evidence. Happy now?' He stomped off, not waiting for my response.

I was finishing up my tea while Albie was in the shower when the phone rang. It was the Monastery, and Jess's doctor, Hilary Dalton, was calling to report that Jess was now responding well both to therapy and treatment and perhaps a visit that afternoon would be beneficial.

'That's splendid news,' I said, pleased. 'And should I bring her son along to see her too?'

'Yes, of course,' said Dr Dalton. 'I was going to suggest that. You could all have tea together in the visitors' lounge. Shall we say around three o'clock? I'm sure Jess will be delighted to see you both.'

She hung up just as Albie came through to the bedroom patting his hair with a towel but otherwise naked.

'Slight change of plan,' I announced.

Albie looked crestfallen. 'What?'

'Well, we're still going for a drive but we're going to visit your mother in the Monastery.'

He frowned and tossed the damp towel on the bed. I looked at it aghast. Fran would never do that.

'Do we have to?' he said sulkily. He stretched and flexed, as though flaunting his firm young torso in front of me.

'I think it would be good. I'm sure she'd love to see you.'

'All right.' He sighed. 'We don't have to stay long, do we?

And can we stop in a lay-by on the way back for some outdoor fun?'

By mid-morning, we were in the Jaguar, motoring through the Kentish lanes on our way to the hospital. It wasn't really warm enough to have the roof down but Albie insisted, and with the heated seats and the hot air blowing on full blast we were cosy enough. I put on Radio 4 but Albie sucked his teeth and muttered, so I told him to put on whatever he liked. He fiddled with the sound system and a moment later loud, trashy disco music was blaring out of the speakers. I winced a little but said nothing.

When we got nearer to the hospital, I switched the radio off and was about to ask him how he was feeling when Albie suddenly said, 'Do you love me?'

'That's a bit sudden,' I replied, taken aback.

'You must know if you love me or not, surely?'

'Are you being serious?' I turned for a moment to look at Albie's face, unsure whether this was just another game to pass the time.

'Well, *I* love *you*. I told you I'd wanted you for years,' he said.

I inhaled deeply several times. 'Yes, you did. You are very surprising, did you know that? You'll have to be a bit gentle with me.'

'What do you mean by that?'

'I'm in shock. Shocked by this whole thing. I'm not saying I don't like it – clearly I do – but it isn't something that has ever, in my wildest imaginings, entered my mind before. You, on the other hand, have been plotting and scheming to have your wicked way with me. And now you have. So there.'

'And the answer to my question?'

'Yes. Yes, I love you.' I said it, but a dark rumble in the pit of my stomach churned uncomfortably as I did.

Albie smiled from ear to ear and leant over to kiss me. He sang the chorus of Kylie Minogue's 'Can't Get You Out of My Head' by way of response. I smiled back but inside me, quietly and out of time with the tune Albie was singing, my inner voice was murmuring a little louder than before: *No, no, no!*

Just then the satellite navigation system instructed me to take the right turn. I glanced at the screen to see that we were only two miles away from the Monastery.

'We're nearly there, Albie.'

He stopped singing. 'So, how do we play this scene?'

'Let's just be as normal as possible. That's what Jess needs now, I think. No shocks or surprises.' I tried to sound relaxed and casual, but I was in turmoil. I was beginning to realise that Albie was someone I didn't know at all; the truth was, I'd had very little relationship with him for the last five years. He was beautiful, certainly, but he was also unpredictable. I was suddenly aware that he might think it a very good idea to announce to his mother that he and I had slept together. I'd assumed that he would understand the need for secrecy but his demand to be told that I loved him had made me uneasy. *You've been very stupid,* a little voice whispered to me. *How are you going to get out of this mess?*

'Do you think she'll be in a straitjacket?' Albie asked with mock naivety.

'That's not nice.' I shot him a stern look.

'Or one of those Hannibal Lecter masks?'

'Stop now. She's not a dangerous criminal. She's still your mother. She's just recovering from what the doctors say is a nervous breakdown.'

'Suppose they send her home? What do we do then?'

I glanced at him. I could see that he didn't want his mother coming between us, spoiling his fun. 'They won't.'

'Oh good.' He looked relieved.

We were waved passed the security hut by a friendly uniformed guard who gave the Jaguar an admiring glance. There was a stone surround over the iron gates and a gently curving drive with lawns and low-maintenance flowerbeds. The Monastery itself was a modest building, as befitted its original purpose. It was built from beautiful grey stone but no fancy carvings or obelisks adorned it. It was a low, one-storey building, with former cloisters spreading out either side of the main, wooden entrance.

We followed signs to the visitors' car park and then made our way to the main door, which opened just before we reached it. A slim, smiling man in grey trousers and an open-necked white shirt greeted us.

'Welcome to the Monastery, Mr Stent, and you must be Jess's son. I know she's looking forward to seeing you both. Do come in. My name is David. I'm the senior duty liaison nurse.'

We followed David into the pleasantly cool interior and down a corridor. Albie nudged me and made as if to grab David's buttocks but I gave him a severe look. Instantly he assumed a pious, almost-funereal expression.

David stopped outside an office. 'I'll just get Dr Dalton. She wanted a word before we go through to the lounge to meet Jess. Shan't keep you long.'

David shut the door behind him while Albie and I sat on two leather chairs to wait.

'I'm rather nervous,' I whispered.

'I don't think my mother's developed psychic abilities. She won't be able to read your mind.' Albie smiled faintly and the mischief in his eyes made me feel even more anxious.

Just then the door opened and a bright, attractive woman in a floral dress came in smiling. 'Hello, I'm Dr Hilary Dalton. How do you do?'

We introduced ourselves as we shook Hilary's hand, and she gave us a quick rundown of Jess's condition. Apparently she was much better after what might generally be described as a severe nervous breakdown with possible personality disorder factors. 'We haven't yet established the precise causes and I'll be recommending some therapy to help isolate that issue, but from what we've learned, Jess's insecurities are more delusional than most. She's been hearing voices and suchlike.' Dr Dalton fixed me with a candid gaze. 'Has she said anything to you about that sort of thing?'

'Not a word,' I said, shaking my head. 'Jess isn't a voice-hearing type, believe me. She's always scoffed at that kind of thing.'

'Mmm. Well, she's been highly affected by the recent change in her circumstances.' Dr Dalton consulted her notes for a moment. 'And there's a suggestion of paranoia, which has aggravated things and caused something of a vicious circle.'

'Poor Jess,' I murmured sadly. Albie said nothing but he looked rather pale.

'But the good news is,' continued Hilary, 'it's all very treatable. We've experimented with a number of mood stabilisers and found one that suits Jess well. As long as she continues to take her medication there shouldn't be a recurrence at all. But if she stops taking it, the consequences could be serious.'

'So hopefully,' I said, being optimistic for Albie's sake as much as my own, 'we'll have the old Jess back again soon?'

'Yes, all being well, but she should also keep a mood diary,' continued the doctor. 'So that if any symptoms start to show themselves, she should be able to recognise them and contact us or her own general practitioner immediately.'

'But will she?' Albie asked, frowning. 'Are you keeping her in for long?'

'Not much longer, no. We just need to be sure that she is fully stabilised and that there are no adverse side-effects to the medication. A few more days and she can go home. Now – would you like to follow me through to the lounge? She's waiting for you.'

The lounge was quite a large, self-consciously cheerful room, with primrose-yellow sofas, pot plants and open windows. Jess was seated in a far corner, and she got up smiling when she saw us. Hilary stood to one side, made a theatrical gesture of presentation, bowed and departed, like a mute messenger in an amateur production of something Shakespearean. We walked over to Jess, Albie a pace or two behind me.

'Darling!' Jess kissed me on both cheeks and, resting her hands on my shoulders to hold me in place, gazed at me searchingly. 'How lovely of you to come.'

I felt awkward and remembered what Albie had said that first night – that Jess was in love with me. It wasn't true, surely . . . and yet I was uncomfortably aware of the heat from her hands. 'Albie's here,' I said, trying to break off her intense stare.

Jess left her hands where they were and turned to look at her son. 'Hello, Albie,' she said, and then let go of me to clasp her son to her chest.

'Hi,' said Albie, smiling. 'How are you, Mum?' He kissed her cheek, and then took a step back to escape her embrace, flushing a little.

'Let's sit down,' said Jess happily. She looked more like her old self, wearing a neat trouser suit and make-up, with her hair brushed and glossy. 'I have tea ready for us. It's so exciting to see you both.'

'I'll pour,' I said, glad to have something to do. 'So you're feeling better?'

'I'm doing very well, quite back to normal,' announced Jess. She frowned. 'I can't think what came over me, it's all very odd. It feels like a dream now . . . as soon as I got here I began to feel better and now I'm feeling myself, as they say.'

Albie giggled at the innuendo. Jess made a face at him and smiled. They looked quite normal together, like any mother and son. I felt relieved that we seemed to have got over everything so easily so far.

'Here you are.' I passed Jess a cup and saucer. 'I could tell straightaway. Jess is back.'

'Yes, I am,' she said firmly. 'I'll be home soon, and back at work. It was . . . some sort of episode. They've given me something to sort it out. And some patches to top up my hormones, or something. I feel amazing.'

She did look like the old Jess again, if a little bloated – but that was no doubt a side-effect of the medication. I was deeply relieved. It had been very nasty seeing my stalwart Jess turned into somebody else entirely. Thank goodness we'd got over this awfulness so easily.

Jess sipped her tea, then said, 'So – is Albie being good?' She looked at him questioningly. 'Have your exams finished?'

Albie nodded. 'I'm home for good. I like it, too. Your new place is nice. And Richard's looking after me.' He sent me a flirtatious look from under his lashes. 'I might stay around for a while.'

I didn't respond but hoped desperately that he wouldn't give his mother any clue of what had passed between us.

'Just make sure you don't cause Richard any bother, that's all,' Jess said reprovingly. Either she hadn't noticed Albie's sly smile to me or I had imagined it.

'He's fine. We all are,' I said quickly. 'We just want you to concentrate on getting well.' Then I said emphatically, in a sudden burst of emotion, 'We love you, Jess. We want you to know that.'

Jess's eyes filled with tears at these words, and she put her cup and saucer down on the table. 'Thank you,' she said. 'That means a lot to me. I'm sorry for all the trouble . . .' She wiped a tear from each eye.

'Sssshhh, now.' I reached over to put my arm around her.

'We'd better go,' said an embarrassed Albie. 'It can't be good to make you cry. Come on.'

Jess's tears were beginning to flow more strongly now, her chest rising and falling as if a desperate sob was trying to escape. A nurse hovered nearby.

'We'll see you soon,' continued Albie, rising from his seat and tugging at my arm, which was cradled around Jess's back.

'Yes,' I said. 'We'll go now. You're doing brilliantly.' I gently extricated myself from Jess's embrace and lowered her back down into her chair. 'Chin up,' I said, lowering my face directly in front of hers and giving a bright smile, the sort that demands a similar smile in response. Through her tears Jess managed a half-hearted attempt, but it crumbled within a second and she bit her lip in anguish.

'Oh, dear,' she said, trembling. 'I feel such a fool. But I miss you so terribly.'

As we said our final goodbyes and made our way back out into the corridor, heading for the door, Albie said, 'Quick. Let's get the freakin' fuck out of here.'

The last thing I saw was Jess collapsing into the arms of the nurse, crying her eyes out and clasping him around the neck.

Scene Five

Summer 1930

Noël

Noël was confident that *Private Lives* was going to be a hit. It was due to première in Edinburgh in August, and he and Jack had only just returned from a luscious holiday in the South of France. Gertie Lawrence, his favourite co-star, had been there, too, and the two of them had rehearsed their roles each day and then sunbathed, getting glamorous tans that would add to the verisimilitude of the play's honeymoon setting.

The certainty that, at last, after a string of flops, he would have a triumph, was comforting but it didn't allow Noël a moment's rest. New ideas were already fermenting in his brain. He had an idea for a play about three people wrestling with their love for each other, and he was keen to ponder it and see what happened. Writing was a compulsion for him; it was his way of sorting out his own thoughts and creating a world on his own terms. He knew that his vision wasn't immoral but it was a challenge to traditional, and established – not to say old-fashioned – moral laws, which excluded him and his way of life. Creating laughter was, Noël knew, the best way to demystify things. If he could draw an audience into his play, entertain them, make them love the central characters then surely, without even knowing it, they would be educated and liberated from the stuffy, conventional view of things the Lord Chamberlain had decided they might be amused by.

It was for this reason that Noël sent his parents and Aunt Vida away for an extended holiday. While the scandal of Arthur's 'filly in the villy' had died down, there was an almost palpable sense of unhappiness around his parents. Their marriage was hollow now, but Arthur had obediently given up his affair with Mrs Cheeseman and was no longer straying – for the meantime, at least. Noël couldn't be bothered with it all, which was why he'd demanded they leave while he and Jack retired to Kent for a brief interlude, so that he could gather his strength ahead of what he hoped would be a long run – though he refused to play anything longer than three months. He didn't want any distractions. Something was bubbling away in his mind, and he wanted to examine it in peace.

Experience had taught Noël that writing was best done in the mornings, so he had his breakfast on a tray and stayed in his room to work until lunchtime, scribbling away on a large white pad with his Eversharp pencil while Jack went off to amuse himself. He stopped, pleased with what had emerged so far. Before he tackled the next scene, he decided, he would take a stroll around the garden.

It was almost midday and a hot early August sun was high in the sky, and the flowerbeds fizzed and buzzed with a variety of insects. The roses were at their brightest, heaviest and most euphoric, and he stopped to admire each perfect bloom, his hand reaching out, cigarette smoke trailing each sweep, his fingertips caressing the moist blooms. He looked around him at his own corner of paradise and his heart sang with undiluted happiness.

Youth, success, wealth – these he had in abundance, but love was the most important thing. As he strolled along the path, stopping every step or two to inhale the beauty that surrounded him, Noël contemplated, or rather experienced, a shining, mesmerising, uplifting gratitude for the love that nested in his heart like a clutch of eggs about to crack slowly open. All around him, in every bush and tree, he could hear the birds calling and communicating, some urgent, some flirtatious. In the fields behind the hedges, the ewes bleated, calling to their almost-adult lambs. In one flowerbed he discovered some chickens luxuriating in a dust bath, pressing their brown, feathery chests down into the dry, powdery dirt and shimmying like burlesque dancers. Noël heard a high-pitched yelp behind him and turned to see his two dachshunds, collectively known as the Coconuts. They ran as fast as their unnaturally short legs could carry them, ears flapping up and down, tongues lolling out the side of their mouths.

'Hello, my poppets,' Noël greeted them. 'Come along with me, let's go and find Master Jack, shall we?' The dogs gracefully received a stroke each and caught their breath, then followed Noël on his mercifully slow walk.

Where was Jack? Noël wondered. Perhaps he would find him looking tanned and breathtakingly gorgeous sitting on the bench overlooking the marsh, the first gin of the day sparkling in its glass on the table before him. But he reached the bench and it was empty, so he wandered on around the garden, inspecting the flowerbeds. He half closed his eyes and saw it all, a profusion of colour and the air rich and heady with a multitude of scents: pink roses, jasmine, lemon thyme and English lavender. Goldenhurst was a work of art, a rustic heaven, the one place where all was well with the world, English countryside as it used to be: steamy, blond and bright in the summer, misty, damp and still in winter. Noël loved his work but was frequently exhausted by it, overcome with the demands of his own talent, the relentless eruptions of creativity that compelled him to lie awake crafting and giving shape to the ideas and scenarios in his mind. In some ways, of course, he celebrated each conception and brilliant idea that grew inside him, but a part of him felt exhausted each time at the prospect of what lay ahead. At Goldenhurst, he felt that he had found a gentler way to be creative. Here, nature was not tamed but harnessed.

With the two dogs waddling beside him, he rounded a corner and noticed the old barn at the end of the garden. It was a soft, sagging wooden structure, no doubt once used to store hay but now a place where bits of abandoned old farm machinery lay rusting and where months-old eggs, laid by roaming chickens attracted by the gloom within, might be found. Perhaps, though, Noël thought, it had potential. Could it be something new and exciting? A swimming pool or a summerhouse? He turned towards it and strolled gently across the grass. The huge door stood slightly ajar, as always, and he slipped inside, not wanting to disturb the slumbering peace within.

It was Jude, the gardener's assistant, he saw first. He was facing Noël as he entered the barn, which was dark after the bright sunshine of the garden. As he entered, Noël looked up at the rafters, waiting for his eyes to acclimatise to the darkness. He heard a whimper, looked behind him in case either dog was the source of the noise, but they were present and correct, sniffing the ground at his feet. Then he saw the pale, oval shape looming out of the grey half-light in the far corner, and recognised Jude. Noël's first thought was that the boy was in some kind of difficulty.

'Jude?' he asked, concerned. Then he saw Jack behind him, frozen mid-thrust, and all became clear. Jude lowered his head as if to pretend he wasn't there, and Jack shuffled backwards, further into the gloom, trying to achieve the same goal. Noël stiffened with shock but darted forward to ascertain exactly what he'd seen. Jude was lying face down on the dirt floor now, wriggling as he pulled his trousers up. He made a couple of throaty noises, then rose up, clutching his waist and backed away at an angle, skirting around the wall of the barn just as Noël moved forward, then he darted, running now, out into the garden.

'Are you all right?' Noël called. Jude was clearly distressed, but the boy had gone, galloping out into the green, hot light. Noël turned his gaze back into the dark corner of the barn.

'Yeah, he's all right. He's very all right,' said Jack, his voice thick and deep. Jack, unlike Jude, had not attempted to pull up his trousers. In fact, his were lying beside him on the ground like a muddy pool. He stood there, brazenly, legs astride, hands on his hips, and his great penis bobbing slowly up and down like a hollyhock in the breeze.

'You cunt,' said Noël slowly and deliberately, the truth at last dawning on him.

Scene Six

Richard

I awoke in the middle of the night, Albie slumbering away next to me, and became aware of a strange, low, guttural hum vibrating through my bedroom. It sounded at first like a lorry throbbing in the distance, but it never came any closer or faded away. The next moment it sounded like a growling dog. I tried to ignore it but after ten minutes I got up, put on my pyjamas and went to investigate. I judged that the noise was coming from the front of the house, maybe the kitchen. I stood by the Rayburn first. Being always on, the Rayburn made a permanent noise, but nothing hum- or growl-like: it purred comfortingly, not unlike someone slowly flicking through a pack of playing cards. Not guilty.

Then I stood by the fridge, head cocked to one side, barely breathing, but it was giving out a higher pitched sound than the one I'd been hearing. Perhaps the cause was in the troublesome cellar, accessed from outside the kitchen door but located underneath it. I put my wellies on, picked up the torch and went out. A fine, cool drizzle was falling. Dawn was getting ready to break.

I opened the door and went down the stone steps. The cellar was dark and dank and strewn with cobwebs that clung to my face and touched my bare arms like babies' breath. This was where the old, lethal, oil-fired boiler used to live, growling and spitting flames. It was gone now, although the oblong outline remained, like a fossil on the ground, a testament to its many years of faithful, fiery service. Inside the cellar, at floor level, a little light broke through from above, to the left, below the kitchen window. Here was once a coal chute, in Noël's day. I thought that was curious, because it was so damp and wet down there, you wouldn't consider it a suitable place for fuel of any kind nowadays. I kept my coal and logs in the barn.

I shone my torch around. It was a large cellar, maybe seven feet high and twenty or so feet square. Mysterious, ancient pipes jutted out from the far wall, back towards the centre of the house. I had no idea where they led from or what their purpose once was, but they had been roughly severed years ago, and were now corroded and rusted, bubbling with limescale and almost organic, fungi-like lumps and bumps. A slow, steady trickle of cold, murky water dripped from them. I had asked any number of builders and plumbers and anyone else who had been down there to try and fathom where the water came from and stop it, but they had all failed to find a solution. Some said it came from an underwater spring, some declared firmly that it was water from a disused tank up in the loft – but I'd had all tanks removed.

I stared accusingly at the pipes as they continued to dribble from the mysterious stomach no one could locate. Then my torch caught a flash of something, and the beam fell on the incongruously new and shiny copper immersion heater, standing proudly against the far wall like a Chelsea Pensioner on Remembrance Day, the low, ominous hum of a giant, butch bee emanating from its core.

'Richard?'

I nearly leapt out of my skin, spinning round to see Albie's half-lit face at the top of the cellar stairs. 'Goodness, you gave me a fright!' I panted, clutching at my chest.

'What are you doing down here?'

'I was trying to work out the source of the humming in the house. I think it must be the immersion heater.' I gestured at it.

'I can't hear a humming in the house. Come upstairs, it's freezing down here.'

I followed him back into the house, feeling low. In truth, I'd been wretched since the day before when we'd seen Jess in the Monastery. Seeing my old friend recovering from her breakdown while I knew I was sleeping with her son was more than a little irksome. Guilt, regret and anguish had almost overcome me. How on earth had I got myself into this situation? I was betraying one of the people closest and dearest to me in an unforgivable way. It was wrong on almost every level, and stupid, too.

'What are you thinking about?' Albie had asked as I drove the Jaguar out of the gates of the Monastery and headed back towards home.

'Oh. Your mother, I guess. How did you think she was?'

Albie shrugged. 'I told you, she's obsessed with you. That's what her madness is all about, really. She can't have you and it's driven her to the point of insanity.'

'She has suffered a breakdown,' I replied, unwilling to go back down that path. 'The medication will sort her out.'

'If she knew about us, she'd flip again. They'd have to throw away the key.' Albie's words sounded oddly like a threat. I glanced over and saw the boy's wicked smile just before it faded.

'Listen to me,' I said firmly. I pulled the car over to the side of the road, stopped and turned to look at him face on. 'If you ever tell anyone about us, that will be the end of it. No one will understand. I don't understand myself. We've both been through a traumatic experience with your mother and I think we've been . . .' I trailed off.

'Comforting each other? Is that what you're trying to call it?' Albie asked, a mocking, disbelieving edge to his voice.

'No, not really,' I said, feeling defeated. I rubbed my head, as if trying to coax my brain into making sense of things. 'This is such a mess.'

'Charming,' Albie observed, indignantly. 'I'm sorry to be the cause of such anguish.'

'No,' I said, well aware that almost anything I said was going to make matters worse. 'I'm sorry. When you get to my age things are a lot more complicated. You're young and everything is an adventure, I suppose.'

'Oh, yes.' Albie's voice dripped with sarcasm. 'Life is one big ripping yarn. Sex with Uncle Richard, what larks!' He opened the car door and jumped out, stomping determinedly away across a field.

'Oh, God,' I moaned. 'Not a bloody drama now, please!' I got wearily out of the car and headed after him. 'Come on, Albie. This isn't helping matters, is it?'

The field appeared to be empty, but as I pursued him to the middle I noticed some sheep lazing in the far corner in the shade of some trees. Just then Albie sat down suddenly on the brow of the sloping field. He slapped the grass with temper, then covered his face with his hands, not crying yet, but cross and confused, building up to an almighty sob of anguish. I reached him just in time and had knelt next to him. It pained me to see the boy so upset and I put my arms around him and had hushed him, telling him everything would be all right.

'I don't want you to be ashamed of me. I don't want to be a horrible secret, a bit on the side or a mistake in your past,' he said, bringing his arms round under mine and hugging me back.

The physical contact melted my heart, and I pushed my face into the boy's hair and inhaled his smell – coconut and hot breath.

'We'll work it out,' I said, feeling suddenly responsible. 'It will be all right. Calm down now. That's better.'

'You don't want me to go mad, too, do you?' he asked, pulling out of the embrace, watery eyes staring into mine. 'It probably runs in the family, you know.'

We smiled at each other. Crisis over, I sat alongside Albie and we both breathed deeply and looked down across the gentle slope to the view below, green trees and fields and the shadowy shape of a country lane snaking around the edge of the field. A few minutes later we returned to the car and drove home. He'd stayed again that night, of course.

The mysterious hum seemed to have disappeared. I tried to put my low mood behind me and enjoy the day with Albie but I felt uneasy all morning and into the afternoon. We had a lazy time of it, interspersed with vigorous lovemaking, but each bout was leaving me increasingly hollow inside. The powerful erotic charge of just a day or so ago was showing distinct signs of evaporation.

In the early evening the Monastery called to let me know that Jess would be ready to leave in two days' time. I said that I would come and collect her. When I put the phone down, I felt like a drink and went to the lounge where Albie was splayed out on the sofa watching an episode of *Family Guy.* I poured myself a vodka, noticing that Albie had already drunk half the bottle.

'I think we should talk,' I said, perching on the edge of the sofa next to Albie's thighs.

'Hmmm,' he said without interest, and then let out a raucous laugh at whatever had just happened on the television screen.

I raised my voice over the sound of the television. 'Your mother is coming home on Wednesday. She'll expect you to be there. Fran is home on the same evening, and then I'm going to France just after that. Things might be coming to a head. We need some sort of plan.'

Albie rearranged his hips with a bad-tempered thump, picked up the remote control and turned the TV off.

'I'll come to France with you. They can both fuck off. How's that?' he said, looking at me with heavy-lidded vodka eyes.

'Er, no,' I said warily, realising the boy was drunk and in a volatile mood. I patted Albie's thigh twice and let my hand rest there. 'Come on, Albie. It's D-Day. Time to face facts.'

'Well, I don't know, do I?' Albie sat upright. 'And I'm not your fucking spaniel so don't treat me like one.' He got up, went to the vodka bottle, put it to his lips and glugged hungrily. When he'd had enough, he said bitterly, 'Talking isn't going to change anything, is it?'

I rubbed my head. 'You can't come to France,' I said quietly. 'You must stay and look after your mother.'

'I don't want to. I want to be with you,' said Albie petulantly before taking another, longer swig, emptying the bottle. 'I love you. That's all I know.'

'Come and sit down. Please,' I said.

Albie swayed over and landed heavily on the sofa beside me. He covered his face with his hands. 'I don't know what to do without you. I'll go crazy. You don't realise, do you? You're everything to me. I've never loved anyone but you. Five minutes without you is more than I can stand. Please take me with you. Please don't leave me.' He was crying now, like a little boy, leaning against me, pawing at me, pleading.

I felt like crying too, but I knew the situation needed careful, mature handling. Albie was overwhelmed with emotion. I needed to take charge, reassure him that I wouldn't leave him, talk him into a plan of action that would, at least in the short term, keep him happy and under control.

'Listen,' I said. 'I have a plan. You and I can be together but it isn't going to be easy.'

Albie stopped crying and looked up, his cheeks wet with tears.

'Really?' he said, his eyes full of sudden hope.

'Yes, really.' I wiped the tears from his cheek. 'Now stop crying and listen to me.'

'I'm listening.'

'While the others are here, we need to be cautious. If anyone finds out about us, at least for a while, all hell will break loose. We must be clever and bide our time – they mustn't suspect anything. Do you understand?'

Albie nodded.

'You go and live in the cottage and take care of your mother. I'll go to France for ten days of filming. When I get back, we'll be able to be together.'

'But what about Fran?'

'He'll be away. He's going back to Los Angeles. We'll be all alone again.' I didn't tell him that Fran had said his contract was almost at an end and he didn't think he would stay in LA if they offered him another one.

'And my mother? Won't she rather spoil our fun?'

'I've thought of that. She needs recovery time. When I get back I'm going to suggest she goes to a health farm and get pampered for a week. Colonic irrigation and carrot juice, you know the sort of thing. That will give us some space temporarily.'

'Love will triumph,' said Albie, convinced at last and sounding calm and happy.

I gazed at him, trying to read his emotions. 'So you agree – we'll keep it a secret?'

He nodded. 'A deadly secret. Now let's seal the deal.' He stood up and tugged me towards the bedroom. Now was not the time to refuse.

Scene Seven

Noël

Noël left the barn, marching imperiously from the scene of unbridled lust and betrayal that he'd just happened upon. His heart was pounding and his fists were clenched as he headed away from the house, down the freshly dug winding track lined with newly planted poplars that were barely two feet high, and which he'd dubbed Twig Alley.

Ahead were the woods and to his left the flat, serene Romney Marsh with the sea beyond it, a pale, grey stripe in the distance that slowly morphed into the high, distant clouds. Once away from the shelter of the house, a strong, warm breeze caressed his face firmly and refreshingly, and loosened his hair from the grip of its greased-back, tight-to-the-skull style. Noël stopped and closed his eyes for a moment, relishing the touch of nature and inhaling the nutritious air. He paused for a while, just breathing, waiting for the cacophony of feelings to calm down and arrange themselves in some order of importance.

He wasn't crying. He was pale with rage. Does this serve me right, he wondered, for writing all those plays about deception and infidelity? The guardians of our morals were right: I have been corrupted by my own talent to amuse. Life is imitating art! How thoroughly inconvenient.

He walked for miles, deep into the woods, unable to face turning back. Coming upon a small clearing, he sat down in a shaft of sunlight on a patch of newly nibbled grass. He was halfway through his second cigarette before he realised that the Coconuts were with him still, sitting a few yards away in the shade, panting and looking decidedly put out.

'All right, girls,' he said aloud, and stood up. 'Let's face the music. Do you have a sense of betrayal in the dog world?'

The two little sausage dogs seemed remarkably uninterested as they trotted on ahead of him, their tails held high.

'You simply have no idea how lonely it feels,' he said mournfully. 'Imagine that the one person you trusted, knew would always be honest and true, has just been caught with his trousers very much down. Not that you have trousers either, although that could be arranged. Lorn could run something up, I'm sure of it.'

Noël chattered away the entire walk home and when they were just a few hundred yards from the house, he said, 'Well, this has been most therapeutic. I now feel much clearer about what has to be done. This problem is nothing that a few sharp words and a one-way ticket to Manhattan can't solve. Thank you for your counsel.' He re-arranged his hair and strode determinedly into the house.

Making sure that the dogs had been provided with a full bowl of fresh water, he went to find Jack and eventually discovered him asleep in a hammock in the orchard. He gazed down at his lover for a moment: the thick dark hair, the long, black lashes sweeping down onto his cheeks, and that handsome, sulky mouth.

'Decorative as you are,' began Noël, his tone only mildly acidic to begin with, but soon gaining speed, venom and volume. 'Decorative as you are with plums hanging just inches from your wanton lips, it is time to WAKE UP!'

Jack almost jumped out of his skin. His shoulders rose up and the centre of gravity for the swaying hammock was adversely affected. It tipped him up and he tumbled to the ground in a semi-conscious heap.

'Fuck!' he said crossly, staring up at Noël from his prone position. 'Did you have to do that?'

'You're wanted upstairs,' said Noël inscrutably.

Jack's scowl became a seductive half smile. 'Oh, really?' he asked.

'Yes, really,' Noël told him. Then, after a beautifully timed pause: 'To *pack*!'

Jack's expression changed to beseeching. 'Noël, darling—'

'You are leaving me, Jack. I cannot have you under this roof for another night, not another hour. Do you understand?'

'Come on!'

'My sentiments exactly.'

'You're throwing me out?'

'You are being called away urgently. A family crisis.'

'Don't do this. Listen . . .' Jack scrambled to his feet and put a hand firmly on each of Noël's shoulders. 'I was bored, I shouldn't have done it, what do you want me to say?'

'Try "goodbye",' Noël suggested sharply, shrugging off Jack's paws.

'Why don't you calm down before you make any rash decisions?' reasoned Jack.

'Rash decisions seem to be all the rage today, wouldn't you

agree? You rashly decide to have your way with the *under*-gardener and I rashly decided it is time you left. Now go and put your soiled underpants into your cheap little suitcase and wait by the gate. I will order a taxi to take you to Ashford Station.'

'And what if I refuse to go?' said Jack aggressively, clenching his fists. 'What then?'

Noël thought for a moment. 'In that case I shall inform the armed forces. I have certainly put myself out for them in the past and they owe me one, as it were. I have connections.'

With that, he turned and marched into the house. The sky was growing portentously dark over Goldenhurst; the sun and the blue sky were obliterated from the north as grey and purple clouds raced in and hung heavily over the knoll. By the time Noël got back to the house large droplets of rain were beginning to fall, clattering on the windows like fingertips on tracing paper. Noël headed straight for the library where he poured himself a large gin and sat in an armchair, seething.

Two minutes later, Jack entered and stood in front of Noël like a naughty schoolboy. Noël looked his lover up and down.

'There is mud on your trousers, your shirt is untucked and you smell of sweat,' he snapped. 'I am very, very angry.'

Jack said nothing.

'If you cannot comprehend how beastly your behaviour is, I am at a loss as to what to say.'

'That's unusual,' replied Jack.

'Not only beastly but reckless. Suppose it had not been me but someone else who had entered the barn? This is a small, sleepy English country village, may I remind you – not the island of Capri,' Noël fumed.

'I know. Sorry,' said Jack. 'I'll have him in the bedroom next time with the curtains drawn.'

Noël gasped and then bit his lip. 'Are my feelings nothing to you?'

Jack paced around on the hearthrug, his dark eyes glittering dangerously. 'Oh Christ, Noël. You're locked away writing with a "Do Not Disturb" sign hanging from your dick all day long. What the fuck am I supposed to do? Sit around watching the grass grow?' He sounded on the verge of exploding with rage, but took a moment to breathe deeply, then said, 'I'm doing what I've always done. We're not husband and wife. I can do what the fuck I want.' He strode over to the drinks cabinet and grabbed a decanter.

'But you've ruined everything,' said Noël, feeling tearful now. He had expected apologies and promises of future fidelity, not this aggressive, brazen self-righteousness.

'I've ruined nothing,' said Jack. 'Except maybe your fantasy that we're Romeo and Juliet. So I fucked the gardener, so what? I see something I want, I go after it.'

'Everything is spoiled,' Noël said quietly.

'It doesn't need to be.' Jack looked suddenly desperate, clutching the cut-glass receptacle so hard his knuckles whitened. 'Why can't you love me enough to let me do what I want and have some fun once in a while? Why do I have to be waiting in the wings all the time, in case you need me to pass you a napkin or administer your smelling salts? My attention wandered while you were busy writing a play or a love letter to your mother, I'm not sure which. It's not the end of the world.'

'Oh, I'm so sorry. I should have offered the two of you cucumber sandwiches, should I? And maybe embroidered a duck-down cushion for Jude?'

'No, I don't mean that.'

'I am heartbroken. Not because of your actions, but because of your thoughtlessness. You didn't care.'

'I didn't think—'

'Exactly!' Noël pounced. 'Thinking did not come into it. We have taken no marriage vows, but I thought we had an unspoken promise to each other to be honest and honourable.'

'But you've slept with other men since we've been together,' Jack countered.

Noël took a deep breath, his eyes half closed, before he replied. 'But not here. And discreetly, among people like us. A quiet knock on a hotel door late at night, an afternoon investigating the more private nooks of *La Grotta Azzurra* with an eager tour guide, but nothing so *bold* as what you've done. I would never dream of anything so dangerous and complicated and foolish!'

'I didn't dream of it either. I did it,' Jack said snippily.

'I believe in freedom. Of course I do. But what you do is unprincipled.'

'You mean freedom has rules?'

'Yes.'

'Then it's not free, is it?'

There was a long pause while Noël considered this. Then he said abruptly, 'Do you love him?'

'No, of course not. I love you. But I – I had to have him. Nothing to do with love.' Jack looked helpless as he tried to explain. He shook his head. 'It doesn't change the way I feel about you,' he said softly. 'Don't make me leave.'

Noël suddenly felt exhausted. 'Goldenhurst has been violated. The home I bought as our exotic island, our place of refuge, is condemned. You have released the serpent into Eden.'

'A bit overdramatic, even for you. Please let me stay. Let's see if we can work this out.'

'I don't know if I can live with the thought of you and Jude in my mind.'

'Stop now,' said Jack, judging the moment correct to place his strong arms around Noël's hunched shoulders. 'You need me. You know you do. I'm not going anywhere.'

'But Jude may talk,' Noël whispered. 'It's dangerous.'

'He won't,' Jack said. 'I promise.' There was a long pause and then he said, 'You don't really want me to go back to New York, do you?'

Noël looked at him, his eyes burning with hurt and confusion. 'No,' he said finally, defeated. 'I couldn't bear it. But you must be more careful in future.'

'I will,' Jack said, quietly triumphant.

Although Noël accepted Jack's apparently harmless 'affair' with Jude, he didn't want to know too much about it. It was the price he had to pay to keep his lover happy and that was that. He would sometimes hear the footsteps going up the stairs and the bed-springs creaking, or see Jack returning from the woods in the late afternoon adjusting his clothing, but he busied himself with his work and tried not to dwell on it. Of course he couldn't resist the odd sarcastic reference but he tried to keep his bitterest thoughts to himself.

'I do apologise if you can smell horse manure,' he once announced to a room full of guests drinking cocktails, 'Jack has been helping out in the potting shed this afternoon.'

It was a relief to get away from the fecund countryside and return to the relatively staid environment of London. *Private Lives* was due to open and Noël had to dedicate himself to his work. He was able to put Jack's behaviour out of his mind while he prepared for the countrywide tour of his new play. When they finally opened in London at the Phoenix in the autumn, Noël's instinct was proved right: they had a hit with the entire run booked out in advance, and the song 'Some Day I'll Find You' boosting its popularity and Noël's earnings.

It was hard work but Noël adored being back at the centre of things, back on top of his world. And what was good for the goose was also good for the gander. Noël, too, allowed himself a number of extra-curricular lovers, although his affairs were discreet: fellow actors – though he tried in vain to seduce the enchanting young Laurence Olivier – or irresistible titled gentlemen, but never the staff employed to serve him. He had standards after all. Trifling with the servants was so *déclassé* – and risky too. But Jack liked to live dangerously.

It didn't matter, though, Noël told himself, fighting the jealousy that rose up inside him in bitter waves. There were no rules to his relationship with Jack – they were not, after all, modelling themselves on more conventional, heterosexual partnerships. And the first, passionate flush of romance had blossomed and faded somewhat. They were no longer headily obsessed with only each other, although they remained closely bound together. Noël had noticed that Jack's excessive drinking was beginning to take its toll on his youthful American good looks, but he still loved and needed him, and Jack remained in charge of all of Noël's business affairs. Noël was grateful that Jack's investment in gilt-edged securities meant that he had been protected from the stock-market crash of '29, and saw no need to change their arrangement.

But gradually, Noël began to contemplate a future without Jack as his constant companion.

They returned to Goldenhurst for Christmas, a large event with the whole Coward family there and many friends too. David Niven dropped by, along with the Bogarts who were visiting England from Hollywood. It was a riotous happy time, and if Jack, high on whisky sodas, slipped away a few times into the chill darkness of the garden, well . . . Noël didn't care, or so he told himself.

One winter afternoon in the new year, as Noël and Jack were finishing their lunch together, Alice came in to clear away the plates and offer the gentlemen port or brandy. Violet and Vida had gone off to the village for a bridge afternoon, and Arthur had stayed in his room all morning with a headache, so the two men were able to enjoy a quiet companionable hour or so together.

'Mrs Ashton says you're leaving soon, sir,' Alice said, placing the decanters in the middle of the table. 'Off to America, she says.'

Noël smiled at her. 'That's right, Alice, in a week or so we set sail. I'm opening my play *Private Lives* on Broadway. It should be very exciting.'

'He's almost as popular as Mickey Mouse over there,' added Jack.

'And how is life treating you, Alice?' Noël asked, pouring himself some port and taking a sip. 'All good I hope?'

Alice flushed prettily. 'Yes, thank you, sir.'

'Good. I can see by your face that you've something to say. What is it?'

Alice went even pinker. 'I'm getting married, sir.'

'I am so pleased to hear that. Congratulations!'

'A toast to Alice,' said Jack, raising his glass.

Noël raised his eyebrows. 'I do hope this doesn't mean you're going to leave us and move somewhere frightful like Ashford?'

'Oh no, sir.'

'Who's the lucky guy?' asked Jack.

Alice bowed her head and gave a shy smile. 'I'm engaged to Jude the gardener, sir.'

Noël's eyes darted to Jack who looked into his glass as if he'd seen a goldfish swimming there. 'A fine young man! You will make a splendid couple. Don't you think, Jack?'

'Jude?' said Jack, vaguely, as if trying to recall a distant acquaintance.

'You know the one,' Noël pressed on. 'Lovely teeth. Spends a lot of time in the cottage garden amongst the sweet peas.'

'Ah, I think . . .' said Jack.

'He's quite tall, sir,' added Alice helpfully.

'That's great news,' Jack managed to say eventually. 'And when does this happy event take place?'

'We haven't set a date, sir, but it will be at St Rumwold's, probably in the spring.'

'You mustn't get married before we get back. I'd hate to miss seeing you in your orange-blossomed finery. Well, how thrilling,' concluded Noël. 'I hope you will be very happy and have seventeen children.'

'Oh, I dunno about that!' Alice blushed. 'Will that be all, sir?'

'Yes, thank you, Alice. And do pass my best wishes to your betrothed.'

Once Alice had left them alone, Noël allowed himself a quiet chuckle. 'A spring wedding,' he said. 'The graveyard at St Rumwold's will be awash with daffodils. As pretty as a picture.'

'I do hope she's gonna wear a veil,' said Jack sourly.

'Try not to be bitter. You had your fun and must now move on.'

'Must I?'

'Don't be ridiculous. You can't interfere with a happily married man.'

'Who said he's going to be happy?'

'I mean it, Jack. Fun and games is one thing. Dabbling in Alice's future happiness, something else. It must finish, and that's that.' Noël turned back to his port, pleased that this was surely going to bring an end to the dalliance that had caused him so much pain.

Scene Eight

Richard

We waited until after lunch to drive to the Monastery to collect Jess. On the journey I went through our masterplan several times to make sure Albie realised how important it was.

'One false slip and we're in more trouble than a Catholic priest in a public lavatory. Understood?'

'Yes,' said Albie wearily, sipping from a Bacardi Breezer, which I plucked from his grasp.

'And lay off the booze. It might loosen your tongue.'

'I'll just drink holy water.'

Once we arrived we were discreetly shown into the office and I was presented with the hefty bill for Jess's care and treatment.

'We are very hopeful that as long as she takes her medication she'll remain stable,' Dr Dalton assured me. 'Jess is very anxious to return home and we think, on balance, that it might be best for her. Any problems at all, please call me on my direct line.' She gave me her card. 'I know she's longing to get home. A country cottage with her son fussing over her is just the tonic she needs.'

'Can't wait,' Albie said fairly convincingly.

'Good. If only all of our patients were so lucky – and so nice.

We've got a rather bad-tempered television historian checking in this afternoon. He has a chronic obsessive-compulsive disorder involving a suit of armour.' She pulled a long face, and then smiled warmly at Albie. 'Now, Jess is waiting for you in the lounge.'

Jess was all smiles and very chatty on the drive home. 'I feel ten years younger, to be honest,' she said. 'Really, I am perfectly fine now. Just sorry for all the trouble.'

'I've tidied up,' said Albie from the back seat. I was constantly aware of his tousled hair and blue, glittering eyes in the rear-view mirror. He always seemed to be watching me. 'I even hoovered!'

'Goodness,' said Jess over her shoulder. 'Did you know which end was which?'

'Very funny,' he said.

The cheerful banter continued until we got home, although I had to admit secretly to myself that the jolly atmosphere seemed just a little bit forced.

'Here we are, home sweet home!' I said nevertheless, as I parked the Jaguar outside the cottage.

Jess was about to enter her front door when she turned and stared at the big house. Her expression seemed to change, and her smile dropped. 'Yes, I dare say,' she said quietly but determinedly.

'What's that?' I asked. 'You dare say what?'

'How lovely to be back!' Jess replied, her wide smile back in place again, and turned to enter the cottage. Inside she cooed and exclaimed at how clean and neat everything was. 'And flowers! How thoughtful.' Every now and then though I saw her turn and peer out the window towards my house. Her eyes would widen as she did so, as if some shocking suggestion had been whispered in her ear. Other than that, she seemed perfectly normal and delighted with everything, and like a happier version of her old self. After a cup of tea and acutely aware that I could feel Albie's gaze longingly upon me, I said I'd better be trotting along the path to the Old Manor.

'It's a day of home-comings,' I said, significantly. 'Fran should be landing at Heathrow about now. He'll be here in a few hours. I'd better go and check there's nothing past its sell-by date in the fridge. He goes into palpitations.'

'The English countryside might be a bit of a shock for him after sunny California,' said Albie dryly.

'Possibly.' I gave him a warning look. 'But I think he'll love it here.'

Evening was fading into darkness and I was mashing the potato in the kitchen for our shepherd's pie supper. The thought of seeing Fran again made my eyes sparkle and a warm, happy sensation spread across my chest, as if I'd just downed a sherry in one gulp. He was due any minute and I was smiling to myself with anticipation when the door opened and Albie rushed in and threw his arms around me.

'I can't do it. I want to be here with you,' he said breathlessly.

'Albie!' I shouted crossly, pulling him off me and narrowly avoiding burning myself on the hot saucepan. 'Albie, please stop this!' I held him by the wrists and stared into his eyes.

'But I love you,' he said, whining like a guest on the *Jeremy Kyle Show*.

I spoke earnestly and hurriedly. 'Fran will be here any moment. Do NOT do this again. Remember what we talked about, what you promised. We can't take any risks, it has to be entirely secret or it's all over. I *mean* it.'

'But—' He thrust out his lower lip petulantly.

'We've been through this all a hundred times. Go home and stay there.' I thought of something. 'Where's your mother?'

'Having a bath. I just needed one kiss. Just one and I'll be all right then.'

'No. You have to be stronger than this. I've told you—'

Just then I heard the sound of tyres on gravel and the bright beam of a car's headlights swung across the window.

'Fran's here!' I said and pulled Albie across the kitchen and towards the back door.

'Kiss me, please!' he cried, digging his heels into the rug and slowing us down as much as possible.

Somehow I got him to the door and flung it open. 'Go! Quietly!'

'Not until you kiss me,' he hissed stubbornly.

'Christ!' I said, my heart pumping violently in my chest, and through gritted teeth gave him a rough peck before finally pushing him outside and shutting the door. I made it back to the stove and my saucepan of mash with less than a minute to spare.

'Honey, I'm home,' Fran said with a smile, as he pushed open the back door and put his head round. He must have seen me through the lighted window and come to this door rather than the front one. I hoped he hadn't seen Albie scurrying off towards the cottage. 'And what a home.' He came into the kitchen, put his case down and looked around. 'You've done a fantastic job – it's even better than the pictures.'

'Very glad you approve,' I said, wiping my hands on a tea towel and hoping that Fran would put my red face and slight sheen of sweat down to the rigours of cooking. I looked at him with a mixture of pleasure and relief. He was just the same. He moved across the room, his long limbs swinging in a slow, expressive way, pendulum-like, assessing with every sway the authenticity of everything within his sensory orbit. His clean-living, open and honest presence instinctively sized up the situation in which he found himself, and he kept his findings to himself, just the merest bite of the lip discernible to those like me, with a bad conscience and a heightened sense of guilt.

He offered me his right cheek and I gave it a brief kiss. He did the same to me. That was how things were with us, despite his long absence in Los Angeles. After all our years together, we didn't rush into each other's arms and do tongues. There were too many separations and reunions for that. I never met Fran at the airport and we didn't rip one another's clothes off and have rampant sex as soon as possible. Nevertheless, a careful observer watching us together would have concluded that we were in love. We smiled and smiled at each other, genuinely happy to be together again, and had we worn electrical monitors an analyst would have noted that our heart rates had both increased considerably, although in my case, the quickening of the pulse might have had something to do with fear of discovery as much as with love.

'How was your journey?' I asked.

'Worked the entire way, of course. I am completely knackered,' said Fran, as if ruling out any notion of an affectionate evening together.

'I'm so glad you're home,' I said, stroking his shoulder.

'Ugh,' was Fran's response. 'I am minging. I'm going for a shower. You'd better show me where it is.'

Later, however, despite the politeness and the seeming indifference between us, we had one of our no-frills but lovely evenings together, both in our dressing gowns, eating shepherd's pie and drinking pink champagne with a single scented candle on the coffee table.

Afterwards we lay together on the sofa in front of the television. Fran sighed, obviously feeling at home in the new place, just as I'd hoped he would. I kissed him spontaneously over and over again, holding him tighter and tighter until he screwed up his face and pretended to gasp for air. These were the rituals of togetherness that we had developed over the years, like primates reunited, freed from transportation crates and released into our natural habitat.

We giggled together as we watched *Crimewatch*, imagining the poor actor's reaction when he got a call from his agent telling him he'd been cast as Bible John, the notorious yet never-identified serial killer who struck in Glasgow in the 1970s. We spooned each other on the sofa, sniffing each other's necks, moaning about work, complaining that we were to be parted once again, in just a few days. So content was I, entwined with Fran, half asleep and smiling, that I momentarily forgot about Albie and all of that messy complication. Fran, exhausted from his journey, fell asleep in my arms and I dozed happily, my nose buried in his hair. An ominous pip-pip of a text message at half past midnight woke us both up. Fran nudged me. I reached for the coffee table and, without having to extricate myself from Fran's grasp, picked up the phone. But then, more awake, I realised the danger of Fran reading the message over my shoulder and sat up to block his view. It was from Albie.

DO YOU MISS ME?

Fran stirred. 'Who is it?' he asked, yawning.

I tossed the phone back on the table and said wearily, 'French film producer. Ignore.'

'At this time?' asked Fran, his usual suspicion evident in his tone of voice.

'Coke head,' I said. 'It's going to be a nightmare job, I can tell already.'

'Well, what does he want?'

'Fuck knows.'

'What did he say?'

'Some bollocks about flight times. I'll leave it till tomorrow.'

'That's not very professional. Shouldn't you reply?'

'Shouldn't you go back to sleep?' I said, pretending to be overcome with tiredness.

'Very suspicious,' said Fran. We lay back down, quiet again, but the atmosphere was different. Fran, I knew, was the only person in the world who could tell when I was lying, even with his eyes closed. His hand moved up my chest, palm spread wide.

'What's the matter with your heart?' he asked pointedly. 'It's going like the clappers.'

There was a pause. 'Maybe I'm having a heart attack,' I offered, hoping we could slip into the usual banter we enjoyed. 'And you're about to do very nicely from my will.'

'I doubt it,' said Fran.

'Or I'm just excited to see you again after all these weeks.'

'Now I know you're lying,' said Fran, exhaling through his nose on to the back of my neck. 'The man at customs control was more pleased to see me than you are.'

'I expect you were flirting with him.'

'Of course I was.'

Our speech was becoming slurred with tiredness so after a couple of minutes and a few more stabs at witty repartee, we managed to raise ourselves up and stagger to the bedroom. While Fran conducted his rigorous bedtime routine of brushing, flossing and moisturising, I quickly answered Albie's text with a MISS YOU TOO, turned the phone to silent and put it in a drawer.

I lay in bed feeling terribly guilty, even if there was a sort of pleasure in the sensation of danger such subterfuge was bringing me. It made me feel alive but I was also surer than ever there was no real future for me with Albie. I must do everything I could do to end it without Fran finding out.

While I'm in France, I thought, that's when I'll think of a way out of this mess.

The next couple of days were wonderful. I loved having Fran back: it was as though sanity had been restored. More than that, the curious noises and hummings in the house stopped abruptly as well. Happy as I was to be with Fran, though, I was also terribly anxious. I was only too aware that despite the outward normality, everything was trembling on a knife blade and inside I was frantic in case I gave anything away. Fran had always known when I was deceiving him but now it was vital that he didn't guess, so I drew on all my acting ability to project normality. I managed very well, I think, using a form almost of self-hypnosis. I trained myself simply to block Albie and my associated guilt from my mind as if the liaison had never happened. That seemed to work but I observed Fran with a watchful eye. For once, he didn't seem aware at all of anything having changed in our relationship, but then he was overwhelmed with jet lag half the time or writing up notes from his 'Integrated kick-off meeting', whatever that meant.

When he wasn't doing that, he spent ages exploring the house and commenting on my various decor choices. It was, I must admit, very pleasant to share it all with him. No one else had been as fascinated by my mood boards, colour palettes or tile selection, and I'd missed having him there to share it all with me much more than I'd realised. Luckily he adored my rather daring choice of frilly pelmets in the guest bedrooms, which pleased me no end.

Then there was Jess, more bright-eyed and perky than ever. She was whisking in and out, looking determinedly cheerful and busy as if to wipe all memory of her little episode from my mind. She practically whistled as she worked, like Snow White doing the housework. I was nervous at every moment, in case Albie had splurged on her shoulder and told her everything, but she seemed perfectly blithe about the whole thing as well. Despite all the cheerful radiance, there was a certain twitchiness about her, and occasionally I caught her standing still and cocking her head, as though listening to a distant radio station that only she could hear. Apart from that, she seemed quite normal.

Then there was Albie who was wandering about the grounds looking sulky. I could tell that he was jealous of Fran's return and he brooded about the garden looking as though he might explode. I kept him in check with secret text messages that promised him a delightfully romantic time as soon as I got back from France while stubbornly refusing to be drawn into exchanges of tormented looks and sighs of longing. I tried to make the clandestine nature of our relationship integral to the romance. But Albie was young and petulant and unpredictable, and I felt that everything could collapse like a house of cards at any time.

All I had to do, I told myself, was get through the last few hours before I headed off to France to do my film. If I could stay afloat, manage to spin all these various plates for just another day, then I was sure I would think up a way to extricate myself from this sticky situation.

And yet . . . it was all rather exciting. I could hardly bring myself to think about the consequences of discovery – I would certainly lose Fran, Jess and what was left of my floundering career too, if the press got wind of it, which they probably would, but I was living dangerously and part of me liked it that way. Maybe this attraction to danger was just a side-effect of approaching fifty, I mused. Otherwise, if one was endlessly sensible and calm and appropriate to one's age, then life, or what was left of it, spread boringly ahead like a great newly mowed lawn. Complicated and fraught with difficulties as my current situation was, at least it was *interesting*.

'Here you are, Richard. The information you wanted on Cheryl Dawkins.' Jess waved a Wikipedia printout in front of me.

'Oooh, my gorgeous co-star. Thank you, Jess.' I took the page and scanned it. I knew a little about Cheryl Dawkins – who didn't? – but I wanted to make sure I was up to speed before I met her. It was simple film-star etiquette to pretend to have seen everything your co-stars had done – seen it and loved it, no matter what a pile of twaddle it really was.

Jess sniffed. 'Cheekbones have a lot to answer for. As you should know.'

That was the old Jess. I smiled at her, and continued reading. Cheryl Dawkins, now thirty-two, had started on her road to fame as a teenager, when she'd been spotted in her hometown of Norwich by a model-agency scout there on a day trip. She had been tall and gangly, with gappy teeth and straight brown hair, but with her flawless porcelain skin, wide-set green eyes, and extremely long legs, she'd definitely had potential. After some dental work, good hair products and a little deportment training, she'd become stunning, graceful and elegant. Her bee-stung lips and wonderful bone structure had designers and photographers clamouring to employ her. After twelve gruelling but lucrative years on the catwalk, she had made the transition to acting and after a faltering start in a low-budget British flop she was now making steady progress.

The film that Cheryl and I were making together was also her first leading role – playing the beautiful wife of a fictional French President, simply called 'Madame'. My cameo role was as her drug dealer, Otto, for a flashback sequence.

It was the night before I was due to fly to Lyon for the shoot and I finally deigned to open the script as Fran and I lay in bed. Fran was reading the *New Statesman*.

'This has gone off terribly,' he said, tossing it to the end of the bed. 'Have you learned your lines?'

'Good Lord, no,' I replied. 'Why on earth would I do such a thing? It's complete and utter crap. I wouldn't dream of sullying my mind with it for a moment longer than is necessary. I'm only doing it to pay for the house renovations.'

'Not very professional,' said Fran, yawning.

'I shall memorise my lines in my trailer before each scene, and forget them instantaneously afterwards. There seems to be a long driving sequence down a French motorway and chopping up lines of cocaine while travelling unfeasibly fast.'

'Very racy,' said Fran. 'Are you going to do a French accent? Let me hear it.'

'*Mais non*,' I said.

'Jesus. Do you not think you're risking your reputation by doing such nonsense?'

'How rude. I'm a working actor. Anyway it might be a huge hit, then you'll be sorry.'

'Any film that features Gethin Jones's acting debut as the President of France is not, in my opinion, destined for a clean sweep at the Oscars.'

'Snob.'

'Has been.'

'Sex?'

'If you're quick. I want a face pack before I go to sleep.'

'All right, let's not bother.'

Scene Nine

1931

Noël

It was early on a bitterly cold January morning when Noël was woken by the sound of screaming. He lifted his head out from under the eiderdown and listened. As far as he could tell, it was Alice the maid making the racket. Despite the happiness of announcing her engagement just a week ago, she'd just recently become highly strung and emotional, given to tears and tantrums. He glanced at the clock. It said 7 am, so he attempted to go back to sleep but it proved impossible. A short while later he heard men shouting, then the sounds of footsteps hurriedly rushing down the stairs and outside. The final straw was the pitiful sobbing that blubbed and bubbled in the background. This he could not ignore, so with a sigh he got up, stoked the dying embers of the coal fire that was just about still alight in his bedroom grate and threw on some more coal. He put his red floor-length winter dressing gown on, straightened his hair and went to see what all the fuss was about.

The various sounds seemed to be coming from the front of the house so he padded along the corridor from his room, through the study and the lounge into the kitchen, a place he rarely visited. He peered out of the kitchen window into the half light and saw Alice shaking with distress, her head buried on Arthur's shoulder as she gave a dreadful high-pitched moan like the cry of a mournful seagull. Noël's father was wearing his pyjamas too, but had his overcoat on top. His hands looked quite purple in the chill wind. Noël didn't look any more. He opened the kitchen latch and went outside. The bitter cold hit the back of his throat.

'Whatever is the matter?' he asked. Arthur looked at him but said nothing as he stroked the top of Alice's hair. He nodded to the right, beyond the barn, where several workmen and Stanley the chief gardener were gathered. Noël saw Jack kneeling down by the edge of the pond.

'Jack,' he called. 'What is it?'

Jack stood up, blocking Noël's view. 'Go back inside, Noël,' he said urgently. 'Something terrible has happened here.'

'What?' said Noël, full of fear. 'Tell me what it is. What's so terrible?'

'No,' said Jack firmly. 'Go now.'

Noël ignored Jack and pushed his way past the workmen. There, on his back by the pond, blue in the face and with green pondweed dotted all over his sodden clothes, was Jude. Or rather, Jude's body. He was very obviously dead. Noël only had time to gasp and cover his mouth with horror before Jack was at his side. He put a muscular arm around him and sharply turned him back towards the house.

'Back inside. I didn't want you to see that.'

'How terrible – how has this happened? That poor, dear boy,' Noël said as Jack pushed him back inside. He began to shake as they went back into the kitchen. 'Has anyone called the police? An ambulance? How did he – was it an accident?'

'We don't know. Alice found him a little while ago. He's covered in ice so I think—'

'Oh, dear God, no!' Noël couldn't bear to hear whatever it was that Jack was going to say. That boy had been vibrant and alive only the day before. Now he was no more than an icy corpse, a collection of frozen organs, his blood turned hard as stone.

'Now listen,' said Jack firmly. 'I think you should go to your room and stay there.'

'This is all so horrendous,' whispered Noël, his skin pale with shock and his hands trembling.

Jack's expression was strong and serious, but he too looked shocked. 'I'll deal with this. Stay out of it.'

'But—'

'Quiet. Go on now, to your room.'

Noël did as he was told. Once in his bedroom he paced back and forth, horror and sadness pulsating through his mind. But there was something else too. Fear. Jack's bit of fun, his seduction of Jude and enjoyment of his fit, young, sinewy body had ended in the most terrible way, and who knew what the repercussions might be. It had been several months since the encounter in the barn, and although it had been plain that Jack had gone on enjoying liaisons with the boy, once Alice and Jude were engaged – and that was only a week or so ago – Noël had been sure that it would be over. He'd asked no questions but assumed that Jack had taken heed of what he had said – that it had to finish. There were many reasons why, not least that if Alice were to find out, who knew if she'd be able to keep her mouth shut.

Why had it ended this way? Had there been a terrible accident? Or had Jude drowned himself? Noël threw himself on the bed, trying to shut out the thoughts that raced through his mind, but it was impossible. His highly tuned playwright's brain demanded an explanation, and the first one it offered – that Jude had killed himself in a moment of guilt and self-loathing as a result of his affair with Jack – was too awful to contemplate.

I should never have let it happen! As soon as I knew, I should have stopped it! he thought, feeling himself growing hysterical. Jack denied the lad his choice. How could he have said no? He probably feared for his job if he didn't . . . If only Jack had left the servants alone.

It had been easy to assume that Jude had been complicit in what had taken place, that he'd enjoyed it and that it had come as naturally to him as to any farmyard animal rutting casually where lust took hold, but perhaps that assumption had been false. Perhaps it had all been too much for him, and he'd taken that icy plunge to end his torment.

Noël sobbed out loud at the thought.

And then something worse occurred to him: what if Jude had left a note, referring to what had been happening to him – one master seducing him regularly while the other assented to it with his silence? What if he had written letters to people explaining why he had taken his own life?

Scandal. Disgrace. Prison, maybe. It would kill Mother. Everything I've worked for, achieved . . . all gone. My career over. Destitution. Desertion.

Panic rose up in him in a sickening wave.

But what, said a little voice in his head, if it wasn't suicide? What if someone else pushed Jude into the freezing lake on purpose? Noël remembered asking Jack if Jude would talk. 'He won't' had been the determined reply. But what if he had threatened to reveal all? Demanded money, perhaps? He was going to be a married man, after all. Perhaps he needed some cash. In which case . . .

Noël's imagination painted a scene for him: Jack and Jude meeting in the chilly darkness. A whispered conversation that turned into a furious row. A punch to the head – hadn't Jack boxed for Yale? – and an unconscious body that only had to be heaved into the lake and the problem was solved. For the moment, at least.

Noël shuddered. 'No, no,' he whimpered. 'Jack would never do such a thing. He would never be capable of that.'

But there were only three possibilities: first, it was an accident. For some reason Jude had been wandering around in the dead of night, slipped and fallen into the pond. But this seemed unlikely – a fit young man like Jude would surely have been able to get himself out. No. Noël could credit only two explanations – either Jude killed himself, in which case both Noël and Jack were surely implicated in the self-destruction, or someone else pushed him into that icy water, intending him to die. If it was someone else, then who but Jack?

Noël buried his face in the pillow so that his anguished sobs were muffled. In the distance he could hear the sound of a police bell heading towards Goldenhurst.

Scene Ten

Richard

My flight from Heathrow to Lyon wasn't until almost five-thirty that day, so Fran and I didn't get up particularly early. We both woke up feeling a little sad. Another separation was imminent. In fact we were still in bed when the front door slammed at precisely nine-thirty. Jess had arrived.

'Shouldn't she be taking it easy? Isn't that what the doctor said?' growled Fran. 'She's been round here just as much as she ever was back in London. You wouldn't guess she's supposedly not working.'

'There's no stopping her,' I replied. 'If anything, she's busier than ever. It's like having a Stepford Wife on speed running my life.'

'Jesus,' he muttered. 'You're employing her. Paying her to make you feel uncomfortable in your own home. Great move.'

'She doesn't make me feel uncomfortable! She's an old friend.'

Fran rolled over on the pillows to face me and said firmly, 'She's not. She's your employee. You're not doing her any favours by leading her to believe any different. I'm telling you, draw the line in the sand and make sure you don't cross it. If that's not possible, let her go.'

I sighed, feeling that he just didn't understand. Jess and I were as tightly entwined as Rupert Murdoch and Tony Blair. It was impossible to imagine life without her – or more to the point, her life without me in it. What on earth would Jess ever do if she wasn't my assistant? 'Don't be so simplistic. She's worked for me for twenty years. I can't sack her. It's a "for better or worse" situation.'

'Mmm. Okay. If I'd known you were already married when we met, I might have thought twice. Now, you'd better get up and pack,' said Fran, clearly not wanting to pursue any conversation about the relationship between Jess and me. It would only lead to an argument and it was too soon in the day for that. Instead he pushed me with the palms of his hands on my shoulder blades and the flat of his feet on the back of my thighs, towards the edge of the mattress.

'No!' I laughed at my sudden, rude ejection from the marital bed.

'Come on,' said Fran, his voice squeezed a little by the effort of stretching out his limbs. 'Chop chop.'

By then, I was rocking on the very edge of the mattress. 'You're vile and evil,' I said, but what I meant was 'I love you'.

'And so are you,' said Fran, but he meant 'I love you too'. 'By the way,' he added casually, 'if they offer me the new contract in LA, I've decided not to accept. I've had enough. Another month or so and I'll be coming home.'

'Here?' I asked, excited.

'Well, I decided against Windsor Castle.' He looked solemnly at me. 'Too draughty.'

*

Half an hour later we were just finishing our muesli in the dining room when I heard the back door open and someone talk to Jess, who was making herself coffee in the kitchen. The voice was mumbled, but I recognised it at once. Albie. So far, since Fran's arrival, he'd kept his distance and stayed out of the house. What the hell was he doing here now? Shit.

'Who's that?' asked Fran. 'Piece of toast?'

'Yes,' I replied, my voice a little more high-pitched than I'd intended. Fran looked sharply at me, but said nothing.

Buttering and eating the toast gave me time to think, but even so I couldn't seem to formulate a plan of action. At any second Albie would walk in, I was sure of it. I felt like a man awaiting the executioner but there was nothing I could do to stop it.

Sure enough, a moment later, Jess came back through on her way back to her office, clutching a mug of coffee with Albie right behind her.

I turned to look at him with what I hoped was a natural-looking smile. He had a strange expression on his face. 'Morning, Albie,' I said brightly. 'How are you?'

'Morning,' he mumbled. He looked absurdly young and handsome in his jeans and a baggy navy blue T-shirt that matched his eyes. But, I realised suddenly, he looked more like a fantasy than the real thing: not like dear, sensible, decent Fran sitting opposite me, who was now staring at the new arrival with his clear, candid gaze, obviously appraising the boy but without a single salacious thought in his head. Albie shrugged, unable to meet anyone's eyes. 'Thought I'd call in and say goodbye, have a good trip, that sort of thing.' He ran a hand through his dark hair, making it more tousled than ever. I suspected the presence of gel.

'Bless you,' I said, more than a little flustered.

Jess smiled at her son. 'That's nice of you, dear.' She looked over at us confidingly. 'Always thinking of others.'

'Hello,' said Fran in a loud clear voice, as though wanting to make his presence felt. 'I haven't seen you for ages, Albie. How are you?'

Albie gazed at Fran. 'I'm fine,' he said eventually. 'Bit of man trouble.' He glanced at me. 'You know how it is.'

'I do, yes,' said Fran, looking surprised. This was the first he knew of Albie's gay-ness, but he was clearly determined to play it cool. 'You shouldn't be suffering angst at your age. A quick grope on the night bus and then eyes across the student disco . . . Nothing more, surely?'

Albie turned and gazed out of the window. 'Right,' he said, dripping with sarcasm.

I looked quickly at Jess to see how she was taking all this, but she seemed rather amused. 'If only I was a lesbian we could call the Old Manor a gay ghetto and get some sort of discount on the rates.'

Fran raised his eyebrows at this rare display of humour from Jess. 'A bidet in every room, naturally,' he added.

Jess ignored him and smiled at me instead. 'Your taxi is booked for two o'clock. I've got all your details printed out for you. Someone called Gerry – a runner, obviously – is meeting you at Lyon airport.'

'Look out for Gerry,' said Albie, his voice bouncing off the window. 'Oxbridge type, no doubt, wearing baggy shorts. Strong pecs from his surfing last summer, violet eyes and manicured nails.'

No one knew how to respond to this comment so a thoughtful silence ensued. Fran looked at me, I stared at the table, Jess continued to smile fixedly, and Albie carried on gazing out of the window.

Jess broke the silence a moment later, handing me a sheet of laminated paper. 'Here's your itinerary, Richard. You're staying at the Chateau Grand Vivaldi for three nights, then you move to the Hotel Esmeralda in Monte Carlo. You fly home on the eighth.'

'I'll be gone by then,' said Fran. 'Hasn't it all worked out well?'

'Terribly,' I said, feeling torn between sadness and relief.

'Perfect,' said Jess.

'Wicked,' said Albie.

There was a sudden loud bang. We all jumped.

'What was that?' I cried, grateful for the diversion.

'It sounded like the cellar again,' said Jess, frowning at the floor. 'I'll go and check. Don't worry about a thing, I'll take care of it.'

I was glad that the awkward moment had passed by without any explosive revelations, although the cellar was not quite so lucky: a sewage pipe had burst and there was some gruesome-smelling gunge all over the floor but, before I could say Pimlico Plumbers, Jess was on the phone and sorting it all out. Albie slipped away in the fuss, and I knew I'd dodged a bullet there. It was a huge relief when the taxi arrived to take me to the airport. I kissed Fran goodbye, feeling certain that the next time I saw him, I'd somehow be free of my little entanglement and back on course, and I would set about making it all up to him.

It was a relief to be on my own in the back of the taxi as we sped along the M20 towards Gatwick. Being away from Albie and my guilty conscience was liberating, even though the texts kept coming from him all through the day. I replied to every one in three, telling him that as soon as I was back, we would be together and he needed to be patient. I sighed to myself. How had I got myself in such a terrible pickle? How was I to wean Albie off me without the whole sorry scandal coming out in the wash, too? A few months ago I'd been living happily in London, secure in my relationship and my career, content in every way. Now I was living in a beautiful but unpredictable house in the back of beyond, embroiled in an unseemly secret affair with my godson. His mother, newly recovered from her nervous breakdown, was practically living on the premises too.

And yet, by the time we passed Maidstone, I was aware of a feeling of longing for the Old Manor. The house had got under my skin somehow and away from it I felt a bit like a fish out of water. I worried about it, the strange bangs and crashes, hums and burst pipes by which it communicated its displeasure, like a great incontinent, prehistoric beast. And even if it meant I was at serious risk of failing to take responsibility for my own actions, I wondered if the house was to blame for the reckless turn my life had taken. The more I thought about this, the more it felt like a revelation that could explain my current situation. There was something rogue-ish and feral about the place. The usual rules and niceties of acceptable behaviour seemed to make it bristle with contempt. But then, if something about the house was urging me on to lustful, drink-fuelled abandon, why was I fighting it? Was it my old, well-mannered self battling to be heard, or another voice, calling at the same time for order and restraint?

And what about all the spirits that Marcia had roll-called that day just after I'd moved in? I'd grown so used to the familiar noises in the house that I almost didn't notice them any longer. It was true that I'd heard some odd whistlings and cries that could have been human, except that they were undoubtedly wild creatures going about their business on my extensive lawns. Noël, despite allegedly residing in my back bedroom, had failed to make much of an appearance in my life. Even listening as hard as I could, I'd never heard so much as a clink of a dry martini. And yet, recently – ever since Albie had arrived, I realised with a start – the house had been humming and playing up like a thing possessed. It seemed that every time he'd stayed the night, I'd woken to some disaster. And the moment he'd walked in today, the pipes had gone bananas.

It was a coincidence, of course. It had to be. It wasn't as if the house were able to cast a moral judgement on what had been going on under its roof. But all the more reason to find a way out of this sticky situation, I decided. At the rate we were going, I wouldn't be able to afford the repair bills.

The airport was quite a culture shock. I had been so long away from crowds and urban civilisation, I was on the verge of a panic attack by the time I'd checked in. I had almost forgotten I had a famous face and when an elderly woman asked for my autograph with the words, 'Didn't you used to be Richard Stent?' I answered, somewhat flustered, 'Yes, I was once.'

'Are you all right, love?' she said, concerned. 'You look like you've seen a ghost.'

'I'm fine, thank you,' I said, hurriedly scribbled my name for her and turned away.

The flight and my arrival in Lyon all went very smoothly, with Gerry collecting me from the airport as promised and whisking me away into the air-conditioned, darkened-windowed privacy of the car. There was no filming that day but once I had settled into my suite at the chateau that evening, I went down to the restaurant to meet Cheryl Dawkins. She looked stunning in a sixties designer halter-neck dress with big orange earrings and not a scrap of make-up, her dark hair pulled back into a simple ponytail.

'Shit,' she said, as I took her hand. 'Let me hug you, please.' Then she clasped me to her chest. 'Thank you, thank you, thank you, so, so, so much,' she began. 'I have loved you for ever and now you are here. I really can't believe it.' She released me but put her bony hand firmly on my shoulder and held me still, determined to have a steady, serious moment with me. 'You? Fantastic. Me? Pathetic. Can't believe I'm working with you.'

'Cheryl,' I said formally, with an embarrassed laugh, 'the honour is all mine. Love your work. Love you.'

That out of the way, we sat down and toasted each other with champagne. Our conversation roamed from mutual show-business friends to the perils of Hollywood and our lives back in England.

'I'm a country girl,' said Cheryl, turning her beautiful face to its best advantage. It was hard not to stare at those wide-set eyes and the extraordinary lips. 'London rather wore me out. Now I'm back in Norfolk. Horses, dogs, sunsets. Love all that.'

'Curious you should say that,' I replied, glad to find some common ground. 'I've recently become a rustic person myself. Kent, though. But it's a worry, isn't it?'

'What is?'

'Well, I mean, no street lights, no police sirens. How do you know you're not dead?'

'You're too divine,' said Cheryl, hanging on my every word. 'But give it time and you'll love it. Go outside in the middle of the night and look up at the stars, see them in all their glory. Listen to the birds, the foxes, the sheep . . . You'll never have felt so alive. It's quite a buzz, trust me.'

I was enjoying the tease and kept my face straight. 'Yes, but in London I can look out of the window, see what other people are wearing and dress accordingly.'

'Well, we don't care in the country. Not about that sort of thing.'

'I'll fit in very well,' I said.

After the first course Cheryl leant towards me and said 'Fancy a line? Just a little palate cleanser? Help you get into character. Follow me.'

I had thought my drug-taking days were long behind me. My fix of choice these days more likely to be a glass of decent Pinot and the latest Heal's catalogue – what Fran called my 'domestic porn'. However, something – whether it was the stress of recent weeks, the threat of my impending birthday, or even the desire not to be thought square by this bright young thing – I found myself saying: 'Why not? I'm nearly fifty and I need to be decadent while I still can.'

Afterwards, in Cheryl's suite, with the added stimulant of cocaine, our conversation inevitably became more verbose and intense, but not necessarily more meaningful or significant. Neither of us worried that the rest of the crew saw us march determinedly out of the dining room and not return. We sniffed and snorted and gulped our way through the mini bar and it was four o'clock in the morning by the time I left Cheryl's room and staggered along the corridor to my own. My make-up call was in two hours.

Cheryl and I met again in the make-up trailer, after my alarm had hauled me from a deep and necessary sleep.

'Precious one!' Cheryl greeted me.

'Morning,' I replied, throwing myself heavily into the make-up chair.

'Thank God for make-up,' said Cheryl, her head moving animatedly from side to side, oblivious to the make-up artist's attempts to paint her eyebrows. She still looked incredible, her eyes clear and her skin fresh. I assessed her jealously. I'd forgotten how robust youth could be. I looked grey and drawn by comparison. 'Listen,' she said. 'This first scene in the car. I thought I could play it a bit manic. Strung out. What do you think?'

'Er, yes, I think that could work,' I replied vaguely. Not having glanced at the script since I was in bed with Fran, I struggled to know what to say. Once make-up was done with me, I imagined I'd have half an hour or more to learn my lines. I was very quick at that sort of thing, usually.

'I am so genuinely thrilled to be working with you,' continued Cheryl as the make-up artist bit her lip with frustration. 'Really.'

'And likewise I'm sure,' I said, aware of that sinking, wonky feeling that comes the morning after the night before and with the realisation that Cheryl was not going to be easy to work with. She was sweet but the constant inane, meaningless talk was not what I wanted or needed. I shut my eyes as if to allow my make-up artist to darken my sockets but really as a means of blocking Cheryl out. The coke the night before had been a mistake and I felt the prickly, hot sensation under my scalp and the clogged, mucky residue in my nostrils. Cheryl may be able to get away with it at her age, and from the look of it had enjoyed a little freshener for her breakfast, but I was too old for such things. I regretted my indulgence. But if I drank enough water and sniffed my Olbas oil inhaler I'd get through it. It was only a silly, cheap film after all, well beneath me if the truth were known. Learn my lines and don't bump into the furniture, that's all I needed to do. Then collect the cheque and go home.

'Acting is such a scream, isn't it?' continued Cheryl, letting the make-up artist at last paint in her eyebrows. 'You get to travel all over the place, pretend to be someone other than yourself and get paid for it. We'll have a nice little bottle of Beaujolais in my room when we're done, if you fancy. Have you got any photos of your house to show me? You must come and stay at mine, too.'

'Love to,' I said sincerely. I had already started acting.

A couple of hours later we were called to the location. The scene was to take place in a brilliant green sports car and Cheryl – or Madame, as her character was known – was to drive. I, as the drug dealer, was in the passenger seat. There was a camera on the dashboard and another camera held rather uncomfortably by a surprisingly porky cameraman called Charlie who was wedged into the back seat, which was designed for nothing larger than a miniature dachshund. Rufus, the director, was in a large truck watching the shots on monitors. He communicated with us via a walkie-talkie hidden down the side of the driver's door. It was Rufus who insisted the film was going to be gritty and real – hence we were all squashed into a real car about to drive down a real motorway, and not in a roomy simulated vehicle in a nice air-conditioned studio or on a rig. I had met his kind before: over-keen and over-ambitious, and I had taken an instant dislike to him. But never mind. This nonsense would all be over in a few days.

'Okay, guys,' came the director's crackly voice. 'Receiving?'

Cheryl grabbed the black brick-sized walkie-talkie and said, as if on army patrol, 'Roger. Receiving. Go ahead.'

'Make your way to Autoroute 7. Crew one, you lead. Cheryl and Richard, follow with Charlie. Crew Two are behind to get some tail shots. Once on the autoroute we have police cover for just a three-mile stretch. We have to fit the scene into that time. Ninety seconds. We have just three takes. Understood so far?'

'Roger, let's go get those motherfuckers,' Cheryl barked in response.

'Atta girl!' responded Rufus. 'I'll give you a "go" to proceed and an "action" for the scene to commence.'

'Roger,' said Cheryl, swallowing hard.

'Final checks, props and make-up,' said Rufus, his pitch higher now. The doors of the Maserati were opened, hair was tweaked and noses powdered. The props consisted of a CD case, placed on the area between Cheryl and me just in front of the gear stick. On the CD cover were a rolled up fifty-euro note and a fake wrap of cocaine. Finally everyone was ready.

'Thank you, everybody. Let's roll,' said Rufus and our convoy set off. After a couple of miles of country roads we joined a dual carriageway and then, via a slip road, the A7.

'Stand by. Gain speed. This shot is with the helicopter. Faster, Cheryl. Cameras to speed, please, and . . . Action!'

The roar of the helicopter hovering just above us made it impossible for us to hear the command and Rufus had to shout 'Action!' several more times before we heard him. Cheryl was staring intently at the road ahead. Eventually she turned to me and said fiercely, 'You ask me how I've been.'

'Oh yes, thank you,' I muttered, seriously alarmed by the speed we were travelling at. 'How are you? How have you been?' I floundered.

'Cut! Cut!' squeaked the walkie-talkie. The helicopter veered away and Cheryl slowed down, and then left the autoroute at the next exit.

'Returning to base,' she said to Rufus and threw the apparatus on the floor. Charlie gave a grunt of discomfort from behind us.

'Really sorry,' I said contritely.

'Light me a snout, would you, darling?' said Cheryl, looking tense as she swung back on to the autoroute from the other side. 'I'm not the slightest bit surprised you couldn't think straight,' she said as I passed her the lit cigarette. Then she laughed suddenly. 'Your face!' she managed to say eventually. 'I thought you'd had a stroke or something.'

I began to laugh too, and by the time we arrived back at the chateau to reset the scene, Cheryl and I were wiping away tears of laughter.

'Oh, dear,' said Cheryl, as we parked on the driveway. 'We really must pull ourselves together. I'm going to have to go for a wee.' She leapt out of the car, grabbed her handbag and sauntered, chuckling, towards the entrance.

'Mind if I get out for a bit of a stretch?' asked a pink-faced Charlie.

'Oh, you poor chap,' I said, pushing forward the driver's seat so Charlie could slither out and rearrange himself. Released at last, he stood beside the car, knees bent, shaking himself from the shoulders down like a grizzly bear. For the next take Charlie wasn't needed, nor was the helicopter.

'We got some good aerial shots,' explained Rufus. 'Don't worry about the dialogue – this is the take we're going for. Dash cam is on, Crews One and Two on. Your close-up, Mr Stent. You got me?'

'I shall be fine without the helicopter, Rufus, I assure you,' I said.

As we sat in the catering bus, each nibbling on a bacon sandwich, Cheryl and I went through our lines.

Otto: How have you been?
Madame: Lousy. Is it good shit?
Otto: The best.
Madame: Let's try some then. Come on. You're not here because I enjoy your company.

[Otto unwraps the cocaine and chops two generous lines. He snorts a line himself before holding the CD case up to Madame, who snorts her own line while still driving.]

Madame: Ah. Thank you, God.
Otto: Is Madame happy?
Madame: She is. Thank you for your most gracious gift.
Otto: You have the money?
Madame: Was Coco Chanel a bit of a goer?

[Both laugh. Cut]

Moments later, after final checks, before the cameras were turned on and as we were revving up on the driveway, awaiting the off from Rufus, Cheryl nudged me. I looked at her and she nodded towards her clenched fist. I looked at it curiously and she turned her hand over, slowly opening her fingers to reveal a more realistic wrap of cocaine than the one set by the props man.

'It'll help, honey bun,' she said, plucking the prop wrap from the CD and replacing it with hers. She smiled. 'No need to act this way.'

Cheryl revved the engine and soon the walkie-talkie crackled into life again. Rufus ordered us to pull out on to the autoroute once more.

'This'll be over in no time,' Cheryl said brightly as we set off.

INTERLUDE

Scene One

Richard

In the chauffeur's cottage at Goldenhurst, Jess was clearing up the sitting room with half an eye on the television news. She didn't usually have it on, but Albie had been watching something and then wandered off, leaving the thing blaring.

Her attention was suddenly caught by the sound of Richard's name, along with that of Cheryl Dawkins. She stopped still, listening intently and watching the screen.

'Our reporter Emily Maitlis reports from Lyon,' said the newsreader solemnly, and the picture changed to Emily wearing a dark-brown linen trouser suit and clutching a Biro in one hand. Her face was cocked slightly to one side, her eyes serious and sad as she spoke.

'The two stars were staying here, at this chateau behind me, filming scenes for a movie called *Madame*. It seems they were shooting a sequence this afternoon on the nearby Autoroute 7 when their vehicle spun out of control, crossed the central reservation and was involved in a collision. French police have closed the motorway in both directions. No statement has yet been made but it looks as if this is a major incident and our sources say they do not expect the road to be re-opened soon.' Emily pressed her earpiece and looked into the camera significantly.

'And is there any indication at all,' said the anchorman back in the studio, raising his voice a little, 'of the condition of Cheryl Dawkins or Richard Stent?'

'A number of ambulances have been at the scene but we don't know any more than that at this stage. Unconfirmed reports say they were filming some kind of high-speed motorway chase sequence. One eyewitness described the crash as "devastating".' Emily looked even sadder.

Back in the studio the newsreader said he'd bring us more news as soon as they got it. He took a deep breath. 'And now the sport . . .'

Jess opened her mouth and began to scream. A moment later, Albie came rushing in to find out what the noise was about and found his mother in a state of hysteria, pointing at the screen and barely able to stand.

Marcia Brown, grim-faced and chain-smoking, picked up the BlackBerry that was juddering and beeping on her desk. It had not stopped ringing all day.

'Hello, Gary, love. Yes. I know, it's beyond awful. All I can tell you is that they're keeping him under sedation in a medically induced coma. His legs are badly mangled. There are . . . head and face injuries too.' She paused to let out a sob. 'But it's still too early. When they can, they're going to fly him back to this country. I'm just taking care of all the arrangements now. Darling, can you get hold of Fran for me? I don't have his number and he hasn't contacted me. He's away somewhere and I don't even know if he's heard. Thank you, darling. Yes, we're all praying for him. That's all we can do, isn't it?'

Later that day, in his bungalow near the village green, Julian Clary was watching the television, one ear glued to his mobile phone.

'I know,' he said down the line. 'It's terrible. Poor Cheryl Dawkins. They've just announced she died at the scene. That gorgeous girl, I can't believe she's gone. And Richard Stent's in hospital in Lyon apparently, undergoing emergency surgery.' He listened for a moment and then said, 'I know. I'm in quite a state myself. It's touch and go whether I'll be up to watching *Deal or No Deal* this afternoon. Poor love. Let's hope he pulls through.'

You might wonder how I knew all this. Who knows? Perhaps they told me. Perhaps, in some curious way, I was with them all, or perhaps I simply dreamed it. But I saw it all as clear as day. I saw Albie sobbing and weeping bitter tears, I saw Jess, white-faced and ranting, clearly losing her mind once again. I saw Fran on his flight to LA and then at the other end turning on his phone as he went through immigration, only to stop dead and drop his briefcase in horror. He ran straight to the desk for a return ticket. I was pleased about that. Wherever I was I wanted him, more than anyone, by my side.

I had my own flight to make, or at least, that's how it felt. I was alongside myself the whole time, as my prone body was stretchered out of the French hospital, past flashing cameras, into an ambulance and away to the airport, a nurse close by at all times to manoeuvre the drip and the electronic box of tricks that was monitoring me – keeping me alive as well, for all I knew. I was grateful that Jess had made all those punctual PruHealth payments. The National Health would never have coughed up for me to be flown home on a special flight. My French wasn't good and it was terribly frustrating hearing the doctors sombrely discussing my prognosis and being unable to understand a word. I gathered I had trauma around 'la tête' area, which didn't sound good at all.

In the plane I hovered over my own body, looking down with interest at my inert self, the face bandaged and invisible, the limbs encased in plaster. I felt no pain whatsoever. Everyone around me seemed very concerned, however, checking my vital signs every few moments. I wanted to tell them I was fine, perfectly happy and in no pain, but then I remembered that no one could see me, let alone have a quick chat. Was I going to die? Was I already dead but no one had noticed? Had I given up the ghost, but the machines were still working away, keeping the technical side of me alive: the heart; the lungs; the mechanical brain?

Time passed strangely. Within a few minutes, it seemed, we were in another hospital, in England this time, in a quiet, dark intensive care unit, and I was transferred to a hospital bed, connected to even more machinery, fussed over and assessed, and finally left pretty much alone as the day drifted into night. I wasn't sure what to do with myself once all the drama had passed. I sat down on a chair nearby and observed Richard Stent in his ICU bed, all broken into little pieces and being mended.

The door opened after a while but it wasn't, as I'd expected, the nurse making one of her regular fifteen-minute checks to ensure everything was still functioning. It was a middle-aged man in a pale suit with a green tie. His rather thin hair was combed back, plastered down with something oily, and he was puffing away on a cigarette.

'You can't smoke in here,' I said, forgetting for a moment that no one could hear me, but the man turned and raised his eyebrows, staring me straight in the eye.

'I beg your pardon, but in my day the doctors would chain-smoke while snipping out your appendix,' he said, 'and balance their martinis on the instrument tray while they were at it!'

I recognised his voice at once. After all, I had spent several months perfecting my award-winning impersonation of it. '*Noël*?' I gasped.

'Sir Noël, if we're being pedantic, but as you're in a frightful pickle I'll let it pass. You don't seem too pleased to see me. Perhaps I'd better leave.'

He flicked his ash on the carpet and turned as if to go, but I called out, 'No, please. Stay.'

He turned back, his thin eyebrows raised up into the wrinkled brow.

I tried to speak but found it hard to get the words out. 'Does . . . does this . . .'

'Spit it out, my dear boy,' he said. 'It's times like this when your RADA training should pay dividends.'

'Does this mean . . . I'm dead?'

Noël shrugged his slightly stooping shoulders. 'Best not to ask me what anything *means*, quite frankly. I can tell you which fork to use at the Savoy or how many diamonds in the Queen Mother's tiara, but that's about your lot.'

'I must be dead,' I said, astonished. 'I'm surprised no one's noticed.'

'Betwixt and between, I dare say. Half dead. Let's settle on that, shall we? You could go either way.' Noël took a puff on his cigarette. 'I'm not an expert on these matters, much as you might wish otherwise. I thought I was somewhere else entirely, if you must know.' He looked around, his expression puzzled. 'I thought I was entering the main bedroom at the dear old house, not this *laboratory.*'

'The Old Manor?' I asked, suddenly filled with longing for the place.

'Yes,' he said in that clipped way of his. 'Goldenhurst. Do you like it?'

'I love it,' I answered sincerely. 'It's a beautiful, restful place.'

He smiled at me, wandered over and sat on the chair opposite, leaning well back and crossing his legs. 'It's a bit of a minx, the Old Manor. Have you had trouble with the drains by any chance?'

'Oh my God, yes!' I said.

'And beware of that fireplace you've uncovered in the French room. There's a very good reason why that was bricked up in the first place,' said Noël in a warning tone.

'Oh?'

'Gases. Through the brickwork.' He rolled his R's excessively, for comic effect. 'My dear Aunt Vida was plagued by them – woke up one morning and she was lavender blue from head to toe. Fill it in, for pity's sake. You'll be rooting around in the priest's hole next.' He inhaled on his cigarette again and gazed appraisingly at me as he blew out a cloud of smoke. 'It is a little naughty of the old girl, but she does this to each and every new resident. Testing your mettle, seeing if you are up to the job.'

'I don't understand.'

'The house thrives on drama. Always has, over the years. It is her lifeblood. More than that, she likes to break in a new occupant. Saw that comedian off in record time.' Noël pronounced the word comedian as if he meant tax inspector. He was clearly referring to Julian Clary. Had he borne witness to Clary's stay at the house too? Noël continued: 'Although I must say she has rather excelled herself with regard to you. I had a death in the garden for my entrance exam. It nearly ruined me, I can tell you.'

'A death?' I said, appalled.

Noël nodded. 'You'd be surprised what the wicked Old Manor can get up to. It can make people behave in ways they never usually would. The under-gardener, Jude, was found dead in the pond. It shook me to the core.'

'How did he die?'

'How does one die in a pond? Drowning, my dear, not shark attack,' he retorted dryly.

'I mean . . . he killed himself?'

Noël took another long drag on his cigarette while his small eyes, even smaller when half closed, regarded me thoughtfully. 'I don't know exactly what I may reveal. There are rules about these things and even I must obey the rules occasionally. Otherwise anarchy might break out and none of us would want that, would we? Let me just say that Jude's death wasn't quite as straightforward as it looked. There were other hands involved.' He leaned towards me in a sudden, fluid movement. 'But that's the house for you,' he said urgently. 'She plays with you, sends your emotions haywire, and then punishes you for it.'

'Is that what happened to me?' I asked.

'A dalliance with someone dangerous? An unlikely, perhaps even forbidden, partner?'

I nodded.

He smiled. 'But this much I know. I saw you, I must confess. I blush to recall it. Albert, is that his name?'

'Albie,' I corrected him.

'Hmmm,' said Noël, his lips twitching with amusement. 'Such, er, stamina in one so young. A credit to the private education system.' Noël cleared his throat and then paused, his expression becoming more serious. 'I know the kind of erotic madness that possessed you. And rather wonderful it is too, at the time. That's the awful thing about temptation. It's so terribly nice to give in to it. But then, once the blood has stopped rushing around all over the place, hither and yon, one feels a little sheepish.'

'Did you give in to this . . . gardener?'

'Me? Oh dear me, no. His fingernails were far too grubby. I was never one for rough trade. Not that rough anyway.' Noël looked pensive. His cigarette, I noticed, never became shorter or diminished in any way. 'Not me. My darling Jack. He was the one possessed.'

'Jack?' I tried to think back to what I knew of Noël's life. The name Jack rang a bell.

He waved his hand. 'Best not to mention his name, dear boy. Or he'll come dashing in here and drink neat cognac out of your bedpan. I've simply come to say that you've survived the initiation and now you may be allowed to return to your old life.'

'Why would the house want to test me in this way? And isn't nearly killing me rather extreme?' I remembered, suddenly, Julian Clary's mention of the seance at Priest's Hole House, as it was then. Perhaps that had been his test. If it was, it was one he failed spectacularly as he'd hightailed it out of there as soon as he possibly could.

'She doesn't do things by halves,' said Noël with a sniff. 'She's a bad-tempered old trout. Seems to have an interest in emotional stress and strain. Probably built on ley lines, who can say? No doubt there is some pagan explanation that mere mortals cannot grasp. Gave me the idea for *Blithe Spirit*, mind you, so hats off to her. But I wouldn't blame your accident on the house. That's not her style at all. Her influence tends to be restricted to her own domain.'

I didn't know what to make of this. If the crash wasn't my initiation, or whatever Noël wanted to call it, then what was?

'It is hard to explain to you while you are still blinking your way through the tunnel back to your present time and place,' he said firmly. 'No doubt it will become clearer. I've come simply to tell you that you must be very careful. The house may test you some more. Make sure you do not fail.' He got up. 'That is all.'

'So – will I die?' I asked, glancing over at my body lying motionless in the hospital bed.

'Eventually.' He waved his cigarette at me. 'I believe it happens to the best of us sooner or later. Now, get some rest. I must go. People to see. Plays to write . . .'

And then he was gone. I was terribly tired, I realised. I needed to rest. I leaned back in my chair and closed my eyes. That was all I knew until much, much later.

ACT IV

Scene One

Noël

'Sir?' Mrs Ashton appeared in the drawing room, her face creased with worry. 'Sir, the inspector is here to see you.'

Noël looked over at Jack, whose knuckles whitened as he clutched his whisky glass a little harder.

'I see. Send him in, please, Mrs Ashton.'

The housekeeper bobbed a curtsey. 'Very good, sir.'

Ever since the discovery of Jude's body the previous morning, the house had been in an awful state. Alice had been taken home and policemen had been roaming all over the garden, probing the reeds around the pond and looking for evidence, and then walking mud all over the carpets. It had all been most unpleasant. Violet's reaction to Jude's drowning was to moan about the loss of Alice's services for breakfast.

'I suppose I shall have to pour the tea myself,' she said, and did so bad temperedly, slamming the pot down on the table, which caused Aunt Vida to let out an involuntary squeak as she passed the milk.

Noël was pale and incapable of eating a thing, still shaking and in shock.

'Snoop, I think you should go to bed at once,' said Violet, concerned.

'It's hardly appropriate,' he answered, his voice high and tense.

'Oh dear,' said Violet, putting down her teaspoon. 'You look feverish. You must look after yourself. You know how tired you get.'

Arthur, as silent as ever but with a grim expression on his face, took a large bite of his scrambled egg and bacon.

'Beast. Brute,' muttered Aunt Vida, shooting him a look of hatred.

Seeing the look, Noël decided at that moment that he couldn't stand it and got up. 'I'm going to my room,' he declared, 'and I shall stay there until Jack and I leave for New York tomorrow. I want everyone to leave me severely alone, do you understand? I need to be by myself.'

He'd walked out, leaving them all staring after him, even Jack. But they had disturbed him to let him know that the inspector intended to call on the house that afternoon. It had sent Noël into a fit of hysteria and it had taken all of Jack's skill to calm him down.

'Listen to me,' said Jack now, as Mrs Ashton disappeared to bring the inspector in. 'Be careful what you say. It was an accident, wasn't it? My guess is that Jude was drunk last night and slipped. It was a simple but tragic event that had nothing to do with us. You're busy writing plays all day. You don't mix with the staff. Keep it vague. Got it?'

'I need a moment to clear my head,' said Noël, grabbing a decanter from the Japanese cabinet and pouring himself a whisky. Jack grabbed it from him before he could take a sip.

'Are you crazy?' he said angrily. 'Want him to smell drink on you at this time of day?'

'I didn't know I was going to be sniffed,' said Noël indignantly.

'For Christ's sake, calm down,' Jack said, putting his own hand on top of Noël's cold one. 'The point is, we're not guilty of anything, so don't act like we are. We want as little to do with the police as possible, right?'

'Do we?' Noël gave him a miserable look.

'Of course we do! You know why . . .'

Just then Mrs Ashton returned, leading a man in a trilby hat and mackintosh into the room. He had a small grey moustache and small grey eyes behind a pair of black-rimmed spectacles, and looked to be in his late forties.

'Detective Inspector Cecil Keaton, sir,' said the housekeeper. 'I will bring tea.' She made a discreet exit as Noël and Jack quickly stepped apart from each other.

Detective Inspector Keaton stepped forward into the room, and said in an unexpectedly strong voice, 'I do apologise, gentlemen. I realise I am a little early for our appointment.' He removed his hat to reveal a waxy bald pate. His eyes were inquisitive and his nose large. The nostrils flared intermittently, as if testing the air for suspicious contraband. He seemed the type that didn't miss a thing.

'How do you do, Inspector,' Noël said, drawing on all his actorly talents to appear composed. He turned on his witty, cynical persona, the one that always served him so well. 'Please, do sit down. Some nice warming tea is on its way. Are you peckish at all? Judging from the smell coming from the kitchen, Mrs Ashton has some kippers on the go.'

'I'll stand, thank you. And I'll pass on the kippers if it's all the same to you. I'm sure you're aware why I'm here. Your employee, Jude Perkins, died here yesterday.'

'Yes, yes,' said Noël. He sauntered over to a small button-back armchair and sat down, moving as though he was on the set of a play. He crossed his legs and reached for a cigarette from the box on a side table. His expression was mournful. 'That poor boy. He couldn't have had a sadder life if he'd been born in Folkestone. Honestly. Have you been there?'

'Shut up,' muttered Jack through gritted teeth, turning away briefly so that the inspector couldn't see his face, only the broad expanse of his back.

'I live there as it happens,' replied the inspector dryly.

'Such a terrible tragedy,' continued Noël, unable to stop himself. 'I have sent my condolences to his family.'

'Very kind of you,' said Keaton, reaching into his top pocket and plucking out a small notepad with a thin brown pencil tucked into the spine. 'Now, sir, a few questions, if I may. What did you know about your gardener's state of mind prior to his death?'

'Nothing whatsoever,' said Noël, remembering Jack's instructions. 'I don't remember having a conversation with him, ever.'

'Mr Coward is rather busy,' Jack put in, leaning against the fireplace and putting his hands in the pockets of his wide-legged tweed trousers. 'He is Britain's biggest star and he's leaving for New York tomorrow to open his latest hit on Broadway. Perhaps you've heard of it. *Private Lives.*'

Keaton bit into his pencil before replying. 'Oh, a very pretty title, I'm sure. But I'm not interested in that, Mr Wilson. I'm not interested at all. Doesn't help me in my job in the slightest.'

'Of course not,' said Noël. 'Silly, silly Jack!'

'How long had the deceased worked for you, Mr Coward?'

'Er, several years. Only ever outside.'

'As one would expect, him being a gardener,' said Keaton. 'And did he seem a happy individual?'

'I told you, I never spoke to him. He was the *under*-gardener. I spoke to Stanley, my head gardener. The snowdrops this year have been exceptional. Have you seen them?'

Keaton ignored this and turned to Jack. 'And you, Mr Wilson. Did you ever speak to Perkins?'

'No, sir,' Jack said politely.

'He only ever saw him from behind,' remarked Noël, tapping his cigarette on the side of a large malachite ashtray.

Jack coughed loudly. 'Excuse me, Inspector. I think I can safely speak for both us when I say we had nothing to do with the gardener, and we're both deeply distressed by his death. It was obviously a very sad accident.'

Inspector Keaton rocked back on his feet and completed his notes before speaking. Then he gazed at Noël and Jack, looking from one to the other and frowning. 'Do you gentlemen both live here?'

'Yes,' Noël said imperiously. 'Mr Wilson is my manager. He looks after all my personal affairs.'

'And, may I ask, sir, whether you are both . . . unmarried?'

'That is correct.' Noël lifted his chin haughtily. 'I am a bachelor. I find there is less laundry that way.'

Jack snorted but quickly produced a handkerchief and blew his nose to cover his amusement.

Noël shot him a look, unable to resist continuing. 'Of course I am tempted,' he said with the same superior indolence. 'As soon as the price of washing powder is reduced, I shall be jumping over a broomstick with Gladys or Gertie or anyone else in a skirt.' He gave the inspector a rather withering look as if punishing him for his impertinence. 'Until then I shall try very, very hard to keep myself nice.'

Keaton frowned and nodded, then looked at Jack. 'And you, sir? Are you of the same mind?'

'Who knows,' Jack said airily, returning the handkerchief to his trouser pocket. 'If the right girl came along . . . Never say never!'

'I see,' Keaton said thoughtfully. 'Now, I need to ask if either of you gentlemen saw or heard anything that might touch on the events of yesterday. Any noises during the night or early morning?'

'I'm no earthly help, I'm afraid,' Noël replied quickly. 'I hadn't seen the boy for days and heard nothing until I was woken by the maid crying, after the body had been discovered.'

Keaton made quick note on his pad. 'And you, sir?'

'The same for me, Inspector. I hadn't seen Jude for I don't know how long. I came out when I heard the shouting, a little before Mr Coward arrived.'

The inspector frowned. 'Jude? Surely Perkins to you, sir?'

Jack gave a small smile, stuffing his fists in his pocket and shrugging. 'I'm American, Inspector. We're a little less formal than you British.'

Keaton stared at him again for a while, then said, 'I see. Thank you. My enquiries will continue. I will be in touch, gentlemen.'

When the policeman had gone, Noël and Jack spent the rest of the afternoon huddled by the inglenook fireplace.

'It's not our fault,' Jack said over and over, whispering, into Noël's ear. 'Believe me. Nothing to do with us.'

'But—'

'No buts. And it'll all be over soon. We're leaving for New York tomorrow and all this unpleasantness will be behind us.

You're on your way to a triumph on Broadway. You're a star, remember?'

Noël was still clammy and weak. 'I keep seeing him,' he said to Jack. 'Poor Jude. How could this happen? Why?' He clutched at Jack's arm. 'Was it an accident, Jack? Really?'

'Yes,' Jack said determinedly. 'It was. I'm certain of it.'

'He didn't kill himself . . . because of us?'

'Don't be silly. Of course he didn't. It was an accident . . . it has to have been.'

Noël gazed into his lover's eyes. There was something dark hidden in their black depths, he was sure of it. 'And the policeman . . . he suspects us. He wants to catch us out. Will he come back for us?'

'Not if I can help it.' Jack had never looked so sure of anything.

Scene Two

Richard

The Old Manor was bustling and busy. From my spot on the terrace, I could see Jess directing operations for the big day tomorrow: tables and chairs were being assembled and fairy lights strung around the garden. I'd been told firmly not to do a thing but conserve my strength. After all, my fiftieth birthday party would no doubt be an emotional occasion and I would be the centre of attention.

It was just over a year since the fatal car crash in France that had killed Cheryl Dawkins and which I had only just survived. For several days, my life had hung in the balance owing to the internal injuries I'd suffered, not to mention two shattered legs and the lacerations to the left side of my face. Cheryl's death, my life-and-death struggle and the entire drama had been headline news for weeks. Then the toxicology reports from Cheryl's post-mortem had been leaked and the media speculation had gone into over-drive. Cheryl became a posthumous icon for our times, the Princess Diana of her day. The footage of our accident was requested by the coroner for her inquest. Some of it was shown on the news but the most controversial parts were not – though, of course, they turned up on various websites, with conspiracy theorists positing all with manner of zany theories as to why Cheryl had been 'murdered'. I never saw the footage myself but I know that it showed Cheryl being thrown completely out of the car. But it was the thirty seconds before that, captured by the dashboard camera, that were most controversial: the infamous coke-sniffing scene. I've never commented – neither confirmed nor denied – and I'm not about to now. The toxicology report – and our dilated pupils – said it all, but out of respect for Cheryl's grieving family, I'll never say more than that. My official line was that I could remember nothing, and I'll stick to that.

After the accident, and the many weeks in hospital, I returned to the Old Manor to continue my recovery. My face and legs would never be the same again, and it was probable I would be on strong painkillers for the rest of my life. I didn't know what would happen to my career but I made an intelligent guess and I was right: it was over. If it hadn't been for a steady stream of income from my Hollywood films, I'd have been destitute. No one wanted Richard Stent. Even Marcia's cheerful, ever-optimistic calls dwindled after a while. I was finished and I knew it. I had the same career prospects as Sid Vicious.

I didn't care much to start with. I was in a wheelchair, after all, and I had a livid pillar-box-red L-shaped scar across my cheek and down to my jawbone. I wasn't exactly expecting to be cast as the new PE teacher in *Waterloo Road*. I knew I looked terrible. I saw it in Fran's eyes the first time he looked at me when the bandages came off. He caught his breath and his eyes filled with tears, then he smiled and said, 'That reminds me, I must get some liver for dinner.'

I knew it too when Albie came to see me. He never visited me in hospital, but when I returned to the Old Manor, he ambled across with Jess one day to mumble his sympathies. His expression when he set eyes on my ravaged face and scrawny frame was one of barely concealed horror. I knew at once that for him, it was completely, entirely over. Whatever dream I had been in his mind – the famous movie star, his magnificent, handsome, unattainable godfather – died instantly and it was obvious that he had no feelings left for me, and certainly not desire. It was with patent relief that he had scuttled away after those ten dutiful minutes he spent beside my wheelchair.

I'd watched him go, half amused and half sorrowful, but entirely relieved. It was over, and now he'd gone away to university in Bristol and our lives had taken the separate paths they were supposed to. I had got out of it by the skin of my teeth, although nearly dying in a car crash had been a rather drastic way to do it.

What was it Noël had said in that funny little dream vision I'd had? I strained to remember now, as I sat in a chair well-padded with cushions against my still-delicate frame. *A dalliance with someone dangerous.* Something like that. Dangerous indeed! Life threatening, as it turned out. But that was all just a morphine-induced dream, was it not? I had mentioned it to no one. Everyone had enough to worry about without me bringing imaginary dead celebrities into the situation.

It seemed to me that the accident had been the outcome of a very reckless, self-destructive phase I had been going through of which Albie had been a part: a dramatic, outward expression, perhaps, of my inner turmoil. When things get out of control the universe sometimes asserts itself and order is restored. Drink, drugs, extramarital affairs: these are all going to tip those who indulge off kilter. When you have a bad back, the osteopath can crack your spine back into place. The car crash was the great osteopath in the sky putting a stop to my imminent derailment. I had learned a lesson and was now graciously permitted to continue with my life. Cheryl Dawkins had obviously been beyond saving, poor girl.

The best thing was that Fran had never known about my madness. Since the accident, he'd been there constantly, sweet, attentive and tactile, dropping kisses on the top of my head when I least expected it and softening his sometimes caustic tone. He had taken leave from his job – that very job that had kept us apart for so long and been so important to him – in order to care for me and be with me. Occasionally I wished for the old days and the self-possessed, sharp-tongued Fran, before he became my carer, but then I remembered what a lesson I'd learned. His love had proved itself when the chips had come plummeting down and I knew now how bloody lucky I was to have it.

Time had passed and my condition had greatly improved. I could walk now, though not for long periods, my scars were healing and the worst of the pain had subsided. But I worried that the past could still come back to bite me. Albie was coming to my birthday party the following day and that fact was making me nervous. He was, after all, unpredictable. The champagne would be flowing, the excitement would be high – would his tongue start wagging too? As I watched people scurrying about getting my party ready, I hoped that this wouldn't be the moment where everything that had been saved from that little affair would be lost after all.

'Richard, how are you?' Jess was coming across the terrace towards me, bearing a glass of chilled apple juice in one hand. The heat was still intense despite the evening approaching. 'Isn't the weather blissful? The report says it's going to be gorgeous tomorrow!' She smiled at me. She looked so young and happy, fresh in her floral dress and espadrilles.

Jess had been a marvel after the accident and I was hugely grateful to her. While I was in hospital, though, I had been aware that I was the object of a power struggle between her and Marcia. From the moment I emerged from my coma, both of them were sitting either side of my bed, clutching a hand each, and when I managed to flutter my eyes open, they took it in turns to say soothing, encouraging words to me. I knew Jess had my right hand and Marcia my left, because I could feel Marcia's nails and her many rings, but both were equally possessive. Who knows what the conversations were between them while I was unconscious but they tried to show a united front when I was awake, although not always succeeding.

'Marcia,' Jess would say in a subtly superior turn. 'Would you be a dear and plump up Richard's pillows for him? We don't want him getting bed sores now, do we?'

'Certainly, Jess,' said Marcia, bristling. 'Did you suffer from those during your hospital stay?'

'No, I did not!' snapped Jess. 'I was not confined to bed, I was up and about.'

'Of course, silly me,' replied Marcia. 'That's the beauty of a padded cell, I suppose.'

Poor Fran was stuck in the middle of all this and eventually he could stand it no more. As he told me later, with award-winning diplomacy he'd persuaded Marcia to relinquish her watch. 'I loathe Jess as much as you do, Marcia,' he confided after following her outside for a cigarette break. 'But having the two of you tussling over him like dogs with a bone can't be good for Richard.

I honestly feel, now he's out of danger, that we can both retreat a little and let Jess be matron-in-chief.'

'You're right,' sighed Marcia. 'My being in a confined space with that bitch isn't pleasant for anyone.'

'The phrase "three cats in a sack" springs to mind,' said Fran with a weary chuckle.

'I'd better get back to Percy anyway,' she concluded. 'He's run out of clean underwear and is threatening to wear my knickers to the House of Lords if I don't go home soon.'

With Marcia off the scene, a triumphant Jess had taken care of everything, arranging my transfer to a private clinic as soon as I was off the critical list and getting me safely home. She also protected me from the outside world as I made my recovery, cancelling all my commitments for the foreseeable future and concentrating on getting me well. From the chauffeur's cottage, she kept a careful watch on all comings and goings, guarding me night and day and shooing away any journalists or sightseers who came sniffing about. She refused to hire a nurse but insisted on looking after me herself, administering my medication and cooking my meals whenever Fran was not around to do it for me. Her dedication to me and her brilliance as a PA had at last come together. In a strange way it was as if the past twenty years had all been a cosmic preparation for this eventuality.

I felt filled with affection for her now as I saw her excitement over my party. She had done the lion's share of the work, of course, and it all seemed to be coming together beautifully. 'I'm fine,' I said. 'Good news about the weather. Any changes to the guest list?'

Jess put the juice on the table in front of me and sat down. 'Oh yes, I meant to say. Julian Clary called. He wants to bring some old bird along with him. He said you'd be interested to meet her.'

I had decided it would seem churlish not to invite the former owner of the house when he still resided in the village.

'Oh. That's fine, I suppose. We've got a hundred coming, so what's another?'

'That's good.' Jess smiled. 'I said exactly that. And Albie's coming, of course.'

She gazed at me with innocent eyes. I murmured that he was very welcome, and I was looking forward to seeing him.

She leaned forward and put her hand on mine. 'Richard,' she said earnestly. 'It's going to be a wonderful day tomorrow. A *special* day. I can just feel it. Can't you?'

I was pleased that she was so enthusiastic but I couldn't help scanning her face for signs that another breakdown might be on the way. Jess had certainly been working flat out for the party, but she had been amazingly stable for months now so the medication was clearly working. I put the thought from my mind. Her slightly manic demeanour was simply heartfelt joy at my recovery and excitement about the party.

'Yes,' I said, smiling back at her. 'I can feel it too.'

Scene Three

1931

Noël

The next morning, while their things were being packed for the trip to New York, Noël went out into the greenhouse to cut some flowers. In the dining room, he arranged them into a beautiful bunch and was just tying them with a pretty white lace scarf that had been left in one of the bedrooms by Gertrude Lawrence when Jack came in, fresh from a morning shave and pulling on his Fair Isle jumper.

'What are you doing?' he asked, inspecting the detritus of stalks and leaves scattered over the mahogany table.

'A bouquet for Alice. You don't think it's bad taste, do you?' asked Noël, uncertain, looking at the lace falling in a foamy waterfall around the stems. 'Given that she and Jude were to be married?'

'What?'

'Well, weddings, wedding dresses, white lace?'

Jack made a dismissive face. 'Well, a pair of black stockings would work. Any of those lying around?'

'Just think,' said Noël, ignoring Jack's suggestion. 'These are flowers grown from bulbs planted by Jude last autumn. The whole business is most upsetting.'

Jack looked at his watch. 'We're leaving soon. You can't spend too long playing with flowers, you know. We have to be ready when the car comes.'

Noël looked at him, almost imploring. 'You're very cool about all this. That poor boy is barely cold. You took your pleasure with him, and now he's dead. Aren't you bothered?'

Jack fixed him with a hard look. 'Sure I am. I hate it all as much as you do – but what's to be done? It's sad but it comes to us all in the end. What do you want me to do? Throw myself to the ground and cry, "Alas, poor Jude, he had a nice, tight arse"? I'm not the sentimental type, I guess.'

'I'll say.' Noël frowned, and then buried his nose in the sea of flowers, inhaling their scent. 'This perfume: so delicious and yet so close to decay. I suppose that's why we decorate coffins with flowers.' He shuddered. 'I'm glad we shall miss the funeral, I don't think I could have borne it. I've given instructions that all bills should be sent here, though. The least I could do.'

'That's good of you. It's the right gesture.' Jack looked sombre. 'Now, let's have some lunch. We need to have a little chat about what happens next.'

They were lunching alone, with the rest of the family still under strict orders to leave Noël to himself, when Mrs Ashton came in.

'Sir,' she said, a worried expression on her face, 'the inspector is back. He says he'd like a word and can't wait. May I show him in?'

Noël shot a startled look at Jack, but kept his composure,

despite turning pale. 'Very well. Yes, please, Mrs Ashton.' He stood up and dropped his napkin elegantly on the table as the housekeeper went out. 'Well, well,' he murmured.

'Just stay calm,' Jack urged him. 'There's nothing he can put on us, nothing at all.'

When the inspector was shown into the dining room, Noël said peevishly, 'To what do we owe the pleasure of your company this time, Inspector?'

'Just a courtesy visit, sir, to let you know how things are progressing,' the inspector replied in a friendly way, gazing quickly at the two men. 'You're still here, Mr Wilson?'

'I seem to be!' Jack replied cheerfully. 'Mr Coward and I are leaving this afternoon for the States – as you know, we're business partners.'

'Yes, business partners. I expect you know each other inside out,' the inspector remarked, grimacing slightly and inclining his head towards Noël.

'What do you want?' retorted Noël, annoyance sizzling through him. He pointedly did not ask the inspector to sit down, but the policeman seemed unperturbed, simply turning his well-worn hat round and round in his hands.

Keaton cleared his throat and said, 'Our investigations are continuing, and the coroner at Ashford has opened and adjourned the inquest. I must say, we've not found evidence of anything other than a tragic accident.'

'Oh. Good,' Noël said with evident relief. 'Just as we all thought.'

'Except . . .' Keaton turned his small, penetrating eyes on Jack. 'I wondered if you gentlemen knew anything about a bruise they found on Perkins' head. Fresh, it looked. And quite a whack too.' His bright gaze moved quickly between the two men.

Noël looked over at Jack. His face had reddened and his knuckles tightened, if only for a second.

'And what importance does that have?' Noël said quickly, to draw the inspector's attention away from Jack.

'Well, we're not in a position to say yet, sir. None most likely. Especially as your little maid, Alice . . . well, she swears blind that the lad hit his head the day before yesterday, banged it on a low branch in the orchard, she said. And I wondered if either of you gentlemen witnessed the incident?'

Jack looked cross now, his dark eyes flashing. 'I'm afraid not, Inspector. I don't know how to make it any plainer that neither Mr Coward nor I has ever consorted with the servants. Bangs and scrapes endured by the working class are no concern of ours. Unless, of course, the tree was damaged in any way. Besides, if Alice has a reasonable explanation, what are you doing talking to us about it?'

Keaton rocked back on his heels, his expression inscrutable. Then he said almost cheerily, 'I can't seem to get it out of my mind, I suppose, sir. If you'd seen the boy bang his head, then I suppose I'd be able to let it lie. But I can't. More's the pity. Still, we have our explanation and there's no need to question the girl's account of it.'

'Then,' Jack said curtly, 'you've no further business here, have you?'

Noël cut in quickly, his voice carefully polite. 'I hope you understand, Inspector, but we're leaving here today. We must be getting on with our preparations.'

'Quite, sir, quite,' replied Keaton, putting his hat back on.

'You're free to go, of course. You must have some packing to do.' He turned as if to leave and then slowly looked back at them. 'Separate suitcases, it is, I suppose, sir?'

There was a short but horrible pause before Noël snapped, 'Of course.'

'Of course,' the inspector said smoothly. 'Everything just as it should be. I'll see myself out. Good day to you both, gentlemen, I hope you enjoy your travels. I'll see you again, no doubt.'

Jack and Noël gazed at each other when he'd left.

'What game is he playing?' Noël said slowly.

'What do you think?' Jack replied grimly. 'He wants to catch a falling star . . . and preferably a musical one at that.' He fixed Noël with a serious look. 'We must be careful. It's a very good thing we're going away for a while.'

That afternoon, they motored to Southampton and boarded the liner to New York, both hugely relieved to be free of the terrible atmosphere that had fallen over Goldenhurst. The crossing was fine, except that Jack, Noël noticed, was drinking more heavily than ever.

We've both had a shock, Noël thought benevolently. It's no wonder he needs to numb himself to it.

New York proved a wonderful remedy to the tragedy that had engulfed them. It was as frenetic and energised as ever, despite the gloom and poverty caused by the Great Crash, and it was a joy to see Gertrude and the young Oliviers again, for Laurence's charming wife Jill Esmond was playing the role of Sybil in this production. The curtain rose at the end of the month to warm reviews and a sell-out run. It was so pleasant that Noël broke his three-month rule and played Elyot through until May, and when he wasn't on the stage, he was at his desk in his flat at West 18th Street, looking out on the Empire State Building surrounded by old copies of *Illustrated London News* and writing his most ambitious work so far, a patriotic piece of nostalgia spanning thirty years that he called *Cavalcade*.

It was writing about home that made him forget the sorrow and sadness, and long to be back.

Scene Four

Richard

It was the night before the party and Fran, Jess, Gary and I were having dinner together in the big dining room. The mood was jolly and full of anticipation for the following day.

'I think the bunting is going to look fabulous,' said Jess with a broad smile, tilting her head affectionately at me.

'Good,' I answered brightly. 'White, is it?'

'Yes, with a big green R on it. Specially made by a peasant woman in Mallorca. I shall put it up first thing tomorrow.'

'Do they know what bunting is in Spain?' asked Fran. 'I always thought it was a rather English thing. Women's Institute and all that.'

'Royal Navy, actually,' said Jess a little snappily. 'But they seem to understand the concept of a triangle in Spanish parts. Coq au Vin, anyone?'

After dinner, Jess and Fran cleared the dishes and disappeared into the kitchen to wash up.

Gary had only arrived that afternoon and it was our first chance to speak together.

'How are things?' he asked. 'You're looking much better.'

'Thank you – I'm feeling much better too. My legs are nearly healed, though I'm still finding being on my feet for any length of time difficult.'

'Well, we all need to sit on a poof from time to time . . . You'll soon be good as new,' Gary said reassuringly. 'And you and Fran look very happy too.'

'We are.' I smiled. 'Things are better than ever, if I'm honest.'

Gary looked over his shoulder to check that the coast was clear. 'Albie?' he whispered. 'What of him? I take it that's all forgotten now?'

'Completely,' I replied, speaking hurriedly, worried we might be interrupted. 'As far as I'm concerned, it's ancient history. But listen – he's coming to the party tomorrow. I'm worried about some sort of confrontation.'

'Why?'

'He's such a drama queen. And possibly a bit unstable, like his mother. I just feel uneasy about it. I don't know why. Will you keep an eye on him tomorrow, perhaps be ready to distract him? I'm worried that something might be said. I don't know—' I stopped mid-sentence and cocked my head towards the ceiling. 'Listen! Can you hear that?' The house had been silent for months now but as clear as anything I could hear a loud humming noise, as though a swarm of bees was trapped in an upstairs bedroom.

'Hear what?' Gary listened as well then shook his head. 'Can't hear a thing.'

The hum seemed to fade a little. I frowned. 'Strange. Perhaps it was the boiler.' Then Fran came back and we talked of something else.

*

I didn't sleep well that night. The house banged and thumped for no obvious reason until the early hours but eventually I managed to drop off. The next morning Fran and I awoke to brilliant sunshine streaming in through the window.

'Happy birthday,' Fran said, giving me a smile and a kiss, and then handing me a package. I unwrapped it to discover a beautiful, handmade, white linen shirt.

'How gorgeous,' I said, delighted. 'Thank you. I'll wear it today.'

'You're welcome. I know about Albie, by the way,' he said casually.

I froze. 'What?'

'I know, that's all,' he said, meeting my worried gaze. He stroked my head reassuringly. 'Don't get upset. I know that you and he had a brief affair.'

'How do you know?' I asked, more amazed than ashamed for the moment.

'Albie told me. Months ago. While you were in a coma.'

'Well . . . why tell me now?' I said, perspiration beginning to spring from my forehead.

'Hush. For goodness' sake, I'm not feeling cuckolded. In the great scheme of things it isn't important. It was a pre-accident thing. I thought you were going to die, remember.'

'But—'

'Shush now, I'm talking,' continued Fran. 'I'm telling you now because I can read you like a book. Albie is coming to the party today and . . .' he paused, considering his words carefully '. . . and you're worried.' He stopped suddenly and looked at me, eyebrows raised, seeking confirmation.

'Well, why aren't you angry?' I asked, almost indignant now.

'Oh, I knew anyway. I know everything, remember. Remember the morning you left for Lyon? Albie came in all tragic and mysterious while you stared at the tablecloth? It was perfectly clear then. Anyway, no matter where I am in the world, I only have to speak to you and I know. I know if you've had a glass of wine or a bottle. I even pride myself on knowing if it is red or white. The year even.'

'Don't be so pompous. So when Albie told you, were you all calm and superior?'

'No one was very calm then. You were at death's door, Jess was guarding you like a Rottweiler and squabbling with Marcia, the doctors were gabbling away and making no sense half the time. Albie suddenly turned up uninvited and hysterical. Jess wouldn't allow him in the room where you were wired up to dozens of machines. She said it wouldn't be good for either of you. Then the nurse got a bit twitchy with all the crying and carrying on and said there were too many of us in the corridor. I took Albie to a bar for a calming drink. That's where he told me.'

'Oh, God. What a mess,' I said, feeling like the bottom had dropped out of my world. So he knew. He must hate me. At that moment, I loved him so desperately, I couldn't believe I had been such a terrible fool to risk losing him like this.

Fran paused and took a deep breath. 'I'm not going to tell you off. I'm not going to ask you what you were thinking of, or how you let such a thing happen. I've no desire to make you feel any more uncomfortable than you already do.' Yet he got out of bed as though he longer wanted to be lying there next to me, touching me.

'But?' I asked, propping myself up on one elbow to look at Fran who was opening the wardrobe and choosing some clothes.

'Your broken legs and punctured lung were punishment enough, wouldn't you say?' Fran answered brightly.

'Is that it?'

'For now, yes.'

'We're not . . . finished?'

'No. But let's be practical. Albie is coming to the party. Be careful. I don't want any hysterical scenes.'

I stared at him, putting everything into my gaze. 'Please . . . don't leave me.'

'Can I go to the bathroom?'

'I mean it. Don't ever leave me. It would be like losing my senses. All of them.'

'You nearly lost your life.' His eyes were suddenly full of tears.

'Fran, I'm sorry,' I said, looking at him beseechingly. 'More sorry than you can ever know. I was an idiot. I can't believe I was so stupid—'

'I know. You don't have to say.' There was a pause heavy with things unsaid. Then, a second later, he spoke in his normal voice. 'I'm going to the bathroom and I may be some time.' He peered out of the bedroom window. 'There are some young men downstairs filling balloons with helium and tying them to the gate. I suppose Jess arranged that. Try not to seduce any of them on an empty stomach. It wouldn't be good for you.'

'Ha,' I responded, deadpan. I knew I wouldn't be doing that sort of thing again in this life. As soon as Fran was out of the room I got up, put on my dressing gown and looked out of the window. It was only half-past eight but there was a hive of activity on the front lawn. Apart from the balloon boys, the caterers had arrived and they were unloading equipment and trestle tables into the barn where their preparations were to take place. Jess was in the midst of them all, supervising and looking tense while arranging large daisies in jam jars. 'No paper napkins!' she shouted to someone non-specific. 'Linen only! It matches the bunting.'

I sat on the side of the bed for a moment allowing my injured legs to twinge and my cheek to twitch. My legs always ached most in the mornings and I should really do my stretching exercises before I walked any distance on them. But I wanted to have a think first, to get my thoughts in order. I found myself gazing at my own reflection in the mirror.

So Fran knew. He had known for months. I thought back over the last year. Despite Jess's almost constant presence and Fran's frequent trips away, we had enjoyed the odd weekend of solitude together in the Old Manor, and when we were alone together the old beams seemed to creak with quiet contentment and the garden bloomed roses just for us. The wattage of our love for each other was suddenly increased so we were like glow worms, charged with an ethereal, pagan goodwill. And all along he had known about Albie. I was suddenly sure beyond any doubt that my destiny lay with Fran. It always had. And if I still had him, then I was very, very lucky.

My ruminations were interrupted by a gentle knock on the door and Jess's voice.

'I've brought you up some breakfast on a tray. Can you open the door? I've no hands.'

I opened the door and greeted a smiling Jess who came in carrying a Cath Kidston tray on which was a steaming teapot, boiled eggs, toast, fruit juice, a copy of the *Independent* and a napkin. A small package nestled in the cup on top of a neat pile of crockery.

'Happy birthday!' said Jess. 'Thought you might prefer to eat up here, away from all the mayhem downstairs. Save your energy.'

'Oh, bless you,' I said, taking the tray from Jess and placing it on the marble-topped Edwardian dresser. 'Everything going to plan?'

'Fingers crossed,' she said, trying to keep smiling but her mouth twitched nervously and she brought her hand up to cover it.

'Can I help with anything?'

'Certainly not,' said Jess firmly. 'It's your big day and everything is going to run like clockwork.'

'Well, don't worry if it doesn't,' I said. 'I mean,' I added hurriedly, 'I'm sure it will but I won't mind if . . .' I gave up trying to make sense. By some tacit agreement we never spoke about her breakdown or her time in the Monastery. In the wake of my accident the focus had very much been back on me. Jess had swung into action as if she'd never been ill and, despite constantly thinking I should talk to her about 'things', it seemed easier to abide by her wishes and, like her, regard everything as back to normal. 'Ooh, is this for me?' I picked up the package and looked at Jess.

'From me,' said Jess, her eyes sparkling. 'Open it. I've been waiting for ages to see if you like them.'

'Aha. It's a *them,* is it?' I said, glad our conversation was on safer ground. Inside the white crêpe wrapping paper was a small, worn leather box. I opened it and gasped. Then I said softly, 'They're beautiful, Jess.'

Gently, between thumb and forefinger I lifted out a thin, gold oval-shaped cufflink and held it up to the window.

'Just stunning,' I said. 'Inlaid with pearl. Where on earth did you get them?'

'Asprey's found them for me. Read the inscription,'

I looked at her in astonishment. 'You naughty thing. Asprey's?'

'Yes. Now read what it says,' said Jess impatiently.

I turned the cufflink over and held it closer to my eyes. 'Can't see a thing,' I said, and reached down to the bedside cabinet to retrieve my reading glasses. Then I turned on the bedside light and sat on the bed, tilting the cufflink towards the light.

'Hang on. Some dates,' I said. '*Sixteenth of December 1930. Goldenhurst.*' I stood up excitedly and picked the matching cufflink from its box. '*To N.C. Always, J.W.* Oh my God, Jess – these were Noël Coward's?'

'And very difficult to come by, I'll have you know,' replied Jess. 'Asprey's managed to track down a previous owner.'

I stared at them. How strange. I knew who JW was: Jack Wilson, Coward's lover and manager. I read about him in the course of my research for the biopic. The two of them had lived here together, enjoying the first flush of their love affair. I frowned. A remembered line of dialogue floated into my mind: *My darling Jack. He was the one possessed.* I only had the vaguest recollection of the curious vision I'd experienced in my hospital room – but this was the Jack Noël had mentioned. What on earth had he meant? Possessed by what? But then . . . it had just been a dream. Odd that I should put a mention of Jack in, though.

I turned the cufflinks over in my palm. From Jack to Noël. But hadn't it ended badly? I couldn't remember now what had happened. But it had not been for always after all. I hoped this wasn't a bad omen for Fran and me.

'Do you like them?' Jess asked.

I smiled at her. 'I love them. Thank you, Jess.'

Scene Five

1931

Noël

It was early summer when Noël and Jack finally returned to England, both tanned from the delightful detour they'd taken to Bermuda, where they'd met up with the Oliviers and enjoyed some rather daring nude sunbathing.

Announcing that the muse was upon him, Noël left Jack in London for a few weeks and retreated to Goldenhurst with Gladys Calthrop, his friend and designer, to work on *Cavalcade*. 'You go and buy a new hat while we're recreating Armistice Night in Trafalgar Square for the stage. We shall see who finishes first,' he said flippantly.

It was lovely to be back, Noël thought wistfully, as he sat at the piano one afternoon when Gladys had gone, dallying with several different melodies and lyrics. He could see the garden from here, and a new gardener working there; nothing like Jude this time – at least sixty and weathered by Kentish wind and rain – and probably all the better for that.

He rippled his fingers over the ivory keys and broke into a new composition, one about a mediocre actress.

'Her career was unremarkable,
Her résumé frightfully dull,
The only moment of excitement occurred,
When she was seduced in her digs in Hull.'

'That's nice,' said a familiar voice, and Noël turned to see Jack standing in the doorway, a broad smile over his handsome face. He walked over to the piano and leaned on it. 'Sounds like a hit to me.'

'It probably will be.' Noël smiled and blew him a kiss while still playing. 'Hello, my darling, so lovely to see you. I've missed you horribly.'

'Me too,' Jack replied. His face, Noël noted, was a little puffier than it used to be. Well-fed and watered, he thought. But still so handsome.

'You've been gone a very long time,' said Noël, a slight crack in his voice.

'You didn't need me. And how is the grand production coming along?'

Noël stopped playing. 'Very good. We open in October, all going well. As long as Gladys manages to fit the Mile End Road on the stage at Drury Lane. Have you been amusing yourself in London? Word reached me that you've been out on the town every night charming eligible bachelors with your extensive selection of Easter bonnets. I look forward to receiving the bill in due course.'

'Is there a drink around here?' Jack said, ignoring Noël's barbed comments and looking forlornly at the empty drinks tray.

'Of course. Ring the bell.'

The bell was answered by Alice, who came bustling in, only to stop short when she saw Jack standing there. Her cheeks paled but she quickly recovered herself and smiled prettily. 'Yes, sir?'

'Bring a bottle of Scotch in here, please,' Jack said brusquely.

Alice bobbed a curtsey and hurried away.

'What a strange effect you had on little Alice,' Noël remarked, running his fingers across the keys again.

Jack flung himself into a chair and reached for a cigarette from the box on the table. 'Did I? I didn't notice anything.'

'She went as white as a farm duck. It was almost like the old days.'

'Yeah? Maybe she's got a crush on me.' Jack laughed but his eyes remained unsmiling.

Noël stared at him for a moment and then said quietly, 'I'm so happy to have you back where you belong.'

It's almost as though we've never been away, Noël thought, when they gathered around the tea-table: himself, Jack, Violet and Aunt Vida – though Arthur, Noël noticed, was markedly more frail and had taken to sleeping in the afternoons and sometimes between courses at dinner.

'Laziness!' said Aunt Vida, nibbling on a sandwich.

'Well, as long as he's happy,' said Noël, already weary from the sniping in which the two sisters constantly indulged. Whenever he was away, he forgot how boring it was to be surrounded by ill humour but he remembered very quickly on his return. He watched as Alice set down a silver pot of hot water, and slipped quietly out of the room carrying her tray.

'Mind you,' said Violet. 'He may well be tired. None of us sleeps well in this house at night.'

'Noises!' agreed Aunt Vida, nodding. 'All night, sometimes.'

'What sort of noises?' asked Jack, tapping the side of a scone that looked as if it had seen better days.

'The whole house is alive,' said Violet disdainfully. 'There's a family of mice or rats or squirrels – I don't know – scuttling about from dusk till dawn in the rafters.'

'Get a cat, then,' said Jack, deciding against a scone and helping himself to some fruit cake instead.

'Or we could have little felt booties made,' suggested Noël. 'Then they could dance the Charleston without disturbing anyone.'

'Other noises too,' put in Aunt Vida. 'Bangs and creaks.'

'It feels as if the entire house might collapse, really it does,' said Violet. 'It's worse than it's ever been.'

'Humming!' said Aunt Vida. 'Torment. And screeching!'

'Yes,' continued Violet. 'A very unpleasant noise. And there's a smell coming from somewhere,'

'Oh, do stop, please,' said Noël irritably. 'All this talk of noises and smells. It's all part and parcel of the English countryside. Or would you rather we all moved to a tent in the middle of the Sahara Desert? And then you would no doubt complain about sand in your crevices.'

Aunt Vida gave one of her involuntary squeaks.

That evening Noël went out for a stroll after supper. He rounded a corner in the garden, the dachshunds frolicking at his feet, when he saw, almost obscured by some bushes, Jack and Alice the maid in deep conversation. Not a word could be heard, only the buzz of Jack's deep voice and the softer answering lilt that was Alice's. He could see only the girl's face, tipped up towards Jack's dark head with a serious expression, quite different to the distraught, ashen way she'd looked last time he'd seen her.

'How strange,' Noël said to himself. He watched for a while, and then turned to walk in a different direction. 'How very, very strange.'

Scene Six

Richard

Despite the heat, I decided to wear a long-sleeved shirt so that I could show off my Noël Coward cufflinks. In the kitchen, tucking into bacon and eggs, I found Gary.

'Morning, birthday boy,' he said with his mouth full.

'Morning.' I said. Then, clasping an imaginary cigarette I assumed the stance and then the voice of Noël Coward:

'I've exfoliated, moisturised,
Deodorised and scrubbed.
My teeth are clean, my hair's a dream,
I've combed it till I blubbed.
My clothes are fresh, I must confess
I'm wearing too much scent.
Tongues will wag that I'm a fag,
But one that's heaven sent.'

'Bravo,' said Gary. 'Getting in the spirit, are we? Was that one of Noël's lesser known works?'

'Well, no, actually,' I replied, reaching for the teapot. 'I made it up in the shower. I've been inspired by these. Look.' I presented my wrist to Gary and showed him the cufflinks. 'They were Noël's. Presented to him in this very house by Jack, his handsome lover. How fantastic is that?'

'Heavens,' said Gary. 'Amazing.'

'Jess found them for me. They've been all over the place and now they've come home.' I stopped and sniffed the air. Suddenly Noël was back, singing in the style of an old sea shanty.

'Home is heaven, it's where I belong,
A haven with crazy paving
Where nothing is wrong.
Home is heaven, who could disagree?
The fire burns and no one learns
About my man and me.'

Gary was shuddering with mirth. 'Deary me, you're on form!'

I looked down at my cufflinks and frowned. 'Do you think I'm possessed by the spirit of Noël Coward? If I can't get through breakfast without a winsome lullaby, they're coming off. I'm fifty, you know, my dear boy.'

'I do,' Gary confirmed. 'Many happy returns. Drink your tea. I'm afraid I only got you a card.'

He handed me a bright pink envelope. I drank some tea and opened it. Inside, in his slanted, sad writing, he had written:

Darling Richard,

I am so happy to be here with you and for you. I hope the day brings you much laughter and joy and that you realise how loved and cherished you are.

I add my love to the mix,

Gary xxx

I put the card on the table and turned to Gary who opened his arms for a hug. The two of us embraced.

'And I'm very glad you're here, too,' I said as we released each other after thirty comforting seconds. 'I may need you.'

'I know. It'll be fine. I won't let any young pups come snapping at your heels. Ghosts from your past.'

'Good. Thank you. It turns out Fran knows what went on.'

'Really?'

'Yup. Knew all along. Told me this morning.'

'Well, why didn't he say anything then?'

'I suppose it was a bit like telling someone they'd stepped in shit. It was distasteful and he didn't like to bring it up.'

'Quite understandable,' said Gary, nodding.

The door opened and Jess came in. 'Have you had your pills?' she asked me urgently.

'Er, no,' I said.

Jess tutted and looked at her watch. 'I'll get them,' she said, rolling her eyes and reaching up to the shelf above the bread bin where there was an array of brown bottles.

'I'll go and check the lawn for badger poo,' said Gary. And with that he left.

'You're looking pale,' said Jess as she unscrewed the first of several bottles.

'Well,' I said, looking at my watch, 'only two hours till the first guests start arriving.'

'Albie is already here,' said Jess, shaking out my dosage. 'He wants to help. He's with the others setting up in the barn. I thought that if he hands out champagne or something, it'll be a nice way to meet everyone.'

'Oh,' I said, swallowing hard. 'Great idea. How good of him.'

'Here,' said Jess, handing me a glass of water and a small saucer with several pills on it. 'Down the hatch.'

I took them and swallowed all five at once. 'Thank you, matron.' I handed the empty saucer and glass back to her. 'I'd better go and say hello to Albie.'

'Yes, why don't you? He'd like that.'

I found Albie in the barn where all the food and drink was being prepared. Lights had been put up, ovens and fridges plugged in. A small generator chugged away behind the far wall. Six attractive young waiters of Latino origin were busy polishing glasses and folding serviettes. Their dark eyelashes wafted up as I entered and twelve sultry eyes assessed me. Albie was amongst them, second from the left, clearly flirting with the most muscular of the waiters. He put his cloth and glass down.

'Richard!' he said, moving around the table, his hand outstretched. 'How are you?' he asked, as we looked each other up and down.

'I'm doing well,' I said, with a smile.

'Me too,' said Albie, with a slightly forced enthusiasm. 'I'm having a fantastic time at Bristol.'

'Good,' I said. We looked at each other in disbelief. It was hard to comprehend that we had been lovers, albeit briefly. It seemed a lifetime ago. There was nothing about this superficial, hard-eyed boy that I found attractive. The desire had curdled, maybe because of the time and events that had occurred since we last met. Who could say? It didn't much matter.

'It's great that you're well,' said Albie awkwardly.

'Listen,' I said, aware that I could only hold my happy smile for a few seconds longer, 'I'll see you later.' I clasped him by both shoulders and gave him a manly pat. 'Great. Really great,' I said as sincerely as I could.

I was relieved that I no longer felt anything for Albie, or he for me, but I still had a sense of foreboding. I tried to put such negative thoughts aside. This was my party and I was determined to enjoy myself. Perhaps a quick glass of champagne would put me in a better frame of mind.

The champagne for the guests was still on ice but I found a bottle of Laurent-Perrier Pink in the fridge, took it upstairs and opened it, then poured into the glass by my bed. I could see Fran pacing about the lawn. The party was scheduled from 1 pm to 8 pm. Half the guests would be arriving by cars and Fran had offered to be the chief car-park attendant. He would line them up in three neat rows on the front lawn. The two Portaloos, male and female, were nestled discreetly under the fir trees at the farthest end from the gate. The front border was brimming with pink and white foxgloves together with deep royal-blue delphiniums and hot-pink lupins. Another seventy or so guests were arriving by coach.

I looked at my watch. It was time to descend and prepare to greet my guests.

Twenty minutes later I was feeling pleasantly spaced out and enjoying my second glass of champagne. The loyal Gary was at my elbow and we had positioned ourselves a few yards inside the side gate where the guests were filtering through. From this position I was able to meet and greet everyone once they'd been parked and photographed by Fran on the front lawn and given a glass of champagne by a waiter. A big trestle table covered with a red gingham cloth was close by and any gifts that were given were then handed to Gary who stacked them on there to be opened later.

One of the first through the gate was Julian Clary, looking a little heavier around the jowls than in his heyday and accompanied by an old lady in a wheelchair. This must be the woman he wanted me to meet.

'Happy birthday. You have been in the wars, haven't you?' he said as he shook my hand rather limply.

'Yes, I have rather,' I said managing a smile. 'But I'm well on the road to recovery now.'

'The house is looking very smart. You've done a lot of work on it. Allow me to introduce Miss Creyse,' he said, gesturing to the lady in the wheelchair. She had an open, rather simple face, mottled with sunspots, topped by a frizz of white hair. She was wearing a floral dress a little too large for her shrunken shoulders. Nestling on her lap was a stylish, if faded and stained, red silk clutch bag.

'How do you do?' I said.

'Very pleased to meet you,' she said in a surprisingly deep voice.

'If you are experiencing any bumps in the night, Miss Creyse may be able to explain them for you,' said Julian mysteriously.

'Oh, really?' I said, surprised. It was the very subject I wanted to discuss with him, but, to my frustration, now was not the time. I couldn't get drawn into a long conversation when there were people lining up waiting to say hello. I also wasn't sure how much I wanted to share with Julian Clary of all people. 'Well, we must make a time to have a really good chat.'

'Miss Creyse used to—' began Julian but was interrupted by a tall silver-haired man slapping him on the shoulder.

'Hiya, Julian, how are you?' asked Paul O'Grady, another near neighbour it had seemed rude not to invite. They gave each other a theatrical kiss on both cheeks, making sure they didn't actually touch. 'You've got a nerve showing your face around here in polite company,' he berated Julian. 'You used to be seen falling out of the Walnut Tree at all hours and showing your arse in the car park.'

'I did no such thing!'

'Yes, you did. You lowered the tone of this village. Now we have a man of culture and breeding at the Old Manor. Thank goodness,' he said, bowing respectfully to me. 'People round here can hold their heads up high once again.'

'One of the reasons I moved to the other end of the village was to get away from you,' Julian retorted, raising his voice to match Paul's. 'It was like living next door to the Dingles. And I don't think you're in any position to talk about culture and breeding.'

'Just cos I wasn't born with a silver spoon up my twat doesn't mean that you're any better than me.'

They could clearly have continued like this for hours but Paul suddenly looked over my shoulder, yelled 'Celia!' and darted off. Across the lawn in a beautiful pink chiffon dress and white gloves was Celia Imrie.

When I turned back, Julian and his elderly companion had melted into a cluster of other guests and our conversation, mercifully, was over.

'We've lost him for now,' said Gary with a sigh of relief.

Jess was bobbing around with a clipboard ticking off guests as if we were all at school assembly. I told her she could calm down and enjoy herself; it was all going swimmingly.

A little later I was chatting to the director Chris Renshaw and his charming partner when Marcia made her entrance. I recognised her voice from several yards away, shrieking with excitement.

'Where is the birthday boy? Where is my darling? Richard!'

I turned to see her sailing towards me in a white sequined kaftan and a huge straw hat, clutching the biggest bouquet of pale pink peonies – each the size of a small cabbage – I had ever seen. She flung the flowers at a startled Chris so she could embrace me urgently.

'Ah, dearest Richard. That feels sooo good!' she said. 'I could cry with pleasure. Happy birthday, peanut. What a fab party!'

'Marcia, thank you,' I said, inhaling lungfuls of her heavenly jasmine scent. 'Beautiful flowers.'

Chris said he'd take them to the kitchen and put them in water and his boyfriend trotted after him.

Marcia looked about at the milling crowds. 'Everyone seems to be here. How fabulous! You look so much better than when I last saw you.' She threaded her chubby arm through mine, leading me down to the far end of the garden towards the new thatched swing and grabbing two glasses of champagne from a passing waiter without even looking at him.

'I feel pretty good,' I said. 'Legs play up sometimes, but they're fine once they get going.'

'That is a *miracle*, darling. And you know I've always found a limp rather attractive in a man.'

'How's Percy?'

'A sweetheart. There's a sale on at Majestic Wine, otherwise he'd have been here.'

We both laughed as we sat down on the swing and began to sway gently backwards and forwards.

'This is such a splendid way to celebrate your half century,' said Marcia, as we watched the guests in all their garden-party finery. 'Let it be the beginning of the new Richard. Time to start living again,' she said gently, giving me an encouraging nudge. 'See how loved you are?'

'By all my friends, at least,' I said.

'That sounds rather cynical.' Marcia looked quizzically at me.

'Part of living is working, that's all,' I said with a sigh. 'I'd like to work. It's a shame that nobody wants me.'

'But you know they do,' she said, frowning.

'What do you mean? I'm a complete has-been. You haven't called me for months.'

'I knew it!' said Marcia, almost spilling her champagne with indignation. She went pink on the apples of her cheeks, like a painted Victorian doll.

'What's the matter?' I asked, alarmed. Marcia didn't often get cross, but when she did her voice took on a steely tone that could send shivers down the spine of James Bond.

'That fucking bitch!' she said, now bright red with anger.

'Who?'

'Jess, that's who. Every time I call she answers the phone. Didn't she pass on my messages?

'No. Not a word.' I was confused.

'You've been offered all sorts of interesting parts. Polonius in *Hamlet* at the National. Toad in *Toad of Toad Hall* at the RSC. A part in the remake of *Peyton Place*.'

'You're kidding!' I said, amazed.

'Did she not even mention *Celebrity Come Dine With Me*?'

'No!' That was too much.

'I'll kill her!' said Marcia. She put her glass down and put her hands over her ears as if to stop the steam from escaping. 'She told me you weren't interested in working ever again. That you wished to be left alone. You were planning to become a recluse.'

'Jess said that?'

'Yes. I was surprised to hear about this party quite frankly.' Marcia picked up her glass again and took a big swig. 'It was only when Fiona Bruce told me at the BBC Current Affairs shindig that she was coming, that I rang Jess and asked if my invitation had been lost in the post. She sounded rather sour about it, but she sent one eventually. Otherwise I wouldn't even be here today!'

'Maybe she was protecting me,' I said weakly. Could Jess really have been turning down all these offers without even consulting me?

Marcia shook her head. 'You do realise you have placed your career, if not your life, in the hands of an over-bearing, conniving lunatic? I have been telling you this for years, decades. Even after she has a breakdown and is confined to a psychiatric ward you refuse to believe me!'

'But she's been so marvellous since the accident. Really she has, I don't know how I'd cope without her,' I said, realising suddenly that those words were beginning to sound a little hollow. The conflict between Marcia and Jess would never be resolved, I'd always known that, and up until now, I'd put Marcia's attitude to Jess down to jealousy. But, the thought occurred to me: perhaps there was more to it than that. Perhaps I had to listen to Marcia and Fran, and even Albie, and accept the evidence they offered me. Maybe it was time to open my eyes and ears. I stared down into the fizzing champagne in my glass.

Marcia put her hand on my arm. 'Richard, what you do about Jess is up to you. There's work waiting for you if you want it. But just look across the lawn. Is your answer not right in front of you?'

I followed her gaze and saw the slim, relaxed figure of Fran waving to us from several yards away. We both waved back.

'He is the answer,' she said very clearly and precisely.

'I love him,' I stated simply.

We paused while we watched him smiling and welcoming new arrivals.

'I know you do. So why don't you do something about it?'

'Like what?'

'Marry him. Make it official.'

'I don't think Fran could live with Jess, though,' I said.

Marcia raised an eyebrow and stroked my leg gently. 'Then don't make him. It is the perfect way to get rid of her. You and Fran are settling down. Jess needs to move on. End of.'

'But after all these years?'

'She is a sinister presence,' said Marcia seriously. 'You know how sensitive I am to these things.'

We sat in silence while all of this sank in. A civil partnership with loyal, lovely Fran and the gentle removal of Jess? I let out a sigh of pleasure at the prospect. God bless Marcia, she had such wonderful ideas.

Tomorrow, I decided. Tomorrow I'll ask Jess about what she's been up to. And if necessary, I'll talk about us going our separate ways. Marcia's right. It is time for a fresh start.

Scene Seven

Early autumn 1931

Noël

Noël was alone in the drawing room, his parents and Aunt Vida out on a drive, and Jack asleep upstairs, still recovering from his recent jaunt in London, which he said had completely exhausted him. While Jack slumbered, Noël was savouring the peace and sketching out dialogue for his new play, *Design for Living,* a piece that had been welling up inside him for a long time. Into this play he was pouring all his conflicting thoughts about sharing love with more than one lucky recipient, although he had a feeling that the Lord Chamberlain would be less than approving. Still, he would deal with that when it came to it – perhaps avoid trouble altogether and open in the States. In the meantime, he was lost in the delicate love triangle between Gilda, Otto and Leo.

When the telephone rang, he was quite startled and stared at it for a while, until he remembered to reach out and answer it. It was a perplexed Lornie.

'Just want to check a few of your – or rather Jack's – out-going expenses,' she said, her voice raspy down the line from London. 'He's spending at quite a rate. Five new suits in a week? Almost a hundred pounds at Claridge's? Lunches at the Ivy with, I'm told, David Herbert, who seems to go everywhere with him at the moment, and twenty-five pounds for a set of cufflinks that were then driven from the jewellers to Goldenhurst by taxi?'

'Oh dear,' said Noël lightly. He glanced down at his cuffs where two gold ovals inlaid with mother-of-pearl glimmered. 'Such an extravagant man! But they are rather lovely. They were waiting for me when I arrived here – a welcome-home present. Engraved too, which was very touching. Very, very chic.'

'I just think—' began Lornie.

'Well, I wish you wouldn't think,' Noël snapped, shutting her up quickly. 'It wasn't something asked of you when you applied for your position. Of course Jack spends my money. He is, after all, a *bona fide* member of the team.'

'As are we all, oh Lamb of God,' said Lornie wearily.

'Just remember, Lorn, dearest,' said Noël. 'Fine words butter no parsnips.'

'Your parsnips are your own affair. I'm just here to issue the cheques.'

'Quite,' retorted Noël.

'So Rose Bud Cottage in Cherry Lane, Aldringham is a team purchase too, is it?'

Noël was flummoxed. 'What?'

'Didn't Jack tell you? I thought it rather odd, as you hardly need another cottage – or do you?'

'I don't think so,' Noël said slowly, his mind racing. 'You'd better tell me all about it, dear.'

Using his power of attorney, Jack had apparently purchased the modest property in Noël's name and signed it over to Alice Creyse, no less. The little maid who had gone white at the sight of him. He told Lorn as brightly as he could that he was sure there was a good explanation and then laid some time on the sofa, staring into space, wondering why Jack would do this without telling him.

He remembered the strange conversation between Alice and Jack he had seen only the previous evening. It was odd, he couldn't pretend it wasn't, and now it looked as though they were in cahoots. Had Jude left a note naming Jack as his corruptor, which Alice had found and now she was blackmailing him? Perhaps Jack was trying to protect him from the maid's extortion. Or – ghastly thought that he could hardly bear to allow into his mind – had Alice seen what happened the night of Jude's death? Was Jack buying her silence? And what about what the inspector had said about the mark on his head? It was Alice who had sworn blind the bump had occurred before the accident. Had the cottage perhaps been payment for that vow?

Oh God, this awfulness hasn't gone away! Noël thought, his face creasing up with worry. He couldn't bear it. But he simply had to know.

He said nothing when Jack came downstairs refreshed from his nap but only watched, particularly when Alice came in to serve them all tea that afternoon, although the girl seemed perfectly composed and there was no sign of any secret communication between her and Jack.

After tea, they went for a stroll in the garden, inhaling the scent of the last of summer, feeling the chill in the air and seeing the first crisp, pale orange leaves on the grass.

Noël said casually, 'You haven't really told me about London. How was it? Did you go to marvellous parties every night?'

'It's been crazy, as usual.' Jack assumed a serious expression.

'Much of it was work, of course. I talked to a lot of people on your behalf.'

'Did you have lots of fun with *David*?' Noël asked lightly, his gaze sliding over to assess Jack's reaction.

'I'm not going to answer that. I saw lots of friends.'

'And spent rather a lot of money. You do like to write cheques on my account, don't you?' Noël sighed. 'But then . . . why not? If it makes you happy.'

'We have a certain style to keep up. When do you come back to London? They're all dying to see you again.' Jack plucked a late-blooming white rose and slipped the stem through his jacket lapel buttonhole.

'I shall be swinging from their chandeliers very shortly,' Noël assured him. 'We're beginning rehearsals for *Cavalcade* next week. You and I can go back together.'

They said nothing for a while as they climbed over a rickety stile into the orchard. Then Noël said delicately, 'My dear, it's been pure delight to have you back . . .'

Jack smiled at him lasciviously. 'Last night was a rather hot reunion, I thought.'

Noël smiled back. 'Yes. Yes it was. But something's troubling me. Lorn called today and told me about Rose Bud Cottage.' The two of them stopped walking and Noël turned to face Jack, noticing a flush along his lover's cheekbones visible under the tan, and a look of annoyance. 'You must have known I'd find out. What is that all about? Why on earth didn't you tell me about it, at least?'

Jack's gaze slid away and he looked uneasy. 'I didn't want to trouble you with it.'

Noël reached out and took hold of Jack's hand. 'Now, Jack,

that's not good enough. You may trouble me whenever you like, especially when you're spending considerable sums of my money. A cottage for Alice the maid? What next – a gypsy caravan for the chimney sweep? I find it strange and I find it sinister. Tell me why you'd buy the maid a cottage?'

'I knew you'd think that!' Jack raised his voice. 'That's why I didn't say anything.' He looked furious and tore a strip from a young cherry tree. 'Listen, I've talked to Alice. I felt incredibly sorry for her. She was going to get married to the man she loved and her whole life, suddenly, has changed: her future has been taken from her. Now she's got no fiancé, no future beyond working herself to the bone, and she's heartbroken, doesn't want any other man. It doesn't matter that it was an accident, I still feel guilty about it. So I thought . . . well, I thought it was the least we could do. This way she's got some kind of compensation, right?'

'I'll say,' Noël replied dryly. 'You've compensated her very generously indeed.' He stared straight into Jack's black eyes. 'Tell me honestly – is there anything more to this than just your tender heart?'

'No,' Jack said emphatically. 'I promise. I swear on my life.'

Noël searched his face for any clue that he was being lied to but there was none. 'Very well,' he said at last. 'But I think that's enough for young Alice, fond as I am of her. The tragedy must be put behind us now. It's time we all forgot about it.' But Noël was quite sure of one thing. He couldn't bear to see Alice any longer. She reminded him too forcefully of Jude's tragic death, his own feelings of guilt and, worse, his dark, secret suspicions of Jack's involvement. She would have to go, and that was that.

When they got back to the house, Noël summoned Mrs

Ashton and asked her to give Alice her notice, giving her a month's wages in lieu so that she could leave right away.

'Coming to work here every day must be a terrible reminder for the poor girl. I feel, faultless though her work has been, that I must let her go.'

'I see,' said Mrs Ashton so passively that Noël guessed she knew about the cottage and perhaps sensed that there was quite another reason for Alice's dismissal.

'I'm not feeling too well, I hope Alice understands that I don't say goodbye,' Noël added. 'And could you see about finding someone else, Mrs Ashton? Maybe someone homely? Though obviously not Irish. Thank you so much.'

Mrs Ashton nodded to Noël and headed for the kitchen looking grim-faced.

Well, thought Noël to himself. I surprise myself sometimes.

A week later, with suitcases on the drive ready to be loaded into the car, and a tearful fond goodbye to his mother, Noël and Jack were about to set off to London. Noël, too, had spent restless nights at Goldenhurst and was ready for the more easily explained disturbances of London life, not to mention the start of rehearsals for the latest show. They took one last stroll about the lawn while they waited for the chauffeur to bring the car round. Hearing an engine pull into the drive, they turned, expecting to see the chauffeur in the Jaguar, but instead there was a police car. The door opened and Detective Inspector Keaton emerged, striding purposely towards them.

'Oh, Christ. It's that idiot policeman,' said Jack, frowning. 'What can he possibly want after all this time?'

'We shouldn't mock the afflicted,' cautioned Noël, before

adding, 'I suspect he may have been dropped on his head at the age of forty.'

The inspector raised his hat as he approached the pair. He turned and nodded at the pile of smart leather suitcases. 'Off somewhere nice, gentlemen?'

'A place called London,' quipped Noël. 'Have you heard of it?'

'Yes, I have, sir. A place, I believe, where anything goes?' replied Keaton with a sly half smile.

'I wish *he'd* go,' muttered Jack under his breath.

'You really ought to visit and see for yourself. Maybe pop in to Savile Row and treat yourself to a new suit? Now, to what do we owe the pleasure of your call?' asked Noël, trying not to rise to the inspector's bait but failing rather. 'It's been some time since we saw you.'

'Rude of me not to call in sooner, but I've only just heard the happy news that you are back. Both of you.' Keaton looked a little sour. 'On my patch.'

'Somehow we've managed without you. But to leave it so long is very cruel of you. A crime, some would say. Jack and I have been crying into our pillows all week.' Noël couldn't help rolling his eyes a little.

'*That's* not a crime, no. But I'm sure you're aware that some things very much are.'

Noël gave a tinkling theatrical laugh. 'Oh, Inspector, I have no idea what you're talking about.' He glanced over to the driveway. 'I see the Jaguar has arrived. We really must be setting off now, if you'd be so kind.' He gestured towards the cars and the chauffeur loading their luggage into the boot.

'I'll only keep you a few moments longer,' said Keaton, digging his heels into the lawn, quite literally.

'The business with Perkins was closed months ago,' said Noël, his tone a little sharp. 'What else can there be to discuss?'

'Well, now,' said the inspector, taking a small, circular stroll around Noël and Jack with deliberate slowness. 'Look at the situation from my point of view. I am, first and foremost, a policeman. Upholder of the law. I'm also a moral man, sir. A man who knows what's right and what's forbidden, not just by the law but by a higher authority. What goes against nature.'

Noël looked at his wristwatch, trying to ignore the nausea that lurched suddenly in his stomach. 'Please, Inspector. I am due at the Dorchester for a meeting . . .'

The two men stared at each other with thinly veiled contempt.

'Yeah, we gotta go,' said Jack.

'I won't delay you much longer. It's just that sometimes in my line of business, one investigation leads to another . . . Funny how that happens. And I've heard reports that your relationship is one that might not stand up before the law, or before the Almighty.'

'What can you mean? What is this impudence?' Noël's voice was freezingly haughty. 'Servants' tittle-tattle, Inspector? I'm surprised at you and I don't intend to listen to any more of your insinuations. Good day to you, Inspector. Come, Jack.'

The two set off across the lawn towards the Jaguar, aware that they were being keenly observed by Inspector Keaton.

'One more thing,' he called out, before they had got more than five steps away from him. They stopped in their tracks and turned to face him.

'What is it?' asked Noël with a sigh of exasperation.

'I'm sure you gentlemen both know where the law stands on the crime of *unnatural acts* between two men? Even in private?'

'The only unnatural thing that happens in this house is

Mrs Ashton's scrambled eggs. As hard as billiard balls,' retorted Noël.

'Your nosc is twitching up the wrong tree, Inspector,' said Jack suddenly finding his voice, speaking firmly and with confidence. 'I'm Mr Coward's business manager, and nothing more.'

'Oh?' The inspector looked disbelieving. 'Well, my dear sirs, I don't know if that's strictly accurate. And let me tell you that if I suspect you two are up to no good, I shan't hesitate to step in on behalf of all that's moral and decent. I hope I make myself clear.'

'Perfectly,' Noël said in a withering voice. 'Good day to you.'

In the car on the road to London, Noël was shaking and outraged, appalled by Keaton's vulgar insinuations. 'As if it matters!' he cried. 'As if it's any of his business, the ghastly man. He has no idea about life and love, none at all. Does he want to deprive me of comfort, affection and pleasure for the span of my natural life because it offends his petty notions of what's decent?'

He went on at some length, his tongue becoming sharper and wittier until he was lashing Keaton and all of his kind in the most fearsome Coward style.

At last Jack interrupted him, saying quietly, 'I'm going back to New York. Alone.'

Noël's heart sank, and his gloved hands tightened involuntarily into fists. 'But why? Don't leave me!'

Jack turned to him. 'You know why. We can't give that frightful man any grounds to accuse us. He might be vulgar and pathetic – probably repressed, the amount of interest he's taking in the whole thing – but he's also the law. He could make life very nasty for us, and if he hinted to the press that you were in trouble . . . well, it's just the kind of scandal they like.'

'But what shall I do when I hear strange noises in the night and you're not there?' Noël asked, with a longing look.

'If I'm not there, then there won't be any strange noises,' Jack replied with a devilish smile. Then he grew more serious. 'Can't you see? We have to live separately for while. He wants our scalps. I can feel it. If he can't pin Jude's accident on us, then he'll get us for unnatural practices.'

'Buggery?'

'Not just now, thank you.'

So it really was as serious as that; even Jack's wisecracks couldn't hide it. Noël said fearfully, 'My dear – would he?'

'I think he's desperate to,' Jack said grimly. 'And that's why we've got to steer clear of the place for a while. And why we should be apart. If I go to the States, we've got proof we're not living together.'

'But if we're in London, how can it matter?'

'I'm telling you,' Jack said stubbornly. 'It's for the best. I mean it.'

Noël stared unhappily out into the darkening evening, watching the countryside fly by the Jaguar's windows. Was Jack telling the truth? Was he returning to New York in order to protect Noël? Or simply to live the high life on Noël's money, without the constraints of having his lover nearby? So that he could drink himself silly in peace?

'I'll hate it, but I'll have to let you go,' he said softly.

'You'll thank me for it in the end,' Jack replied. 'I mean it – I'm doing it for you.'

Scene Eight

Richard

My birthday party was going splendidly. A couple of hours in and everyone was enjoying the luxury buffet, served by the handsome Latino waiters, and the music had been changed to a Noël Coward compilation. I realised Gary was no longer by my side. I scanned the lawn to see if I could see him and spied Julian Clary's elderly companion alone in her wheelchair, parked by the wall in the shade. I felt a pang of sympathy for her, so I wandered over to ask if she'd had something to eat.

'Yes, thank you,' she said with a kind smile. 'I had six of those lovely prawn wraps and some salad and four – or was it five? – mini-cheesy things. Delicious. I'm just having a break before I tackle the pavlova. I get a bit of indigestion sometimes. Very annoying! I have to make sure I don't eat my food too quickly or I repeat on myself.'

I sat down on the lawn next to her. 'So tell me,' I said, 'how do you know Julian?'

'I met him outside the post office soon after he moved in here. My shopping bag disintegrated and I had tins of peaches and bread rolls and tomatoes running all over the place!' She laughed at the memory. 'Luckily Julian helped me. Very kind of him. Then he took me home to my little cottage.'

'You live here in the village?'

'Yes, that's right, dear. Lived here all my life. I've only ever been as far as London and I didn't like it much I can tell you.'

'I don't blame you. I find I'm much happier down here. Julian said you had something to tell me, I think,' I said, warming to her.

'I don't know about that, dear. He probably thought you'd be interested to know that I worked here when Mr Coward was here.'

I felt an immediate spark of interest. 'You did? When?'

'Not long after he first moved in.'

I stared at her disbelievingly. 'In the twenties?'

She nodded. 'I was just a scrap of a girl. Not quite sixteen.'

'Then you must be . . .'

'I'm expecting my card from the Queen this year.' She smiled and I saw for the first time how very old she really was. 'But I seem to have all my faculties. Just don't make me laugh or I'll leave a small puddle on your lawn.'

One of my hands went involuntarily to a cufflink. The synchronicity was extraordinary. A gift that had been given from Jack to Noël. Now here was a flesh-and-blood link to the past. 'So,' I said almost breathlessly, 'You must have known them both – Noël and Jack . . . Jack Wilson.'

Miss Creyse looked around furtively as if to check that no one was in earshot. 'Oh yes. I worked here, in this very house, as a maid for Master Coward and Master Wilson. Two bachelors living together, but we didn't mind. I was so young, I didn't understand about such things. It was all very quiet to begin with, but that soon changed. Mr Coward's parents and his aunt moved in. Then there were the parties. We were rushed off our feet, but it was lovely meeting all the famous people and seeing all the carrying on. Goodness, they knew how to have a good time. It took Mr Coward a few years, but he had this place looking lovely. We all loved working for him. Mr Wilson – Jack – he could get a bit tetchy and loud when he was in drink, but he was American, so we put it down to that.'

My darling Jack. He was the one possessed.

'Then you must have known . . . Jude,' I said, pulling the name out of the depths of my almost-faded memory. That was the name Noël had mentioned when he'd told me of the under-gardener.

A strange change came over the old woman. She jerked upwards sharply and her mouth gaped open, showing worn, yellow teeth in pink, shrunken gums. 'Jude?' She looked as if she were about to cry. 'But how did you know? How did you hear about Jude? No one has said that name to me in seventy years . . .' Her voice grew even deeper, almost a retch.

'I'm not sure,' I said. I wasn't quite ready to admit to anyone that Noël Coward had come to visit me in an out-of-body experience. 'Perhaps I read about him. Didn't he die tragically, drowning in the pond?' I didn't want to distress the old lady further, but the words were unstoppable. I needed to know if there was a real truth to the slivers of memory that were slowly surfacing in my misty mind.

The old woman stared at me, terrified and shaking. 'How did you know?' she almost hissed. 'Who told you?'

'I'm sorry. I don't know whether to . . .' My words faded and I said no more, but stared into the old lady's eyes,

Beneath the heavy, slanted, desiccated lids, her eyes were a faded blue and filled with tears. 'He was my intended,' she said in a rasping voice. 'We were going to be married. The handsomest boy you ever did see. We were very happy. Then he drowns and they said he'd done himself in. A moment of madness in the middle of a freezing night in January. The coroner ruled it was an accident but everyone in the village always said it was suicide.' Her hand reached out and grasped my arm, the withered fingers only centimetres away from the shining oval cufflink. 'But the policeman didn't think so, and neither did I.'

'What did you think?' I asked slowly.

She paused dramatically and then said, '*They* did it.'

'They?'

'They were both guilty! One was making my Jude do unmentionable things, and the other let it happen. And when my lad wanted to stop it all, Master Wilson made sure that he would never be able to tell.'

My mouth dropped open. 'You think . . . *Jack* killed him?'

The old woman nodded. 'Why else would he buy me a cottage to live in, if his heart wasn't black with guilt? "Alice," he said, "it's the least we can do for you now you've lost your precious boy." So that's how I got my little house.' Her face contorted. 'Blood money. But I was poor and young, I wasn't going to turn it down.' Alice gazed at the house and I could see she was struggling to keep control of her emotions.

'Is it difficult to talk about the past?' I asked, trying to take it in.

'So long ago,' said Alice, shaking her head. 'But it feels as if it was yesterday. The heart never mends. I found him, you see. I'd come to work as usual at six that morning. I went outside to get the coal and I looked straight at him. His face was like a rock sticking out of the water. Just the chin, lips, nose and forehead sticking up, his eyes open. He looked so shocked. I think I screamed then. I found myself in the water too, trying to reach him, to get him out. Mrs Ashton pulled me out. Then the old man – Mr Coward's father, I mean – he was there, then lots of people. I can't remember much after that.'

'Was Jack there?' I asked, suddenly eager to learn whatever I could from her.

'Jack . . .' Her expression darkened. She opened her mouth to say something but was interrupted before she could get anything out.

'Miss Creyse! There you are!'

A squiffy-eyed Julian Clary came dashing over, a bottle of champagne clutched in one hand, and some of the contents dribbling down his chin. 'Oh, my goodness, I thought I'd lost you!'

'I'm here,' muttered the old woman, looking a little put out.

'Miss Creyse was just telling me about the old days,' I said, irritated at Julian's badly timed appearance, not to mention the embarrassment of an inebriated guest at my elegant party.

'Ah yes, Noël! Gertie! Prince George of Kent!' Julian shouted, sloshing more champagne on the grass and over the wheels of the wheelchair. 'Happy days. But now, Miss Creyse, I have to get you home.' He let out a sudden burp. 'Excuse *me*,' he said with a sniff. 'This isn't vintage, clearly.'

'Maybe some coffee?' I offered.

'Don't be silly,' snapped Julian, signalling to a waiter to bring him another bottle. 'Don't mind if I take one home with me, do you? One for the road, as they say at the Three Cocky Sailors. I've just seen Miss O'Grady mincing down the road with a crate of cider under her arm. I'll wheel Miss Creyse to her cottage, then I'll be back.' He gave me a wink and lowered his voice. 'I want to ask you about how the ghost is treating you.'

'Ghost?'

'Yes. You know. The ghost of Goldenhurst. The one that bangs and crashes and farts. I thought I was living with Louis Walsh for the first fortnight. Don't tell me you've not been bothered by it?'

'Oh . . . well . . .' I tried to laugh nonchalantly. 'Now you mention it, Noël has been rather difficult to live with.'

'It's not Noël, silly,' Julian said, putting down his glass and gripping Miss Creyse's chair. 'I'll tell you who it is later. Bye for now!'

Fresh bottle of champagne wedged into the side of the wheelchair, Julian set off with Miss Creyse, weaving his unsteady way towards the gate. He was in such an inebriated state I rather doubted he would make it back later. A shame, in a way. I rather wanted to hear what it was he had to say. And I would certainly be looking up the old woman. There was more to uncover about her story too.

By six o'clock the party was going well and my guests were all enjoying themselves or so it seemed. The friends and family were mixing happily with the celebs, and the atmosphere was happy and jolly. My sense of foreboding had faded away. In fact, I was feeling rather light-headed, probably from the effect of several glasses of pink champagne on top of my medication.

Fran came and found me where I was lazing in the Indian tent by the herb garden, chatting to Dame Judi.

'I need a word,' he said quietly, so I followed him out on to a quiet bit of lawn. 'I'm sorry, Richard, I have to go to London. It's work.'

'What? Now?' I said, dismayed.

'Yes. They've got an emergency.'

'But we haven't cut the cake yet,' I said plaintively.

'I'll wait for that, and then I'll have to go. Sorry. It's an urgent matter to do with deliverables. You wouldn't understand. I'll be back as soon as I can.'

'What constitutes an emergency in your world?' I asked bad-temperedly. 'Has someone mislaid their laminated action list?'

He smiled at me. 'Don't get snappy on your birthday,' he said, offering no further explanation. I couldn't be cross with him. He'd given up so much for me already and was only just getting back into the swing of his career. Besides, following my conversation with Marcia I was seriously thinking I ought to marry this man. If he'd have me.

'Have you talked to Albie?' he asked.

'Yes. That's all over. Completely.'

'I know.' He smiled again. 'It's a fabulous party. Happy fiftieth.' He kissed me on the lips.

Jess banged on a gong to summon us all to the patio, where a marvellous cake topped with a firework was wheeled out, spitting golden stars into the air, as Beethoven's 'Ode to Joy' played on the speakers. Everyone gathered round and sang Happy Birthday to me, and then applauded. David Tennant called out an imaginative suggestion for where the candles might go later, and I made a short speech.

'Thank you all so much for coming today. It is lovely to see you. Could we have a round of applause for Jess for organising such a fabulous party?' After a prolonged, vigorous clapping, I encouraged everyone to 'Eat, drink and be merry! I'm fifty and I'm alive!'

More applause and a splattering of party poppers.

Jess passed me a fresh glass of champagne, everyone toasted my fiftieth and the cake was carried off to be cut up. Then Fran came to say a quick goodbye. Gary had vanished off somewhere, no doubt shagging a waiter in the barn. I looked around for someone else to chat to but suddenly the drink got the better of me.

'Richard?' Jess was at my shoulder, concerned. 'You look done in.'

My legs were aching from the unaccustomed hours of standing up, and I felt myself wilting under a blanket of exhaustion.

'You need a lie down,' she said. 'Come on, come with me. You can have a quick rest and come back down to the party later. No one's going to miss you for half an hour, don't you worry about a thing.'

Bed seemed a marvellous idea. A short nap would refresh me. 'You'll tell people where I've gone?'

'They'll understand.' She put a hand at my waist and began to manoeuvre me back towards the house. I could barely keep my eyes open.

'Come on, Richard,' she coaxed.

I put one foot in front of the other but it was a struggle. I hadn't felt this bad since the early days of walking again.

'Help me, Jess,' I whispered.

'I'm right here,' she said firmly. 'Lean on me.'

Scene Nine

1931

Noël

Following the opening of *Cavalcade* (attended by the King and the Queen, no less) and enough parties and soirées at his new Belgravia apartment to last a lifetime, Noël could think of nothing nicer than to pack his bags and sally forth to exotic new destinations.

When friends asked where Jack was, Noël said carelessly that he was looking after the American side of things.

'He's working on my next Broadway opening. The worry is that I may open before I get there.'

When Lorn came over from her Burton Mews office, always kept immaculate and decorated with playbills of Noël's productions, she listened to the true side of things.

'I need him,' Noël said, pacing back and forth between the pale sofas with their brown-and-white zebra print cushions. 'I'm desperate for him . . . and yet – I know what he's up to over there. Everyone does. I have to pretend that I don't care he's sharing an apartment with David Herbert, and chucking my money around like birdseed.'

'Dear little Dab,' said Lorn, using Jack's old nickname, 'does so like to *grab* . . .' She consulted her notebook. 'Ten cheques today, perhaps fifteen tomorrow—'

'Guaranteed to drench my bank account in sorrow,' finished Noël. They'd always like to speak in rhyme to each other and it kept his lyricist's mind sharp.

'Do you trust him?' Lorn asked abruptly. She was sitting neatly in a low chair in her customary plain dark dress. Behind her a lavish arrangement of hydrangea bloomed on the grand piano.

'With what?' countered Noël.

'With your feelings.'

'Like I trust a cat with a pork chop, darling.' Noël stopped pacing and stared at the carpet. 'But I love him, and there's not much I can do about it. Perhaps that's half the fun. But it is rather wearing me out.' He stood wondering for a moment if he should confide his other, darker worries about the events at Goldenhurst, but he couldn't bring himself to voice them out loud. Instead, he opened a silver box on a side table, took out a cigarette and lit it with a very slightly shaking hand.

'You must be careful of your health,' ventured Lorn, noticing. 'You know what happens when you become too nervous, too strained . . .'

'Indeed I do.' Noël looked at her gravely. 'I pop my cork like a bottle of over-agitated champagne and make a frightful mess. And that's precisely why I plan to go travelling. I have a play to finish, and I need to see the sun. Desperately. I'm so thin and pale. Look at my arms: they could be mistaken for candlesticks! I'll go this month and I won't think about coming back for a good, long while. I'll meet Jack in the States, and we'll see how the land lies then. Could you arrange it all?'

Lorn gave a compliant bow and reached for the telephone. 'That's what I'm here for, Master. You must be laid out in the tropical heat and fed macadamia nuts by naked youths with rings through their noses as a matter of urgency. Leave it to Lornie.'

Noël had a smart leather travelling photo frame that folded open like a birthday card. A picture of his beloved mother – smiling for the camera (but looking somehow reproachful at the same time from under the brim of an expensive hat) – occupied one side, and on the other was a photograph of Goldenhurst taken from the top of the knoll across the field. Wherever Noël found himself on his travels, be it a suite at the Cathay Hotel in Shanghai or on board the Queen Mary, the pictures were with him, on his desk. He bid his mother a fond goodnight each evening, but looking at Goldenhurst made him frown. It had, of late, become such a troublesome house and each time it seemed he might be returning home he extended his trip and stayed away for longer, partly because Jack wasn't there, but also to stay well away from the snooping detective and the threat he represented. Sometimes Noël lay awake at night under his mosquito net and his imagination ran riot. He saw himself being led out of the house in handcuffs by a smiling Cecil Keaton, then baying crowds outside a courthouse shaking their fists and finally the heavy clank of a cell door slamming behind him.

Maybe I can never go home, he thought, in those small hours when his darkest fears were at their most believable. Keaton is waiting for me, compiling his evidence even now, planning to arrest me the moment I set foot on British soil.

Sometimes he turned on the lights and lit a cigarette, chiding himself for allowing such peculiar thoughts to take over his mind.

If they started arresting all the homosexuals in the world of show business, there would be no one left. How dare that sordid little man in his grubby coat occupy his thoughts? In the circles in which Noël moved, everyone understood and accepted that what might happen in private was all part of the artistic temperament. It was positively chic, for goodness' sake. His estate in Kent was an extension of Noël's exclusive, liberated world. The idea of having small-minded provincial policemen loitering at his gate year in and year out was intolerable. Noël even had a dream one night that he shot Keaton with a hunting rifle and buried him on the marsh. He woke up smiling but drenched in sweat.

In the morning, though, as he dived off his terrace into the warm sea of the Pacific Ocean, Noël's paranoid fears were washed away, and channelled into his new play about alternative lifestyles. This he decided would be his answer to DI Keaton – *Design for Living*.

By the time Noël reached San Francisco, he had finished the play, and he showed it to Jack when he met him off the boat.

Jack, smiling at the final scene when the three friends embark on their shared life together, pronounced it a triumph.

'Outrageous . . . but a triumph.'

Despite the scorn Noël felt for Keaton and his ilk, the sense of safety and refuge at his beloved home had been tainted. He would stay away, he decided, until Keaton's lascivious interest had died down. Besides, Noël had his suspicions about who might have enlightened him as to the true nature of the bedroom arrangements at Goldenhurst. He left the old house to the care of his parents and Aunt Vida.

Instead, Noël immersed himself in work and travel: life was too furiously busy, with new revues and songs to be written, and Hollywood to woo and be wooed by. They wanted to make a film of *Private Lives*, and of *Cavalcade* too. Noël was at the top of his game, as rich and famous as it was possible to be, and genuinely stimulated and excited by the wonders of the world. If there was a reason he kept on moving, no one would speculate about it in his presence. He was positively erupting with creativity and inspiration, and while there were those like Lorn and Violet who feared there might be a price to pay for all this relentless travelling and working, they were helpless to recall the roving minstrel against his will.

Noël left Britain for months at a time, visiting his friends the Mountbattens in Greece and seeing the world, preferably the hot bits, before returning to New York to prepare *Design for Living*. He and his old friends the Lunts – Alfred and his wife Lynne Fontanne – were taking the starring roles, and it would open on Broadway that year. Noël returned home occasionally to write or to settle disputes between his squabbling family, but the long run and US tour of *Design for Living* kept him in the vice-like grip of what seemed to be endless success. He was away from Jack for a great deal of the time too, but as if to make up for the way their hearts seemed to be drawing apart, Noël bound Jack closer to him in business: they formed their own production company and Jack had ever greater say in Noël's professional life, and an even bigger stake in its profits. Time slipped through their fingers in a whirl of new projects and ambitious undertakings; with every year, Noël underlined his genius with new plays, revues and songs.

He never seemed to stop. Coward was the man with the golden pun.

*

The summer of 1935 was particularly beautiful, the perfect time to spend at Goldenhurst and with the years that had passed since poor Jude's death, it was the right time to return and reclaim it. Noël, home at last after sojourns in Hollywood and more exotic travels, had written *Tonight at 8.30*, a cycle of nine one-act plays, with the intention of showing them in the autumn. Gertrude Lawrence was to be his co-star, and she arrived that August to stay at the Old Manor and rehearse.

'I'm not really a rustic person,' she told Noël, holding a handkerchief over her nose as he drove her to Goldenhurst from Ashford Station. 'I don't have to share my room with a goat, do I?'

'That would be extra,' Noël replied. 'But I have put a cowpat in your bed so you feel at home.'

'Always so thoughtful,' said Gertrude, with a sigh.

Jack took a steamer from New York and joined them, and the three of them spent idyllic days together. The Cowards and Aunt Vida were on their usual month-long stay at the seaside, so there were no squabbles or squawks to disturb the peace, and Noël felt that he and Jack were recapturing some of the bliss they had always felt at the old house. They didn't speak of other infatuations or infidelities; instead they revelled in being reunited. They made love tenderly at night – the wild passion perhaps spent, but the love still remaining – talked for long hours, and Jack sat in on the rehearsals, advising and criticising. After all, he was quite the theatre man now – a producer and director in his own right, setting up revivals of Noël's plays across the States.

While Noël and Gertie delighted in each other's company, and while it was a treat for both of them to be together again, there were times when things became fractious.

'Surely,' said Gertie one afternoon when they were rehearsing 'Has Anybody Seen Our Ship?' after a liquid lunch in the garden, 'you can't rhyme "peculiar" with "hallelujah"?'

'I already have, I think you'll find,' asked Noël icily.

'Well, it doesn't work. And you'll upset the Archbishop of York,' said Gertie.

'Then the Archbishop of York can *fork* off,' replied Noël, pouting.

'I'm going to lie down!' declared Gertie, flinging her script down petulantly on a chair. 'You're being obtuse, I didn't get a wink of sleep last night and my room is positively alive with mice! Scratching and scrabbling till all hours. Unbearable!' She sailed out of the room.

'Let's go out, Jack,' Noël said, once the breeze created by Miss Lawrence's departure had died down, drawn by the shimmering heat and the bright blooms in the garden beyond.

'Take some deep breaths,' Jack said soothingly. 'She's quite a number.'

'Mmmm,' said Noël, not really listening, but turning his face to the sun and smiling as the healing rays warmed his skin. 'That's better.'

'Gertrude is great but . . . jeez,' said Jack, guiding Noël gently by the elbow so they could continue their stroll across the grass without Noël needing to open his eyes.

'I shall rise above our little spat, worry not,' he said.

'You're the star. You don't have to put up with her,' said Jack.

Noël stopped and shaded his eyes, looking at Jack. 'I beg your pardon?'

'You heard. On Broadway if someone questioned the script

and then stormed out like that they'd never be allowed back again, that's all.'

Noël gave a short laugh of disbelief. 'I beg your pardon? Are you suggesting I give old Gert her marching orders?'

'No, no,' Jack protested. 'It's just kinda disrespectful.'

'I shall endeavour to put it out of my mind,' said Noël politely.

The pair wandered further down the lawn and entered the orchard, where plums, pears, apples, damsons and greengages hung from every heavy bough. Noël found himself wondering which branch it was that Jude might have banged his head so heavily on, but chose not to discuss his thoughts with Jack. It was a long time ago now, after all, and they never mentioned it to one another.

'You should come back to the States,' Jack said eventually.

'No doubt I will very soon,' said Noël, wondering if this was Jack's way of saying he missed him.

Jack paused for a moment and then said, 'Well . . . there's a girl I want you to meet there. An actress.'

'Theatre or film?' Noël asked. 'Does she do comedy?'

'Er, film. Both probably. She's a Russian Princess. Got a kinda Garbo thing going on. Soulful eyes, adorable nose.'

'She sounds hilarious. How's her English?'

'Not great. She has an accent you could use as a doorstop. But she was in *Sylvia Scarlett*, the Cukor film, and she knew her words backwards.'

'As long as she didn't say them that way,' Noël sniffed. 'I've heard of it, but didn't see it. Nor did anyone else, I believe. Kate Hepburn was in it, wasn't she?'

Jack nodded. 'Natasha did well, she's as pretty as a picture. I'm just saying you'd like her. A real party girl.'

'She sounds very decorative. No doubt she has some lovely fur hats too.' Noël's eyes narrowed as he looked over at Jack. 'And she is as rich as princesses generally tend to be?'

Jack shrugged idly. 'I guess she's not exactly poor.'

Noël's expression became suddenly quite sad. 'I see. I see. Well, you must introduce us as soon as possible. She sounds quite the thing. Now, let's go inside and see if Gertie's had enough beauty sleep yet.'

'Jack, hurry up! We'll be late.' Noël pulled on his linen jacket and made his way out to where the car was waiting. They were on their way back to London. Gertie had gone ahead of them, and they would resume their rehearsals in town.

As he came out of the house, he stopped short, astonished to see the familiar figure of Detective Inspector Keaton lounging against the gate. Immediately he felt sick, and a horrible sense of being a hunted animal clutched him, but he regained his composure swiftly and sauntered forward. 'Inspector. What a pleasant surprise. It's been an age. I can't think how I've managed all this time without your charming presence.'

'I was told you were back, sir,' Keaton said, resolutely ignoring Noël's ironic tone. 'You and your friend.' He raised his eyebrows. 'Still as close as ever are you?'

'I wonder who told you,' Noël returned coolly. He reached for a cigarette and lit it, letting a fragrant plume of smoke escape his lips before he added, 'A little bird by the village green, perhaps. These little birds do seem to harbour their resentments. Perhaps I should have kept her in her cage.'

Keaton shrugged lightly. 'That makes no odds.'

At that moment, Jack came loping lightly out of the house,

putting on his Panama hat. He stopped abruptly when he saw who Noël was talking to, and then approached with caution. 'Good day, Inspector. What do you want? Surely it can't be anything to do with Perkins, can it? That was over four years ago.'

'Of course not, sir,' Keaton said. 'The coroner recorded misadventure, and there was never any evidence otherwise. I'm here on another matter, along the lines of what we spoke of before. You see, I'm told you gentlemen are sharing a room.' A look of distaste crossed his face. 'That you are engaging in unnatural practices.'

'What a horrible job to have, spying into the private lives of others,' Noël said haughtily. 'And you are quite wrong.'

'That's not the information I have.'

Jack stepped forward. 'Well, your sneaky little informant is wrong. Miss Gertrude Lawrence has been here the entire time and can vouch for us. And there's something else that will put pay to these nasty rumours. You see, I'm engaged to be married.'

Noël couldn't help giving a small gasp and turning sharply to stare at him.

'What?' said Keaton, frowning.

'That's right,' Jack replied coolly. 'Here. I have a picture.' He took out his wallet and produced a small snap that showed a glamorous blonde in an elegant black dress, white gloves and a string of pearls, smiling at the camera.

Keaton looked at it, his mouth open. 'Very nice.'

'Her name is Princess Natasha Paley. She is a member of the Russian imperial family, and a movie star. I have her number in America if you'd like to place a call and ask her for the truth. She'll be more than happy to confirm our engagement.'

'I apologise,' said Keaton, more than a little flustered.

'Congratulations to you and your intended. Have a good trip, gentlemen.'

Moments later they were in the back seat of the Jaguar and setting off at last for London.

'Why on earth did you tell such an outrageous lie?' hissed Noël, gripping Jack's knee and whispering so the driver didn't overhear the conversation.

Jack stared out of the window for a moment and then gently unhooked Noël's hand from his knee, giving him a wintry smile. 'It's not exactly a lie.'

Noël was speechless, his face draining of colour. 'What do you mean?' he managed, when he'd regained some ability to speak.

'It's for the best. I mean it. You'll thank me one day.' Jack turned away to stare out of the window again, and neither spoke again for some time.

ACT V
Scene One

Richard

I awoke in complete darkness, and very uncomfortable. I had no idea where I was or how I had got there. I gave an involuntary groan and registered that I was extremely thirsty. First I tried to move my arm but a searing pain in my shoulder stopped me almost immediately. I groaned again. I peered into the darkness but there was only a small chink of light coming from some way over to my left. I could smell damp and hear a steady drip echoing around the space. The pain from my shoulder throbbed and I began to realise that something was very wrong. Had I fallen down some *Alice in Wonderland*-type hole? The last thing I could remember was the party. Talking to guests. It was my birthday. We'd had the cake. I'd been feeling very tired. So where on earth was I now and why couldn't I move?

I attempted to shift my left leg, but it was stuck fast to the right. I was so dazed and confused I closed my eyes again and hoped I'd wake up soon. This must be one of those unsettling dreams that seem real and distressing but soon pass. I'd probably wake up in a hammock in the garden at the Old Manor and find I'd slept awkwardly and my arm was twisted underneath me. But as I lay there, willing the pains in my shoulder and legs to go away, I heard a noise besides the steady drip of water. Breathing. Someone was nearby inhaling and exhaling quickly in an agitated fashion.

'Hello?' I said. There was a slight echo but no reply. I tried again. 'Hello? Is there someone there? Can you help me because I don't seem able to move.'

The sound of breathing deepened. Whoever was there was now taking deep, satisfying breaths but saying nothing. Suddenly a bright light was turned on, the beam shining directly into my eyes from a few feet away.

'Aah!' I cried involuntarily. My eyes burned with the sudden shock of whiteness and I clamped them tight shut. 'Don't, please!'

The light continued to shine. Whoever was there was clearly enjoying my discomfort. An audible sigh of satisfaction could be heard and the torchlight moved up and down my bound body as if admiring the handiwork. With the light diverted from shining directly into my eyes, I caught a glimpse of thin plastic bound around my legs. From that, I guessed that my wrists must be similarly restrained behind my back. The rough, tight sensation around my neck, I reasonably supposed, was caused by more rope. I looked to my right and caught a glimpse of dirty, sooty bricks: the cellar. That's where I was, the cellar underneath the kitchen. But why and how? And who on earth had imprisoned me here?

'Are you going to tell me what is going on?' I asked.

'We're going to have a little chat, Richard. When I'm good and ready,' said a voice I recognised at once. 'We need to discuss your medical insurance. Your near-death experience in France, together with the reconstructive surgery on your face and the nonsense with your hips and legs has more or less used up what little goodwill PruHealth had towards you. How they'll cope with blindness and amputated toes I cannot say. Such ailments have not been authorised and you may have to throw yourself on the mercy of the NHS. Rather a comedown. Still, it may not come to that.'

So it was Jess who was holding me prisoner in the cellar. Her tone was extraordinarily matter-of-fact, as if she believed we were discussing an admin matter up in the office. The talk of amputated toes and blindness I didn't understand but it frightened me.

My mind raced. Jess was clearly in the grip of some kind of an episode, a new version of her previous breakdown. I had to keep her calm at all costs. I'd read that in hostage situations it was important to keep the kidnapper talking, to remind them of your human feelings, to build a rapport. But surely this was somewhat different, as we had known each other for many years. If I kept Jess talking though, I could assess her mental state and perhaps work out a way to calm her.

'Jess,' I began tentatively, 'do you think you could explain to me where we are?'

Jess's voice came low and steady through the darkness. 'I knew this cellar would be perfect the moment I heard about it. When I gave you your anti-inflammatory pills I slipped you a temazepam in along with them, and another two in the champagne with which you toasted yourself. I made sure Fran was summoned back to London on urgent business. The moment you became wobbly I led you through the house and down here. Rope, gaffer tape, plastic ties and sacking hood were all laid out ready. It couldn't have been simpler.'

This was terrible. Fear churned through me. 'Did no one wonder where I was?'

'Of course they did. And I told them you had too much to drink – against doctor's orders – and I had to put you to bed. It all seemed perfectly reasonable.'

'So it's just you and me now?'

Without answering, Jess moved across the cellar and flicked a switch. A soft, 40-watt light came on and we blinked at each other. Then she said, 'Yes, Richard. And the moment of reckoning has come at last.'

She walked slowly towards me. I was still feeling drowsy and my judgement was not what it might have been: I thought perhaps she was coming to untie me, but it wasn't until the last minute that I saw something glisten in her right hand. She loomed over me. Suddenly, viciously and without warning, she slashed at my face. A sudden, sharp pain struck me like a lightning bolt and I cried out.

Jess grabbed my jaw tightly with her other hand. 'Damn. Missed.'

'What are you doing?' I cried, my face stinging.

'I was aiming for the scar. Hard to miss but I rushed it. Hold tight.' She held what I now saw was a Stanley knife close to my eyes, pushed my head roughly back so it banged against the cold, wet wall. Slowly this time, like a surgeon performing an incision, she pressed the blade deep into my quivering cheek. I couldn't speak but a high-pitched groan reverberated from my heaving chest as I felt the hot blood run down my cheek.

'That's better,' she said satisfied, taking a step back to admire her handiwork.

I began to fight, first trying to bend my damaged legs, my bare feet reaching under me to trying to grip the rough bricks, but it was useless. I was bound at the knees and, as it soon became apparent, almost everywhere else, the ropes holding me against the wall by some rusty, old, gangrenous pipes. Jess laughed as I flailed around.

'Do stop whimpering like a child.'

'Please,' I said, the blood now in my mouth, choking me. 'Please, Jess, think of all the years we've worked together. Don't do this. You're unwell. Let me go and we'll get you some help. You need to be looked after. I—' I couldn't speak any more; the pain and blood trickling down my throat into my lungs prevented me. I slumped, coughing, back on the ground, my damaged cheek resting in a cold, rancid puddle and I cried quietly, afraid to express the agony and fear that I truly felt.

'So,' said Jess, pacing up and down the length of the cellar, circling the light bulb as if she were an actress in a Neil Bartlett production. 'If you can shut the fuck up for five minutes I'll tell you what I'm going to do to you and why.'

'Jess,' I interrupted. 'Get me a doctor. I'm going to bleed to death.'

'Shut up. That's just a little scratch for starters. Entirely symbolic, in fact. Don't you see what I've done? I've opened an old wound. Do you get it?'

'Ah. Very funny,' I said. 'That's enough now.'

'I disagree. Look at this.' She leant over me again, lower this time as I was on floor level. Because she was blocking the meagre light source I couldn't see much and the blood from my cheek was now running up and into my eyes, blinding me. 'Know what this is?' she asked, as if she was a primary school teacher addressing her pupil.

'No,' I said bitterly.

'Well, I'll tell you, shall I? A very old, rusty piece of iron. From the look of it I'd say it was part of an old coal shovel. This was where they kept the coal in Noël Coward's day. I expect you know that. It has lain down here, discarded, slowly corroding, decade after decade. But now I've found a use for it. Shall I explain?'

I didn't answer.

'My first plan was rather lovely. There was a fabulous article in my *Woman's Weekly* entitled "I Lost All My Limbs to Septicaemia". Some man cut his hand while removing a manhole cover. It turned out the manhole cover hadn't been touched for about a century and was poisonous – within twenty-four hours all the toxins began to spread through his system and his body went into shock. Long story short – he had to have both arms and legs amputated!' Jess laughed with delight at the conclusion of her story. 'That was my vision for you – limbless, blind, disfigured, but alive. I call that charitable. And rather amusing. Like an amoeba or a baby panda, waggling your pitiful stumps in the air. Quite sweet, in a way.'

I managed a cry and then a 'Please . . . Please.'

'But then I thought – where will I keep you? No doubt poor stupid Fran or that frightful Marcia would get in the way. They'd come sniffing about, demanding to see you. It was always so much nicer when it was just the two of us. Do you remember?' She sighed nostalgically. 'So I'm afraid it has to be death by slashed throat. But I'm going to use this old piece of iron to do it. And I've got a selection of freshly sharpened knives standing by if your skin turns out to be thicker than I thought.'

'Why?' I whimpered, terror building up in me inch by icy inch.

'Don't you know?' Jess sounded surprised. 'Well, let me see . . . Is it the twenty-five years I've worked for you with barely a thank you? No.' I could tell from Jess's tone of voice that she was going to reel off a great, long list of possible transgressions.

'That's not fair,' I gurgled. 'I . . . I'm so grateful. I told you.

I thanked you. I took you all over the world, gave you presents. I paid you! What more did you want?'

'Oh,' said Jess with relish. 'I wanted a whole lot more.'

Through my bloody eyes I was aware that Jess was reaching down to pick up something else.

'What's that?' I asked, flinching.

'A screwdriver,' said Jess casually. 'All my instruments tonight are pleasingly symbolic. Poetic, I like to think.'

I began to plead with Jess. 'No, Jess. Don't do this! Please stop.'

'Stop?' She raised her voice. And the screwdriver. 'Don't spoil your Duke of Gloucester moment.'

'Earl,' I corrected. I knew my *King Lear*.

'Earl of Gloucester,' hissed Jess.

'And you're the Earl of Cornwall?' I asked fearfully.

'Duke!' snapped Jess, beginning to press the tip of the tool into the corner of my eye.

'Screw you,' she said quietly. 'Just like you screwed my son.'

In the midst of all my fear and pain, I sighed. At least I now understood.

'Oh, Jess,' I said. 'I'm sorry, you don't need to—'

Jess silenced me by pushing the screwdriver in an inch and then flipping the handle up. Somehow I managed to turn my head before the eyeball was lifted out of its socket. We both screeched now, Jess with frustration, me with terror and agony. She began a banshee-like wail, stabbing repeatedly at my face and grunting with satisfaction after each hit.

'Albie isn't careful . . . he leaves his phone lying about, unlocked. I found it and I took a look. Some pictures of his A-level celebrations, that's what I thought I was going to see. But what was it instead? Filth. The two of you, in bed together. You and my son! All cosy and romantic. I decided to kill you right there. What mother wouldn't?' she screamed, almost incomprehensible, jabbing at my bloodied face with each word. Small fish-eye wounds opened up all over my cheeks and forehead as I did my best to twist and turn out of the way. I yelped with each stab, the pair of us almost wrestling with each other, face to face, her weight upon me now, my blood spurting and showering her with every hit. I longed to pass out, to die, to escape from this torture, but it went on and on until both of us were delirious and the noises we made no longer human.

Eventually a blood-soaked Jess collapsed, sobbing on the floor next to me. I was barely conscious but I stirred and stopped breathing when I heard Jess's next terrible sentence. It took her several attempts but eventually she managed to form the words.

'Albie. He is your . . . son!' she said and then she slowly rolled away from me into a dark corner of the cellar, sobbing pitifully.

Scene Two

1938

Noël

Noël was explaining to his mother that Jack would be arriving that afternoon.

'With his *wife*?' asked Violet, sinking slowly on to a chair.

'Yes, Darlingest. Princess Natasha Paley. Or Wilson, I suppose she is now. His wife.'

'I see,' said Violet, blinking slowly. 'If a gypsy had told me a year ago that Jack Wilson was going to marry a Russian princess, I'd have given her a slap for her trouble.' After a moment, she said, 'And is she a real princess?'

'The granddaughter of Tsar Alexander II, no less. First cousin of Nicholas II and all those poor murdered Romanovs.'

Violet shook her head. 'He has done well. Is she pretty?'

'Pretty?' shrieked Noël. 'She's even prettier than me!'

'Never!' said Violet, shaking her head vehemently.

'She's a society beauty, a fashion model, film starlet; a blonde, beautiful goddess.'

'But has she got that extra something that you – that Jack – seeks in a man? I mean, a woman.'

'Well, cunning of you to ask, but I am not in a position to know the answer. Word is that neither of them has stopped drinking since he said his vows three months ago.'

'Oh dear.'

'I fear, Mother, that the weekend may be a little trying. It's lucky that Aunt Vida is away, I'm sure she'd only add to the tension.'

'And your father can't cause trouble, not any more,' added Violet.

'No. That's a blessing. Although I could have sworn I heard his bicycle the other night, outside my window.'

Arthur had died quietly in his sleep (and almost unnoticed) the previous year. He was buried in the local churchyard but Noël had been too busy to attend the funeral. The general feeling was one of relief that they needn't bother about him any longer.

Noël looked at his watch. 'They should be here in a few hours. I shall go and check that Mrs Ashton put some flowers in the French room.'

As it happened, whatever he may have heard about Jack and Natasha, it was Noël who was doing the drinking that day. He had more than two glasses of port after lunch to calm his nerves as he waited for the royal couple to arrive. This was the first time he would be alone with them. He had been at the wedding in New York, of course, but that was amongst all the other guests and he'd managed to slip away right after the speeches and before the mingling began, to avoid any awkwardness. There were questions he longed to ask Jack but he wasn't sure if he wanted to know the answers. A chasm had opened up between them ever since Jack had first mentioned his engagement to Natasha. All at once, things had become brittle and superficial and they hadn't been able to talk properly. Everything had changed.

'I'm doing this for you,' Jack had pleaded with him over a crackly telephone line from America in the weeks before his wedding. 'I don't love Natasha, I love you. This is to protect us. Don't you get it?'

'Just like a headmaster tells the boy it is for his own good before he gives him six of the best?' Noël had replied bitterly. 'Is it her money, Jack? Weren't you content with siphoning all you could from me? Is that it?'

'Don't be ridiculous,' Jack retorted, and would accuse him of not trusting him. But Noël could not believe Jack would really go through with it and when he did, there was no way things could ever be the same again.

Jack and Natasha arrived just after four o'clock, all cheery and loud and fragrant, Jack in a cashmere coat and Natasha draped in furs despite the relatively warm weather. As soon as they were out of the motor, they were hugging Noël and even kissing Violet on both cheeks. She could have coped with this but as she was halfway through a curtsey at the time, she almost crumpled to the floor at the merest touch from the princess. Noël scooped her up in the nick of time and sent her off to lie down before dinner so that he could have a little time alone with the newlyweds.

'Welcome, my darlings! Just fling your hats and coats in the air and let us take tea on the terrace,' said a suspiciously ebullient Noël.

'It is luffer – luffingly?' said Natasha in her thick Russian accent as they settled themselves on the comfortable, cushioned wicker chairs on the sunny lawn. She was quite superbly beautiful, with luminous, sorrowful eyes and a perfect profile. Her hair had been lightened and curled by Hollywood but her exquisite dress sense and grace was all her own.

'Lovely,' translated Jack.

'Thank you,' Noël replied to Natasha before glancing at Jack who was drinking in the view across the marshes. Then Jack closed his eyes and tipped his head backwards, lifting his face to the sun. He gave a little groan of pleasure.

'That is so good,' he said. 'Hot, Kentish sun on my tired, Yankee cheeks.'

'Vanky?' asked Natasha.

'No, Yankee. American.'

'You vank an American?' She seemed very matter-of-fact about it.

'No. Just forget it,' said Jack, a touch irritably. 'Why don't you go find our room and freshen up?'

'Force one up?'

'No. *Freshen* up.' He mimed washing his face and then explained, with a lilting, musical delivery, as if to a five-year-old: 'Clean fucking face, you stupid Russian cunt.'

'Ah! Cunt! This I understand!' Natasha suddenly lashed out and cuffed Jack across the top of his head with her clenched fist.

'Whoa there, Mamma!' said Jack, ducking instinctively, but shuddering from the glancing blow.

Natasha glowered at him, stood up and flounced back inside through the French windows.

Jack and Noël were alone at last.

'Are you in love with her?' Noël said.

'Terribly.'

'Good.'

'We met at a house party in Aspen.'

'Very cold, Aspen.'

'You're looking very lovely in this damned sunlight, Noël.'

'Don't say any more. You're making me cry so dreadfully.'

The two men laughed together at their witty routine.

'So. You did it. Just to spite me, I suppose,' remarked Noël once their mirth had subsided, a sudden coldness to his voice.

'Pardon me?' said Jack wearily. 'Spite you? Hardly.'

'Well, it serves you right if you did. She doesn't appear to understand basic English. How on earth do you get her to turn over when the time is right?'

'We manage, thanks for asking.'

'Does she know about us?'

'Does anyone not?'

'Then what was the point? Besides the buckets of roubles?'

'You know why. You'll thank me in the end. Can't you see? We're perfectly safe now, beyond the reach of Keaton's nasty little spying grasp.'

'Perhaps,' Noël answered.

'Did you see the rumour in the *New York Post*? That you and Garbo are having an affair? I had a copy sent over.' Jack lit a cigarette and puffed out smoke with satisfaction. 'I arranged that. Another little distraction for prying minds.'

'Poor dear Greta – what an unsavoury thought.' Noël laughed and changed the subject.

That was the first conversation: a little barbed, but playful nevertheless. Perhaps, Noël thought, it wouldn't be so difficult after all. Was there a chance that Jack was right – that they could carry on despite the presence of a wife? That Natasha was there simply to provide a shield for them?

We shall see, he thought.

Natasha appeared alone at 7.30 pm to join Noël and Violet for cocktails in a glittering black gown with a low-cut back that exposed her shoulder blades and a hint of the knobbles on her spine. That made Noël think again about what the two must do in bed. Could Jack really perform with a woman? How on earth was it possible? She was beautiful but Noël felt no more desire for her than he would for a porpoise, perhaps less. He shuddered inside. It was unnatural. It didn't bear thinking about.

'Darling, what can I get you?' asked Noël, lighting a cigarette and giving his mother a reassuring pat on the arm as he got up to greet his guest.

'Vodka, of course!' said Natasha, throwing her arms out wide so suddenly that poor Violet flinched.

'On the rocks?' Noël asked innocently.

'No, Jack just fell asleep.'

There was no guessing what she thought he'd said, so he gave her plenty of ice and handed her the drink. She took it, and then danced around the room, spilling her drink on the carpet and humming to herself.

'Beautiful!' she cried, whirling about, almost taking the Dresden piper with her as she went.

'High as a kite,' Noël murmured to Violet as he passed the stuffed Italian olives around.

'I luff London. There are so many great big *pricks* there,' a wide-eyed Natasha was saying.

'Oh,' said Violet, contemplatively.

'Everyone can use them. They are free!' Again, the arms went up.

'I think you might mean *parks*,' said Noël gently.

'That is what I said, of course!'

'Natasha, darling, sit down. I can't afford for you to swing about much more. Ah, here is Jack. Thank goodness. It's time for dinner.'

The dinner was something of a disaster. Jane, the maid recruited to replace Alice some time before, dropped the vegetable dish as she came into the dining room. She then burst into tears and ran out of the room without clearing up the broccoli and runner beans strewed across the carpet and still steaming. Then, just as they were making do with dauphinoise potatoes and roast partridge (greens being off the menu), all the electric lights went out and they spent the rest of the evening swathed in candlelight. There were a couple of strange bellowing noises from the cellars, too. Noël knew he hadn't imagined the noise this time because Natasha clutched her priceless pearls to her elegant neck and gasped with surprise. Declining dessert, Violet stood up and announced that she was retiring for the night.

'See you all tomorrow,' she said, waving a gloved hand as if she were in a first-class carriage heading out of Charing Cross.

Soon after, Natasha, having been hyperactive and somewhat incomprehensible for ten minutes at least, appeared to pass out, forehead on the dining table and snoring loudly.

'How adorably talented she is,' said Noël tartly, cocking an ear to where she lay. 'I do believe she's doing an impersonation of a common grey seal.'

Jack stood up and in one movement hoisted his noisy wife over his shoulder. 'Natasha thanks you for a wonderful evening,' he said formally, her limp arms over his back, swinging like pendulums. Five minutes later he was back, without his jacket or tie. He poured two large brandies and passed one to Noël. 'Just the two of us again. Like the old days.'

'Like the first time we came here,' Noël said softly. 'Do you remember? Let's go outside and look back at the house, like we used to.'

Although rather windy, there was a full, bright moon and they went out through the French windows and wandered across the grass to the croquet lawn. They sat on a bench that faced the house, where candles twinkled at the windows and the low fog-horn of Natasha's snores pulsated through the darkness, mingling with the occasional hoot from a barn owl.

Jack placed a hand on Noël's knee and gave an encouraging squeeze.

'I think not,' Noël said dryly, crossing his legs. They heard a distant rumble of thunder.

'I see,' said Jack, peering into his brandy glass. 'Worried that Inspector Keaton is watching us from the bushes still?'

'It wouldn't surprise me. He still comes sniffing around like a beagle from time to time.'

'Tell him I got hitched, just like I said I would. I'm a red-blooded man. It'll stop all the speculation.'

'Greater love hath no man . . .' Noël said wistfully.

A sudden gust of wind caused the curtains on the French windows to billow out onto the terrace and dance, up and down, like a pair of leap-frogging ghosts. A candle on the windowsill flared up and was then extinguished and a slate suddenly flew off the roof and clattered noisily on the path.

'God-damn house,' muttered Jack.

'Perhaps it doesn't like you,' remarked Noël, and another, closer clap of thunder boomed in agreement.

'It's a fucking house, that's all. It can kiss my ass,' responded Jack indignantly.

Noël chuckled. 'Whenever I return to Goldenhurst after trotting around the globe as I do, the house and land seem to envelop me in a warm and lovely welcome. But then as soon as you show your face—'

He was interrupted by loud Russian screams coming from the upstairs window.

'Natasha!' called Jack and ran towards the house.

A couple of chaotic minutes later everyone gathered in the lounge by the fire, the distressed foreign visitor crying on her husband's shoulder, and Violet, in hairnet and paisley dressing gown buttoned up to her neck, pouring tea.

'It's happened in that room before,' she said, as if that would be a comfort. 'My dear departed husband wouldn't set foot in there. Said it was haunted.'

It seemed that a vase had inexplicably flown across the room, dousing the princess in carnations and cold water.

'Maybe you were thirsty, and in your half-asleep state, mistook it for a glass of water?' suggested Noël, patting her dripping head with a towel.

'I vas sleeping!' said Natasha indignantly. 'Flowers by vindow then – hoar!'

'Hair!' corrected Jack, ignoring the tea and helping himself to the brandy decanter.

'Anthony Eden claims he had his bottom pinched in that room. I blamed Marlene, but maybe I was wrong,' said Noël thoughtfully.

They managed to calm Natasha down but she and Jack abandoned the French room and spent the rest of the night in the second-best bedroom. There were no more disturbances after that.

*

The next day, after an early lunch, Jack announced that they were heading back to London.

'Natasha doesn't think she can do another night here,' he said apologetically.

'Sank you,' she said, 'but I vant big pricks again.'

'I quite understand. Don't we all?' said Noël, secretly relieved that his guests were leaving earlier than anticipated. The goodbye with Jack wasn't painful this time. It was, in fact, quite desirable. Let him go off into this strange new life of his. There was no place for Noël there any longer and it was better simply to forget about it.

That afternoon, blissfully free of visitors, and with Violet dozing in her armchair, Noël went to his desk and within minutes had sketched the outline for a new light comedy.

'This house has given me a rather thrilling idea,' he told Violet as they tucked into their lamb chops that evening.

'Oh, Snoop, how lovely!' replied Violet, her eyes twinkling with affection. 'I thought you looked rather happy.'

'A newly married couple in a country house,' began Noël, relishing his mother's rapt attention. 'But a spiritual medium visits them and summons the ghost of his first wife, Elvira.'

'Then what?' asked Violet.

'Much hilarity ensues, is all I am able to tell you at this stage. But I do have a title.'

'Yes?'

'*Blithe Spirit.*'

'Oh, Noël!' exclaimed an excited Violet. 'It sounds wonderful.

'Thank you,' Noël replied modestly. 'I hope everyone else agrees. I have a feeling we're all going to need a laugh before too long, if things carry on the way they're going.'

'Bad times just around the corner,' declared Violet.

'Quite!'

With a gust of wind, a lump of soot the size of an orange suddenly fell down the chimney and shattered on the hearth, sending a black firework of powder across the room.

'There,' Noël said with satisfaction. 'The house approves. I thought she would.'

Scene Three

Richard

I lay completely still and tried my best to calm my breathing and the quivering, childlike cries that I was making. Jess lay a yard or so to my left, her back towards me, curled up into a ball. She made no attempt to calm her own distressed howls but after what seemed like an hour or more she slowly quietened down. Barely daring to move a muscle, I prayed that she had fallen asleep. Maybe she had taken some of the pills she'd given me as some kind of Dutch courage, or her violent fit had taken it out of her. Whatever the reason, her breathing grew slower and heavier.

What now? I was frightened to move on account of either causing myself pain or disturbing the madwoman who would surely finish me off with her next attack. I didn't know what to think about her ranting accusation. It was not my first concern; that was the screwdriver was still firmly clutched in her hand. I couldn't just lie there and wait to die. I must do something. But what? I had no idea what time it was, but by now I guessed it must be the dead of night. With the lack of activity, my body temperature had fallen and I was cold and numb. I could feel the sticky wetness of my own blood reaching my bound wrists. With the fingers of one hand I began to explore the ties: smooth and hard. Washing line, maybe? I found a knot, pulled too tight for my fingers to loosen. Defeated, I lay there a while longer. A part of me longed for the release and oblivion of unconsciousness, but I fought it. My urge to survive seemed to take over every other sensation or fear. To keep myself awake, and very possibly alive, too, I began to sway slowly from side to side, just an inch either way to begin with. The motion grew and without making any noise, gained momentum. I was delirious, I knew, but even this movement started my blood pumping around my body and more importantly my brain.

Think, I implored myself. This is your one chance.

Suddenly I stopped swaying, stunned by a sudden realisation: although I was trussed up, hog-tied painfully tightly, with my wrists behind my back and my ankles pulled up under my body, there was still a possible way out. The swaying movement had revealed something to me: having tied me up, Jess had not then tethered me to anything in the cellar. I could roll around, shuffle, move! I glanced over to Jess who was now snoring gently, clearly in a deep and demented sleep.

The door to the cellar stairs was just twelve feet away. If I could get a distance away from Jess, I could maybe get onto my knees and from there get a better grip on the knot behind me. I decided I had to try. I began to rock from side to side again and, biting my lip to control the pain that shot through my body, face and eyes with every muscle contraction, I built up the momentum and then gave a minuscule bum jump to the left.

Resting between procedures, I moved five feet in what felt like an hour. I decided that was far enough and gathered my strength. With an almighty effort and a noisy exhalation I pulled myself round and up onto my knees. I opened my mouth wide like a sprint runner, trying to deaden the sound of my desperate, agonised gulps for air.

When I could, at last, control it, I had a terrifying realisation: Jess had stopped snoring.

I knew I had just seconds before Jess woke up properly and discovered my attempted escape. Through my damaged, blood-spattered eyes I looked in horror as Jess rose up onto her hands, coughed and turned to where I had been lying beside her. Then she turned, squinting, to where I now knelt and was on her feet in a second. I did the only thing I could think of and began to make as much noise as possible. First I let out a rather weak, sickly roar. But the second attempt, knowing my life depended on it, was a magnificent, diaphragm-shaking bellow of distress. As Jess flew at me, and before she threw the first of several knuckle-bruising punches; I cried out 'Help! Help!' My voice, given the circumstances, was surprisingly resonant and actorly.

Jess's first punch, smacking into my jaw, was aimed more with fury than with accuracy, and slid over the congealed and scabby surface of my disfigured face and into the darkness beyond. The force of her lunge propelled her forward until she landed in a heap on the other side of me. I seized the opportunity once again and continued shouting. I managed to heave my shoulder against the door and miraculously it flew open. I shouted 'Help! Help me please!' this time facing the door so my voice was carried out into the night. The weak light of the cellar bulb cast a sliver of golden illumination into the darkness outside.

I had no time to say more. Jess was upon me in an instant. She leapt on my back, pulled me over onto my stomach, slapping and punching me into silence.

She leant right into me before she spoke, showing me her

bared teeth between her snarling lips. Her eyes glittered ferociously in the half-light.

'You're staying put. You can't ever leave me. Understand?'

She adjusted her position and then reached across my back and grabbed the rope, jerking it a good two feet outwards, away from me. As an immediate consequence, my head was pulled backwards and my feet reached to meet it. With her other hand, Jess picked up the rusty piece of shovel she had threatened me with earlier.

'Now,' she said. 'Expect a tingling sensation any moment soon.' She raised the jagged remnant and savoured her moment.

'I'm sorry,' I said urgently. 'I shouldn't have slept with Albie. But he made it happen. It was ages ago. This situation is not what you think.'

Jess hesitated. Her arm was raised and she was ready to slash my throat with the deadly piece of metal. She spoke quickly, hardly able to be bothered with spelling out the explanation for what was about to happen.

'I knew you'd say that. But you heard what I said, didn't you? Albie isn't just your godson, he's your biological son. Now do you understand?'

'No, Jess,' I said. 'At least he isn't that. You and I, we've never . . . You know it's just your mind playing tricks on you. I know—'

'Yes, yes, listen to me,' interrupted Jess. 'You have never understood, have you?' She moved the cutting edge closer to her target. My Adam's apple throbbed with fear. 'I have loved you and only you for all of these long years. I used to clear up your bedroom after your nights of lust, remember. I loved you. I was in love with you.' She gently laid the jagged edge on top of my jugular vein.

'This is why I have to do this,' she said, as if pleading for understanding. 'It was twenty years ago exactly – the night of your thirtieth birthday party. You'll recall what a brazen night of flagrant lust that was! The following morning, when you'd gone out with your conquest for breakfast, I took the condom that lay beside your bed. Went to the bathroom and emptied it inside myself and stood on my head for two minutes. I conceived. I gave birth to Albie and you cared for him. As if he were your own. Which he is. As if we were his parents. Which we are.'

I tried to remember the night she was talking about. 'But Jess . . . I don't think that's right.'

'Of course it's right!' she cried. 'I knew you'd try to deny it. That's why I took these, as proof.' From somewhere she produced an ancient pair of underpants, blue with a tiger motif across the front. She looked them almost fondly. 'I've never even washed them,' she said in softer voice.

'I've never seen those pants before in my life!' I protested.

She looked more furious than ever. 'Don't make it worse!' she cried, leaning forward and stuffing the pants into my breast pocket. 'Of course they're yours, don't deny it. You've done a terrible, awful thing. Can't you see you've left me with no choice? I have to administer justice. What else can I do?'

Like an executioner done with the preliminaries, she raised her arm again and prepared to inflict a new, fatal mark on me. She paused and closed her eyes. Just then a tremendous shouting and clattering descended the cellar steps and a silhouette appeared, a thick-set man, hands and legs spread, ready to take on any monster that he could or couldn't see.

'Richard?'

'I'm here!' I cried.

Then there was a sudden flurry of limbs and screams. Jess

screamed and I did too as I was roughly pulled from the ground and up the cellar steps, the cool, fresh dawn air stinging my eyes and my many wounds. My rescuer then abandoned me and rushed back down into the dark and dangerous pit. I gasped for air as I listened to the violent struggle going on a few feet down the stairs. Jess whinnied like a badger in a trap, furiously high pitched and piercing, while another, deeper voice grunted and puffed with Olympian determination. This was the voice that prevailed. When, finally, Jess was silent, my saviour could be heard climbing the stairs and flopping, exhausted onto the gravel beside me.

'Jesus Christ,' said a distorted voice. 'Have I got a hangover or what?'

'Gary?' I asked, incredulous. 'Is that you?'

The pair of us took a while to recover ourselves, sighing with relief before taking in the grim details of our circumstances. Gary looked over my terrible wounds.

'Okay,' he said, trying to sound calm. 'You just rest easy and I'll get my mobile phone. We need to get you to hospital.'

'No,' I moaned, frightened to be left.

'It's all going to be fine now,' he reassured me. 'My phone is in my jacket. Just around the side of the barn. I fell asleep there. I'm afraid the free party booze was all a bit much for me. Unless my drink was spiked. Dunno. But I've been out cold for hours. Until I heard you shouting. You're safe now. Jess won't be bothering you any time soon. She's unconscious. Hold tight here for just thirty seconds. I've got to call you an ambulance.'

'Lock the door,' I said, squeezing Gary's hand.

'Good idea,' said Gary, pushing the cellar door shut and slamming the bolt across.

A few minutes later as I lay cradled in Gary's lap I heard the welcome sound of an ambulance siren piercing through the still Kent night and for the first time I began to think I might live.

'Hello,' Gary said with surprise. 'I used to have a pair of pants like that.'

Scene Four

1953

Noël

Dear Jack,

You will notice at once that this letter is written on black-edged paper. Appropriately mournful, as you will discover. You are probably pausing already to pour yourself a big, fat whisky. Keep the bottle handy – you may need it, dear boy.

As you are aware I can write a play rather swiftly, sometimes in a few days. Songs pop up in my mind almost fully formed, the melody and the lyrics frequently completed in the time it takes a taxi to drive the length of Shaftesbury Avenue. But this letter to you has been longer in gestation than a baby elephant. I have cried ice buckets full of tears simply at the prospect of putting pen to paper. I have stared for hours at the clouds skipping across the skies, gulping like a goldfish, trying to summon the words that will express how wretched I feel. In my professional work I have often been accused and found guilty of being lightweight, fickle, immoral, even. A pleasure seeker who belongs in a world of country-house gatherings and cocktail parties. However I compose a sentence, it seems it can inspire a response no weightier than tinkling laughter and drollery. Well, these pages should be different, much as I regret the fact.

Even now I am beating about the bush, putting off the moment when I write the bitter words that you must know by now are coming. Perhaps I'll just slip them in casually, almost carelessly. It's over. I never want to see you again. There is thunder in my heart where once there was sunshine.

I have come to the conclusion that I am no good at love. It exhausts me and makes me nervous. Eventually. Sooner or later, once it has led me down its twisted path, it leaves me leaden and inert. First, the excitement and the euphoria where eyes glisten and limbs tremble, the paradise of life's meaning found and rejoiced in. Inevitably this cannot last: there is a plateau, a gentler, deeper, less consuming phase where life and love dovetail together. Our days hum with contentment and we slide into glorious nights enjoying hot, scented baths together. But the time comes eventually when a little pool of that water strikes one as slightly tepid. This is the beginning of the end. Love is fading and, try as I might to revive it, it dies in the palm of my hand like a butterfly pulled from a martini glass, flapping desperately once or twice before it lays sodden and still.

You and I were lucky. Our love was sturdier than most and lasted longer. Mainly, I think, because of Goldenhurst. Our charming house in Kent gave love a setting where it could thrive, where nature could let rip. The sun beat down on us in that garden and the part of love that is a life force, the part no one can grasp or comprehend properly, grew and flourished with pagan abandon. It was magical. You remember it, don't you? The house embraced us. It was the only place where we were free. Trying to pinpoint when exactly Eros loosened his grip and allowed our love to begin its descent is difficult. It is such a long time ago, apart from anything else. It may be that one day I withdrew from you a little to immerse myself in the writing of a new play and you felt hurt and abandoned.

Perhaps it was the separation of the war years, with you and Natasha in America and I here in England or off on one of my official jaunts, while Goldenhurst did her bit for the war effort, with soldiers trampling roughly across her soft flowerbeds and a Field Marshal sucking on his pipe in the drawing room – but who knows?

We might as well speculate as to the exact drink you poured yourself that caused your liver to start to curdle. It is quite hard to put this in writing, even though we both know the truth, and I have pleaded and begged you over the years to get some help, but drink is killing you. You're half dead already, Jack. The handsome man I fell in love with is bloated and yellow. And in case you think me unkind, I'll add that the handsome fellow you fell in love with is stooped and nicotine-stained. Such is life, I suppose. And yet . . . love could survive all this. But not other things.

Which brings us to Jude. It occurs to me now that we never really spoke about that tragedy, only in the hysteria of the moment. Not seriously and sensibly. Why was that, do you think? Was it all too upsetting, on every level? It is far, far too late for recriminations and accusations, but you really shouldn't have indulged yourself. That affair put everything off kilter, even before the tragic outcome. Just think of how our lives might have been . . . no suspicions, no Detective Inspector Keaton preparing to pounce on us, no need for you to run away to America, no need to marry Natasha. We might be living happily at the old house now, two cheerful middle-aged gentlemen knitting our own under-garments and growing runner beans.

But Jude did come along, you did give in to temptation and everything changed as a consequence.

We trundled along together for several more decades, though, didn't we? A part of me was always happy to see you. It was, perhaps, just a taste of our former, glorious passion, but pleasant enough, like the delicious scent of a Sunday roast lingering in the pantry long after it has been devoured. I welcomed you and your beautiful if troubled wife into my home, just as you welcomed me into yours. One night when you were three sheets to the wind and Natasha had passed out on the sofa, you followed me to my room and tried to kiss me. I pushed you out of the door and you slumped to the floor crying, telling me you wanted me still, that you'd never, ever made love to Natasha. I don't suppose you remember that. Eventually you cried yourself to sleep, and you stayed there until dawn, snoring outside the door while I trembled inside at the horrible mess you'd made of your life.

But we remained bound together symbolically, through your handling of my American business affairs: a marriage of sorts, in memory of what might have been. There was a comfort in that. Or so I thought.

But now I find out that too was a murky, corrupt, dishonest partnership and it hurts me more than any infidelity or over-indulgence. The dying embers of what was once love and then became faithful friendship were stamped upon well and truly, by you, Jack, in your great big greedy boots. For all your shortcomings, I never once doubted that I could trust you. But I have seen the accounts. You haven't just been incompetent, you have stolen countless thousands of dollars from me. You have betrayed me in the most unforgivable way. My heart is not only heavy, but it is broken. I have done all the crying over you that I can do. It is, finally, over. I never want to see you again and can say with some certainty that I never will.

Noël

Scene Five

Richard

Fran sat beside my hospital bed. I had only just been moved out of the intensive care unit of the William Harvey Hospital in Ashford, but I was still attached to tubes and drips. I had suffered mutilation, a broken shoulder, bruises, shock, dehydration and a fractured femur, all made more complicated by my previous high-impact injuries. In the ICU, I'd developed pneumonia and been at high risk of organ failure, though I'd apparently come through that now. I was still in considerable pain, and only able to see out of one eye. The other was bandaged and they hadn't yet told me if I would ever have the vision restored.

'Well, you've quite excelled yourself this time, haven't you?' Fran said in the dry, reprimanding tone I loved about him. 'I've never known such drama. All I ever wanted was a quiet, productive life. But no. Theatre, films, car crashes, kidnappings, torture sessions in underground cellars. Jesus! Well, I hope you're done now. I seriously can't take much more. Your life makes *EastEnders* look like a Pinter play. We'll both retire gracefully now. Grow vegetables. What do you say?'

'Sounds like pure bliss,' I answered weakly.

'I'm going to read you the newspaper reports to pass the time,' continued Fran. 'You'll be thrilled to know you've been on the front cover of every tabloid and broadsheet for a week. It really is a grizzly story for them to get their teeth into. Here's the *Guardian*. "Actor's assailant was psychiatric out-patient" is the headline.' He began to read aloud. '"Jess Campbell, the personal assistant who last weekend imprisoned, tortured and attempted to kill actor Richard Stent, had sought psychiatric treatment several times over the last year it emerged today.

'"Mr Stent has been in intensive care following the attack, although doctors say he is no longer critical. The incident took place following a party at Stent's home in Kent last Saturday. It is understood that the actor was imprisoned in the cellar of the house for several hours, bound and gagged and subject to a vicious, sustained attack. Miss Campbell was apprehended at the property and is now under police guard in hospital. A friend of Mr Stent who is thought to have raised the alarm is currently assisting with police enquiries."

'Well, they don't know the half of it,' said Fran, closing the paper noisily. 'All we need now is for orphan Albie to sell his story to the highest bidder.'

I had no idea what to say. Fran didn't even know that Jess's motivation was that she thought I was Albie's father. I wanted to tell him and usher in a new age of honesty but I could hardly bear to, it was all so grim. Quite frankly I didn't think he could take another dramatic development. As far as Fran was concerned, Jess had simply lost her mind. In essence, that was right.

When Fran wasn't visiting, Gary came to see me, smelling comfortingly of booze, cigarettes and Jasper Conran fragrance, and at last I could let it all out. Together we worked out that on the night of my thirtieth birthday, I had failed to ensnare the beautiful Canadian student, Grantley, but Gary had ('Huge cock, balls like Christmas decorations. I could never forget that night!'), while I had passed out in the bath, apparently.

'If memory serves me correctly, you'd gone in there to perform a sex act on a closeted Arab prince called Faisal. You then threw up and fell asleep groaning in your newly installed roll-top bath. That's right,' he continued, pressing his temples to help the memories emerge. 'I covered you in towels and slunk into your bed with the sex-on-a-stick Canadian.'

'So it was *your* condom Jess found in the morning?' I interrupted.

Gary blushed a little. 'Er . . . Not exactly.'

'What?' I said impatiently.

'It turned out that Grantley was Arthur, not Martha.'

'You mean it was *his* condom?'

'Well, let's just say,' answered Gary bashfully, 'he wasn't a member of the Canadian *mounted* police force. If you get my drift. And now I think of it, his eyes were very like Albie's.'

We both had a moment of contemplation.

'Is Albie well hung?' Gary asked urgently.

'I really don't think that's appropriate,' I said sternly, but added, 'Actually, yes, now you come to mention it.'

'Then Albie is definitely the fruit of Grantley's loins, not mine!' He smiled with relief.

'Why?'

'Because I'm hung like a button mushroom, that's why.'

'I am so pleased for you,' I said sincerely. 'I'd forgotten about that, but now you mention it, you're quite right.' I wondered if that was an entirely scientific way of judging parentage but I was no expert. 'I had no idea I'd come to see your shortcoming as such a blessing.' I managed to raise my right forearm and we shook hands. Lying back on my pillows, I sighed. 'But I still don't understand how Jess could be so stupid. She knew I was sleeping with several men a week back then. She was the one who chucked them out in the morning. Why would she think that the condom on my bedside cabinet was, erm . . . literally mine?'

'She wanted to believe it,' Gary said solemnly. 'And when you're three parts bonkers, that helps. But those were definitely my pants. I remember that tiger. And come to think of it, I remember waking up in the morning and Grantley had gone, taking my pants with him, or so I thought. It was about seven in the morning. I hauled you out of the bathroom and into your bed, and took myself home for a fry up, a hot shower and a jolly good sleep.'

'That settles it,' I said, satisfied. 'Albie is the son of Grantley, the Canadian student. Well, I'm glad that's cleared up. Thank heaven for small mercies. Poor old Jess.' I took Gary's hand and stared into his eyes. 'By the way, I want to thank you for what you did. You saved my life.'

'You're welcome, old love. Couldn't have you bowing out on your birthday, could I?' He smiled at me. 'I intend to drink your booze and torment you with boasts about my love life for many years yet.'

'Sounds like a plan.' I smiled back. 'Press the morphine drip again, will you? There's a love.'

Apart from Fran and Gary, my other visitor was Marcia. Her ebullient presence was always a joy.

'Have you popped the question yet?' she asked excitedly as she bustled into the room, tossing bags of fresh apricots, grapes and miniature bottles of whisky in all directions. 'I realise you can't exactly get down on one knee, but maybe you could manage an elbow?'

'Not yet. But you'll be the first to know,' I promised, dodging the missiles as they flew in all directions.

'Thank you, sweetness. And in other news, your assailant, the mad, bad and dangerous-to-know Jess is now in the care of Broadmoor prison hospital. Her injuries, unlike yours, were superficial. But she's unlikely to face trial, as she is barking.'

'Well, that's one thing to be grateful for, I suppose. I couldn't face a trial. But . . . poor Jess,' was all I could manage.

'Shall we move on? Don't laugh, but you've been asked if you'd like to be the new face of Lexus.'

'I haven't got much face left, have I?' I asked seriously.

'I think that's the whole point. The tag line is "If only I'd been driving a Lexus". See how you feel when you're back on your feet, eh?'

Albie sent me a dozen stale cupcakes. I strongly suspected they were recycled. I knew I was not his father. Gary's account of the night in question confirmed it, but I was sure instinctively too. Poor Jess had been wrong about that.

At night, when I was alone in my hospital bed, with only the mechanical beeps and whirrs of my support technology to keep me company, I wondered if Noël would return. Perhaps he would come to tell me that I had finally passed the house's test. There couldn't be another after this, surely . . . I mean, we all like a laugh, but enough's enough.

I remembered what Alice Creyse had told me at the party, a few hours before my ordeal – that Jack had killed Jude. I wondered suddenly if it had been Jack's uneasy, guilty spirit that had been causing so much trouble. The house had seemed to protest every time I came into contact with Albie, or even mentioned his name. Had that been Jack, warning me not to become embroiled in a dangerous liaison as he had? It made a strange kind of sense. And who knew, perhaps Jack had urged Jess on to the ultimate wickedness that, if Alice was right, he himself had committed.

Julian Clary had told me that it wasn't Noël who was making things go bump in the night. Who else then, but Jack? I felt the same as if I was stuck on the last grid of a particularly difficult Sudoku puzzle. There must be an answer, I told myself repeatedly as I drifted off into a drug-induced sleep.

Despite my hoping that Noël would return and enlighten me, there was no sign of him.

Scene Six

1956

Noël

The selling of Goldenhurst was torture for Noël. Not only because of the wrench of parting with his magical home of the last thirty years, but because no one wanted to buy it. It was withdrawn from auction twice after failing to reach its modest sale price. He felt indignant that the dear old girl wasn't snapped up.

'Embarrassing for her to be left on the shelf at her age, the poor darling,' he said, as he and his companion approached the old place from the driveway. Noël was staying with friends in Kent and had come to say his last, final goodbye on the dull, grey September afternoon. He stopped on the gravel drive by the gate, hesitating, a dark figure in a padded-shouldered double-breasted suit and sunglasses. Goldenhurst looked battered and beaten after being requisitioned in the war, and afterwards rented out for years. 'Quite a come-down for her,' he remarked. 'Not to mention for my own expectations. I was hoping for a dazzling return on my rural investment. But it was not to be. It seems my charming composition "The Stately Homes of England" has proved prophetic.' But he had sold the place in the end to a retired army colonel, just back from Kenya. 'Perhaps the house will have some fun with the old duffer she belongs to now.'

'Well, at least the whole business is sorted out,' said Graham, who was, and would remain until the end, Noël's gentleman friend. He was dark-haired and good-looking, and much younger than Noël.

'What Mother would say if she were alive I can't imagine. The thought of a member of the armed forces, retired or otherwise, charging around the place is more than I can bear. The whole business has been torture for me.'

'We are in transition. Transferring to a new life in the sun at Blue Harbour. It was bound to be difficult. But it will be worth it in the end, trust me.' Graham smiled encouragingly as they got to the front gate. He pushed back the catch and held it open for Noël.

He muttered as they approached, 'All of my furniture, my paintings. Gone. I feel as if I've died.'

'Now then. Drama alert!' cautioned Graham, clutching Noël's flapping hands between his own and speaking very clearly and comfortingly. 'Calm down. It's the only way to make this work, remember? We're going to go and live in Jamaica, in the sun, beside the sea, and you are going to paint pictures and be happy and contented. It's what you want. Remember?'

Noël looked less fraught, visibly relaxing as he listened to Graham's soothing words. 'Ah yes, my dubious painting. Dubbed "Touch and Gauguin" by Gladys.' He glanced at the younger man. 'I feel the need to wander from room to room, touching the walls, like Madame Ranevsky in *The Cherry Orchard*.'

'Dear room, dear bookcase?' offered Graham helpfully.

'That sort of thing precisely.'

'Would you like me to come with you?'

'No, thank you, dear boy. This is one of those things in life that one must do alone.' Noël was sure there was a witty tag line to his sentence, but on this occasion he didn't bother searching his mind for it. He already felt a wave of emotion sweeping through him, like a mourner arriving at the funeral service, and he wanted to give vent to his thoughts and feelings.

His key turned easily in the lock and he went in, closing the door behind him. Noël looked about, stricken at the dilapidation of the old place. He looked older now himself, with his hair well-receded, carefully dyed and combed back from his high forehead. A tan from the Jamaican sun only added to the leathery impression. He took his sunglasses off and squinted to see better in the gloom. The furniture was gone and there were cobwebs growing from every dark corner and a light layer of dust over the floorboards. He drew in the familiar Goldenhurst smell of burnt wood and earth. The Old Manor felt as if it had been resting, dozing peacefully, and Noël cleared his throat a couple of times, to wake it gently.

He wandered into the dining room just as the cool air stirred, pulled up through the inglenook fireplace as the house inhaled and sighed in recognition of him.

Noël looked to the space where his mother used to sit, her back to the fire, her bright, critical eyes surveying everything, but resting always on him, full of adoration.

'Mother, dearest . . .' he said aloud. Yes, it was right to move on. This house would always remind him of her and he would always expect to see her here, even though she had gone.

Bowing his head, he moved to the next room. Although only in his mid-fifties Noël now had a permanent stoop – a result, he sometimes said, of living here all these years and bending over to avoid hitting his head on the low beams of the ancient doorways. He passed through the library, just glancing at the place where his desk had been, where he had written so many of his plays and songs. He did not feel sentimental about this; his talent to amuse he kept with him, and he could write wherever he was, on a boat or a plane or in a hotel room in Shanghai. He did not owe the house his fortune.

Next, as the floorboards creaked underfoot, he went down the corridor to his bedroom. It was here that sadness finally overwhelmed him. The mark on the wall where his bedhead had stood was what did it. He stood where he had so often lain and looked towards the window, tears glistening in his eyes. A climbing white rose had, with one final effort, produced its last, brown-edged bloom, and it waved at him mournfully from outside the latticed glass. With no furniture in the room to hold on to, he hugged himself for a moment and then sunk to his knees.

'Jack,' he said quietly. 'Oh, Jack.' Noël could see him now, young and devastatingly handsome, coming towards him on the bed, naked and strong. Here in this room Jack had held him in his arms and kissed him until Noël thought his heart would burst with love. They had lain in the bed here for hours, for days, not wanting to let anyone else into their world, consumed with lust for each other and plans for their future.

For a while Noël held on to this image of Jack and remembered how real their young love had been and how it made him happy and content. But, inevitably, the Jack of recent times crept back into his mind and Noël pictured him the last time he had seen him, not long before he sent that letter: bloated and almost demented with the effects of decades of heavy drinking and who knows what else. They had both got older, but how had it all gone so horribly wrong, so septic and poisonous for Jack? The drink would kill him very soon. That much had been obvious.

Suddenly there was a loud cracking sound. Noël, from where he knelt, turned to look through the open door just in time to see a large, dinner-plate-sized lump of plaster crash noisily from ceiling to floor. A cloud of white dust a foot high then billowed towards him like dry ice, stopping gracefully just at his knees.

Despite the shock, Noël plucked a handkerchief from the breast pocket of his tweed jacket and wiped his eyes. He allowed himself a knowing chuckle. 'I hear you, old girl,' he said, raising his eyes to scan the walls and ceiling. 'I'm only *thinking* about him. He's not coming back. Neither am I.'

It was true that whenever Jack visited over the years, cellars had flooded, trees had fallen on parked cars and electrical plugs had sparked and caught fire. Goldenhurst had never taken him to her heart.

Without judgement, without sentiment, Noël allowed the image of the young, handsome Jack he had fallen in love with to hover in his mind: the line of his jaw; the strength in his shoulders; the smell of his skin. He daydreamed for a moment, as the powdery white residue settled on him like frost. What if he had led an ordinary life, out of the public eye, free from fame and all that came with it? Might he and Jack have survived? He tried to imagine them both, without the money, attention, the drive to continue onwards and upwards that came with celebrity; without his mother living in the same house, the first nights, the champagne, the hangers-on, servants and gardeners . . . but he couldn't.

They had always been at risk of discovery and disgrace, and

perhaps that had been the greatest pressure of all. That was, after all, why Jack had got married and gone away. At least, that's what Noël believed. Or wanted to.

And, in the end, it was impossible to forget the man who had, eventually, betrayed him, and who had cost him thousands in bad deals, unwise decisions and mismanaged taxes.

His thoughts were interrupted by Graham's footsteps rushing down the corridor.

'Oh my goodness!' Graham cried when he saw the pile of shattered plaster. 'I heard a terrible noise. Are you all right?'

'Yes, Graham, I am fine. Unscarred by falling masonry.'

Noël's companion stood awkwardly in the doorway. 'I think we should go soon. It will be getting dark and Gladys will be expecting us home for tea.'

'Help me up then,' said Noël, holding up his arms like a baby in a pram.

Graham hooked his arm under the Master's and hoisted him to his feet, accompanied by Noël's exaggerated 'Ooh's and 'Ahhh's.

'Thank you. I do hope I haven't given you a hernia? Or an erection?' said Noël, brushing himself down with the backs of his hands.

'I think we're safe in both respects,' Graham replied swiftly.

'Then take me to my new life!' said Noël with an impish look, and gave Graham a warm, affectionate smile. As they walked together, back through the house towards the front door, stopping every few feet for Noël to gaze around, nod and whisper 'Goodbye,' Graham kept a respectful silence.

Once outside Noël could sense Graham's keenness to get him in the car and away from the place, but he raised his hand in protest.

'The garden,' he said, 'I must say goodbye to the garden,' and set off down the side of the Old Manor. He followed the rag-stone path right the way around the house and then through the woods, constantly looking over his shoulder, as if pursued by ravens. Graham followed at a watchful distance. The last port of call, before getting back to where the car was parked on the gravel driveway, was the pond.

Noël stopped and wrung his hands in anguish. Here, twenty-five years ago, he had seen Jude's frozen body lying on the very stones where he now stood. Noël saw again the skin like marble, the lips blue and the eyes wide open in shock. He remembered it all too well. What was the truth of that night? Jack had never said, and Noël had never been able to ask – not in such a way that would get the answer he needed.

'What secrets are you keeping from me?' he asked, plaintively. He didn't cry, because he knew if he did, Graham would come and usher him away. The dear boy couldn't bear to see him upset. Noël stared into the limpid, slate-grey surface of the pond as if expecting an answer to reveal itself.

Despite the lack of drama Graham stepped forward after a long two minutes.

'Shall we make tracks?' he said gently. Noël, as if awoken from a dream, stared at Graham for a moment, and then held out his hand.

'Take me from this place. Lord knows, I cannot leave by my own will.'

Graham stepped forward and led Noël to the car.

'How are you?' Graham asked once they were settled in the car and several hundred yards up the road.

Noël continued to look out of the window, but replied, 'I am very, very well. Goodbyes are sad, but once the tears have dried the sun comes out again and the future takes on new and exciting possibilities. Now I have a new life to think about. The Jamaican sun will be just the tonic I require.'

Scene Seven

Richard

Finally the day dawned when I was allowed home. Fran made sure this was done via the back entrance of the hospital to avoid the paparazzi. A nurse was waiting at the Old Manor, installed in one of the upstairs bedrooms, and I was lifted into the bed in the downstairs room with Fran, white roses pressing against the window and ivy creeping in through the hinges, waving at me.

'I am so glad to be home,' I said with a sigh, invigorated and terribly happy to be back. And then I fell into a deep sleep.

The next morning, after a breakfast of three spoonfuls of yoghurt, which was all I could manage, Fran helped me on to the sofa in the lounge and put a blanket over me. Then, kneeling in front of the inglenook fireplace, he scraped away the old ashes with a shovel and built a new fire before lighting it.

'A fire on a warm summer's day?' I asked.

'Yes, that's right,' he said, blowing on the kindling, before choosing a hefty log from the pile in the basket. 'That's what you do in these old houses when people are ill or giving birth.

I've seen it on a documentary. Fires are very comforting and cosy.'

'If you say so. I expect they used to burn the placenta. But I haven't got a chill,' I complained, tossing the blanket over the back of the sofa. 'Can we have the window open? I'm sweltering.'

Fran got up and folded the discarded blanket into a neat oblong and felt my forehead. 'Hmmm. I'll open it an inch,' he said, pursing his lips. 'I think you have a bit of a temperature.'

'I will if you insist on broiling me.' Just then I heard the scrunch of tyres on the gravel drive outside. 'Who's that? We're not expecting anyone, are we?'

Fran peered out of the window. 'Oh, it's Marcia. She appears to be dressed in some sort of sheet . . . I'd better go and greet her.'

A moment later, with much coo-ing and aah-ing, Marcia entered the lounge like a giant seagull in a grey, silk kaftan. She dropped a large holdall by the door, gazed at me and spread her arms wide. 'Darling one, just look at you! So dashing and handsome!'

'Marcia, what a lovely surprise,' I said as she approached and swept her wings around me.

She stood back. 'Now I know I wasn't invited. But I decided in the middle of the night that I had to come.'

'Were you worried about me?' I asked.

'No more than usual,' said Marcia. 'But I realised today was the seventh day of the lunar calendar.' She had opened her handbag and was reaching in now, pulling out candles, tea lights and incense.

'Some green tea for us all?' interrupted Fran, bringing in a tray.

Marcia glanced up from her paraphernalia. 'Darling, that is very kind, but I'll just have water until I've finished my business.'

'Business? I hardly think Richard is up to—' objected Fran, but Marcia interrupted him.

'No, silly. Not business as in work. Today, according to the Shamanic Lunar Calendar, is the day of the rooster.' Both Fran and I looked at her blankly. Marcia tutted and proceeded to light the candles and place them around the room. 'On the seventh day, my darlings, demons and black energy are afraid. Darkness is afraid. Secrets are exposed! Am I making sense yet?'

'I think I know all of Richard's secrets,' said Fran, pouring the tea. 'And if there are any more to come, I shall smother him with a pillow and take the consequences.'

'Not Richard,' said Marcia impatiently. 'The house. I'm going to do something that should have been done a long time ago. Cleanse the place. Heal it! Lord knows it's necessary. We may have got rid of Jess – the corporeal problem – but the bad spirits still remain . . . I am glad that you have a fire lit. With any luck all the mischief and sadness will go up the chimney and float away. Now, where's the salt? Ah, yes – in the bag. Heave it over here for me, would you, sweetness?'

'What's going on, Marcia?' asked Fran in his best school-teacher voice, ignoring her request. 'We've just finished breakfast and Richard was going to sit quietly by the fire while I read the paper.'

Marcia raised her hands as if in surrender. 'I know, I know. I'm interrupting. But it must be done.'

'What must?'

Marcia had gone to fetch the holdall herself and was now heaving it to the centre of the room and unzipping it as she spoke.

'I've been up half the night googling how to do this. It shouldn't take too long and then I promise I'll leave you in peace. Real peace I hope.'

'What?' said Fran, raising his voice. 'Tell us what on earth you're talking about?'

I was too weak to do anything but observe and allow Fran to speak for me. I had seen Marcia in this type of mood before – there was little point in trying to stop her. Whatever she was up to she was clearly on a mission.

'I told you. I'm going to cleanse, purify and re-balance this house,' she was explaining. 'Do you have any matches?'

'By the fireplace,' answered Fran. 'I hope you're not talking about some sort of hocus-pocus nonsense because I simply won't allow it.' He didn't hold with such things. He was far too down to earth.

Marcia stopped busying herself and sat down on the sofa where I was lying, squashing my legs somewhat until I moved them. She sighed and shook her head. 'Please let me explain. Sit down, Fran. This house is very old. Many people have lived and died here over the centuries. Some of them, it seems to me, are still here. You're sharing the place with them, whether you like it or not.'

Fran yawned loudly. 'Will this take long? Only Anne Frank is upstairs in the loft and I promised I'd make her a sandwich.'

Marcia gazed at him patiently. 'Okay. Just hear me out, whether you believe me or not. It's for your own good. I promise this won't take up much of your time.'

'You haven't been here much, Fran,' I reasoned. 'You haven't witnessed all the strange things that have happened. The noises and all the rest of it. The first day Marcia came here she knew there were ghosts, didn't you?'

She nodded. 'I did. Half a dozen or so. Not unusual in a house this old.'

'We walked through each room and she spoke to them.'

'And did you play bridge and dance the Gay Gordons?' asked Fran tartly.

'Not all of them are unfriendly, of course,' Marcia continued, 'but there's a malevolent spirit here I can tell . . . more than one perhaps.'

There was the sound of another car on the drive. 'Now what?' asked Fran crossly.

'That will be Julian Clary,' said Marcia, glancing at her watch. 'I told him to meet me here.'

'Jesus,' breathed Fran. 'This had better be good.'

We heard the kitchen door open and Julian appeared in the doorway clutching a dusty shoebox.

'Hello, girls,' he said, smiling nervously and wriggling his hips. 'Room for another small homosexual in here?'

'Hello, darling,' said Marcia, greeting him with a kiss while Fran remained pointedly in his seat. I couldn't move in any case.

'Hi,' I managed, while Fran couldn't even look at him.

'Richard and Fran are a little unsure about what is happening,' explained Marcia. 'I'm in the middle of making it all clear.'

'I didn't think you two knew each other particularly,' I said.

'We didn't,' said Julian with a little smile. 'Until we bumped into each other last week at Ashford Station. Marcia had been visiting you in hospital and I was on my way into town to do a Toilet Duck voiceover.'

'We got talking,' Marcia continued for him, sensing Fran's growing irritation. It was obvious Julian wasn't his cup of tea at all. 'And Julian told me the real reason he sold this house.'

'The bottle of Sauvignon Blanc you had with you certainly helped,' added a simpering Julian as he sat himself down on the sofa opposite Fran and me.

'Tell Richard and Fran what you told me,' urged Marcia, her expression serious. She sank into another armchair and sat like a great snowy mountain.

'Oh, dear,' said Julian quietly, stroking the box that rested on his knees. 'I feel a bit of a fool, really.'

'It's all right, darling,' Marcia encouraged him. 'They need to know.' There was an uncomfortable silence and Julian looked close to tears.

'Out with it,' said Fran sharply. 'It can't be that bad, can it?'

'Well,' began Julian. 'I'm worried that you'll blame me for everything that's happened.' He looked pleadingly at me. 'All your misfortune – it would never have happened if I hadn't been so . . . frightened, I suppose.'

'Whatever do you mean?' asked Fran, his tone a tad more aggressive than before.

Julian took a deep breath. 'The seance,' he said at last. 'You know I told you I had a seance here with some friends of mine, just a few weeks after I moved in. We were all a bit merry and we thought it would be fun. We were stoned, too. Just a bunch of queens celebrating Halloween. But – but it wasn't fun at all.'

'Sounds hideous already,' said Fran under his breath.

'There were six of us,' continued Julian, ignoring him. 'We cut up bits of paper and wrote all the letters of the alphabet on them and put them on a table in a circle.'

'Which room were you in?' I asked, my interest growing. Perhaps, now, at last, things were going to become clearer.

Julian glanced about. 'Here. In this room. We placed a glass tumbler in the middle, upside down. I hadn't done a seance since I was a child. We were just being silly, laughing and carrying on. But—' He stopped and wiped his eyes, clearly distressed at the memory of what happened next.

'Carry on, love,' coaxed Marcia.

'Well, we didn't even get to ask a question,' Julian said. 'Our fingers had barely touched the glass when it started moving.' Annoyingly, he stopped again.

'What did it say?' Fran asked eventually, more than a little exasperated with the delays.

'Sarah. She said her name was Sarah. She was fifteen. We asked her what she wanted and she said "My baby." She just kept saying it: "I want my baby back. My son. Where is he?" Then we heard these thuds and bangs coming from the cellar, the walls, everywhere, it seemed. There were gusts of cold air sweeping across the room and high-pitched, terribly sad, mournful noises, like an animal trapped somewhere. We were totally freaked out. Hector and Paul got in their car and left, even though it was gone midnight. I've never heard from them since.'

'It's a wonder you can carry on,' said Fran witheringly.

'Hush, Fran,' warned Marcia. 'This isn't easy for Julian. Wait till you hear what's next.'

'I'm all ears.' Fran sat back expectantly.

Julian went on, his voice tentative. 'I can't remember everything from that night. A hung-over haze, I'm afraid. But Sarah said her baby was born out of wedlock and her father had taken him from her as soon as it was born. Squeezed the life out of it after its first breath and taken him away – never to be seen again. Then other people kept interrupting, sending the glass all over the place. "Get out!" they kept saying. "Get out! Go! Be gone!" We were very scared. Then the walls seemed to shake. A kind of sawdust fell from the ceiling like mist and landed in our drinks. We stopped it eventually, when the glass flew across the room and smashed against the wall.' He looked white just remembering. 'The whole experience was completely terrifying. We all spent the rest of the night huddled in one bedroom listening to the hisses and thuds that went on all through the rest of the night until dawn.'

'The evils of drink,' muttered Fran.

'Is that why you sold the house?' I asked. I believed him, even though it all sounded incredible. I'd had too many odd experiences not to.

'Not quite,' Marcia answered. 'Tell them what happened a few days later.'

'Well,' began Julian. 'I pulled myself together after that. I didn't touch a drink for several weeks. I put the whole experience down to too much booze and too many spliffs. The house was quiet as well, so I began to think we'd imagined the whole thing. I decided to decorate. Freshen the place up. A friend of mine came to help. Lisa. She's a TV producer – or she would be if there was anything to produce. It's shocking, the state of the industry these days. Channel 4 are only interested in—'

'Could we get to the point?' Fran asked tetchily.

'Yes, I'm sorry,' said Julian contritely. 'So, we'd done the ceiling in Georgian White and were just preparing the walls. Lisa was over there—' he indicated the inglenook fireplace '—to the right, in that recess. She was scraping away the loose plaster when she said it sounded hollow. We tapped on the panel above and below and they both were solid, but the middle section was all echo-ey. Then, as we tapped more enthusiastically, the plaster, which was quite rotten, began to flake away, and before we knew it a hole had appeared.' Julian stopped and looked at each of us in turn. He looked pale and tired. He held out the old shoebox. 'And this is what we found inside.'

With a flourish he opened the lid and we all leant forward to see what was inside. There was lot of yellowish dust and some chunks of old straw like plaster. But in amongst it were what looked like grey twigs and a tiny skull.

'Let me see,' said Fran, taking the box. 'Eeew. Whatever is it?'

'Lisa thought it was cat bones, but I knew at once. It's Sarah's baby,' said Julian almost inaudibly.

Fran almost dropped the box and immediately handed it back to Julian. 'That's – that's just bizarre. Why on earth didn't you inform the police?'

Julian looked upset and guilty. 'Perhaps I should have, but I'd had enough of this house of horrors and anyone involved in all this business must be long dead by now. I was freaked out, not thinking straight, as it were. I just wanted to sell the place. As quickly as possible. If word got out that it was some sort of house of horrors no one would ever have bought it, would they?'

'Then I came along,' I said, realising where I came into the story. 'No wonder Jess was able to knock the price down so easily.'

'I'm sorry, I really am,' said Julian, giving me an apologetic look. 'I was scared out of my mind, almost. If I'd known what was going to happen I'd never have let you buy it. But I took the box with me and hid it. I thought that it would be the end of it, once it was no longer in the house.' Just before he started crying, Marcia silently took the box from him.

'Now then, no one can say that the house has caused any of Richard's misfortunes,' she said soothingly, raising her voice a little so she could be heard over his rather girlish sobs. 'We certainly can't blame it for what happened hundreds of miles away on a French motorway. Let's keep everything in proportion.'

'But,' I said slowly, 'this might sound crazy but I think it may have had something to do with Jess's madness. She always appeared to be hearing sounds here, almost talking to someone. And she was always drawn to this fireplace too – once she said, "I don't know where it's gone". And she talked of "she", as though there was a woman she could hear. I remember quite clearly. I had no idea what she meant. It's too much for a coincidence, isn't it?'

There was a sharp intake of breath from Marcia. 'So the old baggage had some sensitivity in her, did she? I'd never have guessed myself. Poor Sarah must have thought Jess would help her find the child, perhaps because she was a mother too. But as Jess was a bit of a cynic where spiritual matters were concerned – and, let's face it, a bit unstable – it seems to have pushed her over the edge, made her psychically vulnerable.' Marcia shook her head knowing. 'Well, well. A fascinating case. I must write a paper for the Psychic and Spiritual Questing Group. They'd love to hear about this.'

'Pseudonyms only, please, Marcia dear,' I put in.

'We'll all be ruined otherwise,' said Julian, his voice catching on another sob.

'Chin up, old boy,' I said, feeling almost sorry for him. 'Have a good blow and you'll feel much better,' I added, handing him a tissue.

'That's what they all say,' was Julian's 'witty' response. He blew his nose, wiped his eyes and took some deep breaths.

'I don't think we can sue you,' said Fran. 'If that's of any comfort.'

'That's not all, though.' added Julian.' Alice, that old biddy told me the rest of the story . . . it was village folklore in her day. It was said the milk from Sarah's unsuckled breasts curdled inside her—'

'Oh, please,' said Fran, covering his mouth.

'Some say she died of a broken heart,' continued Julian, 'while others say her father, overcome with remorse—'

'Yes, we get the general idea,' interrupted Fran, finally losing patience. Assuming a cod country accent, he continued, 'And some do say she won the lottery and moved to the Costa del Sol!'

'Enough!' said Marcia, looking sadly at the contents of the shoebox. 'I think it is all terribly sad, and the least this poor innocent baby deserves is a proper burial and a blessing. That will free his soul and release Sarah from her torment.'

'If only I'd done that when I discovered him,' said Julian, shaking his head. 'I just went to pieces.'

'Where have you kept the box all this time?' I asked.

'I have an old chest where I keep all my press cuttings,' said Julian, sounding a little awkward. 'It's awful, I know. When I moved I put the chest in the garden shed and tried not to think about it.'

'Jesus,' muttered Fran. 'As if the poor mite hadn't suffered enough.'

Just then the nurse, Erin, appeared in the doorway. 'Excuse me interrupting,' she said tentatively, 'but it's time for Mr Richard's pills.'

'Thank you,' said Marcia decisively, raising herself up and clapping her hands decisively. 'We're almost done here. Julian – you may go home now. Fran? After his medicine, I'd like you to take Richard out for a drive while I perform the exorcism. I don't want him distressed in his condition. Give me an hour. Then I think we may all be able to put this unpleasantness behind us.'

'I need a lie down in a darkened room,' said Julian, getting up and heading for the door with all the speed and determination of a shoplifter under suspicion. 'Thank you all for being so understanding. I'll see you soon.'

There was an awkward moment after he hurriedly kissed Marcia on both cheeks, and both Fran and I went rigid, hoping we might be excused. He read the signs and made do with a little smile and a wave, before letting himself out.

'Right then,' said Fran, hoisting me to my feet by my elbow. 'So much for a restful morning in the countryside. Come on, injured soldier. Let's go to Hythe and peruse the charity shops.'

'Oh, the excitement,' I exclaimed.

'Ahem!' said Erin, poised with a glass of water in one hand and rattling some pills in a plastic pillbox with the other. 'Once these have gone down the hatch and not before.'

'Yes, nurse,' I said compliantly, and obeyed.

We returned to Aldringham an hour or so later, and stopped on the top of the hill to look down at the Old Manor. The sky was watery and palest Wedgwood blue. From our view point, it seemed to me that the roof no longer looked heavy and sagging in the middle but instead sat jauntily over the house, like a protective summer hat buoyed up from within, and the tiles, every shade from honey to carrot, sang like a flock of hatchlings perched on the beams.

'Does the place look any different to you?' asked Fran.

'I do believe it does, somehow,' I said cautiously. 'It's changed . . . wouldn't you say?'

'Mmmm,' agreed Fran. 'Like you, after you had that colonic irrigation. All purified and glowing.'

'Good old Marcia,' I said, as the woman herself came walking towards us across the lawn. She looked as if she'd been wrestling with a whole legion of spirits but she wore a beaming smile.

A week later Marcia returned, bringing with her an old vicar friend of hers. Marcia had explained the circumstances, and he had agreed to bless the grave for us. Together with Fran, we laid the little box to rest under a large oak tree at the bottom of the garden and Marcia's friend performed a simple burial service for the remains of Sarah's baby.

From that day the cries in the night were silenced and although we still heard the odd banging and thumps about the place, it sounded far more like troubled plumbing than tortured souls.

It was some months later, and the end of one of our pleasant evenings together. Fran had done something unusual with a salmon for me, and we had watched a French film until late. Reading the subtitles caused my bad eye to water horribly, but I was determined to get better and live as normally as possible, especially now the house had become so restful and calm. Its mischief was at an end now; only faint and harmless echoes of the past remained.

'I was wondering . . .' I said later, when we'd retired, as he slid under the duvet following his exceedingly thorough ablutions. 'Shall we tie the knot?'

'Excuse me?' said Fran, looking worried.

'Will you marry me?' I asked. I sounded calm but in reality my heart was pounding. Now that I'd said it, I realised I wanted it more than anything. We'd been so wonderfully happy lately, I wouldn't be able to bear it if he turned me down. 'As in, sign a piece of paper and become my civilised partner?'

'Is it finally happening?' said Fran, beaming. 'Yes, of course I bloody will.'

'We'd better do it quickly before I have another drama.'

'I'm not letting you out of my sight,' declared Fran. He took my hand and intertwined his fingers between mine and we raised our joined hands up in the air above our heads and gazed at them.

I was about to speak when Fran shushed me. 'Don't say anything,' he warned me. 'At least, try not to say anything flippant or clever or funny.'

'Am I allowed to say I love you?' I asked quietly.

'Yes you are,' he answered.

'I love you . . . more than I love morphine.'

The next morning, we were seized by excitement at our engagement and spent a happy morning making plans for our forthcoming nuptials. We decided on a quiet ceremony at Claridge's the coming autumn with about fifty guests.

'The graphics department at work can design the invite,' said Fran enthusiastically. 'How about an e-card? We could have a link they click on and see a video of something ironic. Fergie and Prince Andrew maybe? What do you think?'

'Sounds dreamy,' I said, laughing.

'Yes, doesn't it? And after we're married, we'll belong to each other really and truly. You'll be my first priority. Will I be yours?'

'Yes. Of course,' I said. 'Apart from the assisted shower and my lunchtime enema, my body is your plaything. I've never been more receptive.'

We began to put things in motion for our wedding immediately, telling our friends and family who were all, without exception, delighted for us. It was odd to think that Jess, who'd I'd always imagined would be my best woman, was likely to be weaving raffia pot stands in Broadmoor instead, but that was the way it had all turned out. Fran and I spent happy hours choosing flowers, making seating plans and designing matching platinum bands inset with diamonds.

Our relationship had never been better, but while my love for Fran was flourishing, my health, on the other hand, was not so good. It was stubbornly refusing to improve. In fact, after an initial rush of energy, I once walked the entire length of the garden and ate a whole tureen full of Jamie Oliver's gazpacho, I began to sink back into an invalid state, much as I tried to resist it. Fran stopped asking me if I was getting up for dinner and instead brought me an omelette on a tray, teasing me if I couldn't stay awake for *Gardeners' World*. My legs just wouldn't seem to support me and my nurse Erin and her daytime helper Lilia appeared helpless to stop one of the facial injuries from seeping a yellow, bloody liquid that trickled down my cheek like a toxic tear just moments after they had bathed and dressed it.

But despite all of this, I had never felt happier. The Old Manor was quiet and embracing, as was Fran. We huddled together in bed at night, and he wheeled me out into the summer sunshine each afternoon. Sometimes we listened to music (mainly Mahler or Beethoven with the occasional burst of Rhianna) and sometimes – often, if I'm being honest – I fell asleep. Fran took pictures of me, mouth wide open, and showed them to me once I awoke. We laughed and hugged and dissed each other. Soon we would have an engagement party – a small one this time – and I would start to get better. All I longed for was my strength back, the old vitality. But surely that would come with time, rest, nourishment and love.

Meanwhile the house purred contentedly. We were in harmony at long last.

Scene Eight

Richard and Noël

And now we are back where we began, with me spread-eagled under the mulberry tree in the garden, feeling decidedly chilly. I was in a bad state. I lay on the sunbed struggling to breathe.

'Love is a tricky business,' said a voice I'd heard before. I knew it at once. Noël.

I turned my head and looked at him in astonishment. I managed to gasp out a few words. 'What are you doing here?' I'd last seen him in the hospital in that murky, dimly lit intensive care unit, but here he was, as plain as day in my garden, this time wearing a fetching linen suit and a panama hat.

'My dear boy,' said Noël. 'I simply had to come. This is my Elvira moment and I fully intend to make the most of it.' He sat down on a wicker chair by the old tree and crossed his legs. 'There. Now we can have a nice comfortable chat.'

I frowned at him, confused. 'Am I in a coma again?'

'I think not,' he said airily, and then quickly added, 'I thought it would be advisable to clear up a few matters before the others arrive.'

'Others?'

'I wanted to thank you for finally curing the house of its sadness. Poor Sarah has been charging around the place for generations like an extra from *Wuthering Heights.* Since your charming ceremony in the garden laying the poor child to rest, she is as calm and contented as a chocoholic after a Mars Bar.' He hummed a little snatch of the 'The Stately Homes of England', and then sang lightly the lyrics from the later refrain about the baby walled up in the guest wing in 1428. 'Who would have guessed I was so near the mark? So sad. But you and that frolicking comedian friend of yours have sorted her out. So that's one mystery solved.' He gave me a knowing look. 'But I'm sure you're keen to know the rest. What really happened here in 1931. I know Alice had a little word with you at your quaint fiftieth.' He rolled his eyes. 'Mini Cornish pasties? Whatever next?' He shuddered visibly. 'Anyway, she told you that Jack had a hand in poor Jude's demise.' He shook his head. 'Very naughty of her. She was right that Jack had seduced her fiancé, but, darling, if we were all locked up for inadvisable sexual partnerships, the streets would be empty. It seemed blameless at the time. A bit of fun. Where was the harm?'

'But?'

'But then, as the house demands, things got suddenly violent.' Noël dropped his voice and was clearly upset at recounting the events. 'As you know, Jude was discovered one morning drowned in the pond. The poor, dear, young man. I blamed myself. I felt as if Jack had corrupted him and I did nothing to stop it.'

'But he was willing, wasn't he? Even though Jack was technically his boss.'

'Yes, of course. Jack was hardly administering Chinese burns in the meadow. But that didn't mean it was right. Remember the times in which we lived. We were committing an illegal act, as the local police inspector knew only too well. Jack should have contained himself but he didn't. There was a policeman – dreadful fellow, Keaton – he was desperate to bag us. A famous playwright and his American manager – it might have been Oscar Wilde all over again. He knew that Jack and I were *musical* . . .'

'You mean gay?'

'In my day we were *musical* or *so*. Far more poetic, I think, but yes, gay, to use your terminology.'

'Raving, from what I've heard,' I said cheekily.

Noël laughed heartily. 'Yes, thank you. One certainly went as far as one could, given the legal restrictions. No one was bothered by it, not in the circles within which we moved, anyway. But with Jude I felt Jack had crossed a line. Jack should have admired him from afar. He really shouldn't have indulged himself. Too much gin, I'm afraid.'

There was a contemplative silence. Noël seemed lost in troubled thought.

'And it wasn't suicide or an accident . . .' I said slowly. 'Jack did it.'

Noël pursed his lips and frowned before he spoke. 'For a while, I wondered. It drove us apart. Jack did all he could to protect me from the potential scandal and in the end, he even sacrificed our love.'

'How sad.'

'Yes. Even sadder when I realised quite how royally he'd screwed up my finances over the years.' Noël looked around mournfully. 'That is why I finally had to sell this old place. That and the intolerable tax situation. I left England altogether, it was my only way out of the mess. Goldenhurst went and I was left only with memories. But now, free as I am of corporeal matters, I can visit whenever I like. It's rather lovely. England's garden. More or less as it was in my day, apart from Sky TV and the microwave – are they really good for you? Nevertheless, just as I'd hoped, many things are made clear. Secrets are revealed.' He leaned forward. 'I know now that Jack didn't lay a hand on Jude. Not in any violent sense, at least. It was that little minx Alice.'

I twisted my mouth in disbelief. '*What?*'

He nodded. 'There is something about this house, my dear. Quite, quite medieval, no doubt fuelled by that poor girl Sarah. There's nothing stronger than a mother's love for her son, or so my mother always told me. Sarah's grief must have seeped into the stonework and become part of the fabric of the house. And it seems to have had a particular effect where the female of the species is concerned. It brings out the passionate homicidal maniac in a girl – as you found yourself. Alice went quite berserk when she discovered her beloved was indulging in brief but erotic encounters and enjoying them far more than he was with his fiancée by all accounts. There was a frightful row and in a fit of jealousy she whacked Jude round the head with a coal shovel and pushed him into the pond. Then our little darling kitchen-hand blackmailed Jack into paying her off with a nice, cosy cottage by the village green and enough cash to keep her comfortable for life.'

'I can't believe it,' I said, astonished. 'Alice!'

'Oh, yes. And when I sacked her, she went blabbing to Keaton about our bedroom arrangements. It was only Jack's engagement that made him finally desist. I can tell you, I'm very much looking forward to Alice joining us in due course. She's on her last legs. I'm certain she's only kept going this long because she's afraid of what will happen when she has to face the music for what she did.'

I tried to understand. 'What do you mean?'

'You should have listened.' Noël gazed at me meaningfully. 'When you decided to embark on your dalliance with that boy. It had to lead to tragedy. He tried to warn you . . .'

I felt a sense of terrible foreboding. 'You mean, Jack?'

'Jack?' Noël raised his eyebrows. 'No, no, no. He wouldn't dare show his face here, not after what he did to my bank account. Not Jack. He's rarely been back. *Jude*, of course.' He looked over my shoulder, his expression lightened and he said cheerily, 'Ah, here he is now.'

I turned my head and saw a tawny-skinned handsome young lad walking across the lawn towards us smiling.

'You see,' Noël said confidingly, 'there *are* consolations. And dear Marlene often drops by for a chat and a schnapps.'

I knew then. I'd known since the moment he arrived, if truth be told.

'No,' I said pleadingly. 'Not now. Things are about to get better for me, they really are! I'm going to be married. I want to get better, to work again. Please – I'll be good now, I promise. Let me go back.'

'My dear boy, you're not going back. Not this time. You're one of us now, isn't he, Jude?'

The young gardener had reached us now. 'Aye,' he said in a soft warm Kentish accent. 'And you're very welcome, sir.'

Just then Fran came sauntering down the path towards the sunbed under the mulberry tree where I lay.

'Wakey wakey!' he called cheerfully. 'Do you realise you've been asleep the entire afternoon?'

I felt a rush of concern for him, helpless to protect him from the discovery he was about to make.

'Fran, Fran, I'm sorry!' I called out, but of course he didn't hear me. He was just a few yards away now.

'Chop chop!' he said, pursing his lips with mock indignation at what he still thought was my laziness. 'Nurse Ratched is here!'

Noël stood up and leaned against the tree, stroking his chin and gazing at the approaching figure. Jude moved to a respectful distance a few feet away, his head bowed.

'Fran,' I cried desperately. I sat up and climbed out of the sunbed to reach him. I could move quite easily but I left my cooling, stiff body beneath me.

Noël shook his head sadly. 'There's nothing we can do, I'm afraid. He can't hear us or see us.'

Fran knelt by my body, and gave me a gentle tap on the forehead. 'Come along, sleeping beauty.' He froze. 'Richard?' He felt my cheek, took a sharp intake of breath. He shook me by the shoulders. 'No, Richard. No!'

Then he threw himself across my chest, sobbing so violently I thought he might never stop.

I stood next to Noël, crying quietly myself. He put his arm around me.

'All we can do is watch over our loved ones and protect them as best we can,' he said.

'But I love him,' I said quietly, looking searchingly into Noël's blue-grey eyes.

'One day,' said Noël, giving me a comforting pat on my shoulder. 'One day you will be together again. Forever. In this house and in this garden. All will be well. All will be very well indeed.' He slipped his arm through mine. 'I think we both need a cocktail, don't you?' he murmured.

We wandered together arm in arm towards the house.

Epilogue

I shall now have to take you a little way into the future, a place you, dear reader, will never have been, but I have, quite often, and I can assure you it's very nice, though nothing much ever changes in Kent.

You might suppose that was the end of the disturbances at the Old Manor, with the troublesome Sarah and her poor son finding peace at last and me, Richard Stent, now present on the 'other side' and a restraining influence on the rest of the spirits. But you'd be wrong.

There were further 'goings on' and I rather sheepishly admit that it was my good self behind them. To begin with, I busied myself trying to comfort my poor bereaved Fran – I appeared as a beautiful blue butterfly in the days after my crossing over, hovering over him and settling on his shoulder, trying to let him know I was with him still. Unfortunately Fran has never been a fan of the insect world and I realised my efforts were pointless when he chased me around the room brandishing a rolled-up newspaper.

Then, after moping around the house for six months and studiously replying to all of the (gratifyingly numerous) sympathy cards and letters he received, Fran put the place on the market and returned to Los Angeles. I saw off quite a few unsuitable potential buyers with icy cold gusts of air, spooky moans and groans and other tried and tested tricks of the trade, but eventually the Old Manor was sold to a pleasant lesbian couple and their innumerable cats. Abi and Janice are non-smoking, teetotal vegetarians, though, which Noël thought was a frightful bore. (He took to curdling their organic goat's milk and spilling their endless jars of pulses all over the kitchen floor whenever the opportunity arose, which made the cook who haunts the scullery laugh like a drain.)

Sarah kept her distance from us all, confining herself to a back bedroom, bouncing her baby son on her knee and singing him lullabies.

'She's not quite right,' Noël would mouth, tapping the side of his head meaningfully.

Alice Creyse joined us in due course and Noël was as stern and withering as I'd ever seen him, berating the now-young-again Alice for all the problems she had caused, calling her a blackmailer and a police informer. Her riposte was that Jack had seduced Jude first and so ruined her own happiness. Jude sprang to her defence and there was quite an unseemly spat.

When Jack arrived to give his side of the story, I left the Old Manor for a while. Being stuck between two warring couples arguing and accusing each other one minute and locked in passionate embraces the next is not my idea of eternal contentment. I flitted across the Romney Marsh where I took up with a notorious smuggler from the 1740s called Arthur Gray. He was a little rough, it has to be said, but I like a man in a mask.

But then one day, as we were amusing ourselves loosening a choice emerald from the ring of a spinster praying in a pew of St

Mary in the Marsh, I received the news I had been waiting several decades for: Fran, the only man I had ever truly loved, was coming to meet me, back at the Old Manor. I hurried back at once, hoping that Arthur would understand.

When I got there, Noël, Jack, Jude, Alice, even the curious old cook and Sarah (baby in arms) were lined up by the gate.

'Ah, you're here, how splendid,' Noël greeted me, as he straightened his blue spotted bow tie. 'We've missed you. Now, I've arranged a welcome committee for dear Fran. He'll probably be in shock, just as you were. Remember? But isn't it thrilling?' Noël's eyes sparkled with excitement. 'Our cheerful household will soon be complete! We shall have parties every night and play croquet every afternoon.'

'Yes, it is all very exciting,' I said. 'But . . . how? How did he die?'

'One of those tiresome earthquakes, apparently. The whole of Hollywood is under rubble. Rumour has it that Leonardo DiCaprio is now one of us, so every cloud has a silver lining. Now go and arrange yourself decoratively under the mulberry tree and we'll send Fran to you the moment he gets here.'

I did as I was told, ran my fingers through my hair and pinched my cheeks a little to give them colour. Moments later I saw a tall figure emerging from the shadows of the fig tree at the side of the house. My heart beat faster and it was hard to see for the tears that filled my eyes.

'Fran, is that you?'

'Richard?' The familiar voice was wonderful to hear. There was a pause as we stared at each other. Then Fran smiled. 'This had better be good,' he cautioned. 'I was in the middle of a trans-media narrative extension.'

A moment later, he was in my arms and it was *very* good indeed.

PS In case you're wondering about Julian Clary – his career took a dive that Tom Daley would have been proud of. He still lives in his dreary bungalow on the village green. The lesbians of the Old Manor recently took pity on him and he is now employed as the gardener here for two afternoons a week. He is frequently seen behind the barn, drinking gin from a small stainless steel flask.

The End

Acknowledgements

Very special thanks to my editor, Kirsty Crawford, whose steady, manicured hand once again steered me through the choppy seas of creative endeavour.

I am grateful also to everyone at Ebury for their patience and encouragement, especially Gillian Green, Claire Scott, Hannah Robinson and the amusing Andrew Goodfellow.

Sincere thanks to Eugenie Furniss, my literary agent, Donna Condon, my copy-editor, Hector Ktorides for thinking of the title, the Noël Coward Foundation for allowing the quotation from 'If Love Were All'. Thanks also to David McGillivray, Mandy Ward, Kirsty Jones and Merryl Futerman. And Ian Mackley for . . . I forget now.

Bibliography

Noël Coward by Philip Hoare

Coward the Playwright by John Lahr

Coward and Company by Richard Briers

The Essential Noël Coward Compendium by Barry Day

My Life with Noël Coward by Graham Payn

Coward by Sheridan Morley

A Talent to Amuse by Sheridan Morley

The Noël Coward Diaries edited by Graham Payn and Sheridan Morley

The Letters of Noël Coward edited by Barry Day

Noël by Charles Castle

Also by Julian Clary:

Devil in Disguise

How far would you go for fame and fortune?

Would you change your name?

Change your personality?

Reveal your inner drag queen?

Betray your friends?

Would you kill?

Fab, filthy and funny, Julian Clary's *Devil in Disguise* is a tale of friendship, celebrity and the lengths people will go to for both...

Praise for *Devil in Disguise*:

'It's as camp as the proverbial row of tents, but Clary tells a very good story. Funny and absolutely charming' *The Times*

'The comedian's debut novel sold by the bucketload, and this new one is even better – a darkly funny and deeply rude triumph' *Heat*

'Julian Clary combines crime and comedy in his outrageous new novel . . . brilliantly funny and touching' *Daily Mirror*

'Consistently triumphant . . . a brilliant romp' *Express*

'*Devil In Disguise* is a sheer delight from start to finish. I blame Clary for the bags under my eyes and my mumbling late-night mantra of "just one more chapter" . . . it's Showgirls meets Queer As Folk meets Baby Jane. Wonderful' *Pink Paper*

'Absurd, funny and classic Clary . . . witty, derisive, awful, solemn, tender, camp and definitely memorable; *Devil in Disguise* is, in turn, all of these things, which is quite an achievement' thetruthaboutbooks.com

Also by Julian Clary:

Murder Most Fab

Hello, I'm Johnny Debonair and this is my book - *Murder Most Fab*. Buy it. You won't regret it. Everything that has happened so publicly is explained. Of course, I'd prefer it if you remember me as I was at my height, before the past caught up with me so spectacularly – TV's Mr Friday Night with an enviable lifestyle and the nation at my feet.

I hope you, the public, can forgive me and enjoy this sordid tale for what it is – my final entertainment for you.

Praise for *Murder Most Fab*:

'A very funny novel . . . I couldn't put it down'
Janet Street Porter, *Marie Claire*

'*Murder Most Fab* is a slick page-turner, darkly funny, incongruously believable . . . you are completely swept along by it' *Guardian*

'This debut novel is both a shock and rather shocking. Julian Clary does good fiction' *Daily Mirror*

'Black comedy runs riot as a rent boy turns killer and then TV celebrity . . . a hilarious dark ride' *Heat*

'With his high camp and filthy humour, Clary is as entertaining on paper as he is on stage' *Observer*

'*Murder Most Fab* is filthy, very funny and will be adored by his fans' *Evening Standard*

'Clary is a good writer . . . A bit as you'd expect the author himself to be, *Murder Most Fab* has a dirty mouth and scant regard for morals but it is also very pleasant company'
Daily Express

'With all the ingredients that made Clary a success, plus an extra-large helping of sinister storytelling, *Murder Most Fab* is viciously funny and deliciously salacious' *Gay Times*

Also by Julian Clary:

A Young Man's Passage

This is Julian Clary's story, in his own words – the tale of an awkward schoolboy who became a huge worldwide success on stage and screen.

Far more than just another celebrity autobiography or 'funny book', this is a touching, beautifully written and wryly witty account of a unique progression from shy child to comedy icon.

Praise for *A Young Man's Passage*:

'An amazing story . . . a human testament worthy of a hundred of the more luvvy memoirs spouting self-congratulation' *Telegraph*

'A wryly engaging romp' *Sunday Times*

'A witty, charming autobiography' *Heat*

'This is a beautifully honest and sensitive account of a life and career stuffed full of surprising detail. I, for one, never knew Julian was gay' Paul Merton

'Brilliant' Jimmy Carr

'Hilarious and poignant by turns, it's an honest and detailed account' *Sainsbury's Magazine*

Also available from Ebury Press:

Charlotte Street

Danny Wallace

It all starts with a girl . . . (because yes, there's always a girl . . .)

Jason Priestley (not that one) has just seen her. They shared an incredible, brief, fleeting moment of deep possibility, somewhere halfway down Charlotte Street.

And then, just like that, she was gone – accidentally leaving him holding her old-fashioned, disposable camera, chock full of undeveloped photos . . .

And now Jason – ex-teacher, ex-boyfriend, part-time writer and reluctant hero – faces a dilemma. Should he try and track The Girl down? What if she's The One? But that would mean using the only clues he has, which lie untouched in this tatty disposable . . .

It's funny how things can develop . . .

Praise for *Charlotte Street*:

'My top tip for 2012's runaway success, with a very clever twist on the age old story of boy meets girl'
Daily Mirror

'. . . [one of] this year's coolest must-reads' *Stylist*

'Full of funny observations' *Heat*

'We loved this funny romance with a twist' *Closer*

'Here's a chance to look smug among the crowds of *50 Shades* readers, and impress your partner with your devotion to romance novels. A brilliantly funny boy-meets-girl story'
Mail on Sunday

'Looks set to be this summer's *One Day* . . . A delight'
Net-A-Porter

'A light, heart-warming story of one man's struggle with life, work and finding true love' *Top Sante*

Also available from Ebury Press:

Come Home
Lisa Scottoline

Is she the prodigal daughter or a cuckoo in the nest?

Jill had married William Skyler for all the right reasons: love and the hope that she was making a family for her daughter, as well as his two girls. But her husband's devastating betrayal had ripped their marriage apart and she and Megan had lost everything . . .

Now, years later, Jill is engaged to a good man who she trusts to be the step-father Megan's deserves. But then her ex-stepdaughter, Abby, shows up on her doorstep drunk and distraught with the news of her father's death . . .

Abby believes William has been murdered. She wants Jill to help her prove it. But Jill's past is in danger of putting her future happiness in jeopardy. And Abbey is no longer the innocent girl Jill once knew . . .

Praise for *Come Home*:

'You could get whiplash just turning a page. Scottoline knows how to keep readers in her grip' *New York Times Review*

'The suspense and dread builds like a series of tornados flattening all in their path. The pace is relentless, the twists are jaw-dropping and then Scottoline piles ending on top of ending until you turn the last page and just sit there, exhausted on every level. As I closed the novel I thought that, quite simply, Scottoline is a powerhouse' David Baldacci

'Scottoline is always awesome, but her latest book held me spellbound because she has such an eye for describing complicated family relationships (and I know complicated family relationships!)'
Janet Evanovich

'A gripping and compelling novel about . . . the emotional repercussions of going back into a family you no longer know . . . as full of thrills as it is full of heart'
Kristin Hannah

Also available from Ebury Press:

The Adoption

Anne Berry

'I was fourteen when my Mother said that she needed to speak to me . . . And then she told me – just like that. I was adopted. And what I felt was not shock or grief but the most enormous sense of relief.'

Growing up as the only child of strict, God-fearing parents, Lucilla has always felt her difference. But it is not 'till adulthood that she discovers the real reasons behind her adopted mother's oft-times violent indifference.

As for Harriet, she would have readily sent her longed for baby back if she could, having discovered she falls all too short of her expectations.

And then there is Bethan, a young girl in 1940s Wales, whose only mistake is falling in love with the wrong man . . .

Praise for Anne Berry:

"Anne Berry is a wonderful writer with a poetic imagination and use of language; startling metaphors and images flow effortlessly from line to line and, from page one, the plotting is heart-in-the-mouth stuff. What more could you ask?" *Daily Mail*

"Anne Berry takes you to the deepest, darkest recesses of the human condition. Go. Allow yourself to be carried away by her astonishing prose"
Amy MacKinnon, author of Tethered